"*The Pirate's Curse* is a thoroughly enjoyable addition to the Veritas Code series….The author does a wonderful job of building on previous stories. Lauren and Rowan Pierce's family continues to grow, and each member plays a part in the adventure. The story has plenty of twists and turns, and the protagonists must take significant risks to come back together as a family. Great story from a great author, and highly recommended. I'm looking forward to the next."

— MARK EDWARD JONES, AUTHOR OF *PECULIAR ACTIVITIES AND SHADOWED SOULS*

"*The Lost Templar* is a fantastic return to the world of The Veritas Codex series. Kulakowski knocks it out of the park mixing history and the supernatural. No one does it better!"

— R.J. JOHNSON, AUTHOR OF *DREAMSLINGER*

"In *The Lost Templar*, Kulakowski brilliantly weaves the past and present with historical facts in an exceptional narrative that drives the story forward with pounding intensity….This is a fast-paced suspenseful ride that keeps you gripping the edges of your tablet. Tension and family connections that tug at your heartstrings. Mind-blowing twists and turns. Lauren and Rowan are a dream team."

— JENNY SIMARD LABRANCHE, AMAZON FIVE-STAR REVIEWER

"The Veritas Codex is an amazing series that keeps the pages turning and your mind spinning. Suspenseful like Stuart Woods, yet thought-provoking like Dan Brown, Kulakowski has the incredible ability to weave together the threads of fact and fiction and sew them into an amazing literary tapestry that leaves you wanting more."

— BRANDON MARSH, HOST AND
EXECUTIVE PRODUCER, THE PARAUNITY
PODCAST

"The Veritas Codex series is a hearty paranormal narrative entree seasoned with suspense. It satisfied my craving for everything paranormal! Thank goodness there are more in the series—Betsey Kulakowski has whet my appetite and I am begging for more! "

— XANDER ZWEIG, CO-HOST OF THE
XANDER & STONE SCIENCE &
SUPERNATURAL PODCAST

"Realistic heroes and villains. International intrigue. More plot twists than a cup of nightcrawlers. Betsey has definitely raised the bar [in *The Jaguar Queen*]."

— J. DON WRIGHT, AUTHOR OF *BEHOLD!*

"Relatable characters and crisp pace…*The Veritas Codex* combines the intrigue and chemistry of *The X-Files* with the intensity of *The Da Vinci Code*."

— JAZ PRIMO, AUTHOR OF *GWEN REAPER*

"Engaging characters and remarkable plot twists jump from these pages. They pulled me into a thrilling world I did not want to leave."

— JOHN WOOLEY, AUTHOR OF SEVENTH SENSE

"I enjoyed [*The Veritas Codex*]. The writing is well done. I really liked the characters. It kept me engaged to the point I was speed reading (to find out what was going to happen) and I had to slow myself down!"

— TERRI FOLKS

THE KING'S RANSOM

THE KING'S RANSOM

THE VERITAS CODEX
BOOK SEVEN

BETSEY KULAKOWSKI

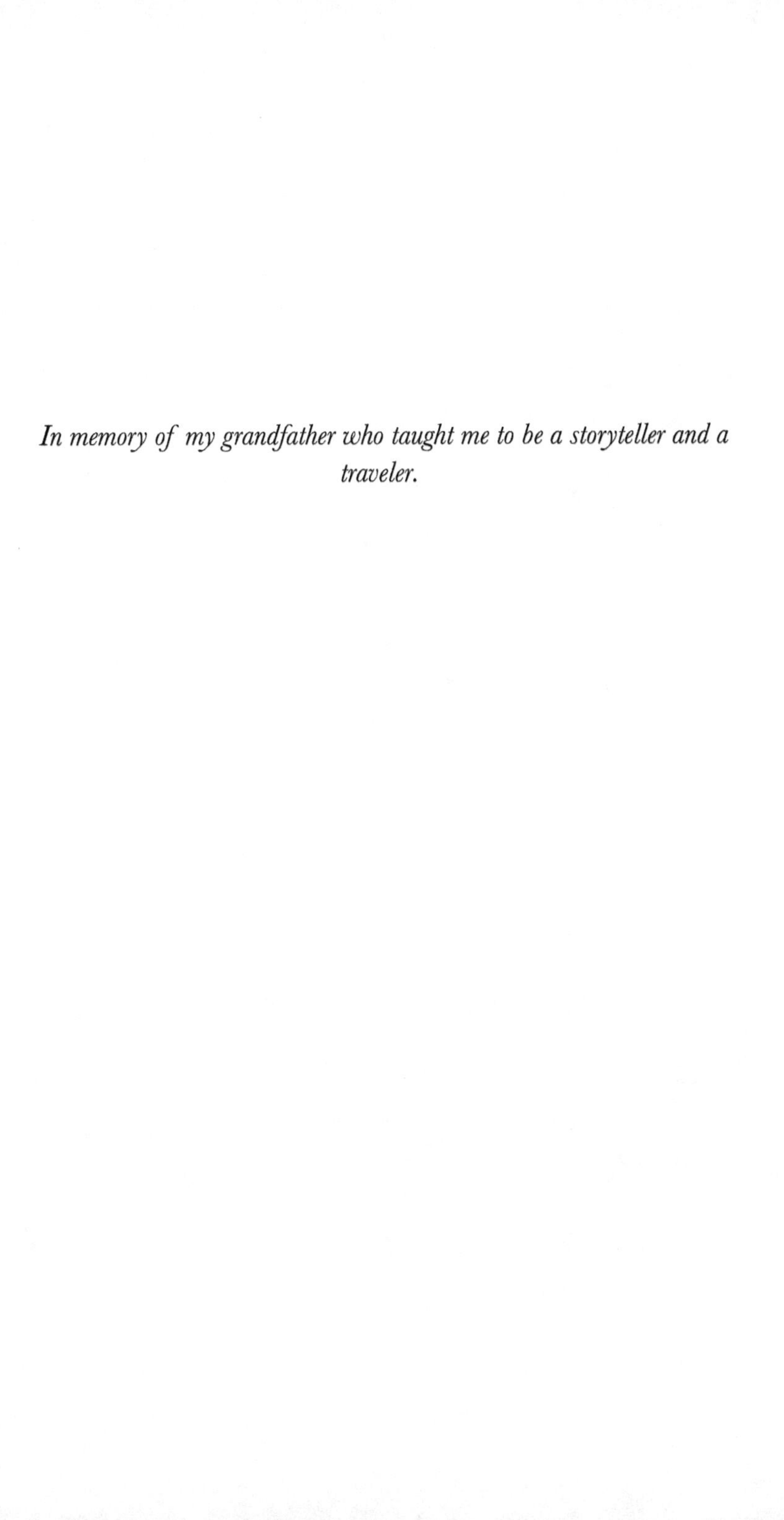

In memory of my grandfather who taught me to be a storyteller and a traveler.

"Travel does not exist without home. They are inseparably married. If we never return to the place we started, we would just be wandering, lost."

— JOSHUA GATES

PROLOGUE

Jordan Island, South Pacific
May 1st

"No Worries to Jonny Quest, copy." Rowan startled when the radio squelched. He nearly dropped the load of firewood onto the toe of his hiking boot. He tossed the load aside and fumbled for his radio.

"You're ten minutes early, Captain."

"Oh, so you're not dead yet? Good. Now I can go to bed and sleep well," the Aussie captain responded with humor in his voice.

Rowan gazed out, scanning the horizon. The good ship, No Worries, was nowhere to be seen as the sky went from muted red to inky black. Darkness came with all the fury and sound that would leave an average adventurer with the sense of being ill-at-ease, and utterly alone. Thanks to the rescue boat somewhere out there, Rowan wasn't so distraught.

He could hear the waves breaking in a rush on the shores in the distance. The nightly arias of bugs and birds created the kind of white noise that left Rowan with a tentative sense of peace as he made camp for the night. "Well, the night is young, and if there really is a monster out here, I haven't found it."

Had it only been a week before, when he attended the opera in Sydney, sporting a borrowed Italian tuxedo? His host —the executive director of the Pacific Archaeological Society —was a delightful companion, but she was old enough to be his grandmother. He spent the entire evening being charming, but he felt like little more than *arm candy*. He'd never had a little old lady pinch his cheeks before, but clearly, his charm had worked. He could only hope the Society had gotten its money's worth in those few short hours. He'd entertained his colleagues with a lecture on the perils of being a traveling adventurer, and field archaeologist. He told a few jokes and answered questions for nearly an hour. Then, he yielded the stage so they could continue their fundraising efforts. He had a boat to catch.

"Find anything today?"

"Old military depot, littered in razor wire," he said. "First time I've ever had to do stitches on myself." He glanced at the track of blue threads up his bare shin that held his flesh together.

"I told ya you'd need a tetanus vaccine on that rock," the Aussie said with a wry laugh.

"Only took me five days to find it," Rowan said.

"Do we need to send a medic with a band aid for your little boo-boo?" The captain was a smart ass, that much was for certain. Rowan had come to enjoy the evening banter.

"I am a medic, and I have band aids," he smirked. "I can manage on my own." A trek into the remotest parts of the world wasn't anything new for Rowan, but to go it alone was extremely rare. The rest of the *Veritas Codex* team had other assignments.

This wasn't the first time he'd taken off alone to see if a mystery was even worth the time and expense of bringing a full television production crew. So far, he hadn't found anything but shadows in the jungle.

Having the chance to speak at the *Pacific Archaeological Society's* annual conference as a keynote speaker helped convince the Network that a quick side trip to this remote island was at least worth looking into. The *PAS* signed a generous check to cover his travel expenses along with a speaking honorarium that only sweetened the pot. It was enough to pay for a boat and guide to take him to one of the most remote islands in the world.

"No ghosts or other boggles out there either, mate?"

"None that I've seen," Rowan said. "As soon as I make camp and get some grub in my gullet, I think I'll break out the REM pod and see about an EVP session."

Legends of this haunted island went back a century. Jordan Island—named for Captain Godfrey Jordan, a British naval captain who commanded the *HMS Gwendolyn*—had earned its reputation based on several well-documented accounts, including stories from the crew of the *Gwendolyn*.

An entry in his journal—made by his first mate—gave some inkling into the poor captain's condition when the ship caught an ill-tide and ran aground on the coral reef that blocked the harbor. *Our beloved captain, who has seen us though many a-storm, suffers ailments that are neither slight nor singular. Beset by fever and ague, he begged for land whereby he could rest. 'If I am to take my final breath,' says he, 'it will be on land, where my bones may bleach in the sun and not become fodder for sharks.'* The captain died shortly thereafter, and many scholars suspected a bout of malaria. His sanctuary became his crew's prison. All hands were lost. Some to disease, and some—to the unknown.

Stories of the crew's ghostly apparitions began some years later, when a Portuguese galleon called the *Esperança Perdida*, reportedly heavy with plundered Aztec gold, wrecked on the same reef in a vicious cyclone. Some said the Aztec gods exacted their justice, others said it was simple karma. When a third ship wrecked on the reef, the survivors made it to land. There, they found the dismembered skeletons of the Portuguese pirates strewn about the island. The bones appeared to have been gnawed on by a large predator that they heard in the dense tropical jungle, but mercifully, never encountered.

Only by the grace of God, the crew of the third ship were saved by a passing whaling vessel. Those survivors provided the source documents for Rowan's research that led him here.

"I know you have a dart gun and a taser for the monster, but what defense do you have for a boggle?" The captain asked.

"Holy water and a crucifix," Rowan said, glancing over at his backpack, wondering which weapon he might need first. He had his dart gun and taser on his belt, but the holy objects were in the kit with the ghost hunting equipment. In all his years as a paranormal investigator, Rowan encountered many things he couldn't explain—ghostly apparitions included—but he wasn't sure he'd ever been truly scared by such a thing. Humans were the real monsters.

One of the crew from the *Esperança Perdida* wrote of the horrors of this cursed island in memoires he found in an archive of whaling ship records kept at a library in Boston. The part about the Aztec gold truly whetted Rowan's appetite, but the possibility of a monster was the real mystery he hoped to solve.

Now that he knew the secret of Bigfoot—no longer a scary monster in his book—he wanted to know what other truths lie in the many legends of creatures and cryptids. An adventurer could not live on sunken treasures alone, and after his recent experiences in the Bermuda Triangle, he preferred to keep to land, even if that meant traveling the most remote oceans to get there.

"Eh, you've probably got more of a chance at finding that treasure than you do a boggle or a beast." That made Rowan laugh. He'd been thinking the same thing himself as he made camp in a clearing beneath a stand of *Pisonia grandis*—a flowering species of trees from the Bougainvillea family. The tropical giants towered nearly a hundred feet over his head.

"I'll keep my eyes out for something shiny when I head towards the beach tomorrow."

"We'll send Ricky in the Zodiac to pick you up at high noon," the captain replied. "Until then, mate, sweet dreams . . . and don't let the boggles get ya."

"Johnny Quest, out." Rowan dropped the radio atop his backpack and returned to setting up camp for the night. A fire was the first order of business.

He was feeding dry coconut husks into the tentative flames when a shooting star sparked across the evening sky above, catching Rowan's eye. He thought of home—and of Lauren—and made his wish. Had he known about this place when he'd planned their honeymoon, he might have brought her here, never mind that it violated their one cardinal rule—there could be no mysteries to solve. The mysteries here came in spades.

Though this island was one of the most beautiful places he'd seen in his life, the ever-present sense of homesickness and dread led him to the kind of anxiety he'd felt certain those stranded sailors must have experienced. It also reminded him he had work to do.

He sat aside the MRE he had yet to prepare and picked up the camera. Flipping the view screen around, he pointed the lens at himself and hit record. He'd made several video recordings over the previous days documenting his findings on this no-man's land.

"There's something exhilarating about being alone on one of the most remote islands on Earth. I know I have help anchored beyond the reef. I can call them by radio or signal flare any time I need them. That's not exactly comforting when legends tell me that something on this island would be more than happy to kill me, eat me and leave my bones to decay in the sand," he said with a half-hearted chuckle, firelight flickering on his face and warming his already sweaty skin. He paused the recording to move the pan of boiling water off the flames. It would need to cool before he could bottle it up and it would provide all the drinking water he would need until Ricky came to pick him up. Then, he returned to his work.

"After a few days, your mind begins playing tricks on you. I've heard all the stories about this cursed and haunted island. I'm starting to believe them. I think I hear whispers in the trees behind me. I catch movement out of the corner of my eye." Rowan paused and looked away from the camera, allowing his eyes to adjust to the fading light. Something was definitely moving. "I try to rationalize my experience by working to debunk what I *think* I'm seeing and hearing," he continued. "Though there are no people on the island, I can't help feeling like . . . like I'm being watched."

Something made a low, deep grumbling growl in the jungle behind him, causing him to bolt to his feet. The camera tumbled to the ground. The ting of broken glass was insignificant compared to the hammering of his heart against his breastbone. Still, he picked up the camera, inspecting it before turning it back on, and directing the cracked lens toward the canopy of trees.

Eyeshine reflected the firelight as something large hovered more than arm's reach above the ground. Rowan swallowed hard and took a step back. Whatever it was grunted, and the palms rustled as it moved closer. Now he knew how a gazelle felt when a lion was stalking it.

His hand rested on the flare gun on his hip. He heard the snap of the buckle come undone as the dark shadow lurched forward. Before he could get his hand around the weapon, he was knocked from his feet even as he spun around to run. The camera flew from his hand and rolled into the underbrush, out of reach. He didn't have time to worry about it now.

His foot caught a rock as he bolted forward. Like a panicked fawn, he ran for his life. Hot breath seared the back of his neck as he dodged a stand of thorny shrubs. He could feel claws swipe at him, snagging and tearing his t-shirt. He still hadn't identified the monster on his heels. At the moment he didn't even have time to make an educated guess. He only knew if he didn't get away, he wouldn't be going home in the morning when the boat returned, and that wasn't an option. Lauren would kill him.

Another zig at just the right moment saved him from becoming dinner as the dark flash of beast rolled and struck a tree. It sounded like a large watermelon striking a telephone pole. A high-pitched bawl of pain echoed off the canopy.

Rowan didn't wait to find out if the monster was okay. He found the trail he'd hiked up to the clearing, headed towards the beach. Taking advantage of the rising moon's mottled glow, Rowan ran as fast as his unsteady legs could carry him. He could still hear the howling and the lumbering sound of *beast*—or whatever it was—behind him, but he'd gained a bit of an advantage until he realized he wasn't headed back to the beach.

Somehow in his panic, he'd made a wrong turn, and the narrowing path began to rise and grow more precipitous. His options became severely limited as he skidded to a stop at the edge of an embankment. Sand skittered from beneath his feet and fell like rain on the foliage below. Ten feet below, was a large patch of sharp swordfern. What lay beneath the fern was impossible to distinguish. Ten feet ahead, the rocky path grew more steep and appeared crumbling. If there was another way down he couldn't see it from where he paused, catching his breath.

Ten or more yards behind, his stalker seemed to know he was trapped. It no longer raced after him, but Rowan was aware of it at the bottom of the path. It seemed content to lurk, to wait for its prey to make its choice. If he leapt into the certain hazard of the jungle below, it could circle around and take advantage of having him either injured or dead. If the beast allowed him to make a feeble attempt at going higher, the end result would be a perilous jump from a greater height. Either way, the monster had him cornered, and it seemed like it was just a matter of time.

"Up here!" A voice called from the top of the path, startling Rowan. He recognized the voice, but it was impossible. *Or was it?* He was alone on the island. Except, *he wasn't*.

"Henry?"

"Up here, Dad! Hurry!" The tone in his oldest son's voice told him he'd should listen. Rowan knew better than to consider this an impossible scenario. He was coming to grips with the fact that his son was a *wizard*—or whatever you wanted to call him—and whether he existed in the flesh or in a metaphysical form, he was here for a reason. "Run as fast as you can and don't stop! Hurry!"

The monster must have known they'd come to a tipping point. Rowan heard it lurch towards him—grunting and growling as it gained traction on the sandy soil. With no time to think, he turned and made a desperate dash towards the unknown, guided only by a voice that sounded like his son. He had nothing to go on, but trust. It wasn't until the rock face crumbled beneath his feet that he had a moment's doubt in his decision. He raised his flare gun above him and squeezed the trigger. As his stomach rose into his throat, so escaped a startled yelp. Then, the world fell away.

HE THOUGHT for sure he was dead when he hit the water, hard. His body went deep before he had the wherewithal to kick off his shoes and fight against the waves that threatened to take him deeper. When he popped up to the surface, a blood curdling roar erupted from the precipice above, echoing over the vast dark ocean. He turned to try to identify the source of the sound, but a wave washed over him. The saltwater blinded him as it pulled him deeper out away from the rocky cliffs.

"You okay, Dad?" Henry's voice found him again.

"Jesus, son." He coughed, fighting to keep his head above water. "You scared the daylights out of me."

"You're welcome," Henry said, amusement in his hollow voice.

"And you saved my life," Rowan said. "Thank you."

"Of course," Henry's voice answered, even though he was nowhere to be seen. "You need to go get on that boat and get home. Now."

"What? Wait? Why?" He'd already started swimming for it.

"Besides not getting eaten by a monster?" Henry said. "Mom needs you home."

"What? Is she okay?"

"Just get home," Henry said. "You need to go home. It may be too late already."

"Can't you just blink me there?"

"It doesn't work like that, Dad." Henry sounded bemused.

Rowan swam a few strokes toward a sand bar that seemed inaccessible from the cliff where the monster's shrieks continued to echo. "She's okay? Right?"

"She's fine," his son assured him. "It's going to take some time for you to get home. You don't want to wait."

A wave caught him, and he had to fight the current that threatened to pull him farther out to sea. "Henry?" He had a dozen questions. There was no answer. "Henry?"

Christ! What was up with that woman now?

1

Lauren took a seat in the wooden chair that looked like something from the 1940s. It creaked when she sat and squealed when she shifted to settle in. It reminded her of the weight she'd gained since giving up her role in the field with the production teams. The years had not been kind to her hips.

After she and Rowan got lost in the Bermuda Triangle, changes had to be made. They had the children to think about and having both their parents jetting off right and left doubled the risk of making orphans out of them. No. Staying home was for the best, more so now. This trip notwithstanding. She had to do *this*, for their family. She hated being here, but she'd set the chain of events into motion. She resolved to see it through to the end, even if this trip took her away from her children temporarily.

The arms of the old chair were rubbed smooth by sweaty palms over the decades, hers included. The chair had no cushion. Any attempts to mold the chair to the human form by the carpenter offered little in the way of comfort.

Nearing the last three months of her fifth pregnancy, she found very little to ease her aching joints, unless it involved her pajamas and her Tempurpedic mattress. Even that lasted a few hours before she grew restless, needing to move. Sleeping in Rowan's recliner—or on the sofa—while he was gone, at least for part of the night, provided options. She often fell asleep in the living room reading or ignoring the television as she gazed out into the yard where the children's bikes and toys were left haphazardly strewn across the patio.

In another time, Lauren would have rounded the children up before bed and scolded them until they put their playthings away, but these days she had no energy for it. Henry might have taken up her banner with the younger children, but he was off on a trip with his school counselors to visit Oxford and Cambridge. His SAT and ACT scores, which surpassed his classmates, earned him a great deal of attention from colleges around the world. Top tier institutions rallied to win his commitment to whichever degree program he settled upon.

He was considered a *boy genius*. Lauren knew how much hard work he'd put in to earn the grades and test scores he'd achieved. She was immensely proud of the young man he'd become and credited the many strong role models he had to look up to. It made her appreciate the effort she'd put in to home-schooling. He could go anywhere he wanted, but she suspected he'd stay close to home. If anything, Henry's devotion to family was strong. He'd expressed an early interest in following his father's path to Colorado State University, which would keep him close to Grandpa John and Grandma Martha in Denver. But Pepperdine, Stanford, and Cal Tech were courting him, too.

He had his parents' full support to make his own choices. To Lauren's delight, his interests leaned more towards physics than archeology, or even anthropology. While he might follow his father's footsteps in his choice of universities, the young man would blaze a trail in whatever he decided to do.

Lauren stifled a yawn, wishing she could take a nap. Last night, she managed to fall asleep in a lumpy hotel bed, but by midnight she paced back and forth between the bathroom and the balcony. The early summer breeze was nice in California, but the New Orleans humidity left her nightgown clinging to her. She closed the balcony doors, cranked up the air conditioning and retreated to the bathroom for a long soak in a warm tub.

"Dr. Grayson?" Lauren glanced up. She was accustomed to being in the spotlight, but this was outside her normal routine. Jean-René, typically behind a camera, sat in a similar chair behind a wooden table next to the prosecuting attorney. Uncharacteristically, he wore a suit and tie. It wasn't at all like the adventure-wear more suited to jungles and forests, or—in some cases—a wet suit and SCUBA gear that he normally wore. "Are you all right?"

"*Ehem.*" Jean-René nudged the woman beside him. "It's Dr. Pierce when she's not on television," he corrected in a low tone.

"Apologies, Dr. Pierce," the attorney said. "Are you ready? Do you need some water?"

"No." Lauren forced a nervous smile onto her face, feeling the thick layer of makeup crack in the creases around her mouth. She hadn't worn makeup in a while.

These days, she avoided the cameras, most of the time. Instead, she did research and pre-production script writing. When post-production finished up with the editing and audio correction for the first half of the season, the Network called her into the studio for filming. There, she sat behind a desk to record the introduction and post-show wrap up—a desk that hid her growing figure. "I'm fine."

The arrangement satisfied her doctor's limitations, though Lauren hated being left at home. *Women her age weren't supposed to be having babies*, her doctor told her, *repeatedly*. He kept her on a short leash, even though there had been no complications, other than heartburn and a sore back. *Advanced maternal age*, the words echoed in her brain.

"Are you ready to begin?" the attorney asked again.

"Yes." Lauren came back to the moment.

A bailiff came over to Lauren and swore her in as the court reporter in the corner began tapping away at her stenograph, her fingers flying on the keys.

"Dr. Pierce, can you tell me about the flyer you received regarding the services of a Mr. Antoine Thibodeaux . . . also known to the court as Tony Thibodeaux . . . also known to the court as *Papa Dauphine?*"

Lauren cleared her throat and nodded. "The flyer came addressed to my husband, Rowan Pierce, sometime before September 16th of last year," she said. "I found it on the desk at our home office when I went to pay bills."

The attorney stepped forward with a plastic covered document. "If it pleases the court, this is item number 01-01-214 on the evidence log." She handed it to Lauren. "Could you please verify this is the document your husband received?"

"Yes." Lauren cringed as she studied the 8x10 glossy brochure, creased into a trifold, the edges worn and curling. Their home address on the label had faded but was still legible. It came to their *home* and that bothered her as much as anything. That con artist knew where they lived. The images of the *corporate team building*, and *leadership training* burned in the back of her eyes like daggers. She'd come so close to losing Rowan to this *scam artist*. She filed a police report without telling him and even today's court proceedings remained a closely guarded secret. If he and Jean-René could sneak off and risk his life behind her back, the cameraman owed her the same discretion. "I can verify the document is the one my husband received."

"And was it addressed specifically to Mr. Pierce? Was it delivered by the US Postal Service?"

"It was . . . on both counts," Lauren said, turning the document over.

"What did your husband do with this flyer, Dr. Pierce?"

"Objection. You're asking the witness to speculate." The attorney at the other table sat beside his client who'd spent the last two months at the Orleans Justice Center, where he'd been held—without bond—pending trial. He was considered a high flight risk.

Lauren used her investigative skills—not to mention some of her sway with government officials who remained unnamed—to ensure he was caught somewhere with extradition. She wanted him prosecuted to the full extent of the law. To her great luck, his arrest was made in New Orleans just after Mardi Gras, and justice would soon come to fruition.

The District Attorney originally planned to charge him with a misdemeanor, but she pressed for attempted murder. The best she could get was a felony fraud charge and using the US Postal Service to commit such fraud. The DA met with her over video conferencing several weeks before and tried to *mansplain* to her what fraud was. "*It involves deception and the presentation of false information for personal or financial gain. Generally, that's handled in civil court, Dr. Pierce.*" She could still hear the derision and arrogance in his tone and the emphasis of her title, *Doctor*.

The conversation with the DA replayed in her head as the attorneys argued over the question on the table. She was glad now for his disinterest. Using her sway, the case had been moved to federal court instead of district court. The prosecuting attorney at the table beside Jean-René had been open to working with them and seemed confident that a prosecution wasn't just possible, it was inevitable.

"*Are you aware that my husband technically died?*" Lauren had pressed harder, still sick to her stomach knowing how close she'd come to losing him. *"His heart stopped beating and his best friend had to do CPR on him until paramedics arrived. They were able to revive him with a defibrillator."*

"Dr. Pierce?" The attorney took the document from her hand, drawing her back to the moment. "Can you answer the question?"

"Sorry," Lauren shifted in the chair. "I saw the document on his desk at the Network. I also overheard him discussing the services of the accused. A discussion about life after death followed."

"Oh?"

"The services of the accused promised to take clients to *a place beyond the gods*. It sounded like an innocent enough discussion. Given the kind of work we do, it's not uncommon."

"And can you tell the court about your work?" The prosecutor made it clear she wanted Lauren to paint a picture for the court—for the jury. Lauren painted a masterpiece.

"Did your husband tell you he intended to enlist the services of Mr. Thibodeaux?"

"No," Lauren said. "I didn't find out about it until after the fact."

"How much did your husband spend for this *experience*?"

"My husband didn't pay for it out of his own pocket," Lauren said. "The Network paid over fifteen thousand dollars. That included the rights to video tape and air the ceremony."

"Objection! Speculation."

"I saw the ACH receipt myself," Lauren snapped.

The judge held up a hand, stopping her. "Dr. Pierce, please allow me to address the objections before you continue."

She blushed at the admonishment. "Apologies, your honor."

"Overruled." The judge nodded, indicating she should continue.

"I believe a copy of the payment is in the evidence submitted," the prosecutor said. "But I don't see it on the evidence log."

There was some discussion between the judge and the attorneys. Lauren waited for the issue to resolve itself, smoothing the fabric of her skirt. A trickle of sweat ran down the back of her blouse. The humid scent of mold lingered in the centuries old courthouse that had been severely damaged during Hurricane Katrina. The miasma of humid air and fungus made her stomach turn.

The defendant sat next to his attorney in a suit that looked like it was two sizes too big. His dreadlocks had been tied back and he was relatively clean shaven, except for the soul patch beneath his lower lip, and the thinnest moustache along the line of his wide mouth.

She wondered where he got the clothing, and suspected the jail kept a stash of court attire—most likely Goodwill finds —to allow defendants to dress in accordance with the court's requirements. She hadn't been so lucky. Her own closet was filled with clothes she couldn't wear. Even the outfit she had on was too tight. It cut into her hips and pulled across her bosom, pinching under her armpits.

Thibodeaux caught her staring. Their eyes locked. Though his face remained placid, his eyes burned with hatred. She sensed the evil in his soul and knew he had every right to blame her for his incarceration. But she hadn't been the one who lured her husband into a trap that nearly ended his life. *Papa Dauphine* was a scam—a con artist—and in time, the truth would come out, and he would be held accountable for his web of lies.

But justice demands repayment for the trouble you and your ilk have caused, Tsul'Kalu's words echoed in her mind. But this monster was no rabbit. Rabbits were tricksters, mischief makers. No, this guy was more like . . . like . . . the *Ka'lanu Ahkyeli'ski. The Raven Mocker*—an evil spirit and the most feared of Cherokee witches. *The Raven Mocker* had the power to rob the sick and the dying of their heart. They were powerful beings with the ability to turn completely invisible or take to the air in a fiery shape. They could mimic the raven's cry and command the wind. For every heart they consumed, it added a year to their life. Like the banshee in Celtic tradition, the *Raven Mocker's* cry meant someone would die soon. If *The People* knew of any defense against the *Raven Mocker*, it hadn't been shared with her.

Lauren broke the stare but wasn't unaware of the evil grin that curled in Dauphine's cheek. Unable to resolve the issue at the moment, the judge instructed the prosecution to continue. They'd find the record at some point. If nothing else, the Network could send another copy.

"That's a lot of money." The attorney returned to the table where Jean-René sat. She glanced at her notes. "Is it a common practice for the Network to pay for such services?"

"We pay fees to film all the time. Sometimes, it's to individual tour guides, subject matter experts, and sometimes it's a government-mandated fee."

"What other costs were associated with The Network's participation in the defendant's . . . *ritual?*"

Lauren swallowed hard. "The Network paid for the travel expenses for my husband and his cameraman. The Network also had to pay for his medical care after . . ." her voice caught in her throat and she froze, trying to keep her composure.

"What kind of medical care did your husband require?"

"He suffered a cardiac episode," she said. "Most likely a drug induced ventricular tachycardia, according to the cardiologist."

"The medical records entered into evidence are from several days after the event. Can you explain the delay in your husband seeing a specialist?"

"There wasn't one available in Port-au-Prince," she said, "And we've had trouble getting records from the hospital in Haiti."

"Haiti?"

"That's where they had to go to meet Papa . . ." she started but remembered the coaching she'd received prior to her testimony. "To meet the accused . . . in Haiti."

"So he had to travel outside the country for this . . . experience?"

"That's correct."

"Dr. Pierce, when did you learn about your husband's . . . *cardiac episode?*"

Officially, she'd been told he died during the experience by Jean-René while they were in Miami, preparing to search for the Network's lost vessel. In truth, Rowan told her himself, when he'd come to her in her dreams. Of course, she could never testify to that in court . . . not under oath. "A few days later, when I met him in Miami. That's when we went to see a cardiologist."

The questioning continued for another forty-five minutes. The attorney for the accused objected here and there—whenever the prosecution asked her to speculate or asked for her expert opinion. She had to give it to the defense, he'd done his homework on her. "Asking Dr. Pierce for her medical opinion is inappropriate. She has a PhD in anthropology, not medicine, counselor," the judge admonished.

"Dr. Pierce," the judge turned to her. "You are instructed not to answer the question." She hadn't heard the question. The baby kicked her full bladder. It was hot. She felt dizzy and wanted to be done. "Dr. Pierce?" Lauren observed the exchange between the judge and the prosecution. "Counselor, I believe your witness could use a break . . . and so could I." The judge picked up his gavel and pounded it on the marble base. "We'll take a fifteen minute recess. Dr. Pierce, can I get you some water?"

The judge was a rotund black man with white hair and sideburns. His accent had the melodic patois of the Bayou.

"No, thank you, sir." She stood as the judge rose to leave the bench, meeting Jean-René halfway across the room.

"You don't look so hot," he said, catching her arm.

"I just need to use the ladies room," she said, pressing to move past him. Jean-René kept her hand in his and led her out of the courtroom to the door of the ladies' room. She knew he would wait outside for her, keeping a watchful eye out for reporters. He was over-protective when Rowan was gone. Lauren didn't think the media would recognize him. He always stayed behind the camera. But if anyone saw her the media frenzy would begin. They hoped to keep this a covert operation, for now.

Lauren splashed water on her face and neck at the sink, trying to cool herself off. That morning, she put her hair up in a tight bun, but silvery wisps had escaped their bonds and slithered down her neck, clinging to her skin. The dark circles under her eyes still show through her make-up.

Her hair grew grayer with each passing year. Before this baby was out of kindergarten, Lauren suspected her hair would be just as white as her mother's.

When Lauren returned to the witness stand, the judge reached over and handed her a bottle of water. She knew better than to argue, or refuse. No one else in the court room had been permitted to have food or beverage. She was grateful for the gesture and took advantage of the comfort. She enjoyed a long refreshing drink as court was called back to order.

"Prosecutor, you may proceed," the judge said.

"We have no further questions for this witness, at this time."

"Very well. Does the defense have any questions for Dr. Pierce?" The judge all but leaned over the bench, eyeing the attorney who appeared as if he'd rather be anywhere else.

"Dr. Pierce, were you there the night your husband allegedly participated in my client's training session?" The attorney began the question before he stood, and the judge looked as if he might have something to say about the lack of decorum in his courtroom.

"I was not," Lauren answered before the judge could say anything.

The attorney sat back down. "I have no further questions for this *witness*."

Lauren caught the look of surprise on the judge's face. "None?"

"No, your honor."

If he meant it as an insult to her, it wasn't. Lauren was relieved she didn't have to go through having her credibility questioned—again. She did not need some half-baked public defender *mansplaining* how her testimony was invalid because she hadn't been there that night.

"Very well. You are excused, Dr. Pierce," the judge leaned down and said politely to her. "The court thanks you for being here today." He dropped his tone and the volume of his voice, as he looked down at her from over his glasses. "If you need to step out at any time during these proceedings . . . or if I can get you anything, please let me know."

"Thank you, your honor."

Lauren rose, intent on returning to the table where the prosecutor sat, ready to call her next witness. As she approached the table, Dauphine launched himself from his chair, past his attorney. Before anyone could react, he charged Lauren. Jean-René, however, leapt out of his chair and vaulted over the table, cutting between the attacker and his boss. Lauren let out a shriek as Dauphine swatted at her, his hand tangling in her hair, yanking it. It appeared he might have been trying to hit her in the face. Jean-René was too fast for him. The photographer wrestled him on the floor and was cussing him out in French. The guards moved in and took over, shoving Jean-René aside. He rolled over and got to his feet, catching Lauren's arm before she could go over.

"Bailiff, remove the defendant from my courtroom!" the judge shouted over the din of angry voices and mutters of shocked surprise.

"*Mwen madichon pou . . .*" Dauphine spat at her as Jean-René shielded her. It took a moment to get Dauphine cuffed and under control.

"Dr. Pierce, are you injured?" The judge came down from the bench standing in front of her as Jean-René helped her to the chair behind the table.

Lauren was trembling, but a quick mental inventory told her she was okay. He'd yanked her hair at worst. Her hand went to her cheek to make sure it wasn't scratched.

"I think she needs a minute," Jean-René said.

"Dr. Pierce, your duty to this court is satisfied. You are dismissed with the court's appreciation . . . and apologies." The judge returned to the bench. "Prosecution, when you're ready, please call your next witness."

Lauren saw the glance between Jean-René and the prosecutor. "I'm okay," she said. "Just a little shaken up. Please. Go on."

"Your honor, the defendant has a right to face his accusers," the defense attorney protested. "I move to adjourn and resume tomorrow, after my client has been appropriately admonished for his outburst."

"Counselor, your defendant lost that right when he attacked a witness in my courtroom. The prosecution may continue."

"But, your honor —"

"Overruled," he said, raising a hand of encouragement to the prosecutor. The judge took his seat at the bench.

"The Prosecution calls Jean-René Toussaint."

He hesitated a moment and Lauren assured him she was fine. Jean-René took his place on the witness stand. The bailiff swore him in.

If anyone could get *Papa Dauphine* convicted, it would be

Jean-René. He *had* been there when Rowan—*died*. He had filmed the video of the event, and despite the defenses' arguments, the judge allowed the tape to be played in full for the jury. Seven women and five men watched the entire two hours and seven minutes of footage that began before sunset as Papa Dauphine and Rowan sat discussing the ceremony and what to expect. Dauphine explained the herbal concoction he would mix, and what Rowan could expect when he consumed it. Jean-René asked the priest questions about what side effects there might be. They also heard Rowan give the cameraman instructions not to interfere unless it was a life or death situation, which is what it became.

When it came to the part where Rowan stopped breathing, the judge nodded as Lauren stood abruptly. His silent dismissal offered her a measure of grace she needed at the moment. It allowed her to avoid witnessing her husband's near-death experience. She made a hasty retreat and found a bench down the hall where she didn't have to listen to the agony of Jean-René's panic calls for help. It was everything she could do not to start bawling.

By the time Jean-René stepped out of the courtroom, followed by the prosecutor, Lauren had worked herself up into a tizzy. She paced back and forth down the same marble-tiled hallway until her feet began to swell.

"Now what?" Lauren asked the attorney.

"Now you go back to your hotel, put your feet up and order room service," she said. "The defense will have a chance to cross-examine Mr. Toussaint tomorrow morning."

"And you're sure Rowan won't have to testify?"

"How can he?" Jean-René asked. "He's out of the country."

"The video Mr. Toussaint provided is extremely damaging to the defense," the attorney said. "I'm certain the defense attorney wouldn't want the victim to testify, either. And, based on what I've seen and what I found in discovery, I'm quite sure

I don't need his testimony to make our case. I have other witnesses that have experienced the same issues with the accused. Besides, that's for me to worry about, Dr. Pierce. Your part is done. Now you need to take care of yourself and your baby."

"Why do I suddenly have a craving for some spicy fried chicken and *étouffée*?" Lauren mused.

"Because '*dis is de Big Easy, baby*,'" Jean-René did his best New Orleans' accent.

"If I may recommend, *Bonhomme Felix* has the best chicken and crawfish *étouffée*. It's just down the street from your hotel."

"We'll stop and get some on our way." Jean-René put a hand in the small of her back and turned Lauren to the elevator. He hesitated, turning to the attorney. "Does Lauren need to be here in the morning?"

"No," the attorney said. "She's done her part."

"In that case, you can sleep in," Jean-René said as the elevator door opened.

2

Orleans Parish Prison
New Orleans, Louisiana
May 2nd

The Dark One's shadow hovered in the corner of the dimly lit cell as Papa Dauphine lay on the metal bunk, staring up at the breakaway hooks where his t-shirt hung. The cell reeked of brimstone and sweat. The memory of the industrial cleaner used to sanitize the facility lingered in the air. The voodoo priest yearned for a stiff drink and a Cuban cigar. His evening meal was at odds with his hollowed stomach. It protested the bland concoction of processed sausage and rice they called *jambalaya* but was, in truth, no better than gruel. *No salt. No spice. Not even fit for de rats.* A mist of sweat clung to the tight curls of hair on his chest and stomach.

The buff colored walls and blue trim should have made the cells bright and relaxing, but the rain and dark presence gave the 9'x9' cell an eerie pallor. The flicker of lightning cut like a knife in the cell. The demon appeared flesh in the brief flash. The voodoo priest's cell mate cried out, cowering by the barred doors, afraid—not only for his life—but also his mortal soul. He cried out and begged for salvation. His voice echoed through the cell block, but no help would come.

"*Dis* is *de* reward I get for *doin'* my lord's bidding?" Dauphine bemoaned his fate in his thick creole accent. "Accused of a felony, and left to rot in prison while awaiting a verdict?"

The New Orleans Parish Prison had a tarnished reputation. Katrina exacerbated the decades of complaints about poor conditions, and inhumane treatment. When the category four hurricane struck the Gulf Coast and the Orleans Parish Sheriff's Office abandoned the jail, over 650 prisoners were left to their fate, locked in their cells with no food, water, or ventilation for days. Five-hundred-seventeen prisoners were later registered as *unaccounted for*, with no explanation of whether they lived or died. Dauphine sensed the presence of the many ghosts who roamed the halls, no longer bound by bars or bricks.

"Your reward awaits you when I retake my place at the All Father's side . . . when I reclaim my place as the rightful heir." Enlil's voice was deep and ominous. "I will call upon you to champion my armies when I unleash the eleventh plague upon the heavens and the earth. When my father falls, and I take my place on the throne, you will sit at the right hand of the new Most High. You will become my judgement and my wrath."

"How many others have *ya* promised such *t'ings* to?" Dauphine sat up, standing, pacing in front of his bunk.

"There have been many who have served me," the Dark One said, his voice moving behind the agitated priest. "Many will serve me before my battle is won. But few have been able to give me what I ask for. I feel the rippling magic of your earthly power tremble in the wind. As all your spells come full circle, I can feel the threads gathering. I sense the time of my retribution is growing near. Patience, my wicked and faithful servant. Your reward awaits you on that great and terrible day."

"What is it you want from me?" Dauphine turned.

"The woman who accuses you is a powerful creature in her own right. You cannot win in a court of man against such a witch. She has the ability to sway the minds of men. The words that come from her mouth are tainted with lies that mortals cannot see."

"So, you wish me to rot in this cell for all eternity?"

"I command thee to bide!" The demon's voice rose into an order so powerful the priest's cellmate shrieked, grasping at the bars—crying repeatedly for help. Dauphine took a step back. When he spoke again, the Dark One's tone settled. "Protect your energy. Your thoughts can give you power, but they can also take from you what you will need most. This fortress is a bastion where your power can grow, with proper tending. I will give you the tools you need, but you must plant the seeds and tend the garden of her destruction. These mortals may seem weak of mind, but you will need them when the reckoning is at hand. When it is time to harvest souls, the patience and care you have put into your work will reap its own rewards."

Dauphine bowed and dropped to one knee. "As you command, my Lord."

"That is my command," he said. Dauphine rose and sat back down on the bed. "The lesson begins now."

"Lesson?" Dauphine recoiled. One eye narrowed tightly.

"First, I will teach you to whistle up a wind," the Dark One said. "Then, I will teach you stormcasting. When you have mastered that, I will teach you to bind storms in your hair and cast lightning from your fingers."

"Sounds like my *kinna* magic," Dauphine said, licking his lips as he stood.

"I will teach you how to manifest famine and hunger. We

will raise the tides and flood the fields and cities with salt water. We will lay waste to crops. The fields will go fallow. We will call forth the plagues of locusts. The suffering will be . . . *delicious*."

"As long as it got some spice, I look forward to *de* feast."

LAUREN FLINCHED IN HER SEAT, startling Jean-René who'd nodded off five minutes after the plane from New Orleans took off. "What?" He looked at her bleary-eyed. He tried to remember if there had ever been a time just the two of them traveled alone, but he couldn't recall.

"Cramp." She winced, digging her knuckle into the side of her belly under her ribs. "Maybe a foot."

"You can't have that kid on this airplane, you know."

"I know," she said. "I'm not far enough along." Lauren's doctor signed a release to let her fly. It wasn't an attestation that she couldn't go into labor on the journey, but an indication that she wasn't *likely* to go into early labor. TSA would let her fly for a few more weeks, but having her doctor's note ensured they wouldn't keep her from reaching the courtroom in time to testify against Dauphine. It was a race against the clock in order to get the case heard before she couldn't travel. Now that Dauphine had been found guilty on two counts of fraud, it would be at least ten weeks before the sentencing hearing. She didn't need to be there for that. She'd done her part, and it would be a long time before that snake-oil salesman could hurt anyone else.

"I need to pee."

"The seatbelt sign is still on," Jean-René pointed out, crossing his arms, and tucking his head down. He closed his eyes and rested his chin on his chest. Lauren glanced back the three rows to the lavatory. She had the aisle seat just so she wouldn't disturb anyone if she had to get up. It wasn't a matter of *if*. As if in answer, the plane hit a pocket of turbulence and jostled but settled. Lauren tried to relax, stretching her legs out as much as she could to relieve some of the pressure on her bladder.

To change the subject, Lauren asked a question she'd been putting off asking since they left San Diego. "I heard Jacob mention something about another project he had for you. What was he talking about?"

"I don't want to tell you," Jean-René stated simply.

"You don't want to tell me? Why? What is it?" She knew something was up. His denial to provide details confirmed her suspicions.

Jean-René took a deep breath and sat up, dragging his hands down his face. Lauren noticed the dark circles under his eyes and realized how much he'd aged in the years they'd worked together. She remembered when he was *her* cameraman, and they took teams around the world. Now, he was *Rowan's* cameraman, and she stayed home with the children. She had made peace with that decision, but it didn't mean she didn't miss field work. "I don't want to tell you because . . . you are not going to like it, and . . . and Jacob told me *not* to."

"Jacob? Told you not to what?"

"Not to tell you about this new show." She could feel her anger rising as it flamed in her cheeks. She wanted to blame Jacob, as much as Papa Dauphine, for Rowan's near-death experience. He'd been the one who'd signed off on the ill-fated expedition to Haiti, and intentionally didn't tell her what they were up to. "And I'm sure *that's* why he told me not to tell you."

"What?"

"The look on your face," he said. "You already don't look happy."

"Why should I look happy, Jean-René?" she snapped. "You're one of my best friends. You worked for me when I couldn't find anyone else crazy enough to follow me into the woods to look for monsters and collect samples of Sasquatch poop. If I'm not happy it's because you're not telling me the truth."

"And that is practically your middle name." Jean-René caught her hand. "I will tell you . . . but I will disavow any knowledge of this conversation if Jacob askes me."

"Okay," she said. "In that case, spill it."

"Do you remember meeting a guy named Doug McGuire?"

"The *Canadian Bigfoot Hunter?*" Lauren asked. She remembered him vividly. The man had all the swagger of Teddy Roosevelt with an ego twice as big as the Yukon. His handlebar moustache was equally grandiose. The Grizzly Adams beard wasn't out of character either. Lauren got bad vibes off of him because any time he mentioned an animal, his first comment was about the best way to kill it. "*AK47 is most likely the best for Bigfoot, but with all the damned government regulations, I'd have to go with a Winchester,*" he'd said. "*Nothing like a good old shotgun . . . with the right ammo, of course. You Americans know how to build a decent firearm, that's for certain.*"

"That's the one," Jean-René said, bringing her back to the conversation at hand. "He pitched a show to the Network and Jacob agreed to produce a pilot. If it goes well, he's prepared to offer a twelve-episode contract with options for additional episodes."

"So?" Lauren shrugged.

"So."

"So, why am I not going to be happy?" she asked.

"The name of the show . . . is *Bigfoot: Wanted, Dead or Alive.*"

Lauren did a double take, her jaw falling slack as she

puzzled over the title. "I suspect there's more than just the title that's going to tick me off. What is it?"

"A lawmaker in Oklahoma passed a bill allowing the Fish & Wildlife Department to issue a hunting license . . . for Bigfoot. That's where they're going to film the pilot."

"Are you . . . kidding me?" Lauren wasn't one to cuss, but she included a powerful expletive in the statement. She slapped her hand over her mouth, blushing. The man across the aisle turned and cast shade in her direction. Lauren gave him an apologetic look. Without even realizing it, she switched to French. "So they're going to go get a license and shoot a Bigfoot?"

"It gets better," Jean-René answered in his native tongue. "This show is going to be like a cross between a game show and a survival contest. There will be teams, and the first team that brings in Bigfoot— dead or alive—gets a one million dollar reward."

"Who's paying the reward?" Lauren asked. "Is it the Network? Sponsors? Didn't they learn anything from the fiasco with Eric and Bish?"

Eric Sherwood, Executive Director of the Oceanic Channel, and Bishop Khan, one of the Network's biggest financial supporters were caught in their illegal games of *intrigue*. The money used to fund a new research vessel called *The Explorer of the Deep*—the ship she and Rowan had been sent to Miami to find—came from a clandestine scheme that involved wealthy men paying large sums of money to party and for *companionship* on a private island, utilizing young women trafficked for such purposes.

Neither would ever be brought to justice. Both were dead. Sherwood died, lost in the Bermuda Triangle—his body found in the *Explorer's* wreckage by the US Coast Guard. Bishop Khan's death was more suspicious. Investigators never determined if the car crash that claimed his life had been accidental, or intentional. Two other people died in the incident, and Lauren blamed Khan.

"Jacob wouldn't tell me," Jean-René said. He sat back in his seat. "I don't want to go, but I'm also afraid if I don't, I can't help you and your . . . uh . . . your *people* out." Jean-René knew everything now. He knew about her father and his history. He also knew about Lauren's abilities, too. "If I can inadvertently make a noise, or warn your . . . *your friends*, I will."

"I don't think you need to worry about that," Lauren said. "I don't think anyone *I know* is in Oklahoma right now. I'm more worried about you."

"Me?"

"Running around at night with a bunch of idiots with guns? Especially Doug McGuire? That can't be safe. You could get killed."

"I wish I had an excuse to be anywhere else but there," Jean-René said. "But when *The Veritas Codex* isn't filming, I'm basically the property of the Network. According to my contract, they can send me on any assignment they want."

"How's your mom?" Lauren asked, seemingly out of the blue.

Jean-René looked at her sideways. She knew the question might seem off-subject, but Lauren believed he would follow her line of thinking. "My mother? She's fine."

"Are you sure? You haven't been to see her since we went to film the piece on the Knights Templar. Maybe she's not feeling well. Maybe you need to go check on her."

Jean-René paused, giving this some thought, and she could tell he understood. "Who could ever really be sure? Not from so far away. I mean, she is almost eighty-seven years old."

"Think about it," Lauren said. "Rowan will be home for a little while, then he is going to Egypt to lecture at the University. He'll be home before the baby arrives and we won't even think about filming until September. You might get assigned to something different if you're already overseas."

"I like how you think, Boss," Jean-René said, leaning his head on her shoulder, yawning. "Wake me up when we get to Phoenix?"

"I'm getting up as soon as the fasten seatbelt sign goes off," she said. "If you fall asleep on my shoulder, I'll wake you up a lot sooner."

3

"**D**id you see the weather?" Jean-René asked, bringing Lauren a cup of coffee. She put her feet up on her carry-on bag, having her shoes off.

She turned to the window. "Sun's shining, birds are singing. What's the Weather Channel going to tell me I can't already see?"

"There's a typhoon in the Pacific, a monster storm. They're calling it a once-in-a-century typhoon."

Lauren tensed. "Jordan Island?"

"Taking the brunt of the storm right now," he said, sipping his own coffee as he sat down.

"Did Rowan get out before it hit?"

"Not sure. But knowing Rowan, he's been monitoring it. They'd evacuate him before it got bad, I'd think."

The silence between them grew heavier as the television above the bank of chairs switched over to the weather. The audio was muted, but the closed captions conveyed the story. Typhoon—or cyclone—season typically started in mid-summer, but it wasn't unheard of to see storms this early in the year. This storm, however, was huge. The eye was located north of New Zealand, but the bands of rain that wrapped around it spread from Sydney to Samoa. Spaghetti models identified a dozen different possible tracks the storm might take, but they all converged on Hawaii, and if the storm held tough, it might continue to the southern US Pacific coast. Such storms weren't unheard of in Southern California, but they were rare. New Orleans' chances of seeing a hurricane were far greater than San Diego's.

"Jordan Island is south of the eye," Jean-René said. "If . . . and I must stress *if*—because I know you worry—*if* he's still there, he's going to have to hold out until rescue can reach him. It may be a while."

Lauren took out her phone, opening up an app she generally used to find her children. "*Find my phone*, don't fail me now," she muttered, trying to ping his cell phone.

Jean-René leaned over and winced when the map flipped and panned down over the middle of the South Pacific. "What does this mean?" she asked, worry heavy in her voice.

"It means his phone is still on Jordan Island," Jean-René pulled up his own phone, dialed a number and pressed his phone to his ear. "No signal," he said. Lauren could hear the error klaxon from the other end of the line.

"Try the sat phone," she said, her voice trembling.

Jean-René took her hand, as he dialed with the other. "Rowan's okay. We have to believe that."

WHEN THE PLANE landed in San Diego, Lauren switched her phone off of airplane mode, and puzzled when she saw a number she didn't recognize. "Where's the 808 area code?" Jean-René asked, seeing the number.

"Hawai'i," Lauren said, opening the voice mail. She felt relief wash through her core when she heard Rowan's voice. "It's Rowan. Christ. He's in Honolulu."

"Out of the frying pan, and into the fire." Jean-René had already pulled up the weather on his own phone. "Well, the good news is, the eye might track south of Hawai'i."

"Or not." Lauren swallowed hard.

———

THE KIDS FLOCKED around her as she came in with her suitcase in tow. Bahati swooped in and scooped up Kate who was being the most vocal about their mother's return, demanding all her attention. Even Shadow, the Siamese cat, mewed loudly. Her deep meow could be heard above the shouting.

John Carter moved in and took his mother's suitcase, taking her jacket along with it. He leaned in and kissed her cheek. "Welcome home."

"We're making spaghetti," Jamie said.

"I can smell it." Lauren grinned. "And it smells delicious."

"*Unca Jean-a-nay.*" Kate reached for him when he came in behind Lauren. The toddler couldn't quite say his name, but no one dared correct her. He'd become rather fond of the nickname. "*Unca Jean-a-nay*, you wanna see my baby?"

"Your baby?"

"Nanhi made me a baby doll," she said. "She's taking her nap."

"Well, maybe after dinner," Jean-René said. "I don't want to wake her up, and I'm starving."

"The garlic bread should be done," Jamie said. "Everything else is ready."

"I helped." Sam tugged on Lauren's pant leg. "I helped."

Lauren groaned as she picked him up. "I bet you ate all of it when no one was looking."

"He's just like his brothers," Bahati said. "I swear his middle name should have been *what else can I have?*"

"I think you grew three whole feet while we were gone," Jean-René said, carrying Kate into the kitchen, taking her to her chair, knowing she'd expect him to sit beside her.

Sam looked down at his legs. "I only has two feet."

Everyone laughed as Lauren took her seat, laying a napkin over her round belly. She was tired and hungry, but more than anything, she was worried for Rowan. They ate dinner and talked about the kids' activities. Lauren signed Sam up for soccer. John Carter was taking guitar lessons and doing Boy Scouts.

Jamie was in Boy Scouts too, but he wasn't the most sporty of boys. He tripped over his feet easily and lacked the necessary hand-eye coordination for every sport he tried. Instead, he'd gotten into making kites. He progressed from paper triangles to more elaborate designs. Before she left to go on *vacation*, Diana taught him how to sew the pieces of plastic fabric. John Carter helped with some of the more complicated structures and when Henry was home, he taught Jamie about physics and aerodynamics.

Jamie became quite a hit with the rest of their scouting troop, and now the scout troop hosted monthly kite flying contests. The whole collection of his creations hung on pegs in the garage.

"Have you heard from your Mom & Dad?" Bahati asked. Lauren knew she wouldn't ask about what kind of peril Rowan might be in around the children.

"No, but that's not surprising."

"I bet they decided to extend the second honeymoon a few more days."

"I appreciate you holding down the fort while we were gone," Lauren said. "I'm glad we finished our business early."

"Did you show that *doodoo dude* who the boss was?" Kate asked.

Lauren narrowed her eyes at everyone at the table who knew what their real mission was. All of them—John Carter, Bahati, and Jean-René—tried to look innocent, and Lauren believed it. Kate often demonstrated the same perceptive abilities Henry did at that age. She didn't seem to possess the same time-place abilities, though.

"Excuse me?" Lauren asked.

"That bad man you went to get in trouble. You made him get in jail, didn't you?"

"That's up to the judge to decide," Jean-René said. "Eat your spaghetti and I'll read you a book before you go to bed."

"In French?" Kate asked.

"*Oui. En français.*" Like her mother, Kate loved languages, especially French.

JOHN CARTER PUT the dishes away after dinner while the adults sat around the table nursing glasses of iced tea.

"What do you mean his phone is still on Jordan Island?" Bahati asked.

Lauren explained she'd tried to ping it. "He better not have lost another one. We've replaced three in the last five years, just for him. The *Apple Protection Plan* people are going to have kittens if we have to file another claim."

"Wouldn't happen if he'd get an Android." Jean-René laughed.

"Please. He wouldn't know what to do with an Android. He's been an Apple user since they first came out," Lauren scoffed, wincing as the baby kicked her.

"Look, Rowan is smart," Bahati said. "If he knew a

monster typhoon was coming, he'd bug out early and we all know it. He's probably sitting on a beach drinking a piña colada and raising his glass to the storm."

"Or his middle finger," Jean-René said.

"That's more like it."

ROWAN TURNED on the charm for the gate agent. She pulled him aside, away from the crowds. "I'm sorry, Mr. Pierce, but all flights to the US, Canada, Mexico . . . they're all being cancelled." He almost made it home before the typhoon caught up with him. He'd been so sure he could catch his connecting flight from Honolulu to LAX before the whole Pacific grid snarled. He hadn't. "You can't get past a storm this big. Besides, it's riding the pineapple express. The storm is headed straight for Hawai'i and should be here in hours, not days. Then it's headed straight towards the U.S. Mainland. You might wish you weren't in L.A."

That was concerning. He thought of Lauren and the kids. Maybe this was the perfect time for them to go visit his parents in Colorado. It was summer and they'd be out of school soon. "So, what are my options?"

"The last flight with an available seat out of here is to Singapore. If you want off the island before this hits, I highly recommend you get on that plane. Otherwise, you're going to be stranded here at least a week," she said.

Rowan went to reach for his cell phone, but remembered it wasn't in his pocket. Whether it'd fallen out in his mad dash to escape whatever had been chasing him, or if it fell out of his pocket when he hit the ocean, it didn't matter now. He was without a phone, and he felt like he was missing half his brain. "What's today's date?"

"May 4th," she said.

Rowan put a hand on one hip, leaning on the ticket

counter with the other one. He stared at the toe of his shoe. "I'm supposed to be in Cairo in a week," he said. "I'd hoped to get home to see my wife and kids before then."

"I've seen storms half this size shut down the whole grid for over a week. If you don't get out now, you'll be late for your meeting in Cairo."

4

University of Cairo, Egypt
May 4th

"Legends told of the powerful kings who ruled the lands of Kish, in the country of Sumer. Kish was the first city to have kings following the Great Deluge. There is an ancient tablet that tells us this. It said, *all of them were Lords*. Yet, there is a passage in the Bible where Enoch—being undoubtedly the most important descendant of Adam—*walked with God, and then he was no more because God had taken him away*. Let us ponder on that statement. What do you think it means?" Tima let her gaze pan over the lecture hall. One hand in the corner went up first, as it always did.

"Yes, Maliqa," Tima said.

"Enoch and Elijah were the only two men in the Bible who were taken straight to heaven. They both escaped the curse of death."

"That is true, but do you know why?"

"No one does," one of the boys on the other side of the room said with indignation.

"Because they are to serve as witness to the final Revelation," Maliqa said. "Here they will experience death briefly."

Tima's brow lifted. "That is an excellent theory, but . . . still just speculation." She hated having to quash the girl's enthusiasm. "Most of us have read about Elijah," Tima said. "Enoch isn't as well known. He was the father of Methuselah, the longest living man, but he himself lived three hundred and sixty-five years, according to the Bible. We later see him in the Hall of Faith. *By faith Enoch was taken from this life, so that he did not experience death. He could not be found, because God had taken him away.*"

"Just as the Bible says all those who walk in faith will be taken during the rapture," Maliqa said. "Enoch walked in faith with the gods and was taken."

"Beam me up, Mr. Scott," one of the American students in the back of the hall snarked. Several other students laughed.

"We do see parallels in Enoch's story and the story of the Revelation yet to come," Tima quelled the teasing. "Now, let us talk about a time when gods walked among men." Tima used the moment to discuss something she'd read in a book Rowan gave her. "Has anyone read *Chariot of the Gods?*"

Tima watched the clock as she led the discussion, and as predicted, it came to its natural end in plenty of time to discuss the real matter at hand. "I have been notified by a colleague at Al Turath University, that there is an opportunity to visit Kish to learn about the first civilizations of mankind." Tima stood before her students. "The Kings of Kish have eluded archaeologists simply because of the political strife in Iraq. But now, in this time of peace, I will be taking a sabbatical." There was a groan that rose to a din above the lecture hall. With their professor on sabbatical, there would be no summer intercession classes, and that might delay graduation for students who might rely on the additional credit hours. "The good news is, I have applied for—and received grant funding that will allow six students to go with me." Hope sprung eternal on the faces of her bright eyed students. "The decision will be made by lottery and students must apply for this opportunity. To be considered, you must be in good standing. Your final exams for this semester must be completed and you must receive a score higher than eighty-five percent. Each candidate must write a dissertation on Sumerian culture and the significance of the city of Kish, along with what you expect to learn this summer and what role you hope to play in this expedition. The contest will be judged by an impartial panel. The twenty students with the highest points will have their name entered into the lottery."

Tima allowed the din of muttering conversation between the excited students to run its course as she prepared for her day's lessons. Forty-six students made up this class. She also taught an *Introduction to Ancient Sumerian Religion* course with twenty-eight students who would be offered the same opportunity. The college professors would not be part of the selection committee, in order to ensure no biases were involved. Instead, she enlisted a panel of uninvolved experts, mostly her graduates.

She paused a moment to think of a few of her favorites, but she had little time for nostalgia. She was looking forward to seeing one in particular. Rowan Pierce was an all-time favorite, and she hadn't seen him since his third son was born. *How old would Jamie be now? Nine? Ten? Had it been that long?*

"Ehem," one of the students in the shadows cleared his throat overtly, and Tima realized she'd been lost in thought for a moment. "Dr. Badr? Are you all right?"

"Yes, of course." She laughed nervously. It wasn't like her to mentally check-out during a lecture. "Just thinking about the final exam for this class." It was a cover, but she did remember something she needed to make sure she told the students. "Your final exams will be based on the next three lectures, including the guest lecture with Rowan Pierce, so be sure you don't miss any of them. I don't want anyone to fail because they didn't show up . . . or pay attention. If anyone needs extra credit, pick up a copy of *Chariots of the Gods* and read it. Then come see me about the rest of the assignment."

TIMA SAT with her feet up on a chair in her office. Her feet ached from a full day spent pacing in front of students. She wore the most sensible shoes she owned, but nothing seemed to help. She was at the age where most college professors retired or died. She had no interest in doing either. Other than her aching feet, and a bit of arthritis in her hands, she was as robust as she'd ever been. She might not be as fast getting around the dig site, but she intended to do her fair share of the work. She already made plans for when her favorite student arrived.

Her cell phone lay between her hands as she debated sending a text. She didn't know where Rowan and Lauren lived these days, or what time zone. Someone said they thought they lived in Hawai'i.

She composed the message, but she hesitated for fear of waking them. She knew Lauren was expecting, but she didn't know when her due date was. If the baby arrived and they were already sleep deprived, it could make matters worse. But then again, if the baby hadn't arrived . . . maybe . . .

Sheesh, Tima. Just send it. She scolded herself mentally, then hit send.

She tossed her phone on the desk, glancing up as one of her students paused to knock. "Dr. Badr? Do you have a moment?"

"Please." Tima waved the girl in. It was surprising to see her star pupil in her office. Maliqa was the last student to have issues, and Tima doubted she was here to ask about extra credit. She didn't need it. "Come in, Maliqa. What can I do for you?"

The girl took a seat in front of Tima's desk and fidgeted with the strap of her messenger bag. "I uh, I'm not sure how to say this, so, I'm just going to spit it out." She paused, taking a deep breath. "I can't apply for the summer research project."

"But you are my best student," Tima said. She was convinced if any of her students would earn a spot on the team, Maliqa Hamza al Khalid would be one of them. Her intellect and work ethic were second only to Rowan Pierce. "What's wrong?"

"My father will not permit me to go. He's sending my Uncle to bring me home to Aleppo."

"For how long?"

Maliqa's round face filled with sadness, and tears threatened to burst from her large eyes. "I will not be coming back."

"Why?" Tima asked.

"My father found out I was majoring in archaeology. He does not feel it is an appropriate career for a young woman. He says I have shamed him and disrespected his wishes. I was supposed to be studying to become a doctor. But, I want to get my PhD and become a professor, like you."

"Give me his number," Tima said. "Let me call and talk to him. Maybe I can smooth this over."

"My father is angry, Dr. Badr. He is also very powerful and vengeful. I would not have his wrath fall upon you. Please. It is best I go and bear the brunt of his anger alone."

"What about your mother? Can I talk to her? Maybe she could talk some sense into him."

A tear ran unchecked down the girl's face. "No, Dr. Badr. My mother is dead, and I will consider myself fortunate if he allows me to simply take over the running of the household."

"And if you are not fortunate?"

"He will beat me. He says he will arrange for me to marry

his *friend* in Iran and send me off to live in the desert and I will never see my brothers or sister again."

"Surely there is something we can do." Tima wasn't ready to surrender.

"Please, Dr. Badr. If you wish to help me, do nothing." The girl launched herself from the chair. "I will not have his wrath fall upon you, too." Tima could hear the sobs echoing down the hall as the student made her escape.

This was not the first Syrian girl she'd lost to an overbearing father. It was a custom of the old days, one that should have died a generation or more ago. Women were not allowed the same freedoms she'd taken liberty of when she'd divorced her husband so many years ago.

Tima wanted to help, but she knew Maliqa was right. Any interference could result in dire consequences from her father. Tima hated it, but she would have to find some other way to help her student. She just needed to figure out what that might look like.

As she tidied up her desk and collected the research papers she needed to grade, her cell phone on her desk buzzed to life. Seeing the caller ID, she snatched it up. "Lauren, dear!" she answered brightly. "How are you?"

"Tired, but I'm doing well."

"And Rowan? How is your darling husband?"

"Trapped in Hawai'i, riding out a cyclone, according to the message I received. I haven't been able to get through to him since." Tima could hear the concern in her voice.

"Maybe I can get through," she said. "I'm on the other side of the planet, but it's funny how things work."

"You're more than welcome to try," she said. "Let me give you the number. He lost his phone on location, but he called me from this number." Lauren relayed the information.

"How is the baby doing? When are you due?"

"Not for a couple of months," she said. "Jean-René and I just got back from a short trip. My feet are swollen and my back hurts, but otherwise, it's been an uneventful pregnancy."

"Thank *Taweret* and *Bes*," Tima said. *Taweret* was the Egyptian deity of protection for women and children, often depicted as a pregnant hippo with the limbs of a lion and the back and tail of a crocodile. She was a fierce being. *Bes* was the goddess of merriment and childbirth, fertility, and war. She offered protection to pregnant women. Lauren would know that. She'd sat in on plenty of Tima's lectures when they lived in Cairo.

"Thanks indeed," Lauren sighed. "I just hope Rowan can have some time at home before he has to turn around and fly to Cairo."

"Were his travel reservations made in advance?"

"I booked his flights myself," Lauren answered. "All from LAX."

"If I reach him, I'll let you know and ask him to call you, if he can. If not, I can relay messages."

"If I don't answer it's because I'm sleeping," Lauren said. "It's been a long day."

"As you should, dear. I'll text and you can call me back when it's convenient for you."

"THANK YOU, TIMA," she said, glancing up as Jean-René came down stairs. "On an expedition? The Red Sea? Oh, yes, I can imagine he'd be quite excited to join you. I could send Jean-René. They could get some footage for the show." She grinned wearily. "Yes, please, if you talk to him, let him know about it. I'm sure he'll do it."

"What are you doing?" Jean-René asked as she finished up the phone call and tucked her phone into her pocket.

"I just got you out of that stupid show," she said. "Tima has a diving trip she wants to take Rowan on."

"But . . . Jacob . . ."

"You let me worry about Jacob," Lauren said curtly. "I'll call him. But it can wait until we get some rest. I'll call you in the morning."

"Not too early," he cautioned.

"Maybe tomorrow afternoon." She yawned. "I feel like I could sleep for days."

"I'll keep that in mind when I'm making reservations for you tomorrow."

"Lucky me," Jean-René groaned.

IT WAS after three o'clock in the morning when Lauren gave up trying to sleep and headed for the recliner. She was surprised to find John Carter in the kitchen, making himself a glass of milk, and raiding her stash of Oreos.

"Better save some of those for me," she said, startling the teenager.

"What are you doing up so late?" he asked, going to the pantry for a second glass.

"Fretting about your father," she admitted. "I saw the weather report and the storm has intensified."

"What?" Joy melted from his face. They both knew what that meant. His father would be delayed getting home.

Lauren reached up and brushed his long hair off his cheek. Her thumb brushed against the three freckles beneath his left eye. They reminded her of the Pyramids of Giza. The marks grew darker over the past few years as his face began to lose the roundness of a boy. He looked even more like his Uncle Michael as a teenager. His face grew more square, and his cheekbones grew more prominent. His brows were thick and heavy, but often hidden behind the flop of raven-wing hair hanging in his eyes. "He said he would help me with my Eagle Scout project this weekend."

"Don't worry," Lauren said, assuring him. "You'll have plenty of help. I'll cover for him."

"You always do, but . . ." he glanced down at her bathrobe tied over her belly. "You can't help with the manual labor."

"I have friends who can," Lauren said. "I've told you before, one of the earmarks of leadership is learning to network and leverage your connections. Jacob, Chance, and Aunt Bahati have already volunteered to help, as have several other members of the crew. Your uncle did too, but I have something I need his help with, so he may not be here either."

"I haven't even decided on a project yet. That's what Dad wanted to help with first."

Lauren reached over him and snatched a cookie from his stack. "Okay, so let's talk about that." While they talked, Lauren put on a pot of water for tea.

"Well, I had a few ideas," John Carter started. Lauren pulled out one of the stools and took a seat. John Carter pushed the package of Oreos over to her. She took one and split it apart, going for the cream filling while he broke down his ideas. Some seemed grandiose, others were simple acts of service. All were excellent ideas. "But first, I need to come up with a budget." *Ah, the boy had been paying attention.*

5

Aleppo, Syria
May 5th

"Thank you for meeting with me," Faadin al Khalid welcomed his Sudanese guest as he entered the courtyard. It was an unusually warm day in the desert. "May I offer you tea?"

"It would be most welcomed," Abdul bin Salman replied, extending his open palm in greeting to his guest, before placing it on his chest and bowing slightly.

The host directed his guest to a table in the shade by a babbling fountain. Here, the air was cooler, and a man-servant poured them hot tea, heavy with bright green mint leaves and plenty of sugar. The host offered up sweets and small bites to the hungry traveler who accepted. Small talk filled the space between them until the host dismissed his staff with a stoic lift of his brow and a harsh glance.

Once they were alone, Abdul asked. "Any word from our *neighbors?*"

Faadin paused, chewing a morsel before washing it down

with a sip of hot tea. "I have allies in the south," he said. "They found your theory . . . provocative."

"Still, there are many enemies between us, my friend. Neither of our forces are strong enough to conquer them through brute strength. We will have to be cunning if we are to see victory."

"I agree." al Khalid took up his own cup, which was hardly bigger than a shot glass, and sipped. "That is why I have sought the council of allies, such as yourself . . . and *others*."

"Do they understand the magnitude of the task you ask of them, my friend?" Abdul asked.

Al Khalid nodded, popping another bite in his mouth. He talked around it as he chewed. "*The Great Accord* is little more than smoke and mirrors. War remains at bay simply because we are all gaging each other's strengths and weaknesses. We are aligning ourselves for—or against—one another, this is how we prepare when the time comes for war again." He popped a finger in his mouth, licking off the sugary syrup and crumbs before reaching for another bite.

"Our enemies think us weak." Abdul rose, pacing in the shade beneath an arch of bougainvillea.

Beyond the walls of the manor house, yellow broom flowers, purple thistles and bright red poppies hid the signs of destruction brought by years of war. The hummocks and dells were little more than aging piles of debris, craters, and trenches. The flowers grew where people once lived, fought, and died. al Khalid's manor was the finest in all of Aleppo—if not all of Syria.

Twenty years of fighting killed over a million people, destroyed whole towns and city districts, and made over half of all Syrians homeless. They lived as refugees in their own country. The people were under al Khalid's thumb, and he liked it that way. It made them more compliant, and less likely to rebel.

In the shadow of *The Great Accord*—a global peace agreement, negotiated by Ambassador Kitty Donovan-Grayson—aid organizations flocked to the region to rebuild and offer hope to what had been one of the world's wealthiest nations.

His forces had taken Aleppo in a siege that lasted forty days and forty nights. The defending armies were slaughtered in battle, leaving the residents defenseless. Many died in the crossfire. al Khalid considered it a necessary sacrifice of war.

Those that remained lacked access to food, clean water, electricity, or medical care. Many perished when famine and disease spread through the region. Since one of the bloodiest conflicts in the Middle East, over 30,000 more lives had been lost. Now, Faadin al Khalid was left with little more than a wasteland filled with walking corpses to rule over. He was the richest man in the country, but his wealth brought him little. He was a king whose peasants were of little use to him. He knew he was not well liked, and perhaps that was why NATO denied him entry. Still, he needed allies. This one though, he wasn't sure of.

Sudan was no better off. The country's name came from the expression *ilād al-sūdān*, or *the land of the black*. It was a nation on the brink of civil war. The recognized government was crumbling from its very core, and those like Abdul bin Salman waited for the crumbs among the rubble. It was just a matter of time before the warlord made his play.

The Sudanese warlord—known by some as *Abdul the Usurper*—had been keen to form an alliance with Syria, even before *The Great Accord*. Now they could meet openly since *The Accord* no longer limited discussions or alliances for the purpose of peace. This was a meeting meant to broker peace, but the methods had yet to be determined.

"The enemy of my enemy is my friend," al Khalid said, out of nowhere.

"What does your *friend* in Iraq say? Did he read the documents I sent you? About the weapon?" Ahmed held his empty cup up. A servant rushed in to fill it.

"He believes the prophesy is true," Faadin said. "He believes the key is to find an archaeologist to prove it."

"An archaeologist?"

"Who better to find treasures buried beneath the rubble of ancient civilizations?"

"Do you have someone in mind?"

"As a matter of fact, I do," Faadin held a mischievous grin. "My daughter has defied my wishes and has been pursuing a degree in the science, rather than attending the pre-med classes I thought I was paying for."

"Your *daughter* will be helping us?"

"Of course not," he said. "But her professor . . . a woman, is supposed to be one of the best."

"Women are easy enough to control," Abdul said with a chuckle. "I have five wives who do my bidding."

"I might have agreed with you until I discovered my daughter's deception. I suspect this woman has been manipulating her. I half expected to get a call from her when I demanded my daughter leave the program and come home."

"Well, that could possibly solve one problem, but there is another pressing need that we have yet to address," Abdul said, sitting back. "An army requires capital. I need funds to purchase weapons. Will your friend in Iraq provide what I need?"

"My friend has his own army . . . and friends of his own," Faadin said. A bead of sweat ran down the side of his face. "Have you considered the United States? They have the resources we need. Their ambassador is the one who brokered *The Accord*. The United States and Iraq have been at odds since the 1980's. They could help you take what you want, if it is in Iraq."

"*Accord* or not, the US refuses to recognize my authority in Sudan," Adbul said. "As a conquering force, they did not look kindly on my right to rule a nation I was born in. My own family ruled these lands for centuries. I simply took back a birthright that was denied me. You have a similar problem. Your rule is not recognized either."

"Not yet," al Khalid said. "In time, however, they will know me, and they will not be able to deny my rule."

"The enemy of my enemy . . ." Abdul thought aloud, scratching his thick beard with his knuckles. "We must not fail to consider the enemies of our allies."

"Russia, you mean," al Khalid said. "We must proceed with caution. The Russian government is under the control of an unstable leader. His predecessor was just as mad."

Faadin al Khalid was beginning to wonder just how mad Abdul might be. He rose and paced in front of the fountain. His hands folded behind his back as he spoke. "While my *friend* in Iraq has heard your story, you have not told me how you learned of this weapon or how you came to possess the documents you sent. I have asked, yet you have not told."

"I had a vision," Abdul said, clasping his hands and gazing up into the brilliant sky. "*The Great Lord of the Ancient Gods* has shown me the cavern beneath an ancient city, where this weapon resides. He bids me to make haste, to find his weapon that I might use it against the *infidels* who would oppose My Lord. When the time comes, a path will be made for us, and *he* will show us the way."

"Allah has shown you these things?"

"Not Allah," Abdul said. "I have seen the face of the god of my ancient ancestors. It is the God, Enlil who beckons me to serve."

DR. KITTY GRAYSON arrived in Jerusalem just days ahead of the annual *Gathering of Nations*. It was the perfect time of year to visit the Holy Land. A comfortably warm air greeted her as she stood at the top of the stairs butted up against the aircraft and descended onto the tarmac. Date palms danced in a light breeze. The sun was bright, and the world seemed full of promise.

The Gathering was scheduled to avoid interfering with the annual celebration of *Yom Yerushaláyim* at the end of the month, also known as *Jerusalem Day*. Kitty had tried to convince leaders that there would be no better time than *Yom Yerushaláyim* for a celebration of peace, considering Jerusalem Day was meant to commemorate the reunification of the Old City, or East Jerusalem and the West Bank. However, local leaders insisted their holiday was too significant to the city to interfere with. The *Gathering of Nations* would remind the citizens—the world, too—of the importance of peace and finding common ground.

Prior to her trip to Jerusalem, Kitty completed a tour of the Asian continent to ensure the world leaders were all on the same page, and to prepare for any possible disagreements that might be brought up. War was easy. Maintaining peace was a whole other thing. Over the years, she had negotiated a number of settlements between various countries and factions. Even corporations threatened to implement trade embargos against countries when they didn't agree with various policies.

"Dr. Grayson! Welcome! Welcome!" The Israeli ambassador, Daniel Segal greeted her as she stepped off the airplane. The wind whipped her scarf across her face, blinding her. She recovered and took five long strides over to the motorcade where he stood under an umbrella, held by one of his staff.

"Daniel," she said brightly. "So good to see you."

"I'm glad you made it," he greeted her warmly. "How was your flight?"

"Long," she admitted.

"Come then," he said. "We'll get you settled at the King David Hotel. Tonight's agenda is open, but there's much to do before tomorrow night's state dinner with the Prime Minister."

"Daniel, you promised," she moaned as he led her to his personal limousine.

"I know you would rather we didn't make a fuss, but the Prime Minister requests your presence. I was trying not to offend him. We need him to pull this week off."

"At least tell me I don't have to be anywhere before noon."

"Our first meeting is at 9:00 a.m."

"What have you got for jetlag?"

"Room service and a cup of tea," Daniel said with an impish grin.

"I'll take it." Kitty laughed.

6

Beijing, China
May 5th

"I'm just so happy to talk to you," Lauren said, when he called. "I'm sorry you won't make it home, but I can work on changing your flights today."

"That won't be necessary. They told me it might take a week before the airport would be able to open again, so I went ahead and changed my flights to head to Cairo."

"So you won't be home?"

"I'd be there if I could, you know that."

"I do." Lauren acquiesced.

"When will you arrive?"

A guttural laugh escaped his throat. "I'm getting to Cairo the hard way. I've got a long layover here in Beijing, if you can call two days a layover. I've got a room in the *Aerotel*. After that, I have a stop in Chengdu before another stop with an eight hour layover in Dubai."

"Well, at least you'll earn some extra frequent flyer miles," Lauren said.

"I have to confess," he said, hesitant to mention it. "I cashed in some of my miles for an upgrade."

"First class?"

"It's a long flight to Dubai . . ." he said.

"You don't have to justify it to me," Lauren said, laughing. "Have you talked to Tima yet?"

"Not yet," he said. "You were my first call."

"I'm sending Jean-René to meet you in Cairo."

There was a momentary pause. "Why?"

"Tima wants to take you on an expedition, if you're willing."

"I never say no to field research," Rowan said. "But why are you sending Jean-René? He's supposed to be taking care of you while I'm gone."

"This isn't about me. I'm rescuing Jean-René. Jacob wanted to send him on a project we don't agree with, and I needed an excuse to have him occupied. He can explain it all when he gets there."

"Okay. I'm sure this will be a great story," Rowan said. "How are you doing?"

"Swollen feet and a ton of Braxton Hicks contractions, but nothing unusual. I'm expected at the college soon, but otherwise I'm taking it as easy as I can considering my mother is off on *vacation* with my father."

That was a code for *time-traveling*. She couldn't stay in his time exceedingly long. He couldn't stay in their time either. A few weeks between the two every now and then had allowed them to reconnect, and it did Lauren's heart good to see her parents happy—finally.

"I better keep this short. I'm sure the long distance bill on this call is going to be exorbitant."

"When you get a chance, go pick up a new phone," Lauren said. "I don't dare put in a call to the warranty company on this last one."

"I'll make that a priority," he said. "I'll see if I can pick one up here."

"But do get the insurance policy," Lauren quipped. He'd been through several phones over the last few years, and the prices continued to skyrocket. She hated having to pay for another phone so soon.

"Yes, dear," he said. "I love you," Rowan added.

"I know," Lauren quipped, and the line went dead.

These past few days of waiting to hear from him, all the while seeing video of the destruction in the Pacific had been gut-wrenching. The storm continued to rage and churn in the deep Pacific, having struck the Big Island of Hawai'i worst. Honolulu had taken it on the chin as well. The storm had started to turn for the US but was now scribbling more towards Japan.

At least now she had something to do that was useful. She turned to her computer and typed in the web address for the airlines to start the process of booking Jean-René's flight.

Cairo, Egypt
May 10th

Rowan arrived at Tima's door late in the evening, looking like a homeless bum—an exhausted one. He all but fell into Tima's embrace, even though he was far from *April fresh*. He knew he needed a shower. Tima clung to him. "I'm sorry I stink."

"Don't be ridiculous, Rowan *darling*." She pushed back, inspecting him. She always called him Rowan *darling*. "But you are looking thin. Hasn't Lauren been feeding you?" She caught his bicep and squeezed it.

"If I'd come home once in a while, she might," he said wearily.

"Good thing I'm here," Tima said. "There is always a place for you at my table."

"Good thing she has room for two." A familiar voice came from the kitchen and Jean-René stepped out from behind the doorway.

"*Mon ami* . . ." his voice faded into a sigh as he crossed the entry way and embraced him with exuberance. "You beat me here," Rowan said. "I thought I told you to stay home and take care of Lauren?"

"She's taking care of me this time," he said. "And I have orders to report back to her once I have been assured you made it safely. You gave her quite a scare when she saw your phone was still pinging from Jordan Island."

"My phone? Is it still working? I thought it'd been destroyed."

"*Tsk. Tsk.* No need to worry about that now," Tima said, wagging her fingers at the men. She turned to Rowan, her hand on his arms to steady him. "Which do you need first? Food, bath, or bed?"

"I don't even know," he said. "I'm too tired to make any more decisions."

"In that case, go to the tub. Jean-René and I have started making dinner, and you can go to bed as soon as you've eaten. How do you feel about knaffeh?"

"Sounds delicious." He leaned down and kissed her head.

Jean-René followed him into the hallway where they could talk. "I escaped from Jordan Island with just the clothes on my back," Rowan said, looking down at his wrinkled shirt. "I'm going to need to do some shopping."

"I brought you some things from home. Lauren seemed to know," he started, but let the words fall away.

"Doesn't she always?" Rowan held his gaze. "I still need to go shopping," he said. "I tried to pick up some things in Hawai'i, but the credit card readers were down, and I was out of cash. ATMs were down, too."

"Don't worry," Jean-René said. "We'll take care of anything you need tomorrow. You look like a zombie, and you smell like one, too."

"I'm off to the bath, then."

Rowan knew enough to know that the knaffeh would take a while, he had time for a long soak. The giant copper bath tub had been his wife's favorite thing about Tima's house. He also knew the tub was big enough for his long frame to stretch out in.

He wasn't at all surprised to find she'd laid out fresh towels, along with a basket containing jars of bubble bath, and bath salts—some of which Tima made herself. The aches and pains of travel melted almost as quickly as the scented foam when he sank to his chin in the cloudy waters. He had almost nodded off when there was a tap at the door. Jean-René poked his head in. "Tima asked me to bring you a cup of chai and to gather your dirty clothes so she can wash them," he said. He came in and set a cup on the table next to the tub. "I want in there after dinner, so don't use all the hot water," he added.

"Tankless hot water heater," Rowan said, with a happy sigh. "Installed it myself."

"Does Lauren know about this tub?"

"She does, and she's used it even more than I have," he mused, reaching for the milk laced tea. It smelled even better than the bubble bath. The spices made it taste like Christmas in a cup. "If I'm not out by the time the knaffeh is ready, check in on me. I've either drowned or fallen asleep."

"I'll know by the snoring," Jean-René said.

ROWAN HAD, in fact, fallen asleep before dinner was ready. He managed to get out of the tub, dried and dressed in a Turkish robe that had belonged to one of Tima's sons. He'd used it before, and he made a mental note to buy one for himself while he was here. Tima dismissed him from the dinner table when he started nodding off, even though he hadn't finished his meal.

By the time breakfast was served, Rowan felt like a new man. Tima left his freshly folded laundry on a bench by the guest room door.

Dressed and ready for the day, Rowan's heart was light. He'd slept better than he had in days, and he felt relieved and refreshed. The first thing he did, once Tima brought him a cup of Turkish coffee, was call Lauren.

He credited his chipper spirit to getting to talk to Lauren, as much as the good night's sleep. Her voice worked magic on him. It eased all the tension he'd carried since seeing Henry—or Henry's *shade*, as Henry often referred to it—finally slipped away. He decided Henry wanted him off the island because of the impending weather. The boy's mother needed him. Needed him to be alive and safe.

If he'd gotten back to Sydney sooner, he might have gotten ahead of the weather, but mechanical issues with the boat and then issues getting a replacement passport at the American Embassy in Australia kept him longer than he would have liked. He wasn't going to get home for another week or so, but he had work to do—commitments to fulfill. Tima would have understood if he had to cancel, but there was a contract between the Network and the University of Cairo for him to appear at a recruiting event. Rowan's notoriety had become a huge recruiting tool for the college. Thanks to him, students were flocking to Cairo in droves, in hopes of getting a scholarship, and maybe even a chance to meet the school's most famous graduate.

Tima happily road on his coattails. Rowan didn't blame

her one bit. She was a distinguished professor, and any student would be lucky to have her as their mentor. Rowan considered himself the luckiest one ever.

A fresh cup of Turkish coffee, laced with cinnamon, cardamom and ginger met him at the table, along with fresh squeezed juice. Tima made jasmine rice with golden raisins, dried apricots, butter, and spices. Rowan drizzled honey over his before topping his bowl with sliced almonds and flaked coconut. It was a feast fit for a king, or one lucky alumnus.

"Well, your lecture isn't scheduled until Thursday," Tima said, watching over her coffee. He'd forgotten about this habit, or the joy she got from his enjoyment of her cooking. Her own sons had been gone from home for over twenty years now, and her hair had gone as white as his own mother-in-law's. "So maybe you would like to see what the students are working on?" Fatima Badr's Egyptian features mirrored Diana Grayson's with a few subtle differences. Her high cheeks weren't apple-round like Diana's—like Lauren's—and her eyes were narrow-set, and he thought for a moment it looked like she had a cloudy cataract in one of them.

"What did you have in mind?" Rowan asked, returning to his meal. "Lauren mentioned an expedition?"

She turned to Jean-René to pose her question. "Do you like to dive as much as my favorite student?" Rowan laughed into his coffee cup but didn't meet his friend's gaze.

"Who do you think he goes diving with?" Jean-René asked.

"Well, then, how do you feel about a dive to see where we've uncovered a potential site for the Pharoah's crossing of the Red Sea from Egypt? It's a bit of a trip, but I have some funding to spend time there before your lecture. I think, if we are frugal, we can stretch the budget for all of us to go."

Rowan's head tilted to the left like a curious puppy dog. "Oh?"

Jean-René leaned in and wrapped his hand around his

cup. "I brought the underwater cameras and an ROV, if we need it."

"Some of the grad students have had some tremendous success," Tima said. "Today, I will take you to the warehouse and show you what we have found so far."

Jean-René and Rowan exchanged glances, both beaming with excitement. "I have some shopping I need to do," Rowan said.

"Of course," Tima said. "I already called for my driver. He'll be here after we've finished breakfast."

7

Porto El Sokhna, Egypt
May 12th

The sun broke the horizon as they arrived at the port. The water was as smooth as glass. Omar had the college's research vessel fueled up and ready to go. He greeted Rowan brightly. "Rowan! Welcome! Pleasure to see you again, my friend!" Omar worked for the University when Rowan was a student. His job was to organize the field research projects, like the dig at the Temple of Bastet.

Introductions were made and alliances established. The mood of the morning was convivial. The weather was beautiful. It was warm, with a light breeze. Wispy clouds dotted the clear blue skies. The smell of the salt and the sea welcomed them, and it made Rowan think of Lauren and their last night in Bermuda.

Jean-René nudged him, passing Rowan his newly purchased backpack, and went back for their equipment, as they made to weigh anchor. "Nice day for a sea cruise."

"It'll take a few hours to get to the site," Omar said. "Might as well get comfortable. There's water in the ice chest, and snacks in the galley. Mohammed packed us a nice lunch, and we'll dive this afternoon and have a moonlight trip back."

"No beer?" Jean-René took one of the seats, and Rowan sat across from him, with Fatima on his elbow. She had taken a liking to the photojournalist. It was evident to Rowan she'd just adopted him, too. While his professor called him '*Rowan, darling,*' his best friend was now known as '*Jean-René, chéri*', which essentially meant the same thing.

"No." Rowan leaned in and explained that Omar and Mohammed didn't imbibe because of their Muslim faith. "Water's better for us anyway. It's likely to get hot."

"Fair enough." Jean-René surrendered.

"So, Tima, tell us what the team has been doing. Why are we going to this site in particular?" Rowan asked, getting comfortable for the long journey.

"Many people believe Moses crossed from Egypt to Jordan," Tima began, taking out a map, unfolding it as they scooted around. "At least that is the interpretation of the biblical tale. However, we know the Israelites wandered through the desert for forty years, yes? This is known?"

"Yes," Rowan said.

"How versed are you in the Torah?"

"Jewish religion?" Rowan had been sitting at the table while Lauren educated their children on all of the world's major religions. He'd written a paper on the influence of Jewish religion on archaeology, but he still considered himself a neophyte in the intricate details of it.

"The Torah has an alternate name," Tima sat back, and Rowan recognized she was about to begin a lecture she'd delivered a dozen times, if not more. "It is called the *Five Books of Moses.*"

"Oh, really?" Jean-René was hanging on to her every word.

"The Talmud refers to Moses as *Moshe Rabbenu* or *Moses our Teacher*," she said. "Moses is a major figure in the Bible, beginning in the Book of Exodus to the end of the Book of Deuteronomy. In fact, he has long been regarded as the author, or at the very least, it's transcriber."

"According to the Jewish Encyclopedia, there are more legends about Moses than any other biblical figure," Omar continued the story. "His people grew increasingly upset with him. They said, *what is this you have done to us, bringing us out of Egypt? Indeed, it is better for us serving in Egypt than to die in the wilderness.*"

"The crossing of the Reed Sea, or as we know it now, the Red Sea, was an important part of the narrative. The Israelites' first journey was from Rameses to Succoth, near the modern city of Quantir. From Succoth they traveled to Etham on the edge of the desert, then they turned back to Pihahiroth, between Miguel and the sea, opposite Baal Zephron." Fatima's finger traced the path of travel on the map.

"But there's no solid evidence to that," Omar contradicted. "The Hebrew name for the place of the crossing is *Yam Suph*. Many think that refers to a salt water inlet between Africa and the Arabian peninsula. But because the story combines a number of traditions, the real path of the Israelites is likely much more ... *phrenic*. They wandered in the desert for 40 years. Clearly they were lost, and it doesn't mean they stayed in Egypt the whole time. There's no reason to believe that *Yam Suph* is contained within the modern Red Sea."

"Omar's theory made us rethink what we knew about history," Fatima said. "An Egyptian Archaeologist named Zahni Hammut authored a paper on the likely path they might have followed in search of the Promised Land. He agrees that as a myth, the written records are unreliable."

"So, I worked with a team of graduate students to run a series of computer models. We used predictive mapping to identify the most likely paths they might have followed, based on terrain, weather patterns, availability of water, sea levels, tides, and even the political climate of the day. In ninety-three of the one hundred simulations we ran, the computer narrowed down the crossing to just a five mile span, much further to the south. Here." Omar's finger tracked down the map and circled an unlikely section of the sea.

"That's where we're headed?"

"Yes," Omar said. "The models also factored in the Pharaoh's armies and their chariots and horses, and that's how we managed to narrow down the search area even further. Preliminary results have turned up some promising bits of bronze consistent with the remains of ancient chariots."

"The Bible speaks of the soldiers chariot wheels getting bogged up in the sea floor. We are hoping to find larger parts of a chariot." Tima added.

"That's amazing," Rowan gasped, glancing at Jean-René.

"That's putting it mildly," Omar agreed.

THEY SPENT the next few hours racing across the calm waters towards their destination. During that time, they discussed and debated every theory any of them had ever heard. Rowan injected a bit of playful banter to pass the time.

Sandwiches wrapped in flat bread and slathered with hummus were served mid-morning, along with hot sweet mint tea. Rowan stretched out on one of the benches and took a cat nap. He awoke when they reached their target.

Efficiently, the team set up the equipment to conduct a LIDAR pass, to verify their dive target for the afternoon. While the LIDAR was at work, Rowan and Jean-René began getting into their wet suits and getting the camera equipment ready. Rowan filmed some impromptu segments discussing the mission as well as his own thoughts on Omar's provocative theory, and his innovative work with predictive mapping.

"So, here's the plan," Tima said, as she spit into her dive mask and cleaned the lens in that fashion. The saliva was helpful in keeping the mask from fogging up. "There are parts of the sea that are over 3,000 meters deep. We're diving on a shelf that ranges between eighteen meters to over sixty meters. There is a coral reef, and the water is highly salinized, which means buoyancy is difficult to manage, so plan accordingly. Your BCD will help with that, but we have extra weights if you need them. Jean-René, your PADI log?"

Jean-René reached over into his bag and pulled out the logs of all his dives, handing them to her. In total, there were six books, held together with a rubber band. He had logged almost as many dives as Rowan had. They'd gone wreck-diving, explored cenotes. They dove in lakes, rivers and even a flooded mine shaft.

Fatima inspected his logs, nodding her approval before she wrapped the rubber band around them and handed them back. She didn't need to check Rowan's. She already knew he was an accomplished diver. "There are some under water currents, hammerhead sharks, dolphins, manta rays, turtles, and thousands of species of fish," she continued. "Now, we are much farther south than most teams have searched. We've crossed the Tropic of Cancer, Rowan *darling*. You should reapply your sunscreen. Lauren wouldn't want me to let you burn."

"The boat is equipped with GPS, and we know this general area is where we previously found the artifacts Tima mentioned," Omar said.

"So we'll have Mohamed monitor us topside. Jean-René, you are with Omar. Rowan, you're with me, so Jean-René can get some footage. We'll go first and they can follow, then when it's time to ascend they can follow us up." She spoke to Rowan directly then addressed the group in general. "Be sure to monitor your pressure gage. We'll want to maintain a minimum of 300 psi in the tank. Breath control will be essential."

Omar stood. "The artifacts we found, the last time we were here, were only about ten meters down. This isn't going to be one of the deepest dives you've ever been on. That means we will have more time at the bottom. I've programmed everyone's dive computers with an ample safety factor included. Check your equipment and do your buddy checks and we'll get started here in a bit."

Omar and Mohamed finished the pre-dive prep while Rowan and Fatima checked each other's equipment and made sure their dive computers were synchronized. They waited for Jean-René and Omar to finish their checks before everyone gave a thumbs up. "Okay," Tima nodded to Mohamed and sat down on the edge of the boat and pulled on her flippers, seated her mask, and flipped over backwards. Rowan followed suit.

In his twenty years doing this job, he'd been on many dives, but this was one that caught him most off guard. Called the Red Sea, he'd expected the waters to be rusty and murky. Maybe he'd spent too much time in Oklahoma, where the red clay contributed to the color of the water, but when he realized how clear and beautiful the sea was, he found himself in awe.

As they approached the bottom, the corals appeared—the softest shades of pinks and yellows. Fish swarmed the reef, darting in unison in vivid and eye-catching colors. "This is amazing!" Their masks had a built in communication system, and Rowan took advantage of it. "The Red Sea isn't red."

"It's very beautiful here," Fatima agreed, as Rowan rolled over onto his back, hovering in the water, watching Jean-René with the camera as he and Omar descended. "Let's travel along the bottom and see what we can find, Rowan *darling*."

Rowan followed her lead, scanning the coral reef to an

area where the sandy bottom commanded the terrain, and seemed to ripple in the current created in the valley between two banks of coral. Something caught Rowan's eye and he swam over to it, pushing the sand aside with the tip of his finger. He did so timidly at first, until the glint of something caught his attention. He dug with fervor and was rewarded when he reached down and produced a long white, petrified bone.

"Fatima! Look here."

"What is it, Rowan darling?" She turned and had to fight the current to get back to him, as Jean-René came up over his shoulder. He and Jean-René had done this enough times they had their moves synchronized. Rowan knew he had the camera panning down on him.

"Is that a femur?" Jean-René gasped.

"It looks like a femur," Rowan said tentatively.

"Dig it up! Dig it up!" Jean-René moved in with the camera.

"That is a femur. A human femur!" Rowan gasped. "*Unfreakingbelievable!*" Rowan's signature catch phase had caught on with the fans, and they used it on his social media accounts every chance they got. The children had too. They thought it was funny that they could get away with saying something like that, instead of cussing.

Fatima began digging nearby herself, and within a few minutes, they had several other bones lined up on the sandy bottom. "Here's a metal detector, Rowan," Omar brought him a small hand-held meter. It was orange and looked like a carrot. Rowan inspected it a moment, then put it to work.

"Hey, check over there." Jean-René pointed a meter or so ahead of Rowan, just to the left. Rowan took the bone with him as he swam ahead, with the metal detector in the other hand. He waved the carrot along the sea floor and the device made a muffled bleep as it passed over the spot Omar had seen. Rowan drew the device away and came back over it, confirming the hit. He tucked the device into his weight belt pouch and moved his hand to brush away the sand, raising a cloud in the process. He got ahold of the dark piece of coral-encrusted metal and began working it loose. Rowan withdrew a long object, roughly the size of his hand, shaped almost exactly the same.

"Would you look at that?" he exclaimed. "That is a spear head!"

"You found it!"

"Rowan, the Egyptian charioteers preferred short spears, roughly the length of a man's height," Tima said. "While not their primary weapon, the spear had a prominent place in Egyptian warfare. It was useful for ranged and close quarter combat."

"There's another bone," Jean-René said, just as Rowan saw it. This bone was oddly shaped and determined to not be human.

"That's a horse ... a jawbone," Omar said.

"That is incredible." Rowan grinned through his mask.

"Let's keep looking," Tima said. "Rowan *darling*, bring your metal detector."

8

Papa Dauphine palmed the bones from the fried chicken they'd been served for dinner. He'd gnawed the legs and thighs clean and made sure the guards weren't looking when he approached the tray return and dumped his food wastes into the disposal bin. After working in the prison laundry room all day, he was exhausted. It was hot, hard work and he'd come to the chow hall ravenous. He'd have gone back for seconds, but that wasn't permitted.

The warden made sure everyone knew, the State of Louisiana paid a little over $3.00 per day to feed an inmate, which meant they didn't budget for second helpings. The quality of the food reflected the budget. The budget didn't allow for luxuries like cayenne pepper, salt or anything that tasted good, not even a dash of tabasco sauce. In Dauphine's opinion, the food was gross, and he was quite certain a dog couldn't live off what they provided, much less a man. This was the first meal he could remember that looked like it hadn't come out of a factory.

The prison had a farm where they raised chickens—mostly for the eggs—and fresh vegetables. The products from the farm were sold to compensate for deficiencies in the State's budget. The warden assured them they'd be grateful for that when winter came, and the prison's old steam boiler broke down. They had to pay for repairs somehow.

The fried chicken had come as a result of one chicken testing positive for bird flu. The warden decided if the whole flock had to be culled, they might as well have a feast. He assured the inmates the high temperatures of the pressure friers would kill any virus that might have spread to the flock. The inmates—despite their reservations—considered the fried chicken a treat, and no one turned it down, not that Dauphine saw.

When he got back to his cell, he took the bones and hid them in a slot beneath his bedframe where he hid the bandana that held a handful of salt his cellmate, Jimmy, had absconded from the kitchen in return for Dauphine's promise of protection. The man had seen everything, and his silence was important. It would do the voodoo priest no good to kill him. They'd just assign him another cellmate, and the next one might not be so easy to coerce. He had Jimmy under control. Jimmy was proving to be useful.

Dauphine had his treasure hidden, and settled in with his book to read until Jimmy returned and the guards made their nightly bed checks. The prison library had an extensive lending library and he'd found a Dean Koontz book that was just up his alley. He liked books that gave other people goosebumps. They gave him ideas.

He'd been working on a spell, and he needed a few additional items before he could execute it, but he was getting closer. If he could pull it off, it would please his Lord and set that insufferable woman on a path to face her fate. She had wronged him, and he would have his justice—one way or another.

"You want a magazine?" he heard from the hallway. "New batch came in today from the library."

Dauphine rose and sauntered out to the cart a fellow inmate piloted between cells. The voodoo priest was satisfied with his book but news from the outside might lift his spirits. He'd been brooding for days over his situation and his inability to change it. The Dark Lord told him to bide, but that didn't mean he had to sit still. He was a powerful bokor, after all. Prison walls could not tame his rage. He would continue to serve the loa with both hands, which meant he could practice both white and black magic. Dauphine had been wronged, and black magic could give him the justice he was due.

Beneath the issues of *People Magazine*, *Time*, and *National Geographic*, he spied a familiar logo. The *Exploration Channel's Magazine* was some years old, but right there on the cover he found something he'd never imagined he'd be able to find—something useful. Rowan Pierce and Lauren Grayson posed on the cover in costume. Rowan was dressed like an 18th century Scottish trapper, while Lauren was dressed in a blue calico dress with her hair in braids. They looked like a modern version of Lewis Meriweather and Sacagawea—a very pregnant Sacagawea. The main coverline said, ***Exploring Your Roots***. Beneath it, the plug said, ***Walking Where Your Ancestors Walked***.

"That it?" The fellow inmate seemed impatient. He cocked his head to look at the magazine Dauphine was drooling over. "Hot chick."

"Oh, yes," Dauphine cooed. "This will do."

Before Dauphine could sit down with his prize, Jimmy hurried in. "I got it," he panted. "I got what you asked for."

The bokor turned and lifted a brow at the scrawny man. "Which item?"

"All of them," he said. Dauphine glared at him with cautious hesitation. Jimmy lifted a tin can from beneath his shirt. "Corn meal," he beamed, handing it off before digging into the crotch of his pants, drawing out a tin can. "Soil from an executed man's grave." Dauphine took the can and allowed his brow to sink lower. "I caught a snake in the kitchen . . . a big one! It had a rat in its maw." He unfolded the hem of his pant leg, producing a severed head with a rat in its fangs.

Dauphine inspected it. Venomous snakes lived throughout Louisiana, but cottonmouth water moccasins, rattle snakes, and a few types of coral snakes were most common. Dauphine knew this species well. He'd lived in the Bayou as a boy, and often encountered Harlequin coral snakes like this one. He'd never seen one near a city. Still, it wasn't unheard of. This one was larger than most he'd seen. If he had to guess, Dauphine thought this one might go three and a half feet in length, but with just the head it was hard to say for sure.

"That's everything you asked for, right?" Jimmy fidgeted like a dog waiting for a treat.

Dauphine didn't let his emotions show often, but he allowed his servant to see his teeth as his lips curled into a wicked smile. "Well done," he nodded. "Well done, indeed."

"I told you I could do it," Jimmy beamed. "I told you."

"Now you have earned your rest," Dauphine said. "I have work to do."

"Better put that stuff away before bed check," Jimmy said. "Do you need me to help you?"

"No," Dauphine said, realizing the man was right. "I will take it from here. Tomorrow I will see if I can find some way to reward you."

"Thank you, Papa. Thank you."

"Now, go to bed."

Long after bed check, Dauphine rose from his cot and took out all the things he needed. The niches and nooks in the cell were big enough to hide most things. The can of cornmeal had to be hidden under his pillow as he feigned sleep when the guards came by to do a headcount of the inmates in their cells.

Now he worked efficiently. He made a circle of salt around himself, before taking out the cornmeal. He gathered a handful of it, letting it slip from beneath his thumb and forefinger as he drew the vèvès—sacred symbols—needed to cast his spell. Satisfied with the intricate design, he took the voodoo doll he'd made of Lauren Grayson. He'd used the stuffing from a threadbare pillow he'd found in the laundry storage area. A scrap of ticking made the dress. He made the effigy full with child, just as he had last seen her. He had one treasure he'd hidden in a gap in the bricks. The circle of salt-and-pepper hair had been coiled around his finger like a ring when he'd been returned to the jail after his trial. He uncoiled the hair he'd snatched from her head and tied it around the doll's waist like a belt, hanging it from his fingers as he inspected it. "I name ya before Bondye. I name thee, *Lauren Grayson*. Madonna of the Cursed. *Iwa* will know thee." He hissed the words, breathing on the symbol of his hatred, the target of his revenge. "I call upon the Rada. I have no *ounfò*. I have been denied the justice I deserve. I ask for justice." He plucked the dead rat from the snake's maw and squeezed it in his meaty fist. Dark black blood, already congealed, oozed from between his fingers. He dabbed a bit of it onto the head of the doll, then took the picture torn from the magazine's cover. Using the blood to bind it, before tying it into place with a thread from his bunkmate's blanket. He laid the doll on the vèvè, careful not to disturb the cornmeal pattern. The second voodoo doll represented Rowan Pierce, her husband. He didn't have the man's hair, but he didn't need it. He had the picture from the magazine, adding the cut-out of his target's face. "I name you before Bondye. I name thee, Rowan Pierce. *Dimballa Wedo* will know thee. I ask only for justice—justice I have been denied."

In voodoo tradition, snakes were not seen as a symbol of evil. Instead, they were holders of intuitive knowledge. But a great bokor like Dauphine had intuitive knowledge of his own. He took the dismembered snake head and prayed to *Li Grande Zombie* for forgiveness for taking the life of his minion.

Normally, he would have an altar to his ancestors, and to the gods of the Rada. He had no such luxury. Prayers of protection, however, could never be skipped. He whispered to avoid the attention of the guards, just in case they hadn't fallen asleep at their posts. "I pray, my ancestors, you know me. I am the son of a bokor. The grandson of a bokor. I honor all of those remembered and forgotten, who are associated with my ancestors and my friends. I pray to the Dark Lord who commands me bide. Allow me this favor as it is meant to magnify thee. For all who suffered so that I may carry on these traditions, bless me. I pray this so my ancestors may rest in peace through the intercession of the Seven African Powers." He went through the motions of purification. Normally he would burn a twist of herbs and use the smoke to cleanse his skin and his soul. There was enough dark energy left behind by the visit from his master to serve his purposes.

He said prayers to the Seven African Powers, and then finished with a prayer of his own, asking for an abundant return of blessings, and protection from any ill-power that might come back. He did not fear retribution from the Rada. He was the one who had been wronged.

If he had water, he would pour it on the ground and say "*Ache!*" Then light candles and let them burn out, but tonight he didn't have the time, or the materials needed.

"*Baron Samedi,*" he called to the loa of the dead. When he did his *corporate leadership* events, this was the god he emulated.

He wore a top hat, dark vest, and white skull-face makeup. It was a god of debauchery and merrymaking. He was the loa of death, of sex, and dirty jokes. "When I called thee, in the name of Rowan Pierce, you came to him and gave him what he asked for. I was not at fault. I did as he asked and took him to a place beyond the gods. This is my defense. You are the Lord of Death, the last resort for healing. I come to you for Justice. I speak your name, *Baron Samedi* and confess I was innocent, yet I have suffered." He took the snake head and held it above his makeshift effigies as he bowed to the loa. With great care, he pried open the snake's jaws, and forced the fang out from its mouth, then stabbed the fetish of Rowan Pierce with the fang. "I demand justice!" He took the other fang and stabbed the abdomen of the woman. "I demand justice denied me! Justice tenfold!"

He could feel the trembling of magic swirling around the room. Like tiny fingers crawling from the ether they spread out into tentacles, swirling, and fanning out into the space behind the cell, reaching to a place he could not go. He knew he had to allow the magic to do its job.

He wasn't done. *Not yet.*

9

Aleppo, Syria
May 12th

Abdul bin Salman took his coffee in front of the television in the suite he had been given by his host. Al Khalid seemed interested in his plot, but as of yet, no action had been taken. His daughter had yet to return from Cairo, though she was no longer answering calls from her father. The Syrian feared the girl had tried to escape to Israel or perhaps, Greece.

"What troubles you, my king?" Saiesha, his first wife, came and sat down in the chair beside him. No one ever questioned him, except Saiesha. She wasn't the oldest or the smartest, but she was the prettiest and most loyal.

"I am thinking of bad things," he said. "Things that are of no concern to a woman."

"You are thinking of war, and we both know it." Maybe she was smarter than he gave her credit for. "It shows in every line on your face."

"Perhaps another campaign like Soba would secure your rule," his wife suggested.

Perhaps she was right. If Syria would not play his little game, he could gain attention in his own country. He'd already raided the city of Soba and slaughtered anyone his armies encountered. From there, his juggernaut moved from village to village, facing little resistance. He became known, however, for the attack on Soba. It brought him great delight when word reached him of his new moniker, *The Psychopath of Soba*. It was a fitting title for a conquering ruler like himself.

Something on the television caught his attention. "Famed Archaeologist Rowan Pierce arrived in Egypt ahead of his upcoming lecture in Cairo," the anchor said.

The video cut to a field reporter at the airport. He raced to catch up with the famous explorer and stuck a microphone in Rowan's face. "Dr. Pierce, what will you do while you are in Egypt?" The excited young reporter asked, completely botching Rowan's title.

The celebrity forced a smile to his haggard face. "I've been in the field for the past few weeks, so I hope to get a hot shower, eat some good food and sleep for three or four days, then maybe we'll see what adventure has in store for us," he said, wearily.

"Will you be going on any digs with the college teams while you're here?"

"Who knows what my hosts have in store for me." Rowan was courteous, but curt and never stopped moving as the eager reporter peppered him with questions. The interview ended when he disappeared into the men's room.

"Dr. Pierce will be lecturing at the University of Cairo next week and appear at a fundraiser for the University's Archaeology program. Tickets are still available on the Uni's website." The anchor said as the shot came back to him.

Abdul glanced at his wife, seeing the look on her face. This American was a handsome man, but those weren't stars in his bride's eyes. They were dollar signs. "You could use an archaeologist or two, if you are to achieve your objective. Couldn't you?"

He remembered al Khalid's words, but now it was about testing his wife. "What good would an archaeologist do me?" He already knew the answer, but he wanted to hear what his bride had to say. She made a good argument. The professor at the University of Cairo—the one Faadin's daughter studied with—and this American celebrity could be useful . . . if he could keep his wives away from him.

"Those with ancient knowledge are a blessing to you, but that man," she pointed to the television. "I have seen him in my own dreams. He will bring you all you desire . . . all you deserve."

"I have no need for an American celebrity," he said, now fearing his wife was more enamored with the American than himself.

"Those are prideful words, husband. He is of great worth, a man needed in his own country," the woman said. "If he will not help you achieve your quest, he will bring a high ransom to fund your own mission. There are others who will do your bidding, as your generals have in Soba, once they recognize your courage and your strength. If America will not pay you, make them fear you."

Yes. She was brighter than he gave her credit for.

CAL-TECH UNIVERSITY, *Pasadena, California*
May 12th

"Welcome, Dr. Pierce." Dwight Gray, the current Dean of the Anthropology Department at Cal Tech glanced up at her as Lauren entered the lecture hall. The hall was as familiar to her as her own living room. She'd spent many happy hours here drinking in lectures and panel discussions from learned professionals in her field, so many years ago.

At present, the hall was empty and stage lights illuminated the auditorium. Lauren put down her purse as the man crossed the stage to meet her. "I'm so glad you could make it."

Lauren chuckled pushing back her suit jacket as she put one hand on her hip, the other hand on her full abdomen. "A month or so later and I'd have had to bow out."

The man seemed stunned. "I wasn't aware you were expecting, Dr. Pierce. Congratulations." Dr. Gray was attractive, in a bookish way. He had mushroom brown hair that brushed the collar of his brown suit coat. There was a bit of gray starting to fill in around his temples. He wore wire framed glasses and reminded her of John Boy from the Walton's.

"Thank you," Lauren beamed. She'd met him once over Zoom, and she'd kept her *condition* on the downlow—even from the Network—throughout most of the production year. It was easy enough, since she was working from home and taking most of her meetings via video conferencing.

"Is this your first?"

"Sixth," she said with a bemused grin. "And . . . most likely the last." *Of course she'd said that every time since Jamie was born.*

While Lauren's doctor made sure she knew she was too old to be having babies, convincing Rowan was another thing. They hadn't been *trying* and no one had been more surprised than her when it happened—again.

In the past few months, she'd finished her second PhD through an on-line program at Oxford. Technically, it was a DPhil—making her a Doctor of Philosophy, this one in classical ancient languages and literature. She'd been working on it, secretly, for a while, as her schedule permitted. She could have gone to England with Henry to walk with her graduating class, but it conflicted with the trial in New Orleans, and that was her priority.

Her dissertation on the Anatolian languages, an extinct

branch of Indo-European languages from what was now modern Turkey, had received acclaim and would be published by the Oxford Press as part of a series of classical monographs.

Academia had been calling, too. She'd been offered positions at several distinguished universities from Harvard to Heidelberg. Some were for professor positions, but in a few cases, she'd been offered a more elite status as a Dean of the Department. While it was tempting, Lauren had her hands full at home. Five children kept her busy, but writing, directing, producing, and co-hosting a television show was her second priority.

Lauren had been excited to go back to doing some field work with Rowan when she got the news that she was expecting. She'd thought the doctor would tell her it was menopause, but low and behold, she was twelve weeks along when she went in for her pre-production-year checkup.

"Do you have children, Dr. Gray?"

"Two," he said. "Ginny and Kevin. They're five and nine."

"My younger ones are about that age. My oldest just graduated from high school and he's headed to college in the fall. He's just sixteen, but he's already completed enough credit hours for an associate degree in applied physical sciences."

"Impressive," the Dean said with a nod. "Will we be seeing him in our Anthropology program here?"

"He's visiting several colleges abroad, but I think he's leaning towards Colorado State. It's his father's alma mater," she said, pleased by his options. "He hasn't quite decided on a major, but he's planning to study physics, I think."

"Oh, well. Too bad. Enrollment is down but having you here today should spark some interest, which was our goal, if I'm being honest. The registration list was full over two weeks ago. We had to start a waiting list. Perhaps this fall you could come do another lecture."

"Is this the last one of the academic year?"

"It is," he said. "This class includes mostly freshmen or sophomores. I have a few students who needed the extra credit, so grades for today's lecture require them to be present and to ask thoughtful questions at the end to earn their points."

"Oh, I'm glad to know that," Lauren said.

Lauren liked getting to places early when she had to speak, but it always felt uncomfortable to be the first one to arrive. "So, who else is on the panel today?" she asked, making small talk. She stepped aside as the Dean resumed his efforts to set up the microphones on the table at the center of the stage.

"You are my scientist and field researcher," he said. "Then I have Retired Lt. Colonel William Huey from the US Navy. The last member of the panel is Dr. Mia Flückiger. I believe you may know her?"

The name rang a bell, and Lauren said as much. "What's her specialty?"

"Well, you could say she's an environmentalist, but you could also say she's your everyday nay-sayer."

"Hmm. I can't remember how I would know her," Lauren said. She might have heard the name, but she hadn't slept well, and trying to keep up with five kids while her husband and mother were both out of town, left Lauren out of sorts. She'd almost forgotten about this whole symposium and if Bahati hadn't taken the kids today, she might have had to bail at the last minute. Lauren hated having to cancel anything.

"You beat her out for an award once upon a time," the Dean said. "Do you remember that?"

That's when it hit her. Mia Flückiger was the child activist, a vocal critic of world environmental policies. A few years ago in Washington, they arrested her for participating in a protest that became violent. Since then, she'd gone to college and become an educated scientist. Lauren wondered if she'd ever outgrown her reputation as a haughty young environmental activist with no leg to stand on. They'd met back when Lauren and Rowan won the *Society of the Modern Scientist's* coveted *Scientists of the Year* award. An award the thirteen-year-old girl had been nominated for as well.

The chances of a teenager beating out a real scientist to win such an award was infinitesimal in Lauren's mind. Yet, the teenager had slammed *The Society* for overlooking her. It came as no surprise that *The Society* hadn't nominated her since.

Lauren had seen some of her videos on YouTube and she honestly didn't think much of the girl. She was mousy and plain, with a perpetually sour expression on her face. "So she's got her PhD now?"

"She graduated at twenty-one," the Dean said. "She was quite the *wunderkind*, kind of like your boy."

"From Cal Tech?"

"She did do some of her studies remotely with Dr. Boyd, for a brief period of time," he said. "All our panelists today are alums, more or less."

"Oh," Lauren sniffed. That was interesting. Why would *that brat* come to Cal Tech, when there were so many terrific and highly reputed colleges for science in Europe—closer to home? She suspected the girl wanted to muscle in on Lauren's turf. If she was bitter about losing to a paranormal researcher, she wouldn't put it past the girl. "Well," Lauren said, stepping aside as Dwight put out name tags in front of each mic. "I guess I better go find the ladies room before we get started." She glanced at her watch. She had about fifteen minutes before the students would begin to arrive.

Dwight hesitated and pointed. "Just down the hall to the right," he said. *As if she didn't know.*

"I'll be back in just a bit."

As she washed her hands at the sink, the door of the restroom opened, and Lauren recognized the woman who entered. Mia Flückiger hadn't changed much since she was a teen. She still had that same smug and sour expression on her face, and a false smile never seemed to brighten her countenance. Her frizzy hair was the color of dirty bathwater and looked as if she hadn't washed it—much less combed it—in weeks. She wore it pulled back in a low ponytail, but whisps of it escaped and hovered around her face like mist. Mia's attire was just as plain. She wore a brown wool skirt and a tan corduroy jacket that was two sizes too large. The blouse beneath was a brown floral pattern. Her shoes could best be described as *comfortable*, but Lauren wasn't one to judge when it came to foot attire. Along with black flair-legged pants and a suit jacket with a red floral top, she wore her favorite red Chuck Taylors, only because it was the last pair of shoes that fit, and Jamie had tied them for her when she got dressed this morning. Otherwise, she might have worn sandals.

"Dr. Pierce," the woman said, curtly stopping at the first sink to apply lipstick. The line about *putting lipstick on a pig* came to mind, but Lauren kept her head down as she let the warm water run over her hands long after they were clean.

"Dr. Flückiger," she said, as cordially as she could muster.

Mia said nothing else as she fluffed her frizzy ponytail and tied to slick back the whisps of hair around her face with her damp hands. Lauren didn't say anything either. She reached for a paper towel and dried her hands. Mia stopped and watched with judgement etched into her features and Lauren knew the reason. The media and industry had blasted Dr. Flückiger for trying to eliminate paper hygiene products in government and public buildings through ill-conceived legislation that she'd actively supported. She'd even appeared before a legislative panel on Global Warming while she was in Washington, just days before her arrest.

Paper manufacturing companies and lumber producers

paid lobbyists millions of dollars to fight the rules in the US and had won an equally vocal battle for public support. Lauren—who considered herself a conservationist, though not an extremist—tossed the paper towel in the receptacle marked *Recycle* on her way out the door.

"I AM TELLING YOU—THE world's governments worked together to hide the truth from the citizens of Planet Earth. The aliens *are* here, and *we* have made first contact." The naval officer stood, pounding his meaty pointer finger into the table at Lauren's elbow. It resonated through the lecture hall, carried on the mics through the sound system.

She hadn't expected the conversation to go this way, but this military guy was a big stuffed-shirt. He claimed to have seen alien spacecraft and participated in a secret operation that contacted alien life. This was supposed to be a discussion on the likelihood of life in the cosmos, not a dissertation on alien life *here*.

"I find that highly unlikely," Dr. Flückiger said drolly in her arrogant Swiss accent. Her expression was flat, and she sounded genuinely bored. "We have done so much damage to *this* planet. Why would an alien life form want anything to do with a planet that will most likely self-destruct in our lifetime?"

"Dr. Pierce," Dr. Gray brought her out of her thoughts. "You've been awfully quiet. What do you think of the likelihood of alien life already being here on Earth?"

Lauren knew she had to be cautious here. *She* had been part of the team that had made first contact, along with Rowan, her brother, Michael and her sister-in-law, Dr. Kitty Donovan-Grayson. It was one of those things she was bound —by a legally-binding government gag order—not to tell. She also suspected more than one of the students had their cameras on and anything she said would end up on YouTube or TikTok, if not the evening news. "As a paranormal investigator, I have to confess, I'm interested in the possibility of alien life, but as a linguist, I have to wonder how we would communicate if they did come here." Deflection seemed the best course of action. Taking the approach of a linguist, rather than a paranormal investigator or biological anthropologist provided her legal protection.

"You don't think we could have a conversation with them? Negotiate a peace agreement?" the Lt. Colonel asked.

"Unless they somehow magically know how to speak one of our thousands of lang —" Lauren started but stopped abruptly.

"Dr. Pierce?" Dr. Gray realized something was amiss. "Are you all right?"

Lauren's hand went to her side as a contraction hit. She sucked in her breath and let it out. "Sorry," she said wincing, once the moment passed. "Braxton Hicks. I'm fine." She forced her voice to be bright.

"You're a scientist, Dr. Pierce," Mia snapped. "Aliens won't magically learn our languages, and I'm stunned that—you of all people—might suggest *magic* has anything to do with anything."

"Yet, you don't even believe in alien life," Huey said before Lauren could get a word out. "It's my opinion that they've watched us for centuries. I suspect they've already learned enough about our languages to communicate. No magic to it."

"Is that possible, Dr. Pierce?" Dr. Gray asked.

"It's plausible," Lauren said. "But we don't have any frame of reference for their language, so . . ." Another contraction hit her, but she tried not to react. "So, they'd have to start the dia . . . dialogue."

"Lauren," Dwight came over and put a hand on her shoulder. "Are you okay?"

"Yes," she said, not certain if it was true. "But perhaps it's time for a break."

Dwight turned to the hall full of students. "We've started a little over an hour ago. Let's take a break. When we come back, I'll open the floor to questions. As you formulate your queries, remember you're being graded, so now's your chance to throw out your theories, and get input on your arguments."

LAUREN MADE it through the Q&A session and decided she must be dehydrated. She drank a bottle of water and grabbed a second for the two-hour drive home. She arrived to an empty house. Bahati and the kids hadn't made it back, but that wasn't concerning. All the kids loved the museum and they hated to leave. It was also about to start raining. The fingers of the storm that kept Rowan from getting home were reaching as far as San Diego. The skies were dark, and the wind was picking up. She could hear it whistling in the tree tops of the large palms that shaded the pool deck.

With dinner still an hour or two away Lauren decided she had time to get comfortable, put her feet up and maybe take a nap. If she were lucky, Bahati would feed the kids before they came home. If she weren't, there was leftover lasagna in the freezer she could heat up.

Shadow, her Siamese cat, met her at the bottom of the stairs where all her *toy mousies* were lined up on the bottom step. "That won't keep me from going up stairs and putting on my pajamas," Lauren said brusquely to the cat, who challenged her to pass her by without stopping for pets. "You know I can't reach the floor," Lauren said, with a snicker. "Come on. We'll have a cuddle once I get these blasted shoes off."

Settled in bed, Lauren patted the pillow beside her, and the cat jumped up on the bed with a deep *mrowr*. The purring began before Lauren could even reach her. A hand over the cat's head swept down her back and over the tip of her tail before the cat turned, made circles, then curled up on the pillow against Lauren's belly. The mistress scratched her chin as she stretched, *making biscuits,* kneading with her claws against her. Lauren sighed and melted into her Tempurpedic mattress, relieved to be home. She'd talked to Rowan the night before and knew he'd arrived safely at Tima's door. He'd told her all about what happened on Jordan Island—at least enough to know he was lucky to escape, but not lucky enough to get back to the mainland before storms began to rage and then promptly shut down air travel leaving him stranded and unable to get home.

IT WAS LATE when Lauren woke up from her nap. The room was dark, and the house was quiet. Shadow was curled up against her stomach, purring in her sleep. As usual, the urge to pee was ever-present. Lauren rolled over and sat up on the edge of the bed, upending the cat, who voiced her displeasure.

This baby wasn't as aggressive as its siblings. It kicked enough to let her know that it was well. A rumble of thunder resounded in the distance and rain began to pitter-patter on the window. It was spring and this was the time of year she was most homesick for Oklahoma. She didn't miss dodging tornadoes, but the rain was different here. It never had the same intensity to the thunder and lightning, but the rain, when it came, could last for days. California was supposed to be sunny and warm, but the chill found its way to her as she waddled into the bathroom.

A warm bath never sounded so relaxing. The jacuzzi tub here in San Diego wasn't as nice as the clawfoot tub they'd had in Hawai'i, but it was deep, and the jets hit on all the right spots. She had an ache in her back that she couldn't get rid of, and her feet were swollen. She'd done all of this before, and she knew a nice warm soak was just what she needed. The annoying Braxton-Hicks contractions had started back up, and a bath was the litmus test to see if they were just mock contractions, or something worse.

As Lauren soaked, it became increasingly evident that it might be more than just Braxton-Hicks contractions. They didn't stop, even in the warm foamy water. The clock on the wall ticked audibly, even over the thunderstorm building outside. She counted the minutes between contractions and was relieved that they weren't very regular, and roughly five to six minutes apart. It allowed her to relax and sink back into the foam. Her eyes darted back to the clock with each contraction.

When the water went cold, she let some of it out and refilled the tub with warm water. This couldn't be happening, Lauren decided. She'd had five babies. She knew what labor felt like, and she knew when it was time. While this felt like labor, it wasn't time, ergo it couldn't be labor.

The contractions were growing stronger. It wasn't until a contraction stole the breath from her lungs that she realized her cellphone was in her purse down in the garage. *This can't be happening*, she insisted. Still, the nagging feeling in the back of her mind had her running through the steps it would take to deliver at home—alone. *Okay, Lauren. The first thing you need is to get your phone. You'll need to call 911 . . . if you are in labor. Then, you need to call Bahati. They should have been home by now.* Her mind was racing. *You'll need clean towels. Paramedics should arrive before you need to worry about cutting the cord. That can be delayed.*

She waited until a contraction passed, then said to herself, "Okay. Let's get the phone."

It took a great deal of effort to get out of the tub, but when she did, a sharp pain ripped through her, and her water broke. She shrieked in pain and surprise. The suddenly-cool water turned pink, then darkened to red. *This can't be happening! No, no, no!*

10

The Red Sea, Egypt
May 13th

By the time they neared the end of their safe dive time, Rowan had a net bag full of wonders they had found. It included bones and bronze chariot pieces and bridle bits. The last piece unearthed appeared to be a bronze spoke from a chariot wheel.

It was no surprise to anyone that Rowan's air alarm was the first to sound. In his excitement he'd expended his air supply quickly. "Let's head up," Tima said calmly. "Mohamed?" The assistant top-side was monitoring their com. "Mohamed, we're headed up. Make ready."

There came a muffled response as the radio broke up. Rowan recognized the closest thing to an Arabic swear over the radio and then it all went dead. "Sounds like Mohamed is having trouble," Tima said. "Let's head up and see if he needs help."

"I want some footage of you two ascending." Jean-René turned the camera upward. They were so deep that the surface was just a blur. "Take your time. We'll follow in a few minutes."

"Roger that. Let's head topside," Rowan said, knowing the soundbite might come in handy post production. He tried to speak in soundbites when they were filming, even though he didn't know if the video they gathered on this trip would end up in an episode, as part of a special or just a little something extra for the fans on their YouTube channel.

Rowan was the first to reach the surface, and just in time. His mask sucked to his face just as he reached to pull it off. His tank was empty. He turned in the waves to look for Fatima and found her as a hand came down and grabbed her by her long silver braid, yanking her out of the water. She let out a hoarse scream through her mask as guns were leveled at Rowan by five extremely angry—extremely large men.

One of them shouted at him, waving him toward the boat. Rowan could see Fatima struggling against the captor who wrestled her to her knees, shouting at her in a language he couldn't understand. *Jesus*, he scowled. *Where was Lauren when he needed her?*

"He says to get in the boat, or he will shoot you," Fatima gasped as she was dragged to the side of the boat to translate.

"I'm coming." Rowan raised his hands over his head. He'd already dropped the bag containing the bones and metal fragments in his startle. He realized a second boat was moored alongside the research vessel. As he was hauled up onto the back landing, he realized how dire their situation really was. Mohamed lay on the deck, with a single gunshot wound to the head. He was dead. The gray matter splattered on the equipment cases was sufficient to confirm Rowan's diagnosis. "Let's just all take a deep breath," he said, more to calm himself and Fatima than anything. "What do they want?"

"I don't know," Tima said, then yelped when the one standing closest to her struck her across the side of the head.

The man got in her face, shouting at her, and she shied away. He turned and scowled at Rowan and started shouting at him.

Rowan raised his hands defensively, trying to make sense of the whole situation. "I don't understand!" He shielded his head with his hands. Hands grabbed him, digging into his flesh and yanking him to his feet. Two other men moved in and shoved him to the side of the boat. Men on the other boat reached over and grabbed him, hauling him over the side, scraping his flesh and bruising his muscles as they did. He landed hard and was yanked to his feet. Fatima met the same fate.

A very large black man came from below deck and stood considering them both as they were forced onto their knees. Fatima's hands were on her head and Rowan followed her lead.

"Name?" The man demanded. Neither rushed to answer. The man nodded to one of his henchmen and the butt of his gun came down on the back of Fatima's neck. "Name."

"I am Dr. Fatima Badr," she groaned as she lay face first on the deck.

Rowan reached for her but heard a gun cock. "Name," the man repeated.

"Rowan Pierce," he said, glaring down the barrel of the gun.

"American?"

"Yeah. I'm American." He rolled his eyes. "And you?"

The man began screaming at him in Arabic and the gun went to his temple, pressing into his flesh. Rowan's heart leapt in his chest, drumming an erratic tempo and he closed his eyes. It surprised him when the gun backed off, He'd half expected that to be the end, but the man finished yelling and backed up.

Rowan noticed them moving a crate from this boat to the research vessel and he scanned the water for Jean-René and Omar. They were nowhere to be seen. Suddenly it seemed the crew was no longer worried about them. Rowan took the moment to help Fatima back up to her knees. "Are you okay?" he asked softly.

"I've got a hard head," she groaned.

"Who are these guys?"

"Not sure." She swallowed hard as he inspected her with a medic's eye. "I think they are speaking Sudanese Arabic. But I can't be sure."

"What do they want?" he asked as the pirates came back over to them.

He yanked Rowan up then slammed him back down, flat on his face. "No talk!" One of the goons yanked his arms behind him, wrenching his shoulder as they tied him up. He realized Fatima was face down beside him. They shared a terrified gaze as the boat launched forward, almost upending the aggressors on top of them.

Rowan closed his eyes for a moment in a silent prayer for Jean-René and Omar. Then, he made the effort to reach Lauren. He'd done it once, but at the time he was drugged and on death's door. On the other hand, she found him in the dark before, but only when she needed him most. He needed her now.

He opened his eyes just in time to feel the force of the concussion as the research vessel exploded behind them. Debris rained down around them, and Rowan suddenly felt extremely sick.

Lauren, wherever you are, I need you. Now!

THE PHONE RANG with an urgency that seemed unnatural. Kitty woke instantly.

"Have you turned on the news this evening?" Frank said without preamble.

"It's eleven o'clock," Kitty said. "I spent the evening at a

State Dinner I didn't want to go to. I just nodded off about twenty minutes ago." She sat up and flipped on the light. "What's going on?"

"There was an explosion in the Red Sea," he said. "A research vessel registered to the University of Cairo was destroyed. Three people are missing. Two were injured."

"A terrorist attack?"

"Possibly," he said. "One of the two people that were rescued might be someone you know."

"Me? Who was it?"

"Does the name Jean-René Toussaint ring any bells?"

"That's my brother-in-law's best friend," she said, now fully awake.

"Your brother-in-law is one of the missing," Frank didn't mince words. He never sugar coated anything.

Rowan was in the Middle East. She'd seen him on the news the night before. "What happened?"

"Not a lot of details, but here's what we know," he said.

Kitty sat listening intently as he related what could be gleaned from the cameraman who'd suffered a head injury.

"And you think it was on the evening news?" Kitty said.

"We hope not," Frank said. "No one's come forward claiming responsibility . . . yet. If it's some war-monger trying to get attention, the best thing we can do is squash the story as soon as possible."

"Has anyone notified Lauren?"

"We're working on that," he said. "For now I need you to maintain radio silence but monitor your *Accord*." If even one stitch of *The Accord* had unraveled, it would take every sharp needle in her kit to hold the fabric of peace together.

ROWAN LOST track of time as the boat raced across the sea, the water growing choppier as they traveled. He and Fatima were jostled, unable to brace themselves with their hands tied behind their backs, face-first on the deck. He'd tried to check on her once, to offer some word of comfort, but got kicked in the ribs for his efforts.

It was dark when the boat slowed, much to Rowan's relief. An uneasy nausea washed over him, and he wanted to puke, but his stomach wouldn't do him that simple kindness. Still, he was grateful for not having to lay in his own vomit.

The men exchanged angry words over them, and Rowan recognized an argument when he heard one. As a father of four boys and one strong-willed little girl, he'd heard plenty of them. He wasn't sure what the problem was, but someone wasn't happy and was taking it out on the others.

"You okay?" He managed softly, while their captors were preoccupied.

"Not really," Fatima swallowed hard. "I'm afraid."

"Any idea who they are?"

"Sudanese pirates? That's my theory." She rolled her head where she could see them then returned her gaze to Rowan. "There are rumors of a possible coup in Sudan, but we were not in Sudanese waters. We weren't that far south."

"You're sure?" Rowan glanced up, realizing the argument had cooled down. He lay his head back down, trying not to raise attention to himself.

Tima sensed the same but managed a quick nod before the men came over and yanked Rowan up to his feet. His equilibrium failed him. His knees buckled, but one of them yanked him up by his shoulder, torquing it painfully. The pirate didn't seem to care when he cried out. He slipped down to his knees. The large man that Rowan had decided was the leader came over and squatted down in front of him. "You are American?" Rowan nodded. He was reluctant to tell them anything, but he figured for the moment, a guarded measure of cooperation was in order. "*R-r-r-ow-ahn Piercce?*" His thick accent chopped off his first name in the middle and drug out the end of his last name. Rowan was impressed with how he rolled his R's. "Where is your passport?"

"It was in my duffle bag . . . on the boat your people blew up," he said. His wallet and brand new cell phone were in his bag, along with a change of clothes.

"You are television star, yes?"

"I'm an archaeologist," Rowan corrected.

The man arched a brow at him and then looked up at one of his henchmen and said something. A moment later, the man came over and handed him a phone. He looked at it and then turned it to Rowan to see. It was his Wikipedia page. "That's a horrible picture of me," Rowan laughed nervously. The shot was one Jean-René took when they were filming in Virginia, just before John Carter was born. He'd been over-whelmed with the production schedule, a magical toddler, and a pregnant wife. Nothing had been within his control at that time, and life had taken its toll.

The man nodded at him, then turned the phone back around. "You were fat." He laughed, his teeth brilliant white against his pitch black skin.

"Yeah, well you know," Rowan said weakly.

"Who is your woman?" He pointed with his chin toward Tima as the thugs got her up on her knees beside him.

"This is my college professor," he said. "She's an archaeol-ogist, too."

"She is your woman? Your ...wife?"

"No." He shook his head. "She is my teacher."

The pirate looked down at his phone again and scrolled up on his Wikipedia page, hesitating and arching a brow. He turned it back to Rowan. Lauren's picture. "Your wife?"

Rowan pursed his lips. "For now." If this didn't end well, Lauren would kill him. The pirate arched a brow again as he inspected her picture, licking his lips. Rowan hung his head, more to avoid having to watch the man ogle his wife, but also thinking of her safety.

Rowan realized he could hear the hum of an approaching vessel. The leader looked up and then grinned menacingly at Rowan and Tima. He stood and waved at the approaching cutter, going to help bring the boat alongside their craft. This boat was a larger vessel, and all the men on it had guns—big guns.

Tima and Rowan shared a cautious glance and Rowan could almost hear her comment. *Out of the frying pan, into the fire.*

Their ship was boarded, and Rowan sat back on his heels, his head slumped over as his strength waned. He knew they were in trouble. It was everything he could do to keep his heart from galloping in his chest. The new men shared a heated conversation with the pirates and Rowan got the distinct feeling that these men were even worse than their captors. Their leader was tall and gangly, his head looked like it was five times too large for his thin long neck. His upper teeth protruded over the bottom, giving him a buck-toothed expression. To compound things, his head was bald. His face was pock-marked and scarred. One of his eyes was cloudy.

After exchanging words with the pirate leader, this new menace locked eyes on Rowan, his gaze darting back to the pirate. Rowan had the distinct feeling they were talking about him, and he kept his attention on these two, afraid of what they were plotting. He almost didn't notice one of the pirates come up behind him until he heard the rattle of the man's rifle, just before it came down over the back of his head. Lightning crackled in his skull and the world went black around him.

11

San Diego, California
May 13th

Lauren managed to get herself onto her hands and knees in the tub, draining the water she no longer needed. It took everything she had to reach a bath towel nearby. She rolled it up and used it to rest her chest and arms before the next contraction washed over her.

She couldn't deny what was happening. She was in trouble. This baby was coming now. Lauren had no way to call for help. With each contraction, she could feel the baby's head moving farther down and she suspected once she started pushing it wouldn't take much to get this kid out. Henry and the twins had come early, but neither had arrived this early. If the twins were any indication, this baby would be less than five pounds, and terribly premature. Lauren could only hope both of them would survive.

There was so much blood. In all five of her pregnancies, she'd delivered in a clean, sterile hospital. She'd never had to witness anything beyond the swell of her stomach. She didn't know if this was normal, but everything in her mind was screaming that it wasn't good. *Not good at all.*

"Tsul'Kalu? Are you there?" She cried out to the universe as the next contraction wracked her body. "Dad?" The void around her was silent and it served to remind her that no help was coming. She was convinced now, more than ever, that she had done something to fall from the gods' favor. If Anu cared for her any, she wouldn't be in this mess. Enki said she would never be alone, that she would have all the tools she needed to complete her mission, but over a decade had come and gone since her battle against Enlil in Slovenia, and nothing had happened.

She glanced over at the cat who sat at attention, as if waiting for instructions. She mewed at Lauren when their eyes met. "Lassie, go get help," Lauren grunted.

In the midst of feeling sorry for herself, she felt the all-consuming urge to push. The effort left her in agony, breathless and terrified. In the midst of her panic, a calming voice found its way to the back of her mind. "You are safe, my daughter, and you are not alone." *Was that . . . her mother?* "What you are doing is ancient. It is as your mother; your grandmothers and their grand-mothers have done since time began. Your ancestors hear your cries and are proud of the magic that flows through you. You are beautifully strong and wonderfully made. Be of good heart." No, that wasn't her mother. *Was it?* She couldn't be sure. Her head was swimming, and a burning pain pierced her abdomen just below her belly button. "Magical things will happen when you allow what is to be, to become what is. Step aside and let it happen. You need to breathe and trust in the truth of this moment."

Comfort and calm washed over her, as she listened to the wisdom of her ancestors. When the next contraction began, Lauren took a deep breath. The pain seemed to fall away, and she focused on the energy the voice gave to her. She could feel the presence of her ancestors, and all fear escaped. The pressure of the baby's head told her one more push would be all it would take.

"You are strong, but it is safe to let go." The voice now sounded as if it was close. Lauren glanced up at Shadow sitting patiently in front of her like the very Goddess Bastet herself. The cat purred loudly, as if in blessing, and the next contraction came.

With one last push the baby arrived. Lauren reached down and caught it before she collapsed into the tub. Clutching the baby to her chest, she took a moment to regain her composure, trying not to panic about how much blood there was. Turning her attention to the baby, she reached for the towel and pulled it over them both.

Everything from that point on blurred in her memory. The baby wasn't breathing, and it turned blue in her arms. But Lauren was trained for such emergencies. She made sure the baby's nose and mouth were clear, then began CPR. Only once the soft whimpering cry came, and the baby pinked up, did Lauren collapse and begin to cry, overwhelmed with what she had just accomplished.

"Lauren!" A voice echoed through the house. Shadow looked back to her mistress then disappeared in a flash. Lauren did what she could to cover herself and the baby before a dark face peeked around the corner. "Lauren? What happened?" Bahati looked horrified.

"Call 9-1-1," she said. "The baby came early." She peeled back the towel showing her the small dark head on her chest as Bahati dropped to her knees beside the tub.

"I'll call," she heard John Carter's voice outside the doorway.

"Is the baby okay? Are you okay? I've been trying to call you for hours."

"It's breathing. Finally," Lauren said, tears still damp on her cheeks. Her hair was soaked with sweat and the room had a humid pallor that reeked of new-life and death-held-at-bay. Lauren lowered her tone. "It gave me quite a scare."

"I can imagine," Bahati took her hand. Shadow appeared beside her, dragging a blanket from one of the kids' bedrooms. It was pink, so it had to be one of Kate's.

"Good kitty," Bahati said, taking it, before the cat disappeared again.

"Where are the kids?" Lauren asked, rubbing the baby through the towel to keep her warm.

Bahati leaned back and glanced up. "Right here," she said. "I knew something was wrong when you wouldn't answer your phone. John Carter insisted we come home and check on you."

"What time is it?"

"After midnight," Bahati said.

"I knew it had to be," Lauren said. "It's so dark. Is it raining?"

"This has to be one of the worst storms I've ever seen in Southern California. The bridge at Mission Beach was washed out. We had a hard time navigating around it with all the other traffic. So many people came out to the museum for the kite festival."

"Someone should go meet the ambulance," Lauren said.

"I'll go," she heard Jamie say.

"Is it a boy or a girl?" Lauren heard Kate's small voice from the other side of the door.

"Can we see the baby?" Sam added.

Lauren gave Bahati a cautious look that told her *no*. "Not yet, darlings. We need to get your mother cleaned up a bit." She turned back to her friend. "Do they have a sister or another brother?"

"Honestly, I didn't have time to look," Lauren said, leaning back in the tub, trying to force her legs to stop shaking.

"As long as you are both okay," Bahati said. "Let's see if

we can't tidy up things a little bit." She went to the cabinet for more towels and a washcloth. She dampened it with warm water from the sink and handed it to Lauren. With her hands trembling, she tried to clean the baby and herself up, but it was a feeble attempt. Her jaw clattered and her legs shook. She recognized the signs of shock.

"They're here!" Lauren heard John Carter's voice coming up the stairs. She let out a relieved breath she hadn't realized she was holding.

"How about a couple more towels?" Lauren asked, reaching for the one in Bahati's hand.

***

ABDUL ANSWERED THE PHONE. "We have found him and the Egyptian woman," the voice on the other end said.

"Where?"

"On a research vessel in the Red Sea," the man said. "My brother found them. I have seen them myself. I will deliver them personally to you."

"Well done, Belial. I will see you richly rewarded."

"I ask for one thing alone. I would have a place among your armies," he said. "I have heard the voice of the gods telling me to take arms by your side. Our reward in heaven will be the greatest of all. I will serve you as your sword and shield."

That was what he was looking for! If his friend in Syria would not take arms with him, he would find his own allies at home. He would need friends like this more than anything else. "Bring me your hostages and come prepared for the war that is to come."

Abdul stayed up late, reading about this American archaeologist. He was famous and his name was known around the world. He was married to a scientist, and a father to many children. All that added to his worth as a hostage. He would also know how to find the weapon he needed, but his worth also meant his government would be likely to pay the ransom he would demand.

"Now the nations of the world will listen to me. America will listen. Egypt will listen and they will know me. I will show them the blood of my enemies. I will bathe in it. I will take delight in their suffering. I will show no one any mercy."

"As you wish," Belial said. "We will bring back the old gods and they will rain down their blessings upon our people and restore the ancient kings to power."

Abdul liked the way this man thought. "As it is written, so let it be done."

"So mote it be," Belial said.

"So mote it be." Abdul felt his victory secured. He had his archaeologists, and they would help him . . . or else.

* * *

ROWAN WASN'T the most careful explorer on the planet. Lauren had known him to take some crazy risks in order to get a shot or find an artifact. He'd managed to get lucky, most of the time. He'd talked his way out of a few tense situations and more than one narrow escape. On the other hand, he had more scars and metal hardware holding his bones together than most men. He considered them badges of honor, a sign of his courage and a mark of each adventure—like stamps on a passport.

Lauren hated that aspect of his character, but she wasn't one to talk either. She'd had her fair share of mishaps, despite her more cautious reserve. She'd been trained to analyze everything in her environment and anticipate every potential outcome. She knew enough about risk-versus-reward processes to make a scientific decision before she jumped into the fray. But then again, she could be impulsive, though not to the degree of her husband. Her worst injuries had come at the hands of others, when she'd underestimated the human element.

Even animals were more predictable than humans. She could read a wolf or a bison and extrapolate from its body language what it might do. Humans gave some signs, but animals had no sense of guile. Their goal was not to deceive, but to communicate their intentions, and she'd only once had an issue with an animal.

Grizzlies were the exception to her rule about animals. She had a run in with one in Alaska, and despite following every accepted theory on how to behave when encountering a bear, the female—a sow with cubs—had attacked her tent and left her mauled and bleeding hundreds of miles from any help.

That was the first time in her life she was certain she might die. She'd had that same passing thought a few hours earlier. Now that she was at the hospital, while doctors tended to her premature newborn, she was a little more at ease.

Her biggest concern now was for her baby. She also needed to reach her husband and let him know what was going on. Instead, she got his voicemail. *"This is Rowan. I'm off on another exciting adventure. Leave a message!"* Normally she loved hearing his voice but something about the recorded facsimile grated on her nerves. He'd called her from Egypt as soon as he got his lost phone replaced. *Why wasn't he answering now?*

"Hi, honey. It's me. Please call me as soon as you get this. Please. It's urgent." The message was short, but he would recognize the concern in her voice, and she knew he would call as soon as he could.

"Good morning, Lauren," her OBGYN, Dr. Miranda, appeared in the door of her hospital room. "You just couldn't wait a couple more months?" he asked as he paused to wash his hands at the sink. He wore a white dress shirt and a yellow tie and looked like he was headed to the office.

"I wouldn't have minded waiting, but, this baby seemed a

bit impatient." Lauren swallowed hard as he came over and pulled up her chart on his iPad. "I didn't have time to get downstairs, even."

"Your kids don't like to wait," he chortled.

"I went full term with two of them," Lauren said.

"Let me guess, Rowan is traveling?"

"Of course he is," she said. "But, this is the first one he's missed."

"I'm sure he'll be heartbroken," Dr. Miranda said.

"Maybe that will teach him a lesson." Lauren hadn't realized exactly how she was feeling about his absence until that moment. She was angry.

He'd had six months to reschedule his summer obligations, but he'd done nothing to get out of even a single one of them. He seemed happier on the road than at home, and Lauren hated that she even felt that way.

"Let's take a look and see how you're doing," he said, donning gloves. "How do you feel?"

"Drained," she admitted. She'd lain awake all night, and exhaustion was starting to close in. She'd lost a lot of blood and she felt dizzy. The baby was still in the NICU, and she hadn't had a chance to nurse her yet.

Lauren endured his exam. It wasn't any worse than the nurses massaging her abdomen to get her uterus to contract, which minimized bleeding, but increased the pain. "The paramedics reported quite a bit of blood loss," he said, peeling off his gloves, washing his hands again. "I'm going to order some labs. Your blood pressure is still low, so I want you to drink plenty of water. We're pushing intravenous fluids. I'm going to add Pitocin to help your uterus contract, and we'll continue monitoring, so I'd like to keep you another day or so, just to make sure there are no complications. I'll stop by and check on you tomorrow morning." Lauren nodded. "How's the baby?"

"They took her to the NICU as soon as we got here," Lauren said.

"It's a girl?"

Lauren smiled happily. "Finally. Kate is going to be thrilled to have a sister."

"Congratulations," he said. "I'll stop in and check on her before I head out."

"Thank you." Lauren sighed.

"Need anything for pain before I go?"

"I wouldn't say no," Lauren admitted. If they were going to give her Pitocin, she'd need it, and she knew it.

"Well, try to get some rest." He patted her shoulder and took his leave.

Lauren lay back, feeling the exhaustion in her body grow heavier. Something about her call to Rowan left her unsettled. She didn't have time to ponder it. She heard a shuffling outside the door to her room. There was a knock and a little voice called, "Mommy? Are you in there?"

"Yes, sweetie," she answered. Sam peeked his head around the corner and was bypassed by his sister and older brothers. Bahati followed, scooping him up. He looked distraught and Lauren could understand why. "Is everyone okay?"

"Sam is a little shaken up," Bahati said. "But there is your mommy, and she is fine." She set him down on the foot of her bed. His hand went to Lauren's foot. "More importantly, how are you?"

"The doctor says I'll be fine." Lauren wiggled her toes to reassure her youngest—second youngest. There was a new baby now.

"I want to sit with you, Mommy!" Kate jumped up and down, reaching for her mother to pick her up.

Bahati intervened, picking her up, but not setting her down. "You need to sit very still. Can you do that?"

"Yes, Aunt Bahati." Kate calmed and let Bahati put her next to her brother.

"The ambulance guys were nice," Jaime commented.

"Paramedics," John Carter corrected him.

"That's what I meant," Jamie said.

"Yes, they were, and I was very proud of all of you for staying so calm," Lauren said, reaching for Jamie's hand. "Thank you for helping me when I needed you."

"Where's the baby?" Kate asked, wiggling. A sharp look from Bahati made her settle.

"There's a special nursery for new babies," John Carter said. "She's there while the doctors make sure she's okay."

"Is she sick?"

"No, but she is very small," Lauren said. "Four pounds and two ounces."

"How big was I?" Sam asked.

"Almost two pounds more," Lauren said. "And you were a twin. Kate weighed almost the same."

"How much did I weigh?" Jamie asked.

"Closer to eight pounds," Lauren said. "John Carter was the biggest. He was almost ten pounds."

"Whoah!" Jamie gasped.

Lauren noticed—not for the first time—how much John Carter had grown over the winter. He was now every bit as tall as Henry, his older brother. John Carter hesitated for a long moment and opened his mouth as if to ask a question.

Lauren knew what he needed to ask. "She looks just like you, John Carter," Lauren said. "She has lots of black hair and dark eyes."

"Like me?" He'd always felt like the odd child out, and Lauren knew it. "I think she's going to be your best friend." The smile that cut his dark features made Lauren's heart swell. She lay her head back on her pillow, basking in the joy and exhaustion as the children chattered among themselves in excitement. It was only then that Lauren allowed herself to think about her absent husband. *God, she wished he could be here*. Of all the pregnancies to have complications with, it had to be the one where he was on the wrong side of the planet.

Rowan wasn't here. Her father wasn't here. Her mother wasn't here. Henry wasn't here.

"I'm here," Henry strode through the door, even though it never opened. "I'm sorry I couldn't get Dad home. I tried."

The twins jumped down from the bed and rushed him. His older brothers were a little more patient, but not by much. They realized quickly that he had come in his *shadow-form* and wasn't physically there. It was easier for him to *travel* this way and it expended less energy.

"Okay guys, that's enough," Bahati said. "Let's go down to the cafeteria and get something to eat so your mother can rest and visit with your brother."

"Do they have Jello?" Kate asked.

When the smaller children were gone, Lauren turned her attention to her two oldest boys.

"So, do I have a brother or a sister?" Henry asked.

"Like you don't already know," John Carter snarked.

Henry smiled. "She's adorable."

"Have you seen her?" Lauren asked.

"We've met."

Lauren didn't need to ask what he meant. She knew better.

"Are you okay?" Henry asked.

"Tired, but, I'm okay."

"I wish I could stay with you today," he said.

"Don't you have somewhere to be?" Lauren asked. "Isn't the tour at Oxford today?"

"I've already finished the tour," he said. "But you know as well as I do that I'm not going to Oxford."

"You could," Lauren said.

"But it's not *my* school," Henry said. "I'm going to Colorado State."

Lauren sighed, knowing that it was no use arguing. For

one thing, it was Henry's choice. For another, once Henry made his decision, nothing could sway him. He had a keen sense of his future, and Lauren had to wonder if he'd already seen it for himself. His ability to *travel* was just as powerful as her father's. Though he was just sixteen, his fate lie in his own hands. They'd raised him to know his own mind, and make his own choices, knowing full well that his parents would be there to support him and love him no matter the outcome— good or ill.

"Mom?" John Carter pulled the doctor's stool over and threw a leg over it like Will Riker on Star Trek. "Did you and Dad have a chance to decide on the baby's name?"

"Yeah," Henry said. "What are you going to name her?"

"Well." Lauren lay her head back on her pillow and felt the heavy weight of exhaustion in her bones. "We did have a few conversations about it," she said. "We didn't have a final decision made because we expected your father to be home in time. Whoever thought she would come so early."

"Do you want me to tell you her name?" Henry asked.

It shouldn't have surprised her, but the question caught her completely off guard. "You know?"

"Of course I do," Henry said, sitting on the edge of the bed. "Her name is Sarah Connor Pierce."

"Dude! Is she going to have to fight Skynet?" John Carter snarked.

Lauren sat trying to puzzle this revelation out. She'd dissed every Star Trek and Star Wars name Rowan had on his list. After five children with science-fiction-related names, Lauren knew it was too late to change the naming convention now. *Marion Ravenwood* was eventually ruled out. But *Deja Thoris* was the hill Rowan was prepared to die on, and she knew that.

Still, nothing he pitched felt right to her. But this new option made Lauren's pulse calm. It felt right. In the brief time she'd had with her daughter, Lauren gaged her as a wise old soul who'd seen many worlds before coming into *this* life.

She could sense the magic her daughter would yield. Sarah contained the souls of her ancestors, and they were ancient and powerful. Sarah would be, too.

"Sarah," Lauren nodded. "Okay. Thank you, Henry."

That was the end of the discussion. Henry leaned his head towards the door as he looked to his brother. "Mom needs to rest," Henry said. "You and Aunt Bahati should take the little kids home. Make sure Bahati gets some rest, too."

"Who's going to look after mom? You can't stay all day, and we both know it." John Carter's hands went to his hips in a pose that mimicked their father when he was determined to stand his ground.

"Your brother is right, but I have doctors and nurses to take care of me," Lauren said. "If you can reach your dad..."

"I'm staying with you, Mom." John Carter's tone made it clear he wasn't going anywhere.

Henry seemed resigned to the fact they were right. "I'll check on him when I get my strength back." The physical travel to a different place or time drained the boy. He was tall, like his father, but lithe, almost rail thin. He couldn't possibly eat enough calories to maintain his physique and his magic, even though he tried.

There was a knock at the door. The nurse entered pushing a basinet with a tiny bundle wrapped in a blanket. "Here she is, Momma," the nurse announced. Henry disappeared in a twinkle of dust that the nurse didn't even seem to notice.

Neither Lauren nor John Carter reacted to his sudden departure. John Carter rose from the stool, as the nurse lifted the bundle and lay it in Lauren's arms. He stood back, inspecting his sister, who was wide awake. Lauren watched in awe at the interaction between the matching siblings. Each of the raven-haired children gazed into the other's eyes and it seemed they were already acquainted. The baby squirmed in her arm, kicking her feet before settling.

"Do you want to hold her?" Lauren asked. John Carter took a step back, with hesitation written in his eyes.

"She's so small." He swallowed hard.

"She's still your sister," Lauren said. "You've held babies before."

"Come wash your hands first," the nurse reminded him. He complied and then came over and sat on the edge of the bed, taking the baby gingerly into the crook of his arm, supporting her head and grinning broadly as he settled. The nurse left them to get acquainted.

He was an excellent big brother. Lauren relied on him even more now that Henry was about to head off to college and was often gone to tend to his training. His hair flopped over his face as he bent over her and tickled her cheek with a long thumb.

"She's so cute," John Carter said, his voice breaking. A tear dropped from his face and pattered against the baby's blanket.

"She looks just like you," Lauren said.

"Mom?" John Carter moved closer. "Does she look a little blue to you? Around her mouth?"

Lauren's heart flipped in her chest as he handed her back over. Lauren pulled the blankets back, finding her fingers and toes. "John Carter, go ask the nurse to come back in, please." It took every inch of control Lauren had to keep her tone measured. She didn't want John Carter to panic, but he darted out of the room. She could hear his voice echo down the hall.

The baby's lips had gone cherry red and the skin around her mouth tinged dark. Lauren leaned down and blew a puff of air in her face. There was no reaction.

For a second time, she began CPR on the baby. After a few breaths and compressions, the baby's eyelids lifted, and she startled. Immediately, her lips turned rosy and the skin around her mouth lightened.

The nurse came in with the frightened teenager behind her. "Did she stop breathing?"

"Yes," Lauren said. "I got her back though . . . again."

"I was holding her," John Carter said. "I thought she died."

"She didn't die," the nurse said calmly, putting her stethoscope in her ears, listening to the baby's heart. "She's just learned to breathe. Newborns, particularly preemies, sometimes just forget to do it."

"Are you sure?" Lauren asked.

"I'll take her back to the nursery and give her a little oxygen. We'll take care of her for the next thirty minutes or so. She hasn't nursed yet, has she?"

"No," Lauren said.

"We might need you to pump, so she can eat when she gets hungry," the nurse said, collecting the baby. Lauren was more than ready. The pressure in her breasts was becoming uncomfortable.

"I can do that," Lauren said.

"You haven't eaten yet either," the nurse said. "I'll come back and bring you the breakfast menu."

Lauren realized she hadn't eaten since breakfast the day before, but she really wasn't hungry. Just the thought of food made her queasy. It might make her feel better, or it might make things worse. At this point, she was too tired to care.

"Mom," John Carter said, taking her hand as he sat down beside her. "She's going to be fine. Right?"

Lauren nodded, but realized she had tears building in her eyes.

"Your only job is to take care of yourself. Let the doctors take care of Sarah. She's safe." At the moment, everything was crashing down on her—Rowan's absence, the baby's health, her own fatigue, and surging hormones. "Mom, you need to sleep. You'll feel better when you're rested," John Carter said. "I'll go check on Sarah."

HENRY WAITED for his brother outside the door. John Carter didn't acknowledge him. He wasn't sure if anyone else could see him. He knew it was only his *shade* walking beside him. He waited 'til they were past the nurses station to say anything. "It'd be awesome if you could go get Dad," John Carter said.

"Yeah, about that," he said. "Something's going on with Dad, but . . . with Mom's energy expended like it is, I'm having trouble focusing. I can't stay here much longer. My energy is draining quickly."

"What can I do?"

"Just make sure Mom keeps it together. Sarah is sick, and it's not going to be easy. You gotta stand in for Dad. Once Nanhi gets back, it'll be better."

"What do I do?"

"Just take care of Mom," Henry said, his voice fading into oblivion.

12

A black cloud formed around him, and the sour tang of cannabis and black magic filled his nostrils. Drums echoed in his head. He heard someone chanting around him. "*Ban pouvwa, mwen sipliye . . .*" The chanting voice was deep with a Haitian French-Creole accent. "*Mèsi pou bwa a. Tanpri, ban mwen pouvwa, Bondye. Mwen rele nan nwa a . . . ban m pouvwa soul mòtèl sa a pou m ka sèvi w pi byen . . .*" Somewhere in the back of his pounding head, he remembered where he had heard those words before. *Papa Dauphine.*

"Yes, Rowan Pierce," the man rolled the r's as his evil smile appeared in the darkness like the cheshire cat appearing in the tree. The light caught the gold crown on his front tooth, making the image all the more menacing. "You *remembah.*"

"You tried to kill me," Rowan tried to sit up and push himself back on his elbows—to put as much space between him and the voodoo priest as he could. He couldn't seem to move.

"I didna wanna kill you before," he said, sitting down in

front of him, cross-legged. "But revenge is a dangerous *ting*, and if I wan you dead, den dead you will be."

Rowan was certain he wasn't dead. His head throbbed too much. "Then you must not want me dead."

His smile curled into an evil gaze as he leaned in. "Maybe I take your woman first . . ." he chuckled, his arrogant laugh grew into a crescendo and he rolled back onto his elbow, clutching his stomach. The laughter became deafening, and it sent a chill through Rowan's countenance that wrapped around his spine, twisted around his stomach then reached up like an icy claw around his heart. "Keep your grubby paws off my wife!" Rowan snarled. "And your evil black magic, too!"

"Ya reap what ya sow." His laughter faded.

"You'll need someone to sew you up if I get ahold of you," Rowan snarled, trying to kick out at him. He fought against whatever forces held him down. "Leave me and my family alone!"

Dauphine was standing over him, his fetid breath in Rowan's face. "Karma . . . ain't it a *betch*?" The laughter resumed then faded into the darkness, along with the vision of the voodoo priest himself.

A piercing ringing added to the throbbing in Rowan's cracked skull. His whole body burned like fire. His muscles and joints screamed with the same kind of pain he'd felt when an improvised explosive device had gone off in his face. It also reminded him of something else that happened in his military career.

As a young soldier, Rowan went to basic training at Fort Benning in Georgia. There, he made friends with an Italian kid from Bayonne, New Jersey. Private Joseppi Cannizzo was what the drill sergeant called a *Grade A, First Class F-Up*. Joe liked to pull practical jokes on his fellow recruits. Nine weeks into his eighteen week BCT, Joe thought it'd be funny to do a *ball tap* on his ol' buddy Private Pierce, just as the drill sergeant came into their quarters for inspection.

Rowan was still down on one knee with a hand over his offended junk, puking his guts up when the NCO yelled, "Attention!" He puked on the NCO's boots. His only revenge came when *Nizzo* got to clean up the mess and ended up adding to it.

He knew from that experience someone had kicked him in the crotch when he'd been *manhandled*. It wasn't the worst of his injuries, but it was familiar—and just as painful as it had been when he was eighteen-years-old.

The room was hot and sweat poured down his face—or maybe it was blood. He reached for his chest to see if he still had on the skintight wet suit he'd had on when they hauled him from the Red Sea. Instead, he realized he was naked.

"Rowan." A frightened voice echoed off the walls. He stiffened and a sharp pain cut through his shoulders like a knife. It forced him to try and open his eyes. "Are you hurt?"

"Tima?" he croaked, unable to see her in the blackness. He could get one eye open, but it was dark, and he didn't know if they were in a cave or a cellar. "Where are we?"

"Are you hurt?"

"God . . ." he groaned when he tried to roll over. This time, the pain hit him in the ribs and his breath caught in his throat. "Yes . . ." he managed. "You?"

"I haven't taken a beating like this since I left my husband," she said flatly. He could hear something in her voice he'd never heard before. She'd never talked about her ex-husband with any kind of sympathy. He knew she'd left him, but she'd never said why. He'd assumed the man was a complete fool and cheated on her. He never imagined any man raising a hand to the fiery Dr. Fatima Badr. "But I don't think I'm as bad off as you. They only used fists and feet on me. They came at you with boots and what looked like a club."

"What'd I do to tick them off?"

"I don't think either of us did anything to deserve this, Rowan-*darling*."

Tima's voice cracked and he knew she was trying to keep him from knowing just how severely injured she was. She wasn't a young woman, and at her age—he could only assume she was about the same age as his parents—any blow could do significant damage.

His father had taken a bad fall in the back yard last September, and his mother sent pictures of his black eye almost every day for a month to show Rowan how well it was healing. It only reminded him that the years were ticking away for his parents, and his time with them was limited.

At eighteen Charles Pierce survived a motor vehicle crash that killed two. He survived getting shot in the leg in Vietnam when his plane was shot down over the jungle. Charles spent the better part of a year in a POW camp. His men tended to him, and treated his wounds, even giving up their own meager rations to ensure their Captain survived. After he recovered, he led a daring escape and all but one survived.

Through his actions, Captain Charlemagne Pierce saved twenty-nine airmen. His injuries earned him a Purple Heart, but his courage earned him the Air Force Cross. It also earned him a promotion and a ticket state-side.

Rowan remembered watching them pin the award on his father's chest, even though he was young. He remembered them talking about his father's heroism in the face of an opposing force, and his personal sacrifice. It didn't mean much to a toddler, but Rowan came to learn what his father had done, and how it shaped him into the man he was proud to have as his dad, though he called him *The Colonel*, like everyone else.

Unable to return to combat, he began teaching leadership and survival tactics. He taught those skills to his children, though Rowan just thought of it as his dad teaching him something every boy scout learned from their father. He realized now, he would need those lessons more than he had in the Pacific Northwest, or the jungles of Cambodia.

"Tima?"

"Yes, Rowan . . . *darling*." He could hear her swallow hard.

"Do you know where we are?"

"A bunker, I think, but I'm not certain where," she said.

"How did we get here?"

"I don't know," she said. "But we seem to be the only ones. I've been trying to wake you for what seems like hours."

"Do you know how long we've been alone? Or how long it took to get here?" He knew if they were going to survive, they would have to escape. He also knew his injuries wouldn't permit them to get far. He suspected Tima was in worse shape, despite her brave front.

"I'm not sure," she said. "How badly hurt are you?"

"What makes you think I'm . . ." he started to protest, but she didn't even let him finish.

"I've heard you moaning," she said. "That's how I knew I wasn't alone here."

"What about you?" Rowan began taking a mental inventory of his own injuries. *Boot to the groin, and to the ribs.* He'd been clobbered over the back of the head. He suspected a bruised sternum, but he didn't think anything was broken, yet. He was certain he had a concussion. His left eye was badly swollen. His face ached, but manual inspection of his nose told him it wasn't broken.

"Eh," she managed. Rowan wasn't buying it.

"Tima, I need you to be absolutely honest with me," he said, groaning as he pushed himself up to a seated position, leaning against what felt like a concrete wall. The room spun but he willed it to settle before he continued. "What are your injuries?" There was a long moment of silence before her voice broke into whimpering sobs. "Tima?" his heart sunk into his stomach, and he felt sick. "What did they do to you?" His voice trailed off.

The sob tapered into a trembling whisper. "Unspeakable things . . ."

———

KITTY SAT at a conference table at the American Embassy as Frank White, the Secretary of Homeland Security in D.C., stared back at her from a computer screen. "Kitty, I don't have to tell you that this is about to escalate into more than just an international conflict. This terrorist in Sudan attacked a civilian research vessel in the Red Sea," he said. "Two injured, one dead, two missing."

"Please tell me this information hasn't been released to the media," Kitty said, fearing the worst.

"Not yet," Frank said. "We can't keep this concealed for very long."

"Has anyone claimed responsibility for the attack? This *Psychopath of Soba*, perhaps?"

"Not yet," Frank said, folding his hands on the table in front of him. His gold tie-pin caught the fluorescent lights in his office, flickering as he leaned forward, crinkling his blue and red striped tie. "But we need to begin notifications of . . . the *next-of-kin*. Dr. Pierce and Mrs. Toussaint shouldn't have to hear about it on the news."

Kitty cringed. *It should be her, of course.* She knew the families. She was part of the family. "You want me to take the lead on that." It wasn't a question. She was prepared to fly back to the US.

"No," Frank said. "I'm handling the notification. I want you to begin the diplomatic process. Find out who this *Psychopath* guy is and what he wants. What's his end-game? Work your magic. Broker peace and get these people back to their families."

"And if I can't do that?"

"I know a guy," Frank said. Kitty did a double take,

thinking he sounded like he was about to call in the Mafia to handle the situation. "I've already got a request into his office."

John Carter sat quietly in the corner when they brought his new baby sister back from the NICU. It had only been a few hours, but his mother insisted she needed to nurse the baby as soon as possible. John Carter had pressed the issue, advocating for his mother. They finally complied.

He watched from beneath the curtain of his bangs, peering through his dark hair. His mom looked pale, and she had dark circles growing under her eyes. It was after dinner time, but he'd yet to go down to the cafeteria to get a cheeseburger or something to eat. He hated to leave her alone. Until she finished feeding the baby and eaten something herself, he wasn't going anywhere.

He knew from watching her care for his brothers and sisters, that the first time nursing could be hard for both mom and baby. Sarah seemed to take to it quickly and his mother settled back, letting her eyes close as the baby nursed.

He realized her eyes were on him and he sat up. "Do you need something?"

"No," she said. "Aren't you hungry?"

"Not really," he said, yawning. His mother eyed him down. "What?"

"You can't fool me, John Carter Pierce," his mother snapped. "You haven't eaten since you got that candy bar out of the vending machine four hours ago."

"I'll go eat once you've had a chance to eat your dinner," John Carter stood and walked over to inspect the tray by her bed. The meatloaf, mashed potatoes and green beans had gone cold an hour ago.

"I'll give you twenty dollars to go get us some tacos," Lauren smirked.

John Carter sat up in his chair. "Are you serious?"

"All I can think of is a little carne asada with white onion, sliced radishes and pickled carrots from the *Paquito Burrito*." She sighed, laying her head back. "I could eat a dozen of them."

"Me, too. It's close enough I could walk over there." John Carter's face brightened. "Can I get us each a real Coca-Cola in the glass bottles? The ones from Mexico."

"I would love that," Lauren said, smiling. "There's money in my purse but be careful crossing the streets. It's not still raining is it?"

"A little, but I have my rain slicker," he said. "I'll be back. Do you need anything else?"

"No, but if you'd stop by the nurses' station and ask her to come see me when she gets a minute, I'd appreciate it."

"Sure," John Carter said. "I'll be back in about twenty minutes or so."

"Take your time," his mother said. "I just want you to be careful."

John Carter leaned in and kissed his mother's cheek. "I'm always careful."

JAMIE SAT in the living room floor with his video game controller between his hands, trying to defeat the evil villain Malfael. The whole *Star Battalion*—Jamie's allies in the massive multiplayer online game—had fallen and he was the last man standing. He fired volley after volley of magical weapons, clicking the green button to pop a potion when his own life force began to drop.

"Resurrect!" he shouted at the others through the mic

attached to his headphones. "Come on guys! Hurry up! Can't you see I'm dying?"

"He's at thirteen percent!" a voice answered back. "Keep going! Pop another potion."

Jamie followed instructions, all the while dodging the villain's attack. He tossed a time bomb at the boss and ran away so the damage wouldn't affect him, then turned back, and continued his magical volley. Tiny sparkling bits of *fel energy* did a minute amount of damage to the boss, but Jamie's health bar was still ticking down. Then the time bomb went off. Jamie's avatar was knocked off his feet. It depleted another five percent of his life force. The boss' went to one percent, then ticked down to nothing. The icon over the villain's head turned red and the monster staggered, groaned, and collapsed, creating a shockwave so strong, Jamie's avatar took another ten percent hit, leaving him hanging by a thread. One of his Star Battalion's avatar, a female pixie named *Tinkie Winkie* flittered over and sprinkled him with pixie dust, but it was too little, too late. His icon went red, and his avatar collapsed and disintegrated with a spark. It didn't matter. He'd won the hard-fought battle, and the cheers through the headphones nearly deafened him.

They'd tried every night for the past week to figure out how to defeat the final boss in the most epic quest ever created in any MMORPG. They'd come close the night before but hadn't even made it to the last boss before the group had to disband due to the late hour. Even Jamie knew he'd better get to bed before his Aunt Bahati caught him in the living room. Tonight he waited until everyone else was in bed before he snuck down to join the group. They'd defeated the *sickest* boss ever! *Finally! Not bad for a monk.*

"Where's the spellcasters? Let's get everyone resurrected so we can loot the boss," Jamie said. Something moved out of the corner of his eye as the magical spells were being cast and one by one members of the team returned to their avatars.

Shadow, his mother's cat, came down the stairs, and he realized something was wrong with her. She stumbled, falling over the last step, collapsing into a heap on the floor. Her blue eyes met his. He saw a desperate plea for aid in her expression. A weak mew came from her chest, and her eyes closed.

"Shadow!" Jamie yanked off his headphones and bolted to the cat, hesitating to touch her. "Shadow?" He watched and notice her chest rise and fall in the dim light provided by the television. He stroked her gently and her eyes lifted ever so slightly but closed just as quickly.

"Aunt Bahati!" He shouted up the stairway. She was staying in Henry's old room while his mother was in the hospital and his father was gone. He could hear the door open as he scooped his kitty up into his arms, holding her to his chest, petting her gently. She was breathing, but it was faint.

"Jamie?" Bahati came down the stairs tying her robe. "What are you doing up? Don't you know what time it is?"

"Something's wrong with Shadow," he sobbed. Tears spilled down his cheek. "She came down the stairs and just collapsed."

Bahati rushed down and put her hand on the cat's chest, reaching over and flicking the light, inspecting her. "She doesn't look good." The limp cat hung in Jamie's arms. "Who's your vet?"

"Dr. McIntosh lives two doors over," Jamie said. "He's her vet."

"What's his phone number?"

"There's a book with all the emergency numbers in the kitchen," he said, growing more panicked. "I don't know if it's in there."

"Knowing your mother, he's in there." Bahati moved past him and hurried to the kitchen to find the brown leather book in the built-in corner desk. She thumbed through it and found the number. She retrieved her phone off the counter where she had it plugged into the charger and dialed the number.

The phone call was brief. The answering service took down the information and her phone number and said they'd relay the message to the doctor. "He'll call back with instructions," Bahati said. She and Jean-René didn't have any pets, so it wasn't something she knew anything about.

Jamie found one of Kate's blankets on the sofa and used it to wrap Shadow up. The cat was no longer responsive, but she was still breathing. "What do we do?"

"It's three in the morning, Jamie," she said. "They'll wake the doctor up and he'll call us as soon as he . . ." A knock at the door interrupted her and she bolted for the door.

"Dr. MacIntosh!" Jamie cried out. Relief was evident in his voice. "Something's wrong with Shadow." The doctor, still in his pajama pants and slippers came in, setting down his emergency kit. He took the cat from Jamie. Carrying her over to the counter. He began the painfully slow process of examining the now limp cat, taking out his stethoscope and donning it so he could hear her heartbeat.

"Has she eaten anything unusual?" his tone was calm but urgent. "Had any vomiting, diarrhea?"

"With four kids in the house?" Bahati recoiled.

"No," Jamie said. "Only cat food. Momma said not to give her any people food. None of us would do that. I haven't seen her get sick or anything."

"Has she gone outside?"

"Not today," Jamie said, glancing towards the screen door to see if it was still raining, but it was too dark to see.

"Any chemicals she can get into?"

"Have you met Lauren? This place is more childproof that Fort Knox," Bahati retorted.

"Okay. Go do a quick inspection of the bathrooms, storage cabinets, check the garage for anything out of place— open containers of antifreeze or motor oil. I'll get her stabilized and then take her to the clinic where I can start running tests and get her treated." He pulled a card from his bag and tossed it on the counter. "Call me once you've checked every-where. Look for chemicals, check the houseplants to see if she's chewed on them. Make sure there are no human pills she could have gotten into."

Jamie and Bahati jumped to their tasks.

LAUREN WAS RELIEVED when the nurse came shortly after John Carter left. "Everything okay in here?"

"No," Lauren handed the baby off to her. "I just got extremely dizzy. Something's wrong. It's like the room is spin-ning. I can't make it stop." She could hear the panic in her own voice.

The nurse put Sarah in the bassinet and moved it to the side, jumping into action. "How long ago did this start?" She leaned down and took Lauren's face in her hands, inspecting her eyes. "Stick out your tongue." Lauren did. "Any blurred vision?"

"It just started a few minutes ago . . . everything is spin-ning . . ." Lauren closed her eyes and licked her lips. "I just . . ." A circle of darkness closed in on her field of vision. Her head started pounding and she felt weak. The nurse hit a button on the wall behind her.

"Code Red. I need the attending or on-call in room 1333."

"Unfreakingbelievable," Lauren muttered. *Any room but that.*

"Lauren?" she could hear the nurses' voice as it moved farther and farther away. She felt herself slipping, consumed by the void.

She found herself standing in the middle of a graveyard, in her bare feet and a white nightgown. She glanced down at her hands, realizing they were covered in blood. She could feel eyes on her, and she turned cautiously.

Papa Dauphine sat on a crypt in the same outfit he'd worn in the video Jean-René had shown in court. White pillar candles burned on the ground around him, illuminating the cemetery she recognized as Saint Louis No. 1 in New Orleans. It was where Marie Laveau was buried, and one of the most iconic places in the world. "What did you do to me?" She demanded. She knew something was wrong, but she couldn't tell what. Now everything made sense. Rowan not getting home. Her inability to reach her father. Her baby's early delivery. Her own failing health.

"I didn't do no'ting," he said. "Karma though . . . ain't she a *betch*?" A wide white smile broke across his dark features.

"Karma?" Lauren puzzled. "Justice and karma go hand in hand. You're the one who tried to kill my husband."

"Oh, I might get him yet," he said, chuckling. "Way I see it—de universe owes me a t'ing or two. You have offended my honor. You have not said the words, but you did not have to. You questioned my abilities as a great and powerful *bokor*. You will know the power my ancestors have granted me. You will know the dark lord who commands me bide. You will know suffering and you will know death."

"Well, I know something you don't know," Lauren muttered, clenching her hands, and trying to draw the same force she'd used against Enlil when she'd confronted him in Washington D.C., so many years ago. She expected the heat in her arm to drive through her hand and to force him down, but the heat only reached her fingers, then seemed to dissipate into nothing.

She tried again.

And again.

The last thing she heard was the voodoo priest, laughing.

13

Frank stood at the elevator to await his guest. The old gears and levers creaked and moaned before the doors stuttered open as the bewildered guest stumbled out of the car that stopped a quarter of an inch below floor level.

Frank caught him and set him upright. "Sorry about that. I put in a maintenance request on that thing a month ago," Frank said to the man, as he regained his composure.

Andrew Miller stuck out a hand, introducing himself.

"Frank White," the director returned the favor.

"How is it the head of Homeland Security is calling me off a case in the middle of the night?"

"This one is personal," Frank said, leading him down the long hallway. "For you, too. Look, you can decline the assignment, but I already talked to your chief and she's willing to loan you to me for this case."

"What's up?" Andrew tucked his hands in his pockets. At this late hour, he was dressed in jeans and a button up plaid shirt. Frank had expected as much and felt comfortable leaving his suit jacket and tie tossed over the back of his leather office chair.

"I believe you know Dr. Lauren Pierce and her husband Rowan?"

"I do," Miller said, looking even more puzzled. "It's been a while since I saw them though."

"We've received information from the Embassy in Cairo that Mr. Pierce was involved in a possible terrorist attack," Frank said. The man was stunned. Frank waved a hand for him to follow and led him down the long corridor to a room labeled, *Evidence*. Frank already ran his security clearance if only to verify it was sufficient for this assignment. It was.

"Involved in a . . . terrorist attack? What happened?" Andrew asked, concern creasing his features.

Frank explained. "His camera operator and one of the college researchers were rescued, but there is at least one confirmed fatality."

"What about Rowan?"

First name basis, okay. "We received a letter late last night from a rogue warlord in Sudan—some nut job with delusions of grandeur—claiming responsibility." Frank flipped on a light and led Miller over to the evidence locker, using his thumbprint to unlock the cabinet. He brought over a covered metal box half the size of a standard lunch room tray, setting it on the stainless steel workbench. He reached for a pair of gloves and tossed them to Miller, before donning his own.

Once properly gloved, Frank opened the lid. He'd already viewed the evidence and knew what to expect. Obviously, Miller wasn't so prepared. He blanched visibly at the severed finger laying in the tray, with a wedding band still *in situ*. It was a thick white-gold band inlayed with small diamonds. "Is that . . . Rowan's?" Miller gulped, swallowing hard. Frank noticed him blanch but he didn't seem at risk of tossing his lunch. Not yet, anyway.

"We are certain the ring is his," Frank said. "The techs were able to scour the internet for a picture of Mr. Pierce's ring and are confident it's a match. The finger, however, remains in question."

"Oh?" Andrew glanced up.

"The techs are running DNA analysis, but we don't have anything to compare it to when the results come back. From what they're telling me, this specimen came from an older female." Frank reached down and picked up the severed digit. Whoever did this sliced off the finger neatly, just below where the ring rested. The flesh had gone dark and mottled, the tip almost black beneath a pink painted nail. "There's evidence of arthritis in the joint, and last I checked, Rowan Pierce didn't wear nail polish." He pointed out the flaking paint. "The tech tells me this is a polish color called *ballet slippers*."

"That's the same color Queen Elizabeth wears," Miller observed.

Frank didn't expect him to know something that random. "Queen Elizabeth? The Queen of England?"

"Yes," Miller said. "It was the only color she deemed appropriate for someone of her station. It's a classic pale pink with a subtle sheer finish. The manufacturer has been in business since the early 1980's. They discontinued the color until the Queen's valet reached out and asked them to continue it. Joan Rivers wore their brightest red, *jelly apple*."

"Why do you even know that?" Frank put the finger back in its tray and peeled off his gloves.

"When I was a rookie in Boston, I investigated a crime where a woman was murdered and run through a wood chipper. The biggest fragment we could identify was a fingernail. The blue nail polish was identified as *bikini so teeny*. It was one of the Essie polishes. It became the number one selling nail colors of all time in 2013. The girl I was dating worked in a nail salon and she knew this brand inside and out."

"Did you ever identify the victim? Because of the nail polish?"

"Only through DNA analysis," he said. "Annabelle Leigh was a wealthy socialite. We were able to determine that her husband had a gambling problem. He fell in with the wrong kind of loan shark, if you know what I mean."

"Is there ever a good kind of loan shark?"

"Some are worse than others. Some have families. Big *Italian* families."

"Oh," Frank realized what Andrew meant. *The Mob.*

"So when he couldn't pay up his gambling debts, collection officers came to the house intent on a shake down. When Mrs. Leigh came home early from her nail appointment, she interrupted the attack on her husband. In Mr. Leigh's testimony, he claimed she tried to reach her husband's gun, but one of the thugs got to her first. He watched while they turned their rage on his wife, beating her half to death."

"Let me guess," Frank sniffed. "When he couldn't or wouldn't pay them their money back, they killed his wife and ran her through the wood chipper? Did they make him watch?"

"Yeah, and worse," Andrew said. "They didn't kill her first."

"Oh." Frank's jaw dropped.

Miller turned his attention back to the case at hand. "So if the finger isn't Rowan's, I have to ask, where's Lauren?"

"She's at home in San Diego, pregnant with their sixth."

"Sixth?" Miller shook his head. "Dang!"

"Rowan was in Egypt to do a lecture for his college professor, Dr. Fatima Badr. She was with the team when the research boat was attacked. We're working under the premise that this belongs to her. She's one of the missing people from the expedition."

"So what else do we know about this Sudanese *warlord*?"

"Not a lot," Frank said, returning the tray to the locker.

He withdrew a document sealed inside a plastic evidence bag. He brought it to the table. "This is the letter that came with the finger."

Miller picked it up and flipped it over, to look at the envelope it came in. "He sent it to the President of the United States?"

"Ballsy, I know," Frank said, leaning against a desk nearby as Andrew continued to study the hand written address. "Wait 'til you read the letter."

Miller glanced up and turned the document over. "Dear America, you call yourselves the greatest country in the world, but I have your people. You will pay—in cash or in blood—it's up to you to decide. You think yourselves so mighty, that you mandate peace, while people suffer under failing governments. You will see for yourself the destruction your policies have wrought. Rowan Pierce is mine. If you want him. You will pay." It was signed, *The King of Sudan.*

"What?" Andrew scratched his head. "King of Sudan. Sudan isn't a monarchy."

"Like I said, this guy's got delusions of grandeur," Frank said. "I've already talked to our ambassador. She's in Jerusalem but she's making diplomatic connections in Sudan now."

"So, let me guess, you don't need another negotiator," Miller said.

"I need options," Frank said. "I need to bring Rowan Pierce home to his wife."

"You've met Lauren, too?"

"Yeah," Frank said. "She's an amazing woman."

"You've got that right," Miller said. "Has anyone told her?"

"Not yet," Frank said.

"I'll go," Andrew offered. "She shouldn't hear that over the phone and . . . I'm going to need her help."

"I've already talked to your supervisor about a mutual aid

agreement," he said. "Keep track of the time you spend working on this case. You'll process your expense report as normal. Homeland Security will reimburse the FBI."

"Lassiter already mentioned something about that when she called me."

"You have full discretion for any expense. No questions asked. Of course, I don't need to tell you, this case is a matter of National Security."

"Global Security, from what I can see," Andrew said. "*The Great Accord* has almost put me out of business. They've had me working domestic missing persons and potential human trafficking cases."

"Dr. Kitty Grayson, our ambassador, will be working closely with you on this case. The two of you report to me and to me only."

"That's Lauren's sister-in-law," Miller said. "Do you think it's a good idea to have someone so close to the family work this case?"

"Only Dr. Grayson will understand the magnitude of this case," Frank said, gruffly. "She'll meet you in Jerusalem after you've taken care of Lauren and the children. She will brief you fully. Anything they need is also authorized."

"We'll keep you posted," Miller said.

Frank reached into his pocket and took out a small electronic device. He tossed it to Andrew. "Only use this phone to contact me," he said. "It's a secure burner phone with global capabilities. All tracking abilities are switched off, so don't rely on it to get you out of a pickle. It will let you call out, but no calls in. If we need to do any covert ops, I'll set you up with a secure sat-com."

Miller flipped the phone open and inspected it. It looked like the phone his mother had given him in the late 1990s when he was a teenager. There were buttons, and no touch screen. "No texting?"

"No texting," Frank confirmed. "I've got a plane standing

by at Capitol Airpark. It'll take you to San Diego. When you're ready to head to Jerusalem, let me know. I'll get you aboard a military transport."

"Will it count towards my platinum status on United? I'm working my way into the premier lounge."

"No lounges, no points. You'll be lucky if you get a seat with a restraint. You might end up in the cargo hold, depending on what's available."

"Gee," Miller said, looking sheepish. "Thanks."

"WELCOME BACK, DR. PIERCE," Dr. Miranda said, leaning down over the bed. "You gave us quite a scare."

"What happened?" Lauren felt numb and her body felt heavy. The room was brightly illuminated, and the doctor had an aura around him from the lights. "What is this place?"

"You're in recovery," he said. "You lost a lot of blood. I had to take you back to surgery. There was a uterine tear. You needed a transfusion of red blood cells. Your son was a perfect match for your blood type and insisted we use his."

"My son?"

"John Carter," he explained. "From what I'm told, the ladies in the phlebotomy lab have taken a liking to him. They're giving him plenty of fluids and snacks so he can provide an additional donation, if you need one. In the meantime, we're pushing fluids and working to get your blood pressure back up. You may feel groggy for a while."

Lauren lay there blinking back the blinding light overhead. Her head ached. The room was freezing cold. Her jaw began trembling and her teeth rattled together. She was aware of a burning sensation in her abdomen and the heavy ache that spread through her core and into her limbs.

"Let me get you a warm blanket and then I'll top off your pain medication," she heard a voice, as if an angel from heaven. A moment later, she felt a warmth wrap around her that her mind could only define as *delicious*. And after a few more beats of her thundering heart, the warmth spread within her veins. It allowed her to relax and calm her chattering teeth. A shadow moved between her and the bright lights.

"Is that better?" The voice sounded familiar.

She forced herself to focus. The red-headed man in the blue scrubs looked strangely familiar. "Jamie?"

"Don't say anything." His voice was deeper, and he was so much taller than she remembered. "Just listen. We're under attack. Enlil has found a weakness. You need to be strong and get well. We're doing what we can to protect you. You just have to hold on."

"Call . . . call your . . . father . . ."

"We're trying," he said. "Just get better. We need you."

BAHATI PACED THE WAITING ROOM, while the twins occupied themselves with the coloring books and crayons. Jamie, who'd stayed up all night worrying about the cat, collapsed on one of the sofas and was sound asleep. Dr. McIntosh couldn't find anything wrong with Shadow but kept her in the clinic so he could monitor her condition and give her IV fluids. He promised to bring her home later in the day, if the family was home and she continued to improve.

Meanwhile, Lauren remained in the recovery room and John Carter was downstairs, being pampered in the phlebotomy lab. Sarah's condition was stable in the NICU.

Bahati took out her cellphone, noting that the battery was down below ten percent. She'd tried calling Jean-René, again. She hung up when it went to voice mail. *Jesus Christ. Why didn't he answer?*

"Aunt Bahati?" She turned at John Carter's voice. She

rushed over to him, falling into his arms. He almost stumbled and she backed off. "Hey. It's okay."

She brushed the tears off her face. "I can't reach your father." She sniffed as he guided her over to one of the sofas and sat her down. "Or my husband. Have you seen your mother since she came out of surgery?"

"No. Have they said anything?" he asked.

"They told me they were still trying to get her blood pressure up."

"I've given all the blood I can for today," he said. "They hoped it'd be enough now that she's out of surgery."

"Have you *talked* to Henry?"

"We saw him after Sarah was born, but . . . not since Mom got sick."

"I've tried calling everyone I can think of," she said. "I can't get anyone to answer."

"Mrs. Toussaint?" An unfamiliar voice drew them out of their discussion. Bahati stood abruptly. "Yes?" She realized this was not a member of the medical team taking care of Lauren or Sarah. "Can I help you?"

"You don't remember me?" He lifted his brows. "Special Agent Andrew Miller, FBI."

Bahati took a step forward, her head tilting like a curious Boston Terrier. "Andrew Miller? From Washington State?"

"Well, I'm originally from Texas, but I did live in Seattle for a while."

"What are you doing here?" she asked.

Miller looked at the boy beside her. "If you aren't the spitting image of your mother, I don't know who is." Andrew said to the boy as he stuck out his hand. "Andrew Miller."

"John Carter Pierce," he said.

Miller's eyes narrowed. "You have an older brother, am I right?"

"Henry," John Carter said.

"He looked more like your dad," Miller said.

"Still does," John Carter said.

"Is he here?"

"No," Bahati said. "College tour in England."

"Cambridge or Oxford?" Miller's surprise showed in his features.

"Both," Bahati said.

"Impressive," Andrew said. "I didn't think he was old enough for college."

"That's our little *golden boy* . . . graduated early," John Carter quipped.

"You will too," Bahati patted his arm. "We have more than one *wunderkind* in this family."

"Knowing their parents, I'm not surprised." Miller laughed. "Speaking of, I understand there's a new addition to the Pierce family? How's Lauren doing?"

"Not well," Bahati said, her voice cracking. "They had to take her into surgery. She's still in recovery, and it's been hours."

"Whoah," Miller let out a breath. "What about the baby?"

"Sarah's in the NICU," John Carter said. "She's so little."

"Wow," Miller said. "Then what I've come here to tell you isn't going to help anything."

"What?"

"What's wrong?" Bahati asked.

"Better sit down."

14

Aleppo, Syria
May 15th

The light came on, startling Rowan as he heard the rattle of metal on metal. The cell door swung open, and two men were on him before he could react. They dragged him from the cell and down a long corridor to another room. The floor changed from dirt to tile, and that was about all he could make out with his one functional eye. The other was swollen shut and his face throbbed. The room had a humid, almost musty smell to it.

A sudden spray of cold water hit him and his whole body tensed. He let out a yelp of pain as they tossed him down on the tile floor. He curled into a ball, protecting his gut and other delicate parts in anticipation of a second attack on his person. Maybe it was the third, he'd lost count.

"You have ten minutes to shower and dress," one of them —a large black man with a scar across his face—spat the words at him. The water warmed and soon began to ease his aching body enough for him to push himself up onto his hands and knees. There was soap and a thin scrap of cloth, and he considered them both. The water that circled the drain was tinged pink. He reached for the back of his head, finding a goose-egg and dried blood, just as he'd suspected.

The water though, soothed his aches and pains. He knew from his time in the military the mental health aspects provided by a hot shower. It was the one simple pleasure offered to every soldier at the end of a long day of training. He managed to wash himself of the worst of the blood and grime. He took a mental inventory of the cuts, scrapes, and bruises as he came to them. By the time he was done, he had the strength to get to his feet and stagger out of the shower to a bench where a thread-bare towel was folded, along with clothing.

Time had no meaning. If he'd exceeded his allotted ten minutes he couldn't tell, but he managed to dry himself and dress in the white boxers, and what looked like a pair of poorly constructed scrubs. The fabric was thin, and if it weren't for the draw string, the pants would have ended up around his ankles. There was even a pair of slip on shoes that weren't too tight. He was just about to put them on when the men burst back in and hauled him back to his feet.

"Take it easy, will ya?" he cried out as they undid all the healing he'd gotten from the shower. He'd been manhandled before, but he knew now exactly what that meant. *Scar Face* grabbed his hands and pulled them together in front of him, binding them so tight he lost feeling in his fingers.

He was hauled into a room arranged with two chairs facing one another. The man sitting across from him was every bit as black as *Scar Face*. He was smaller than Rowan but not gaunt. He wore a black kurta that appeared to be silk, with intricate smocking and gold trim. His pants were ruby red with similar gold embroidery. The man said nothing but sat glaring at him.

"*Alaikum Asalaamu.*" Rowan did his best to put his hand over his heart with a weak bow. The goons forced him into the chair, then stood behind him where he couldn't see what they might do.

"Your Arabic is impressive," the man said in English, though his accent was quite pronounced.

"That's about all I know," Rowan said, not ready to let the man know he knew a few highly offensive curse words.

"You are Rowan Pierce," he said. "I have seen your show."

Rowan forced a saccharine smile onto his battered face. "Always nice to meet a fan," he said. "Do I have the honor of knowing your name?"

"I am Abdul bin Salman," he said.

"Look Abdul, I'd love to sit and chat, but I really need to get home." He started to get up from the chair, but a meaty hand came down on his shoulder and pressed him down. Rowan winced but settled back into the chair.

Abdul seemed to consider him a long moment. "I'm afraid it's not going to be that easy, Mr. Pierce." Rowan hadn't expected it to be, but it was worth a try. "You are going to help me find something."

"Oh? I am?"

"Yes," he said. "And I think you will find it of great interest."

"I doubt it."

"Have you ever heard of Sadam Hussein's Stargate?"

That caught his attention and made him pause. He'd heard stories while stationed in Al Anbar province back in the 80's. But Rowan knew not to play all his cards. "Is that a television show? No wait. It was a movie. Am I right?"

Of course, he knew about the conspiracy theory that suggested the former president of Iraq found an ancient device within the ruins of Babylon that was a portal to other worlds. The movie, and later the television show *Stargate* played on the ancient Sumerian legends.

The US Military apprehended Saddam Hussein in December of 2003 following the fall of Baghdad. A British tabloid got ahold of the pictures of the fallen leader in his underwear—pictures that were considered a violation of the Geneva Convention. He was held over for trial for crimes against humanity, and other offenses. He was found guilty and executed.

The conspiracy theories had begun, even before he was captured, convicted, and executed—theories Rowan gave little credence to. He wasn't a *conspiracy-theory-guy*. He was an archeologist. Still, most Americans had no clue how much of a megalomaniac Saddam had truly been.

Saddam had an unhealthy penchant for casting himself as the reincarnated King Nebuchadnezzar. Nebuchadnezzar was the biblical king who ruled the Babylonian Empire—modern day Iraq—from 605 BC to 562 BC. Saddam also liked to compare himself to the Muslim ruler, Saladin whom the Templars faced in the Third Crusades. But his fixation on Nebuchadnezzar was the most pathological.

To promote support for his war with Iran, Saddam focused on projects like the rebuilding of Babylon. When Saddam heard that Nebuchadnezzar had stamped the bricks of ancient Babylon with his name and titles, he ordered that the reconstruction mimic this practice.

Rowan had learned that fact in one of Dr. Fatima Badr's classes. When President Bush ordered U.S. forces to invade Iraq in 2003, they occupied Babylon and turned Saddam's castle into their command center. Rowan heard stories of the military causing extensive damage to the site, looting precious artifacts, and running tanks over ancient ruins. Rowan was assigned to a unit that operated out of the airport, and never saw the destruction of the palace himself. If he had, he hadn't realize that was the original site of Babylon. He hadn't been interested in archeology back then, though he always had a proclivity for history.

Babylon was one of the most glorious cities in the ancient world. It's walls and mythic hanging gardens earned a place on the list of the *Seven Wonders of the Ancient World*. Founded around 4,000 years ago, the ancient city was once home to ten dynasties in Mesopotamia—the cradle of civilization. This was the birthplace of culture, writing and literature before the fall of its empire and centuries of plunder, neglect, and conflict.

It was a wonder to modern day archaeologists. Rowan heard rumors Iraq was considering opening up the site to the worlds' archaeologists now that *The Great Accord* had provided decades of peace and resolution to conflict. The ongoing discussions that held back the research circled around owner-ship of the antiquities. Under American occupation during the Gulf War, Iraq argued their treasures were plundered or destroyed. They called for the return of all Babylonian antiq-uities. Many remained unaccounted for. This was a sore spot —on both sides.

"Please, Mr. Pierce." The man rose and paced behind his chair; his hands folded behind his back. "I can see the hunger in your eyes."

"Oh good. I don't mean to be rude, but . . . is there anything to eat?" Rowan feared his smart mouth would be the death of him, but at this point, it was a race between that and his stomach. He wasn't sure how much time passed since he'd eaten, but it had to be days.

The man looked up at *Scar Face*, and the goon brought a heavy fist down across his already offended head. The room spun and his ears began to ring. He fell sideways from the metal chair, but before he could hit the floor, a hand caught his shirt and sat him upright.

"This is no time for jokes, Mr. Pierce," Abdul bin Salman said. "Perhaps you do not realize the severity of your situa-tion." He snapped his finger and the man on Rowan's left moved away, returning a moment later with a wooden container, no bigger than a cigar box, but thinner. The man opened it. Inside, three severed fingers, each with three or four golden rings, lay on a bed of red velvet. "Perhaps you will recognize the owner of these rings." Fatima Badr wore at least two dozen rings along with a dozen gold bangles on her arms. The bracelets were never worn on an expedition, but the rings had never come off her fingers. Now her strange response to his questions made sense. It was only then that he realized his wedding ring was gone from his finger. "Yes, I see that you do. Then you will understand that I have no problem taking her life in pieces, if it will encourage you to do what I want. If her life is not sufficient to motivate you, I have other means. My allies stretch far and wide. I understand your wife is pregnant with your sixth child?" Rowan felt the heat rising in his face at the implication. "I have no problem killing women or children," he said. "I have done it before. I can do it again."

Rowan forced his anger back, trying to convince himself this man's threats were empty and worthless, but the *what-ifs* were too great. "What's your game? What do you hope to accomplish?"

"World domination," he said. "Power beyond all imagination. With that *stargate*, I will become the *Son of Nebuchadnezzar*. I will rule over the new Babylon. I will bring the glory of Babylon to my country, and we will rule not only the region, but the world."

Sudan? Tima said they weren't that far south? How had he ended up in the hands of a Sudanese captor? Abdul's diatribe continued, but Rowan no longer heard him. The longer the megalomaniac talked, the more convinced Rowan was that he would have to find a way to save Tima and get them both out of here. He would need time, and he would need information if he were to succeed.

"So, again, I command. Make your choice."

Rowan allowed resignation to weigh down his shoulders. "I don't know what you think I can do. I'm only an archaeologist."

"We have allies here in Aleppo," Abdul said. "That is all you need to know."

Aleppo? It was more than enough.

Syria was a hotbed of political unrest prior to *The Great Accord*. Kitty had even referred to it as a humanitarian catastrophe. Violent extremists groups posed a major threat to its people, and the conflict created an instability for the national and regional economy.

ISIS was once the most clear and present danger prior to *The Great Accord*. However, once peace was brokered, the terrorist organization seemed to dissolve, almost overnight. Rowan always thought it seemed too good to be true. Kitty had said as much to him one night sitting around a campfire after everyone else had gone to bed.

"Many of the conflicts between Syria and Iraq stem from water," Kitty explained. "Both the Euphrates and the Tigris rivers have their source in Turkey, before crossing Syria and Iraq, with Syria contributing 90% and 10% of the Euphrates' water flow respectively. The Tigris on the other hand, flows from Turkey to Iraq. Iran, Turkey, and Iraq all contributed to its water capacity. Infrastructure like dams once acted as a driver of fierce fighting and eventually led to fragile compromises. There was a time when water was one of the greatest weapons in the region."

The current terrorist in charge in Syria—Faadin al Khalid —stood accused of instigating a cyber-attack that led to the release of over 500,000 gallons of raw sewage into the Tigris near Bagdad. Hundreds of thousands were sickened. Thousands died. It was considered the worst terrorist attack after 9/11.

It was an attack that shouldn't have happened. The wastewater treatment plant in Sadr City had been Iraq's first fully automated water treatment plant, built at a cost $65 million. Constructed by the US Army Corps of Engineers in 2008 as part of the post-war restoration efforts, the facility could process 25 million gallons of water a day, bringing it up to US standards of quality. While citizens in the US used on average 161 gallons of water per day, prior to the new plant coming on line, the average resident in Sadr City had only 12 gallons of water per day.

"Mr. Pierce?"

Rowan looked at the stone faced man and surrendered. "What do you need me to do?"

"You will lead the team of workmen provided by my allies to find the *Stargate*. When it is secured, you and your professor will be released."

"I have a few conditions," Rowan said.

"You are in no position to negotiate."

"Dr. Badr needs medical attention. Under *The Geneva Convention* and the terms of *The Great Accord*, you are required to allow a team from the Red Cresent to provide aid to prisoners of war."

"This isn't a war, Mr. Pierce."

"Not yet it isn't," Rowan retorted defiantly.

"When this becomes war, Mr. Pierce. It will not be just any war. It will be *The War to End All Wars*. Mr. Pierce, this . . . is the apocalypse, and when this war is over, only Sudan will be left standing. I will build my palace upon the bones of my enemies." Rowan was surprised by that statement. "*A red horse went out; and to him who sat on it, it was granted to take peace from Earth, and that men would slay one another; and a great sword was given to him.* You recognize that verse from your Christian Bible? The red horseman is the second in the apocalypse. It symbolizes war. Peace has lingered far too long. It is time to unleash my Lord's command and open the stargates to the armies of the gods."

That's when it hit Rowan. *This nutjob was working for Enlil.*

15

San Diego, California
May 16th

Andrew Miller entered the hospital room with a bouquet of flowers and a box of cigars, just as he had at the hospital in Mexico City when Henry was born. Lauren lay with her head turned to the window. She had a faraway look on her face. Still, she appeared pale and groggy.

"Is it later yet?" he asked, breaking the silence.

Lauren turned her head towards him, a dopey expression on her face. "Andrew," she said, her voice gruff.

He put the flowers and cigars aside and came over perching on the edge of the bed, taking her hand. "You made the first one look so easy."

"They've all been easy, up to this point," Lauren said, a tear slipping from her eye and running into her hair.

"Oh, come now." He reached up and brushed the tear away with his thumb. "No need to start the water works."

"I'm sure it's just hormones," she sniffed. "I can't stop the tears."

He took a tissue and dabbed at her cheeks, brushing her hair aside. "Well, I think you've earned maybe one or two," he said, realizing this was not the time to tell her about Rowan. He'd have to tell her eventually, but he just couldn't do that to her right now. "I hear you have a new daughter."

"Sarah Conner Pierce," she said. "Henry named her."

"John Carter told me he's off touring prestigious colleges in Europe," Andrew said.

"He came home long enough to meet his sister." She sighed.

Miller lifted a brow. "Oh?"

"He's a wizard, you know."

"Like Harry Potter?"

"Sort of," Lauren said dreamily. "Just like me. I promised you answers, Miller. It's about time you had them."

"Maybe I should let you rest a little longer," he said. "I think the pain medication has you a little loopy."

"When you and Rowan were in Mexico, trying to catch Santiago Mateo, and I was at home pregnant with Henry, I used my magic to try and escape Stephanie Wentworth before she could kill me, but . . . somehow, she came with me. It was out of the frying pan and into the fire." Her voice was flat, deeper than usual and she spoke with a sober calmness that wasn't her normal manner. "But, I couldn't have done it without Henry. Even then, he was a powerful wizard."

Miller sat back, considering her for a moment. He stood, letting her hand slip from his as he turned and paced, as he tried to reconcile her words with his reality. "Wow, Lauren," he said. "That's a whole lot of truth all at once."

"And I'm sorry it's taken me so long to tell you," she said.

"It's understandable why you thought you couldn't," he said.

"It's a truth you've needed to know."

"Why do you say that?"

"Why else would you have come all this way? You're not living in San Diego now, are you?"

"I've been bounced around for the past few years," he said. "*The Accord* has changed my role in the agency."

"Then why are you here, Andrew."

"I didn't know you were sick when I agreed to come," he said, hesitating. He realized he had no choice but to lay all his cards on the table. "I wish I didn't have to tell you why I'm here."

Lauren said nothing. He stood with his back to her for a minute, then turned around and returned to the side of the bed. "Lauren, something's happened to Rowan."

When Andrew thought she couldn't be any more pale, the remaining color drained from her face and her eyes turned red. Her hand lifted but fell back to the bed. She was trembling. "What . . ." she squeaked, her voice breaking as tears flooded her face. "What happened?" Her question was almost inaudible.

Andrew squeezed her hand. "There was an *incident* . . ."

ANDREW TOOK the twenty minute scolding the nurse gave him with contrition. He preferred not to tell Lauren what had happened to her husband, but he knew it wouldn't get any easier—for either of them—if he waited. When he'd told her the worst of it, she just nodded, wiped her eyes, and said softly, "Thank you for telling me the truth, Andrew. I'd rather have my heart broken by the harshest truths than crushed by one cajoling lie." That was what broke him. Both of them were in tears when the nurse came in with the baby from the NICU.

Once she got Lauren settled down, the nurse dragged him to the nurses' station by his ear. She sent someone else to tend to Lauren and Sarah, then let him have it. "So what do you have to say for yourself? What was so important that you had to upset my patient when she's already fragile."

He blinked back the ferocity of the question, then explained the magnitude of the situation. Bahati came down the hall in time to hear the end of it, with her eyes equally red. "I just talked to Jean-René," she said, when Andrew turned to her. "He's going to be okay."

"Thank heavens," he said. "I'm relieved to hear that."

"How's Lauren? How did she take it?" Bahati started to move past him, but he stepped in front of her and caught her arms.

"She's not doing well," he said. "I didn't want to tell her when she was already so weak, but it would have made it worse if I waited to tell her later. They've given her something to help her sleep and taken the baby back to the nursery."

"How is she doing?"

"Better," he said. "She's a strong little girl."

"Would you expect anything different?"

"Considering her mother? No," Andrew admitted. "The worst of it is, I need a sample of Rowan's DNA for the lab in DC."

Bahati paled at that. "Why would you need his . . ." she stopped, as it sunk in. "But . . ."

"There was a ransom demand," Miller said, even though it wasn't entirely true. "We always want some *proof of life* before we'll talk to anyone making demands like this. The terrorist sent Rowan's wedding ring . . . there was blood on it."

"W-w-who's blood?" Her hand went to her trembling lip.

"That's what I need the DNA sample," he said. "To compare." He took a deep breath and pulled her into him, sensing she needed it as much as he did. She and Lauren weren't just anyone to him. They had history and he'd gotten to know the entire *Veritas Codex* team during their investigation in the Pacific Northwest after Lauren was abducted by a double-dealing diamond thief, and a hoax-monger in a monkey suit. Hard to believe it was almost twenty years before. "It can be a hair from his brush, or . . ."

"What about my blood?" John Carter asked. "If it helped Mom, maybe it can help my dad."

"Your blood?" Bahati stepped out of Miller's embrace, wiping her eyes.

"We've been studying DNA and paternity testing in my biology class," he said. "I get half my DNA from my dad, so if they need a sample of his DNA, I have some."

"You're a smart young man," Miller said. "Unfortunately it can take weeks to get results from paternity testing, and we need the mother's blood, too. I don't think your mother can spare a drop at the moment."

"I don't see why it wouldn't work," John Carter shrugged. "I mean, most of our DNA is identical to the DNA of others, except for the inherited regions of DNA that vary in each individual. It's short tandem repeats, or STRs, that consist of a string of repeating nucleotides that are usually two to five bases long, if you didn't know." Miller did know. He was required to attend training on DNA evidence, how it could be used, and what it couldn't do. "My chains of CAGs might repeat five times, but yours might repeat eight. Compare enough of them to my dad's and you might find that his repeat five times, too. It's kind of like sheet music, if you think about it. By analyzing the SRTs in my DNA, you can tell if I inherited my dad's DNA. If the alleles in my DNA matches your sample in those polymorphic regions, you'll know it's my dad's blood. Does the FBI analyze 20 STRs when you create a DNA finger print?"

Miller's brows grew millimeters wider and higher as the boy explained, and when he finished his eyes floated towards Bahati. "That's some kid," he said, grinning. "And yeah, we do."

"I saw that on an episode of *Criminal Minds*. It's my mom's favorite show."

"I seem to remember her saying that," Miller said, shaking his head. "All right, let me call my lab in DC and see if that'll work. But we may not need any more blood out of you. You need to save that for your mother. If it'll work, cheek cells may do."

MILLER CHECKED INTO A HOTEL, despite Bahati's and John Carter's protests that he should just come stay with them. The Pierce house had plenty of room, but he already felt like he'd imposed enough. He had the hospital lab collect the cheek cells needed to test for DNA, but also managed to get a hair sample from the comb Rowan used on his beard. Though the copper colored whisker was tipped in white, it was the unmistakable color of Rowan's distinct facial hair. The lab thought the cheek sample might work, but they were also concerned about the time it would take to go through the forensic genealogy, though rapid DNA protocols could be implemented. As he settled in for the night, the evidence was already in the hands of a certified courier on its way to the FBI Crime Lab.

Rowan's DNA wouldn't be on record in CODIS, the National DNA database, or none of this would be necessary. Rowan entered the military before the US Armed Forces began collecting DNA on its service personnel. He'd gotten out at the height of Operation Desert Storm/Desert Shield before routine DNA collection was a thing.

Today, thanks to modern forensics, the military regularly used DNA to identify remains of fallen soldiers. The goal was to ensure the military never had to bury another service member in a *Tomb of the Unknowns*. Since 1992 when they began the practice, over five million samples had been collected from airmen at Maxwell Air Force Base in Alabama alone. A sample of the airman's blood would be collected, smeared on a card with his or her name, social security number, and other identification. Technicians stored them in sealed vacuum-sealed pouches under sterile conditions to prevent contamination, then placed them in a freezer set to minus twenty degrees. Specimens were stored for fifty years. Most remained untouched until a soldier died or went missing, and they needed the sample to match to human remains recovered from combat. If the military could analyze those samples and compare them to a soldier's remains in twenty-four hours or less, Miller hoped the FBI could do the same kind of magic.

THE PSYCHOPATH of Soba refused to meet with Kitty in person, but he did agree to a video conference. Kitty went into the meeting with confidence that her counterparts in the Cyber-crimes unit at Homeland Security could trace the signal in less than 90 seconds. She took a deep breath and logged into her video conferencing site. She'd already sent the link to the email address she'd been given, kingofsudan@guerrillamail.-com. *This guy had some nerve.*

Her reply email included a seemingly benevolent virus that would be transmitted the moment he clicked on the link. The link would create a digital beacon that the team would be able to track back to its source. No matter how many times it bounced from server to server—a common means used by the criminal underground to hide their location—it would continue to ping until it reached its source.

"You are clever, Dr. Grayson," a voice said but no image appeared. The voice sounded digitized. "How can we broker peace when we cannot trust each other."

"Trust must be earned," Kitty said cautiously.

"How better to gain trust than to provide proof of life," the voice said. "Did you not receive my letter?"

"A severed finger and a ring doesn't necessarily build trust," Kitty said.

"I have given you proof of life . . . along with proof of my resolve. If you will not give me what I want, I will give you back your people, in pieces. Trust me when I tell you this is truth. I am not one to trifle with."

"So what do you want?"

"I will be recognized as the rightful ruler of Sudan," he said. Even the robotic tone assured Kitty he was demanding, not asking. "I will accept weapons that will aid me in my war against my enemies."

"Haven't you heard?" Kitty cut him off. "There is no war. The world is at peace. We have moved past wars to settle our differences. Allow me to set a place for you at the negotiating table and . . ."

"There may not be war at present, Dr. Grayson," he said. "But I will have my war—with or without the aid of the US Government."

"If you are asking me for weapons . . ." Kitty started.

"The only question you must ask yourself, is this. Are you my enemy or my friend?"

There was a click and bleep, and the call ended. "Somebody tell me we got a trace?"

"The virus is still bouncing between servers" A voice came through her earbud. "It's searching for the source."

"How long should it take?"

"We should have had him within moments," the computer nerd in the control room said. "I've never seen one take this long."

"If you were him, how would you derail our efforts to find him?"

"I'd run my signal through a complex program that would send it leaping to servers around the globe to try and throw my tracker off," he said. "I accounted for that. It's like . . . like . . . smoke and mirrors!"

"So, we didn't get him?"

There was a pregnant pause. It spoke volumes. "I'll keep tracking it, but . . . it looks like he gave us the slip."

"Let me know the minute you find something," Kitty said, trying to stay positive.

"Dr. Grayson." One of the administrative assistants opened the door and peeked in. Kitty turned. "There's a call on line three for you."

"Who is it?" she asked, hearing the exhaustion in her voice as she rubbed her eyes.

"It's Dr. Pierce," the assistant said.

Kitty perked up. *So Lauren knew. Jesus, she wasn't ready for this conversation.* Everything she'd was told had been worst case scenario. Lauren had a new baby, and they were both suffering complications. *How could this be happening? Where was Michael when she needed him most?*

She reached for the phone and hit the red blinking button under the number 3. "Lauren?"

"Kitty." The woman's voice was weak, gruff. "Tell me you know where my husband is."

"I'm working on that," she said. "I'm doing everything within my power to broker a reunion."

"As will I," Lauren said. "But at the moment, it seems I'm under attack. I can't *reach* Henry, or my father . . . not even my mother."

"I can't *reach* Michael either," she said. She didn't have the same powers Lauren and the rest of her family shared, but most of the time she could get word to Michael—Lauren's brother—when she needed him. Being married to *a champion of the gods* had its challenges. When Michael was *working*, he could be gone for what seemed like months—to her. She knew for him, the time passed differently, and he didn't always realize how long or how lonely the time could be. "But I'm working on that, too. I hear you had a rough delivery."

"That might be an understatement," Lauren sighed.

"Is the baby okay? How are you doing?" Kitty had so many questions.

"Improving," she said. "Both of us."

"That's good," she said. "Boy or a girl?"

"A girl," she said. "Sarah."

Kitty's heart lifted. She would have loved to have a daughter. As a mother of a boy, she knew they could be challenging. Gabe was a great kid, but she'd had her fair share of emptying worms and frogs from the pockets of his jeans. She got tired of the extra sound effects he liked to add while playing video games on line with his cousins. He was high energy, and—like most teenage boys—ate everything in the house. She wouldn't trade him for anything in the world though. "Kate must be thrilled."

"Not as much as John Carter is," Lauren said. "She looks like him."

A mental picture formed in Kitty's mind. She could imagine a dark eyed, dark haired little girl with a sober Wednesday Addams expression. "What do you need? Anything I can do?"

"Just find my husband," Lauren said, the exhaustion even heavier in her voice. "Bring him home."

"I'll do that," Kitty said. "On one condition." Lauren didn't say anything. "You need to take care of yourself and your baby. You can't get well if you're worried about Rowan. Trust me. I will find him. I will get him home."

"I'm counting on that."

16

Aleppo, Syria
May 17th

Rowan sat at a table in an unadorned conference room. The floors were compacted dirt, and the walls were made of corrugated metal that arched overhead to create a ceiling. He'd seen rooms like this in Quonset huts the military used on temporary installations. The metal door closed behind him and locked from the outside. He'd paced, now free of chains, for what seemed like an hour, before fatigue set in, and he collapsed into one of the heavy metal chairs that reminded him of his high school principal's office. He'd spent plenty of time there. He had the same sense of dread back then that he had now. He was in trouble.

Back in his cell that morning, he overheard the sound of women's voices as they tended to Tima in what he could assume was a similar cell. He couldn't understand the language, but he recognized Tima crying out, but he also recognized the other women's attempts to soothe her.

"Tima?" Rowan moved to the blade of light from a lantern they'd brought in. "Is she okay?"

A woman appeared in front of his cell. "Be silent!" she snapped angrily. "We will tend your mother. As you requested of my husband."

Rowan sat back in the inky darkness, relief washing over him. Tima would be cared for, as required by the Geneva Convention. That was the best he had hoped for. It was everything he could do not to cry with relief.

Then, a key rattled in the door of his cell and *Scar Face* stood at the portal. He motioned for Rowan to stand. It took a moment, but he got to his feet. The chains around his ankles were unlocked, but his hands remained shackled. Nothing was said, but he fell in behind the guards, with *Scar Face* behind him. They took him back to the room where he'd met Abdul, and he expected a similar meeting. Instead, a man in a plain white outfit stood with a medical kit, much like the one Rowan carried when they went on expeditions. "This is the doctor," *Scar Face* said in a thick accent. "He will tend you."

The doctor motioned to the chair indicating Rowan should sit.

Rowan bowed and lifted his hands to his heart. *"Alaikum Asalaamu."*

The doctor returned the greeting but did not smile. He snapped something at *Scar Face* and that's when the goon removed the chains from his hands. The doctor examined him and seemed most concerned about the knot and laceration on the back of his head. Rowan thought nothing of it, when he took out a syringe and a vial of medication. He assumed it was lidocaine and it would be used to numb the laceration so he could stitch it. Rowan was wrong.

That's what I get for assuming, he thought now. How many hours had he been sedated? Rowan wasn't sure. He wasn't even sure he was still in the same building. The floors were similar, but everything inside his pounding skull told him he'd been taken somewhere in those lost hours—maybe days.

The door rattled and Rowan got to his feet, backing up into the corner, as five men entered with trays of food, and jugs of beverages, laying a banquet. There were baskets of flatbread covered with a towel, and a large tray of what appeared to be couscous with some kind of stew poured over the top of it. There was a basket of fruit, and a salad of cucumbers, tomatoes, olives, and chunks of feta cheese. The feast smelled amazing, but Rowan was cautious. No one had offered food or water since he'd been taken hostage. He knew his body needed sustenance, but he also knew that it could be dangerous to gorge himself.

Rowan stood away from the table, even as the men left and closed the door behind them. He heard it lock. He turned away from the feast, if only to prevent the temptation. He allowed his mind to go back to his medical and survival training. He knew that after eight to twelve hours; his body had burned through its glucose reserves. After two or three days, his liver would begin to synthesize ketones in his body to break down fat stores. Eventually, all the cells in his body would metabolize proteins into amino acids. Once fat stores were exhausted, the body would begin metabolizing muscle—the last remaining energy source. He wasn't there yet. Starving to death was a slow process. It could take as little as twelve weeks to several months depending on several factors.

Rowan was generally healthy. Over the past ten years, he'd maintained his weight within ten pounds of his ideal body weight. He worked out and when home, ate a balanced diet. Lauren wouldn't allow anything else. On the road, however, his weight tended to drift upward because he ate what he could grab in airport lounges, or whatever the local cuisine would allow.

MREs weren't exactly low-cal. They weren't intended to

be. They were fighting fuel for America's armed forces, and that's what he'd survived on while exploring Jordan Island.

Tasting the world's culinary best was another perk of the job. The seven or eight months he spent filming and on tour usually required three or four months of solid workouts at home to overcome.

Rowan knew, though, that most people denied food and water for long periods did not ultimately die of hunger. They died from cardiac arrhythmia or cardiac arrest due to the degrading tissue and electrolyte imbalances.

He also knew that eating after long periods of starvation could trigger hypokalemia, which could also trigger cardiac issues and result in death. After his health scare in Haiti, he remained overly concerned about his heart health. Still, the food smelled so good his mouth watered. His stomach growled audibly, then the door unlatched again.

"Please," a familiar voice said. "Don't wait for me. Eat, Rowan. This feast is for you."

Rowan turned to face Abdul bin Salman. Today, he wore a military uniform laden with ribbons and medals, stripes of gold up the wrists of the jacket sleeves, and gold-laden epaulets. "I feel a little under dressed for dinner." Rowan glanced at his threadbare attire.

Abdul smirked but said nothing else. He took a seat at the table and reached for one of the jugs, pouring himself a glass of red liquid. Rowan knew it couldn't be wine. Alcohol wasn't permitted in this culture. It was illegal to bring spirits into the country. More likely, it was *karkadeh*, a cold hibiscus tea. His *host* drank and Rowan was madly aware of how dry his mouth was. His lips were chapped and cracked, and he needed fluids as much as he needed food. Abdul poured a second glass and pushed it across the table before refilling his own.

Rowan watched, cautiously as he pulled a piece of bread —Rowan thought it must be *kisra*, similar to naan bread in India—and used it to scoop up a bite of the stew and couscous instead of using a spoon. Rowan had eaten many meals like this when he'd traveled in middle eastern countries. Arabic foods were often eaten in this fashion. The perfumes of chili peppers, garlic, onions, paprika, cinnamon, coriander, and cumin found their way to his nostrils, and he realized it was futile to resist. He was hungry.

Patience, he reminded himself. *Small bites. Eat slowly.* That was easier said than done. He took a tentative sip of the drink, confirming it was extremely sweetened tea, then drank greedily, draining the glass. The sugar would help stave off starvation by itself, but he needed the fluids as well. Abdul smiled, refilling his glass.

"My wives are excellent cooks," he said, patting his stomach. "They will be offended if we do not enjoy this fine meal."

"Where are we?" Rowan asked, not moving.

"That is no concern of yours."

"Did you move us while I was sedated?"

"The doctor insisted you be provided with IV fluids and nourishment," he said. Rowan glanced down at the inside of his elbow and found a bruise he hadn't noticed before. There was a pinprick in the middle over his vein that confirmed Abdul's claim.

"Then why knock me out?"

"We had to do the same for Dr. Badr," he said. "She refused treatment. She punched my wife in the face." Rowan wasn't sure he was buying that story. Tima was so weak she couldn't even lift a hand . . . and they'd mangled her dominant one. It hit him how many things she wouldn't be able to do now. Writing, typing, braiding her hair . . . his stomach churned at the thought.

"Please, Rowan. You must come join me," Abdul said.

Rowan reached for a piece of bread and followed his hosts example. The meat was lean, well-seasoned in a spicy tomato-based sauce. It had a slightly sweet aftertaste and was a little gamy if he was being honest. In this part of the world, it wasn't likely to be beef. Instead, it might well be goat, but it wasn't as stringy as goat tended to be.

"How do you like the camel?" Abdul asked.

Rowan swallowed hard. "Camel?"

"There was an old cow with a sour disposition I had dispatched. If she would not serve my army by hauling her share of the load, I figured she could serve my guests."

"So, is that what I am?" Rowan asked chewing. He had to work to swallow the bite, now that he knew what it was. He had a sorted history working with camels. They were all creatures with sour dispositions. That didn't mean he cared to eat one. "Your . . . *guest?*"

"That is up to you, Mr. Pierce," he said, leaning back, tapping on the door.

A moment later it unlatched, and the door swung open. Tima stood, looking battered and pale. Her hair was combed back and hung to her knees. She wore a bright brocade robe, fit for a queen, but it hung on her. She held a bandaged hand in the other. Rowan stood, furious to see her in such a state. She kept her head down and shuffled into the room. Abdul rose and pulled out a chair for her. She sat but did not look up. Abdul sat and poured another glass of the red tea, pushing it in front of her.

"Dr. Badr will be helping me translate the ancient text," he said, leaning against her, putting an arm around her. He pulled her in and kissed her head. He took up the glass and held it to her lips. She did not fight, but she did not gulp the liquid. Rowan recognized someone who'd had their spirit broken. *My God, what had they done to her?* Anger boiled in his chest. The food formed a stone in his stomach and threatened to rise into his throat. He swallowed hard to force it down.

The door flew open. A man Rowan had never seen entered in a flutter of long black robes. He was tall and reminded Rowan of Jafar from the Disney Aladdin movie, though he really didn't look much like him. It was the swagger.

He came in and took the seat at the head of the table. Abdul gave him a polite nod.

"Faadin al Khalid, my friend," he said, pressing his hand to his heart. Rowan noticed Tima wince, and glance up, but she averted her eyes. "Allow me to introduce you to Dr. Fatima Badr, professor of Archaeology from the University of Cairo." He slighted her in the introduction. She was the Dean of the department. Fatima didn't look up. Rowan was worried about her. She'd never acted subservient to any man, so far as he'd observed. She was a strong woman, but even strong women could be broken. Rowan knew that. He thought for a moment of Lauren but turned away from her in his mind. He couldn't handle thinking about her. Not yet. He needed to keep his focus. "And this is her student, Rowan Pierce."

"You are the American?" al Khalid asked.

"From the great state of Colorado," he said, forcing his tone to stay light. "God Bless America."

Faadin's brow lifted, but his expression never changed. "Do they know where the *artifact* is?"

"We'll get to that," Abdul said. "We've come to an agreement, though. That is the first step."

"And what agreement is that?" Faadin asked, his tone sour.

"They will help us," Abdul said. "And I won't cut them up into bits and pieces." Rowan noticed Tima's gaze lift to the man. Malice was etched in her features, but Abdul bin Salman was too busy eating to notice. Her gaze darted to Rowan but moved away just as quick. "Eat. Eat. You must keep your strength." Abdul insisted.

Tima's head lowered. Rowan lost his appetite.

THE NEXT MORNING, Tima was already at the table when Rowan was escorted into the room. A stack of ancient books and several weathered scrolls took the place of a feast. The door closed behind him. Rowan took advantage of being left alone.

"Tima." Rowan dropped to one knee beside her chair. He reached up for her hair to brush it away, but she recoiled from him. "Tima. Look at me." She did, but he wished she hadn't. Her face was a mottled mass of bruises. Her lip was cut. His gaze went to the bandaged hand in her lap. The gauze was stained with dried blood. All four fingers were gone, severed at the junction of metacarpals and phalanges. Tears dripped from Tima's face. But it was the look in her eyes that broke him, and he felt his tears build.

"Have they given you anything for pain?" Rowan asked, forcing his voice not to crack.

"They tried," she said. "I won't take anything they offer me."

"Will you at least take some food and water?"

"No," she said. "I will not allow my enemy to offer me comfort so long as we are held here against our will." *So her spirit wasn't completely broken*, he thought. Like Lauren, she had a stubborn streak that often got her in trouble.

"Will you take comfort from me, at least?"

"I take great comfort in knowing you are alive," she said. "Please . . ." Her voice trembled, and it took a moment before she continued. "Whatever they do to me, do what you must to go home to your wife and children."

"I won't leave here without you, Tima. I swear it."

"I am already gone, Rowan . . . *darling*. What happens to me . . . is of no consequence now."

"You can't talk like that, Tima. Mental fortitude is vital to survival in a situation like this."

"And you have that fortitude."

"I need you to have it, too. I can't lose you. I need *you*." Tears flooded his eyes and ran over his cheeks into his beard. "I will fight for you, but I need you to fight for yourself."

"I will do what they ask of me, if only for your sake," she said. "Now, sit and go through these books. Tell me what they are looking for."

Rowan stood and paced behind her, drying his face with his hands. He paused, standing with his hands on his hips, staring at his boot. He made his mind up to get this done and get it over with so he could go home—so they could both go home—in time to coach Lauren through delivery. He still wasn't ready to think about her, but he needed that objective to keep him alive. He needed to get home to Lauren, and he wasn't going without Tima.

"Do you know about Sadam Hussein's *Stargate?*"

Tima looked up. He saw something behind her broken façade that suggested she knew something. "The legendary portal to alien worlds?" Tima sniffed. "It's the stuff of Hollywood, not history."

"Not according to some," Rowan said.

"*The Journal of History* published a paper by Frederic Von Kreger—and Egyptologist from the University of Heidelberg —called *The Stargate Speculation: Ancient Astronauts, Egyptians, and Myth.* Did you read it?"

"If it wasn't on your required reading list, no. Not likely," Rowan said.

"According to the movie, and later the television show, the stargate is a threshold to the universe. You simply enter the correct combination of the thirty-nine symbols on the gate, which opens up a portal to a specific place in space and time. But, this *artificial wormhole theory* has a flaw."

"What's that?"

"It relies on the *Einstein-Rosen bridge theory*, which remains unproven."

"You've often said, myth is based on truth, or at least one culture's version of it. Just because the theory hasn't been proven doesn't mean that's not how things work."

"In the past ten years, the internet has been alight with

speculation that a chart-like carving in Anuradhapura is a *stargate*."

"Sri Lanka?"

Tima managed a weak nod. "There has also been some comparison between the stargate there, and the near identical shapes and symbols found at Abu Ghurab in Egypt, and La Puerta de Hayu Marka in Peru."

"Okay," Rowan said with cautious reservation.

"In ancient Sumerian legend it was said Enki had access to a stargate," Tima said. Rowan's interest was piqued. "The stargate was said to be hidden somewhere in central Iraq, placed there by the Anunnaki gods for ancient Sumer. It is said, when Nibiru, the theorized twelfth planet, is closest to the earth, the Annunaki will use the portal to come to earth and set up their encampment in Iraq."

"I guess I missed that legend when we covered Sumerian history," Rowan said, but he was thinking of Enlil and what that monster might do if given access to a stargate. Lauren had already fought him once. Over fifteen years before, Enlil was weak. Since then, they'd been preparing for him again, and Rowan feared his strength would be much greater now. He had used minions on earth before, too. The *Psychopath* was under his influence now.

"I've heard the speculation that the US Government invaded Iraq because they thought Hussein had a stargate and a grandiose ambition to create a New World Order."

"Some think you have a similar stargate at Area 51 in the United States," Tima added. "According to the television show, there are twelve of them."

"Well, then," Rowan sat and pulled the first book off the stack. "I guess I better get started."

Tima started to reach for a book with her uninjured hand. Rowan rested his on top of it. "I can do this," he said.

"So can I," Tima insisted.

Rowan held her gaze for a moment, then took the second book and opened it, laying it in her lap.

They worked silently, each focused on the documents provided to them. Rowan managed to work through three of the books, all were histories of Iraq, Sudan, and Syrian. The fourth book was a thesis on the rise and fall of the Neo-Babylonian Empire. "Did you know Babylon was once the largest city in the world? It was perhaps the first city in the world to reach a population above 200,000."

Tima lifted her head and he realized she must have dozed off. She blinked at him blankly. "Do you know where the name Babylon comes from?" Tima asked, her voice heavy. Rowan shook his head. "The Greek *Βαβυλών* or *Babylon*, comes from the Akkadian word *Bābilim* . . . it means *Gate of the Gods*." Rowan's jaw fell. "The logogram for *gate* looks much like the logogram symbolizing the god Anu."

"*The most high*," Rowan muttered. "Unlike Enlil . . . his son." Now that he was certain the dark god was involved in this whole fiasco, he needed Lauren more than ever. She was the *hand of the gods*, and if anyone could defeat Enlil, it had to be her. *Dammit!*

"Ah, so you were paying attention in my class," Tima said. "Ironically *gate* and *god* are almost the same word in Akkadian."

"That terrorist must be associating *gate of the gods* with . . . the *stargate*," Rowan said.

"Perhaps," Tima said. "It is an interesting concept."

"How so," Rowan said, closing the book in front of him.

"*Babylon, the jewel of kingdoms, the pride and glory of the Babylonians, will be overthrown by God like Sodom and Gomorrah,*" she said, closing her eyes. He was instantly taken back to the lecture hall in Cairo where she performed many of her presentations. Tima had the heart of an actress, even now. Still, she paused and took a deep breath. "*She never will be inhabited or lived in by following generations; no Arab will pitch their tent there; no Shepherd will rest his flocks there*. That comes from Isaiah 13:19-20. While Jerusalem was the *heavenly city*, Babylon was the *demonic city*."

"That makes me think Babylon is where we need to go then."

"That may be a bit premature," Tima said, her voice heavy. "If the *Stargate* belonged to Enlil it might not be in Babylon at all."

"I'm not following." Rowan scratched his beard, bumping a bruise on his chin.

"In the Sumerian creation stories, it talks of a time when Enlil's city had not been made, Ekur had not been built."

"Ekur?" Rowan asked. "I don't think I've ever heard of that."

"You might also know it as *Duranki*, it means *Mountain House*," Tima said.

"Wait," Rowan grabbed one of the books he'd already skimmed through. "That's the place where the Ziggurats are built atop mounds, isn't it?"

"Yes." She forced a proud smile onto her wounded face. Her student had done well. "The University of Pennsylvania Museum of Archaeology conducted excavations of the site and found several Babylonian inscriptions."

"Did that happen to include an excerpt from an exorcism?" he asked, still thumbing through pages, flipping back and forth before tossing the book aside and grabbing another one, repeating the efforts to find something he'd read earlier.

"The Ekur of Enlil at Nippur . . . but it could just be an extract from a larger text that was never discovered.

Rowan stopped and stabbed a finger into the page. "Or the Hymn to Enlil," he said, excitedly. "Written on clay tablets late in the third millennium BC."

"Well done, Rowan, *darling*," she said, but her enthusiasm was over-taken by her fatigue and pain. She hadn't eaten or drunk more than a sip, and Rowan, in support of her hunger strike, didn't eat anymore either. Rowan felt bad for her, but the work seemed to give her a purpose, and she hadn't complained at all. Rowan opened his book, turned the page, and kept reading, "*Enlil's commands are by far the loftiest, his words are holy, his utterances are immutable! The fate he decides is everlasting, his glance makes the mountains anxious, his* ... this part is blank," Rowan hesitated. "*His . . . reaches into the interior of the mountains. All the gods of the earth bow down to Father Enlil, who sits comfortably on the holy dais, the lofty engur, to Nunamnir, whose lordship and prince-ship are most perfect. The Annunaki enter before him and obey his instructions faithfully.*"

"Keep going," Tima encouraged him.

"*When you mapped out the holy settlement on the earth, You built the city Nippur by yourself, Enlil. The Kiur, your pure place. In the Duranki, in the middle of the four quarters of the earth, you founded it. Its soil is the life of the land.*"

Tima moved as if to lift the book out of her lap but couldn't quite manage the load. Rowan saved her the trouble and collected it from her. He set it aside and rapped on the door until the lock rattled and the handle turned. He took a step back to allow *Scar Face* to enter.

"What is it you want?" *Scar Face* demanded.

"Tima needs to lie down," Rowan said. "She needs food and water."

"I will have none of it," Tima protested.

"You see." *Scar Face* started to back out of the room.

"Wait," Rowan insisted. "Tima, please." He dropped to one knee beside her. "I can't do this without you. You need your strength. I will get you out of here, but you need to trust me and do this for me. I can't let them take you from me, not like this." Tima bowed her head. He leaned in and kissed her crown, pulling her into his arms. "You haven't even met the rest of my family yet. You're their *Auntie Tima*. If you won't do it for me, do it for Henry, for John Carter and his *wockets*. Do it for Jamie, and for Sam and Kate. Lauren will want you there when the new baby comes. I'll take you home with me and you can see how big the boys have gotten. You'd be so proud of them. Please, Tima. Please."

A tear trickled over her cheek, and he saw her walls come crashing down. She nodded. "You will have to do this, Rowan . . . *darling*. I haven't the strength. If you can do this, I will do what I must."

Rowan looked up at *Scar Face*. "Please, take her back to her cell. Have them bring her food and water. Nothing too heavy, maybe some bread or rice."

Scar Face called back to someone in the hallway. Two women in black birkas came into the room. Rowan stepped aside. They gathered her up and helped her to her feet. Rowan watched in horror. She'd become so weak. It broke his heart, but it also made him angry. He wanted to punch *Scar Face* in the gut and claw out his eyes. It looked like someone had already tried. *Scar Face* stared him down, but turned away and locked the door behind him. Rowan turned to his work and tried not to think about his tentative position.

Their lives relied on him now. He had to figure out this mystery and find something that might not even be real. Was there a *stargate* in Babylon? *Damned if I know.*

17

San Diego, CA
May 18th

Lauren paused to catch her breath as she sat on the edge of the bed, debating how to reach her shoes. They were in a locker across what had to be the largest birthing suite she had ever seen. She hadn't expected to have such grand accommodations, considering she'd given birth at home, but she wasn't about to complain.

Sarah slept in the plastic bassinet beside her, freshly washed, wrapped in a tiny pink outfit that was one of Kate's, with a bow tied into her shock of thick black hair. Lauren had changed her and fed her before she began efforts to clean herself up, get dressed and get ready to go home.

"Just where do you think you're going?" Bahati's voice startled her.

"Home, if I can get my shoes," Lauren said.

"Home? Does your doctor know about this? It's only been four days since you had major surgery. Surely you're not ready to go home."

"He signed my discharge papers," Lauren said, holding up the release.

Bahati snatched it out of her hand. "This better not say *against medical advice*," she snapped.

"Would I leave a hospital AMA? Really?" Lauren said.

"You've tried it before," Bahati said. "Don't pretend you don't remember. The point is, I do, and I won't let you get away with it this time." She looked over the paperwork, then looked up with cautious reservation, handing it back.

"You didn't let me get away with it last time, either."

Bahati considered her for a moment. "Any word from Agent Miller?"

"No," Lauren said. "Not yet."

"Did you talk to Kitty?"

"I did," Lauren said. "But I still haven't heard from Henry, or my mother, my father . . . or my brother."

"Jean-René was released from hospital in Cairo," Bahati said. "He's staying at the request of the Egyptian authorities, to facilitate the investigation."

"You should go to him," Lauren said.

"Are you kidding?" Bahati gasped. "I'm not leaving you. You've just had a baby and surgery. Without your mother or Rowan here to help, however will you manage?"

"I have John Carter and Jamie to help," Lauren said.

"But they're still just boys," Bahati protested.

"I'm old enough," John Carter came in on the conversation. "I got the car seat installed, just like you taught me."

"Where are the rest of my children?" Lauren asked.

"With Evelyn McIntosh," Bahati said.

"Our vet's wife?"

"Dr. McIntosh is taking care of Shadow. The kids wanted to see her, but Mac wanted to monitor her another day or two."

"Shadow? What happened to Shadow?"

"He thinks she had some kind of a seizure or got into

some unknown toxin, but all his tests came back inconclusive. She's stable now."

"Uber for Mrs. Pierce." The nurse arrived with a wheel chair. "Ready to go home?"

"It's Dr. Pierce," Bahati corrected before Lauren could. Lately she'd cared less and less about the title, now that she had two.

"Of course, forgive me for making you basic, Dr. Pierce. What's your specialty?"

"Great apes," Lauren said. She didn't offer more. Not many people could comprehend that real scientists might study unidentified species of great apes like Bigfoot, Yowie, or Yeti. "I'm an anthropologist, not a physician."

"Cool," the nurse said. "That makes you *extra*."

"*Extra* what?" Lauren asked.

"It's an expression, Mom." John Carter laughed, smiling at the nurse. Lauren and Bahati both saw it. John Carter was definitely growing up. He could be extremely charming, just like his father. "Can I carry the baby?"

"Did you bring her car seat carrier?"

"It's in the car," he said. "Once I got it installed, I wasn't sure I could put it back in right."

"Then she has to ride in the wheelchair with her mother," the nurse said. "Hospital policy. I'm also a certified car seat technician. I'll have to verify the car seat hasn't had a recall and that its installed properly before we can let her go home."

"It's a brand new car seat," Lauren said. "I checked for recalls when I bought it a month or so ago."

"Do you remember the brand?"

Lauren recited the make and model like it was her favorite poem. The nurse took out her phone and did an internet search. A moment later, she looked up. "No open recalls," she said. "Very good."

Bahati helped Lauren into her shoes and finished packing the few items Lauren had, along with the diaper bag John

Carter had also brought from home. Sarah watched silently, squirming as John Carter moved over her to smile. She held his gaze, but never fussed, never squeaked.

"So, where did you learn to install a car seat?" The nurse asked John Carter as he took his mother's arm and helped her to the wheelchair. The last two days she'd made two laps around the floor, just to prove she could. It was one of the conditions that had to be met before she could go home. Additionally, her blood pressure had to remain stable, as well as her red blood counts.

"Mom taught me," he said. "She and Dad took a class."

"Oh?" the nurse asked, as she handed Lauren the baby. "Where at?"

"It was a few years ago . . . more than a few actually," Lauren said, "But it was when we lived in Virginia."

"Well, I'm sure you did a fine job, but State law requires me to verify the car seat is properly installed." She turned to John Carter. "A licensed adult has to drive the baby home. Hospital policy. I'm pleased to see how you did with the car seat."

"He isn't even old enough to get his permit," Bahati said.

"I will be old enough next year," John Carter said sheepishly.

"I'll go pull the car up to the door," Bahati said. "Hopefully we can get ahead of rush hour traffic."

ROWAN HAD his nose buried in one of the books when the door opened sometime later. A simple plate of food sat at his elbow but had gone cold as he remained focused on his mission. The glass of hibiscus tea also remained untouched. He glanced up, surprised when his captor entered with a plate and glass for himself. "Find anything interesting?"

Not one to mince words, Rowan said, "Nothing yet." He

had a theory, but nothing he was ready to share. "Are we sure the answers can be found in *these* books?"

"The books and the scrolls are said to contain clues to the whereabouts of the *Stargate*. They came from the personal library of Saddam Hussein. He studied them for decades."

"Did Saddam ever find the gate?"

"There were rumors," Abdul said, drinking his tea.

"But nothing conclusive?"

"No," he said. "But there are credible witnesses that say he did. The United States President being one of them."

"The president?"

"Not the current one, no. George W. Bush," he said. "He invaded Iraq to keep him from using the gate as a weapon."

Yes, Rowan knew that tall tale. "Some say that's just a lame conspiracy theory."

"Your military raided his palace and took many of his things . . . including these books."

"Where did you get them?" Rowan asked.

"Off eBay," Abdul said with a hearty laugh. Rowan was in no mood for jokes. "What does it matter? I have verified these were indeed his books."

"So what happens if I find something?"

"You will find something," he snapped. "And when you do, we will go and take it."

"You're just going to hop over the Red Sea, drive across the deserts of Saudi Arabia, and go right up into Iraq and take it?"

"Ah, you do not know where we are," he said. "We have come to visit my friend in Syria. The journey will not be so difficult."

"Syria?" Rowan said, realizing in the lost time they'd transported them out of Sudan. That would throw off anyone who might be looking for him there. "Why Syria?"

"The food in Aleppo is delectable," he said, putting a morsel in his mouth, chewing with enthusiasm. "I have friends in many places—high places. How we get to Iraq is no concern of yours. I simply need a destination."

"I need assurances Tima will be cared for, and not harmed."

"You are in no position to negotiate, Mr. Pierce. I thought I had made that apparent."

"I've already agreed to help you. I've given you *my* word. I expect you to give me *yours* that she will receive medical attention, adequate food, and water, and she will not be harmed."

The man narrowed his eyes at Rowan as he sat back from the book. "You've found something," Abdul said, with realization. "Tell me. The sooner I get what I want, the sooner you get what you want."

"How familiar are you with the *Epic of Gilgamesh?*"

"I've heard of it," he said.

"Never read it?"

"Cover to cover? No. Tell me. What have you found?" he insisted.

Rowan decided to humor him with something he'd found after Tima had returned to her confinement. "Humbaba was a figure in Mesopotamian mythology. In some places the story refers to him as a monster, or a giant. Sometimes it says he's like an ogre. He's portrayed as the guardian of the cedar forest —a glorious realm of the gods. Here, Gilgamesh dared cut down trees from its virgin stands. The epic says that Gilgamesh traveled east, presumably to the Zagros Mountains of Iran, a place called Elam. On each day of the six day journey, Gilgamesh prayed to Shamash—later known as Anu. Shamash sends him oracular dreams during the night." Rowan flipped the book back a few pages. "*The skies roared with thunder and the earth heaved, then came darkness and a stillness like death.*" Rowan emulated Tima's lecturing style as he read the passage. "*Lightning crashed and fire blazed out from the stone bābu.* I'm not sure but I think that means door. If it were *bābi*, it would mean to enter. I don't read the language, but I think this sign," he pointed to a picture of a stone tablet on the *folio recti* across from the text to a series of hashes and ticks that looked like something made by sandpiper feet. He'd heard Lauren talk about the ancient language so often over the past few years that he could recite some of her favorite passages of text—and their meanings—by rote. "This is cuneiform, and I think this is *KÁ*, the logogram for gate, or doorway."

Abdul's brow rose and his face lit up. "My *stargate?*"

Rowan shrugged. He was totally making this up as he went. He avoided giving away too much too soon. He'd read enough to convince himself that the gate lie closer to Babylon, but he wasn't assured Tima wouldn't be harmed, and he wasn't ready to give up his only bargaining chip. "In the *Amarna Letters*, the man authoring the letter is called the *yabitiri*, or the gatekeeper. So that made me think we needed to look there. But Amarna isn't in Iraq. It's in Egypt." He had paid attention in Tima's classes all those years ago. He remembered enough to build a tower of lies and throw their captors off until he could be certain about his other theory. He didn't know if this megalomaniac intended to drag Tima off into the desert with them, so he was trying to buy her the time she needed to regain her strength. He needed his as well.

He knew, if anyone knew they were missing, and he had to hope Jean-René had survived the attack, that someone—if not Lauren herself—would come looking for him.

His sister-in-law was one of the greatest diplomats in the world. Kitty would be involved in brokering their release, if nothing else. He was a soldier, and he knew the military would need time to figure out where he was, and to send a rescue team. He wasn't sure how long he could stall, and he wasn't going to be rushed, but he also knew he couldn't delay for too long.

"I don't read Akkadian—*cuneiform*—but Tima knows some." Rowan sat back in his chair. "I need a pen and a notepad, so I can take notes and try to sort all of this out."

"It is done," Abdul said, standing. He opened the door and called out to the hallway, barking orders. Rowan could hear feet shuffling outside, which told him they weren't really alone. "Please, eat your meal. When your woman has rested, she can help you," he said, enthusiastically. He sat and continued eating. "Tell me more of the *Epic of Gilgamesh.*"

As they ate, Rowan told him about Shamash and the giant's encounter with Gilgamesh, fabricating the tale to give himself time to create is false narrative so it was believable. Part of that tablet remained missing, so there wasn't much fact to go on anyway. Rowan hated that he was sharing a meal or lifting a glass with his enemy. It violated the ridged *Klingon* code—yes the one from *Star Trek*—that said, *drink not with thine enemy.* But Rowan knew he had to earn a measure of trust in order to facilitate their escape, or aid in their rescue. He never knew when an opportunity might arise. Rapport would be hard won, but he could only hope it would pay off in the end. "…and Gilgamesh and Enkidu cut down the cedar forest and used the tallest trees to create a magnificent gate for the city of Nippur. Then, they built a raft and floated the Euphrates. *And they all lived happily ever after,*" he ended the tale with a sardonic expression.

"Another gate?" Abdul asked, excited by the concept.

"Possibly," Rowan said. "So, you see why I still have some work to do. I've found references to several gates."

"Then your work has not been in vain," he said, wiping his plate clean with the last bit of his bread. He tipped back his cup and drained it, then set it atop his plate. "I will leave you to it."

Rowan considered him as he left, wondering what game he was at. *What made it normal for a monster like that to want to have a meal with a hostage as if it were a casual business meeting?* No, nothing about this was *normal.*

Rowan glanced at his plate. He'd hardly touched his food. Despite his hunger, he no longer had much of an appetite. He pushed the plate away, so the spices were less overt, and picked up the book he was reading. Maybe the gates of Nippur weren't that outlandish after all.

HOURS LATER, he felt like the entire Sahara desert had infiltrated his tired eyes. Still, he had a note pad full of ideas, including more of a false narrative he had written in an intentionally poor version of his own chicken scratch. He hoped he wouldn't need to use it, but again, he needed to buy time. That was the only thing keeping them alive at the moment, and he knew he had to make the most of it.

Rowan, though, was tired and couldn't stop yawning. In a room without windows, a clock or even his missing watch, he had no indication of how much time had passed. He could have been in that room for hours, a day, maybe more.

Wearily, he rested his head on his fist, propping his elbow on the table. For the first time since this ordeal began, he allowed himself a moment to think about Lauren and his family. Keeping her at arm's length wasn't easy. She had to know he was missing by now. He could only hope it didn't upset her so badly that it put the baby—or her—at risk.

Tears welled up in his eyes, but he fought to keep them at bay. As he had so many times before, he tried to reach out to her across the expanses of time and space to let her know he was okay. Only once had he ever felt like he'd reached her in this manner. "Lauren," he spoke her name like a prayer to every goddess in the universe. "If you're out there, I need you."

DIANA GRAYSON SAT on the stone step of the log lodge house beneath a brilliant blue sky. A field of wildflowers stretched out for miles, and mountains with their snowcapped peaks bordered the distant horizon. The perfume of honeysuckle and columbine wafted by on the breeze.

Her arthritic fingers wove long fibers of willow into a basket. The work actually improved her flexibility and minimized her pain. The fact that she'd sipped on willow bark tea that morning hadn't hurt anything either. It provided a subtle analgesic effect, but also reduced swelling and increased circulation.

John worked a dozen or so feet away. He spent the morning cutting wood and his naked torso glistened with sweat. His long hair hung in dripping cords. While the days grew warm, the nights in high elevations could turn chilly, if not downright cold.

The years hadn't been kind to either of them, but they were both strong and healthy, which was more than most people their age could say. This escape from time and place had allowed them to reconnect, and for Diana to understand the draw of time on her husband. Here, closer to his own time-place, John had more vigor, more endurance. He could chop wood all day and make love all night in a way they'd never been able to when he came to her time-place. This respite seemed more like a proper honeymoon than they'd had when they first married.

Not long after they wed, Diana was pregnant, and the family grew quickly. Now, they were grandparents, and they didn't have to worry about birth control. In this time-place, they also didn't have to worry about interruptions. John assured her there was no one for hundreds of miles, or hundreds of years.

"Before the night cools, let's go to the river and see if there are any fish to catch. Rainbow trout sounds good for dinner," Diana suggested.

John hoisted the ax, splitting another log into quarters. He turned as she went into the house, the door still open. "I could use a cool drink of water," he said. "Perhaps if the fish aren't biting, we could go for a swim." He had a few logs left to split.

Diana gathered the supplies they would need to fish, but also put together an afternoon snack of cheese, crusty bread, cured meats and apples she'd foraged from a nearby orchard. She didn't know how an orchard came to grow in this region of the Pacific Northwest, at least not in this time place, but she knew John had a penchant for collecting seeds when he had been back in her time-place, and suspected he was a patient gardener. She also knew he had the ability to go back in time, plant a tree, then return to his original *time-place* to reap the harvest, without having to wait. It was a clever trick.

When she stepped out of the house, he'd just placed the last quarter of wood into the rick alongside the lone building. There would be enough to last most of the winter, if she stayed that long. She couldn't though. Her daughter would need her soon, and as much as she loved being here with John, this wasn't her place. It wasn't her time. It never was. She would have to go back sooner or later.

"You worry too much," John said, giving the ax one last heave over his shoulder, burying it into the stump he used for a block. "Lauren is a capable mother. She can manage without you, you know."

"I know," Diana said. "And she has plenty of help. Still, do you blame me for not wanting to miss the birth of my grandchild?"

"We have so many." He laughed. "Have you missed the birth of any of them?"

"Yes," she said. "Too many of them. Lauren contemplated having a home birth this time, but I don't think she'd consider trying it without me there as a midwife."

"Have you attended many births?" he asked.

"A few," she said. "I delivered the last three of George's, and all of David's children, only because Aunt Mary's health was failing. Someone in the community needed to know the

Cherokee way of delivering a child into the world. The old ways are sometimes the best ways, you know."

"This is true." John took the flannel towel she handed him and used it to wipe his brow. He grabbed his shirt from the tree branch where he'd hung it, and they fell into companionable silence as they walked the path to the river. The path fell away twenty yards from the water's edge. The banks were sandy and soft, the water ran calm along the bank, but rocks and boulders created a current on the other side.

Diana paused at the bank and slipped off her leather moccasins John had made for her. She kept her modern attire in a basket beneath their bed. Here, they lived within the customs of their ancestors. It was a simple life, and she could see why John enjoyed it.

"Forget the fish," John said, still damp with sweat. "Let's go for that swim first." He kicked off his boots and took off his clothing. Diana followed suit.

The water was cool and refreshing and soon, they were neck deep in the gentle current at the middle of the wide expanse of water. Diana brought a woven bag of herbs and soaps she'd made. She washed her hair and then did the same for John. A warm hand snaked his way up her side and came to rest on her breast. "Maybe I won't wait until tonight to have you," he said, leaning in to kiss her.

Diana smirked. "Who ever said you had to wait?"

"If you prefer the comfort of a fire and a warm bed, I will understand," John's lips traced down her neck, pulling her into him.

She drew back and glanced at him through the frigid water. "It is so cold," she said. "Perhaps we should retire to the banks and let the sun have its way with you before I do." He was a wizard, but even a wand such as his could do little magic in the cold.

"I know a clearing just up the way," he whispered in her

ear. "Where the grass is soft, and the sun is warm, and not even the birds and squirrels will bother us."

Diana nodded. "Let me rinse my hair and you may lead me wherever you will have me."

AFTER A LONG LOVEMAKING session beneath the open skies, Diana returned to the water to wash, dampening her hair that had dried and become disheveled in their reverie. She picked bits of grass and leaves from her long silver tresses, then joined John on the blanket they shared. He'd donned his clothes and held out her dress, helping her pull it on over her head. She thanked him, then sat, taking out the comb he had made from an elk's antler, and patiently set to work combing her hair while they ate their post-conjugal snack.

"I will miss these days, when you return to your *time-place*," John said. "We never had such leisure when we were young."

"It's true what they say about distance making the heart grow fonder," Diana said. "I love you more now —"

Her voice cut off as John sat up abruptly, the apple falling from his hand. Diana turned and stared at him. A crack of lightning echoed in the distance above them. "What was that?" she asked.

"I'm not sure," John said, rising to his feet without much effort. The apple rolled away as his foot kicked it and he moved toward the center of the clearing. A young man's form appeared and tumbled out of the nothingness in front of him, taking out John's feet. The old man landed on top of him, and they both made a pained huffing sound as the breath was knocked from their lungs. Neither of them moved for a moment.

Diana scrambled to her feet, not as lithe as her husband, but she was more spry than a woman half her age. She rushed over and checked on John first, then the boy. "Henry? Are you okay?"

Henry rolled over onto his back as John pushed him off of him. Henry groaned. His lids fluttered and lolled like a doll's eyes. A second crack of lightning illuminated the sky, and a scream from above echoed across the meadow. "Look out!" A flailing comet raced across the sky, just missing them, but plowing into the soft ground less than twenty feet away. A cloud of dirt and grass erupted into the sky around the juggernaut as it tumbled across the meadow and came to rest against a tree.

Diana sat on her knees, her hands still on Henry as she turned to take in the spectacle. Michael rose from the dust cloud, his hair disheveled and his clothing torn. He shook off the effects of the impact as he walked towards them. His mother thought he looked angry.

"What happened?" Henry groaned as Michael's shadow fell over him.

Diana was torn. She wanted to wrap her arms around her son, but her oldest grandchild lay in a daze at her knees, and her husband was staggering to his feet.

Michael saved her the trouble. He caught his father and pulled him down as he dropped to his knees by his mother. He scooped up his nephew and pulled them all into his arms. "Is everyone okay?" Michael hugged them.

"What just happened?" Diana asked, running a hand over Michael's scraped cheek, before turning to inspect Henry's. "Where did you both come from?"

"I'm not sure," Michael said.

"Mom's under attack," Henry panted, coughing, and catching his breath. "I wasn't sure when she had the baby early, but then . . ."

"The baby?" Diana suddenly forgot Michael. She grabbed Henry by his shirt sleeves. "No, it's too soon."

"Yeah," Henry said. "She's okay, or . . . she will be . . . I think." Diana helped him sit up. "The baby was very small . . . but just before . . . whatever *this* is started . . . I sensed there was a problem. I was about to *travel* home to check . . ."

"I sensed Kitty needed me and was about to head *home* myself," Michael said.

"So," John sat back on his own knees, assessing the situation. "The only magic-wielder at home is Lauren?"

"Gabe," Michael said. "But I'm not sure his powers have fully matured."

"John Carter hasn't found his skills yet, but . . . there is Sarah."

"Sarah?" Diana asked.

"My sister."

18

Syria
May 18th

Abdul sat on a tufted sofa watching Al Jazeera—the evening news—after he'd taken his evening meal alone. There was trouble in the world, but not all of it was his making. He wasn't sure if he should be concerned or angry. Russia was threatening to take back another former Soviet bloc country since its efforts to retake Ukraine had failed. Estonia was looking increasingly like the obvious target after an Estonian spy was involved in the assassination of a Russian cosmonaut. Abdul thought this preposterous. Georgia would make a better target. It would align Russia with Azerbaijan, which had broken away from the Soviet Union in 1991 and there were rumors that the KGB was still active in the republic. The other rumor was, ISIS and the KGB were plotting a coup.

Trouble was rising in Gaza. Colombian drug lords were raiding villages and slaughtering civilians. The virus of dissent was spreading, and *The Great Accord* seemed in immediate peril. This was all his doing. He was the catalyst that would allow his

Dark Lord's power to grow, and yet he was getting none of the credit? *His name had not been spoken in the news for days? How dare they?*

Curses upon them and upon the hairs on the chins of their women! Abdul thought to himself. *Was he not the Psychopath of Soba? He loved that nickname, but the media seemed to tire of it before he was ready. Where was his headline? Why was there no breaking news on the capture of an American television show host and an Egyptian Archaeologist? Where were his allies? Why weren't diplomats and world leaders prostrating themselves before him?*

Maybe one or two archaeologists weren't enough. Maybe he needed to learn from his great role model, Saddam Hussein.

"Belial!" he shouted, his voice reverberating in the metal building. The dark man with the scarred face entered a few moments later. He bowed in front of his commander.

"Find out who the leader of this KGB is," he said. "I will have an audience with him. ISIS and al-Qaeda, too. I will entertain any of the forces that might stand against the *Great Accord* and aid me and my Lord in the destruction of Enki and anyone who would serve above Our Master, Enlil."

Belial stood with a blank expression. "KGB was disbanded in the 1980s. Since Osama Bin Laden was murdered, Al Qaeda has no clear leader. They fight like dogs for scraps of what is left of their terrorist organization. ISIS is like a hydra. There is no one leader. There are many. The more their enemies kill, the more heads spring up."

"If you wish to serve me, this is what I ask of you."

He considered Abdul for a long moment. His cloudy eye and pocked and scarred face gave him the appearance of the monster Abdul knew him to be. He'd watched him chop off the Egyptian woman's fingers while she screamed for him not to. Her screams were more overt when he reached for Rowan's hand as he lay unconscious on the floor. He didn't take fingers, instead, he took the man's wedding ring. She protested even louder, and he turned and stomped her mangled hand with his boot, blood spattering the walls and the woman's face. When Abdul didn't think she could scream any louder, she did.

Abdul had left his prisoners to the mercy of his men, knowing they had none. He left them with only one edict, *do not kill them*. He needed them to accomplish his goal, but he could do nothing until they were broken. Belial assured him of that.

ROWAN LAY with his head on the table when *Scar Face* dragged Tima into the room.

Abdul entered behind him. "What is taking so long?" he demanded.

Rowan sat up and blinked the grit from his eyes. *Scar Face* slammed Tima in the chair beside him. She shrieked but regained her composure, though she clutched her injured hand to her chest. Rowan could see from the bandages that the wounds were weeping a mixture of blood and infected pus. She needed better medical care than she was getting. As a military trained medic, he was running through what care he might be able to provide with limited resources. He needed to see the injuries beneath the bandages, but he hadn't been given an opportunity. Getting the patient out of the combat zone and into improved medical care now took priority.

"I think I found something," Rowan said, no longer caring about whatever this man's game was. Time had run out. He needed to get Tima home to Egypt. Her daughter was a doctor there. She needed a doctor. Tima cast him a cautious glare, shaking her head subtly as if to tell him not to say anything. "I think your *Stargate* is in Kish . . . or more properly, under Kish."

Kish? Tima's eyes widened and Rowan saw the realization that he might be right. It was written on her face.

"That's more like it," Abdul said. "Tell me more."

Rowan opened up one of the large tomes beside him. The ancient book was brittle, fragile. The print was fading, and the pages yellowed. It had a musty smell that reminded Rowan of the acrid scent of mummies.

He turned to a page near the back and pushed it over to Abdul.

Tima swallowed hard, then managed to pick up the story. She must have read his mind. "Legends told of the powerful kings who ruled the land of Kish. They were some of the first kings in history. It was a saga of divine power, war, and conquest. Today, we have access to the lost city of Kish to learn of the first civilizations of mankind."

"There is a well in Kish," Rowan said, tapping the black and white aerial photograph dated May 28, 1948. "This is called a keyhole well. But there's some correlation between these structures and the fiery furnace."

"Explain," Abdul looked like a hungry man, salivating over a T-bone steak.

"You're familiar with the story of King Nebuchadnezzar?" Rowan decided to play on his vulnerabilities. If he likened himself to Saddam Hussein, of course he knew about the biblical king. "In the story of Nebuchadnezzar, it talks about the fiery furnace. There are those who claim that it was the *stargate*."

"Yes! Yes! Keep going," Abdul sat back, grinning.

"It happened during the time of the Jewish exile to Babylon. King Nebuchadnezzar attacked and subdued Jerusalem," Tima said, her voice measured. "Nebuchadnezzar ordered all in his kingdom to, upon command, fall down in worship of the gold idol the king had built of himself. The penalty for not doing so? To be thrown into the fiery furnace. Some of his astrologers, who hated the Jews, reported to the king that there were three young men—Shadrach, Meshack, and Abednego —who refused the command and would not worship the statue."

"In line with the first and second commandments—thou shalt have no other gods before me, and though shalt not make unto thee any graven image," Rowan interjected.

Tima continued, though her voice trembled as she spoke. "This made the king angry. He was so, furious, he ordered the three brought before him." *The Three?* An image of the alien creatures they'd encountered after the incident in Africa came to Rowan's mind. *The father, the son, the spirit . . .* he wasn't sure which one Enlil was, so calling it a holy spirit seemed wrong. *Perhaps Enki was the holy spirit?*

He turned his attention back to the matter at hand. "When they still refused, he threw them into the furnace, but they didn't burn. Do you know why?" Rowan asked, now fully in tune with Tima's narrative.

"They were not the mother of dragons," Abdul smirked, a stupid grin made his teeth glow against his dark skin.

Rowan wanted to let the *Game of Thrones* reference slide, but he was attempting to cajole a psychopath. "Exactly, and we know *fire cannot kill a dragon*. The king could see the men walking the fire, but there was a fourth figure accompanying them."

"But how is that possible?"

"It wasn't a fire at all," Tima said.

"It was a *stargate*. They weren't walking through fire. They were in an alternate dimension . . . in the company of the gods."

"This is the weapon I am searching for!" His face brightened. "You are certain of its location? Tell me, Dr. Pierce!" His enthusiasm made Rowan nauseated. When he hesitated the psychopath slammed the book shut, crushing Rowan's hand between the pages, leaning his weight on it. "I demand you tell me!"

Rowan cringed but refused to cry out. He knew Tima's hand was in much more pain, and he refused to show suffering if only as a signal to her that he knew as much. He clenched his jaw and stared the man down. "Yes, it is in Kish," Tima said. "Under the ziggurat. And I already have an invitation to meet a team of archaeologists there."

"How convenient," Abdul grinned maliciously, taking his weight off Rowan's hand. "I'll make arrangements for transportation." He rose and left them. The door locked behind him with a click.

"What are you doing, Tima?"

"Saving your life," she said. The pain of everything was etched into her olive face. "I'm in no shape to go, but you are. You have to find the gate and do whatever you need to do to get home to Lauren. She needs you."

"I'm not going anywhere without you, Fatima Badr, and that's not up for negotiation." Rowan flung himself from his chair, regretting it as his knee protested the sudden movement. "I can't protect you if you're not with me."

"You can't protect me, Rowan . . . *darling*." She held up her wounded hand. "If they want me dead, they will kill me, and there is nothing you can do."

"Then I won't help them."

"You don't have a choice," she said. "You don't . . . and you know it."

HENRY SAT UP, propped on a pillow in the middle of the bed in the one room cabin, a cup of willow bark tea in his hand. Diana sat beside him, inspecting him for injuries. "I'm fine, Nanhi." The boy repeated the assurance, but the scrape on his cheek was growing darker as the blood that oozed from the wound began to dry. Diana had already cleansed the wound with a tincture of witch hazel, but it still appeared angry and sore.

"When *your* magic involves healing, you can tell me you're fine," she said. "This is my *magic*."

Henry was silent for a minute. Diana glanced up at him. His blue eyes were troubled. "My *magic* failed me."

"What do you mean, sweetheart?" Diana brushed a lock of blond hair from his eyes.

"I was trying to get back to my mother . . . her and the baby . . ."

"The baby? What's wrong?" Diana sat up.

"When I left, they were both doing better—after Mom had her at home—but . . . I got the feeling something was wrong. I tried to get back to her. I didn't make it. I don't know how I ended up here."

"What's wrong with your mother?"

"She lost a lot of blood . . . when Sarah was born. But there was something else . . . I couldn't quite figure out what it was, but there was a dark force between us, and I couldn't see past it."

"Was your father with her?"

"No," he said. "A storm kept him from getting home. He's in Egypt with Aunt Tima . . . but I sense something isn't right there either."

John stood in the door, his shadow cutting across the room as the sun made the slow descent over the back of the mountains. "What do you mean *something isn't right*?"

Henry moved to sit up, but Diana kept a hand on his chest. "I think we're under attack," he said, prompting his grandmother's hand to fall away as he came to sitting, wincing at the effort.

Michael sat at the table, his back to the fire. "Attack? From whom?"

"I don't know," Henry said, panic in his voice.

"We knew this day would come," John said, more to Michael than to Henry.

Diana leaned to kiss her grandson, wrapping her arms around him. "Your parents knew, too." She tried to comfort him.

"What day? What's happening?" Henry asked.

Michael rose and brought his chair to sit in front of Henry. He took the boy's hand and clasped it between his. "Remember all those years of lessons? The time you spent with me, *up there?*" He lifted his eyes towards the ceiling. Henry nodded. "We weren't just playing games. I wasn't teaching you how to cheat on your science tests or how to use time travel to improve your abilities to study and finish high school two years early. I've been preparing you for a coming war."

Diana's gasp seemed to startle the boy as much as his Uncle's message. She covered her mouth and tried to stay calm. She knew their family was different, but she didn't even know about this.

Michael continued. "The forces of the universe are always in conflict. Water versus rock. Day versus night. Youth versus age. Life versus death. Creation versus destruction. Good versus evil."

"What are you saying?" Henry's voice trembled.

"The gods have shown us favor," Michael said, swallowing the last word as his voice cracked. "But the forces that oppose us are strong. The enemy will stop at nothing until they see our world destroyed . . . our race destroyed . . . our family destroyed."

"They tried that before," Henry said. Diana wasn't sure what he was talking about. "You said they'd try again. We won't let them win, that's what you told me."

"It's not for me to say if we will win or lose. The gods have prepared your mother—and your father—for this war. I sense the time is at hand, and I suspect the enemy has banished us so that we cannot interfere with what is to come."

"We can leave, can't we, Grandpa John? I just need to rest and then we can leave."

"We can try," John said. "But it may not be that easy."

"Why not? We were strong enough to save Mom from Chaos," Henry said to his uncle. "You convinced Poseidon to let her and Dad go. You're the *Champion of the Gods*. You can stop this. You can take us home." The boy's agitation escalated, he reached for his uncle, grasping his sleeves. "Take us home! I want to go home. Mom needs us! Dad needs us!"

John crossed the room and sat beside his grandson, placing his hand on his chest. "You need to rest, Henry. Sleep."

The words seemed to work like an anesthetic and Henry collapsed into his grandmother's arms. For as lean as he was, the boys' dead weight seemed doubled, and it took John and Michael both to lift him off her and help get him settled back in the bed. The family stood around watching him for a moment before John turned to his son.

"He's right," John said. "I need to get you all home."

"What about you?" Diana asked.

"I can do more good from here," he said. "My strength will wane too fast in your time. Yours is waning here."

"What can we do?" she asked.

"We will need to rest and eat," Michael paced behind the table, stretching his sore muscles, turning his back to the fire once more. Diana suspected it soothed his aching body. "We will try to get you and Henry home tomorrow."

"What about you?" Diana turned to her son, looking up at him.

"I will return to my place at Anu's side and see what can be done to help my sister," he said. "It may not be too late to disrupt the tides of war."

19

Aleppo, Syria
May 19th

"Excuse me, my king," Belial stepped into the room. "A moment of your time, if I may disturb you?"

"What is it?" Abdul flipped the television remote around and turned the news off. He sighed as he ran a weary hand over his beard.

"There is a call from NATO. Ambassador Grayson is trying to reach you," he said. "Her call was routed through secure lines. Will you speak with her?"

"It's about time they came groveling to me," he said, a wicked grin turned the edges of his moustache up. "I was starting to think no one cared about these hostages." His hand lifted to the blank television screen. "And I have no intention of letting them go. They are taking me to Kish to retrieve my weapon."

"The highest diplomat in NATO and the US is on the line. Is this not what you wished for?"

Abdul considered this a moment, then rose. "It's about

time they paid attention to me. They'll regret ignoring me, eventually. Put her through to the office."

Now in residence in Aleppo, hosted by his ally, he had run of the south wing of the ancient fortress. Reconstruction efforts included modernizing it to include running water and electricity, even satellite television and high speed internet. The balcony doors were thrown open wide, to allow the afternoon breeze to cool the room as the sun warmed the bricks on the west-facing tower. He sat at the desk and gazed at the phone, pausing a moment before he reached for the receiver. "Hello."

OUTSIDE THE OFFICE, on the balcony, Faadin's daughter, Maliqa, sat behind a potted bougainvillea listening. She had been waiting a long time for this moment. She'd suspected something was amiss not long after she'd returned surreptitiously from Cairo. Her father had asked many questions about her professor, and she'd heard him talking to a visitor about her. They'd also been talking about an ancient weapon. She'd have listened longer, but one of her father's servants came with refreshments for his guests and she had to come up with an excuse so it wouldn't appear she was eavesdropping. When the servant announced he was not to be disturbed, she promised to come back later to speak with him.

Since her return from Egypt, her father had been bitter—if not downright cold—towards her. She feared his wrath and had to wonder if his attention was drawn away from her by this visitor. She could almost be grateful, but she needed to calm her racing mind and soothe her anxiety by resolving the tension between them. At heart, she was a peacemaker. She hated conflict and the sooner she could make things right with her father, the better.

Then, this morning, as she lay in bed scrolling through

TikTok she learned something that troubled her even more deeply. A series of videos from an obscure Egyptian Journalist told of the kidnapping of an Egyptian professor and an American archaeologist, supposedly by the same Sudanese warlord who'd attacked the city of Soba.

Maliqa wasn't supposed to be using TikTok. Her father forbade it, but while in Egypt she'd set up an account with the pseudonym *Cleopatra's Library*, so she could scroll through *booktok*. As an avid reader, she found more great book recommendations here than at any bookstore in Cairo. She'd hidden the icon for the app deep inside of a folder within a folder on the second page on her iPhone.

For a moment, she had to wonder if her father was somehow involved in her professor's disappearance. The longer she thought about it, the less she doubted. If it were true, she knew she had to help. Her father had the reputation of being a very bad man, though he always justified his actions as being in the best interests of the greater good. She'd seen the atrocities he could inflict. She'd been a victim of his anger on more than one occasion.

This man, this *guest*, however, she didn't trust him. He looked Sudanese and he had the air of a man who thought more highly of himself than anyone else. He could be the so-called *Psychopath of Soba*. Maybe.

ONE HAS, I think, to reckon with the fact that there are present in all men destructive, and therefore anti-social and anti-cultural, trends and that in a great number of people these are strong enough to determine their behavior in human society. The line from Sigmund Freud ran through Kitty's head as she sat while the phone clicked and pinged. She wasn't sure where the line came from, but probably one of her psychology classes.

Andrew Miller stood behind her, simply to observe. "Is this kind of thing normal?" he asked, biting his thumbnail.

"What? Calling a narcissist with delusions of grandeur on a Tuesday afternoon to get my brother-in-law out of his clutches? Yeah, but usually not so personal."

"Do you think he's all right? Rowan, I mean."

"Hard to say," Kitty leaned her head on her fist, resting her elbow on the desk. "The lab tests came back. The finger was female, so most likely Dr. Fatima Badr—Rowan's professor from the University of Cairo. The DNA tests will take a little longer. The blood type is a match, so I'm afraid it's a given. What's hard to know is if she was alive when the finger was cut from her hand, but it looked to be a clean laceration. I'd wager it took more than one finger. The knife— more likely a sword or a cleaver—was exceptionally sharp."

"But the ring was Rowan's?

"The lab confirmed it based on photographs," she said. "Jean-René verified it too. He's refusing to leave Egypt and is working with authorities there to track down any clues to who might have done this."

"How can I help?" Andrew said. "I've got *carte blanche* on this one from my superiors. I can offer the teddy bear or the pistol."

"The teddy bear or the pistol?" Kitty puzzled.

"I can take the soft approach, or I can go in loaded for bear."

"Maybe you should load up for a *dragon* . . ." Kitty started, but the phone clicked differently.

"*His Majesty* will speak with you. One moment," the heavy voice on the other end of the line said out of nowhere. The phone clicked again.

His Majesty? Miller mouthed the words. Kitty just shrugged, rolling her eyes. The pause was more than a moment. It was almost fifteen minutes before the rattle of the phone receiver picking up signaled the line being picked up.

"Hello."

"To whom am I speaking?" Kitty asked.

"This is the American Ambassador?" the man said, his voice deep and his accent thick.

"Dr. Kitty Grayson," she said. "And your name, sir?"

"I am the King of Sudan, Abdul bin Salman , the great *Hero of Soba*."

Hero of Soba? Hero? What about the slaughter of 6,000 innocent men, women and children made him a hero? Kitty knew better than to challenge him. *Teddy Bear*, she thought. Let's start with the *Teddy Bear* and save the *pistol* for another day.

"It is an honor to speak with you today," she said. "I am calling to negotiate the release of Dr. Fadima Badr and Rowan Pierce. Am I speaking to the person who can facilitate that?"

"You are, Ambassador," he said. "But their release will not be easily won. I have need of them here."

"Where is *here*?" Kitty asked, keeping her voice innocent and passive.

"In Sudan," he answered, almost a bit too quickly. Kitty suspected deception at once. "My armies are gathering, and your scientists are helping me arm them with weapons unlike anything the world has ever seen."

"We are at peace, sir. As you may know, Sudan signed *The Great Accord*. Are you preparing to breach the diplomatic agreement? To end over a decade of peaceful relations with the rest of the world?"

"A false and fallen government signed the treaty," he said. "I did not. Sudan is now under *my* control and if you wish to negotiate a treaty with me, I may be open to discussion. But I have conditions."

Kitty knew she would have to tread lightly here. His rule over Sudan was not recognized and she could not negotiate a peace treaty with a power that was not the recognized leader of a nation. She could only negotiate for the release of hostages. "Perhaps in time, that is a discussion we can have. Today, I'm only authorized to discuss the release of Mr. Pierce and Dr. Badr."

"I am not prepared to release them," he said. "They are too valuable to me."

"Are you demanding a ransom?" Kitty asked.

"Their value to me is inordinate, Ambassador. But if you insist, we could start with a price of one billion American dollars."

The United States does not negotiate with terrorists, it took Kitty everything in her core not to say the words. She avoided letting him know he was already considered a *terrorist*. After the attack on Soba, his name was moved to the top of every most-wanted list in global law enforcement.

"I'm not authorized to negotiate a payment," Kitty said. "But I will take the information back to NATO for consideration. Can I reach you at this number again?"

"You may try," he said. The line went dead.

MALIQA SAT BACK on her heels, having heard the whole conversation over the speaker. This man had taken Professor Badr and the American archaeologist who was coming to lecture to her class. *Were they here? Why? What did this man have in mind? How had her father fallen in with this monster?*

She froze when the man walked out onto the balcony, watching the sunset as he leaned on the railing. Maliqa was confident she was well-hidden, and she could see little through the gaps in the pink flowering plant. She noticed he had a cell phone. He punched in a number. A moment later a deep voice answered. "Yes, my King?"

"Are we prepared to leave for Kish?" he asked.

"There will be a caravan waiting for you and our guests in the morning," a man answered, the call on speaker mode.

"And will our troops be waiting for us when I arrive?"

"They have already been deployed to take over the site," he said. "They'll secure the dig site and squash any resistance before you arrive. Your experts can work without interference."

"Excellent," he said. "Let them fear me with all the might and fury of Enlil himself."

"So it will be done."

The man went back inside, leaving Maliqa to try and make sense of it all.

* * *

ROWAN SAT on the floor against the stone wall, shackles around his wrists and ankles. The chains that secured him to the metal wall were heavy and rusted. They cut gouges in his flesh and bruised into the bone from their weight and scraping when he tried to move.

Tima sat across from him, in similar restraints, though her manacles were only around her ankles. "There's something I have to tell you," Rowan broke the silence with a hesitant tone in his voice. "Lauren is . . . *special.*"

A weak smile came to her lips. "That is no secret."

"Not just because she's an amazing wife and mother, or a painfully beautiful woman that any man would be lucky to have. She's special because of her . . . *powers.*" Tima tilted her head in silent inquiry. "She's got the ability to do things most women can't do. *Magic* isn't even a strong enough word for the things she's capable of. The things she's been through and been able to survive. The enemies she's defeated."

"You're not speaking metaphorically. Are you?"

"No," he said. "Her ability to speak and read any language was the first of her gifts. That happened after she went missing at Mount Saint Helen's." Rowan went on to tell about her ability to travel between place and time, the gifts of the ancient All-Gods, and then there were the children. "Henry, in particular, has his own *powers*. His mother and I have suspected he's using it to get ahead in school, and to prepare for what is to come." He told her about their encounter with Enlil and Enki's command to prepare. That was a much longer story, but they seemed to have time. As he told her every little detail, the cell grew cold. He realized night had come. After spending what he estimated to be a full 24 hours in the room with the books with almost no sleep, he was beyond the point of exhaustion. He couldn't choke down the camel, once he knew what it was.

"I always knew there was *something* about her," Tima said with a weary smile. "You, too."

"Me? I'm just a man," Rowan said. "With a woman I can't handle." He stood, his chains rattling as he moved, stretching as much as he could. His tailbone ached and he felt woozy.

"She never needed to be handled," Tima said. "She only needs your love, and your support."

"She's always had that," he said. "And she always will."

"Of that, there can be no doubt," she shifted, wincing as she tucked her arm to her chest.

"How's your hand?" he asked.

"Still there," she said. "Most of it."

"Can I see it?" he asked, moving as close as his chains would permit. Tima looked at him dubiously, but then presented her injured hand for inspection. A sodium light outside gave the room a subtle glow, but it was enough. In the pale yellow light, her skin was sallow all the way to her elbow. But from elbow to wrist, the skin flamed red. He could feel the heat in it. Infection was setting in. "Tima," he started.

"It's bad," she said. "I've known it for a while. That is why you must do what you can to get home to Lauren."

"I'm getting you home to your family, and I won't argue with you about anything except that," he said.

"But what can you do?" her voice broke, as he backed up and sat back down —

exhaustion weighing on him.

"I'll figure out something," he said. "I don't know how, but —"

The door rattled and it startled them both. But, it didn't open. It rattled again. "Hello?" a small voice came through the corrugated metal. "Dr. Badr?"

"Who's there?" Tima's voice was weak. Rowan repeated the message with more forte.

There was a pause and the voice seemed to move closer behind Tima. "Dr. Badr, it's Maliqa al Khalid."

Tima perked up. "Maliqa? What are you doing here?"

"I told you my father was a horrible man," she said. Her voice broke.

Rowan posed the question with his eyes. "Maliqa is . . . was . . . one of my students. Her father made her quit the program and come home. He was furious with her for studying archaeology instead of medicine."

"Can we trust her?"

"Do we have a choice?" Tima posed.

"Maliqa, Dr. Badr is hurt, we need a doctor or at least some antibiotics."

"I can't get the door open," she said. "Listen, there isn't time. There is another man here who says he's going to find Kish and you're going to help him find something."

"He's forcing us to find a stargate," Rowan said.

"A what? Like . . . the one in the movies?" the query was followed by a scuffle outside, like shuffling feet. Rowan froze, hoping their potential ally hadn't gotten caught. There was a long pause of silence as the door to the building rattled, along with keys in the lock. The door opened and a woman entered carrying a tray of food and cups of tea. Rowan studied her in the dim light, noticing the bruise on her face. Abdul's wife.

The one Tima had struck. He noticed the smirk on his professor's face as she saw him put the pieces together.

The woman said something harsh in Arabic, as she set the tray haphazardly on the floor. The soup spilled, as did the tea. She didn't seem to care.

"She needs a doctor," Rowan said, not understanding the woman's words. He pointed at Tima, then at his own hand. "Doctor. She needs a doctor."

The woman just scowled at him. Behind her, a girl in her late teens or early twenties appeared carrying blankets. The woman turned back, staring at her. A protracted conversation ensued, and the girl looked sheepish, as she answered the woman's questions. Finally the woman turned and stomped out, done with the whole fiasco.

The girl stood hesitantly, glancing back over her shoulder until she was sure the woman had gone. "Dr. Badr . . ."

"Maliqa . . . thank God you are here," Tima said. "What was that all about?"

"I told the woman my father sent me with the blankets. I saw them in the back of one of the cars just outside. I told her he sent me because I spoke English." She knelt beside them and placed a blanket in front of each of them. She saw the bandages on Tima's hand and recoiled. "What did they do to you?"

Tima didn't hold out her hand.

"Look, Tima needs a doctor," Rowan took over. "At the very least, she needs antibiotics."

"They're taking you to Kish," Maliqa said. "I heard a man I didn't know talking to someone on the phone. I think he must be important because his women have taken over our house and my father has given him the office in the tower to use."

"He's Sudanese, and he's dangerous," Rowan said. "You need to stay away from him. Can you help Dr. Badr?"

"I can look. Maybe one of my sisters or my father has some antibiotics," the girl said. "I'll bring it as soon as I can."

"Maliqa was the brightest of my students . . . this term," Tima said, directing the comment to Rowan. "Maliqa, this is Rowan Pierce."

"It's an honor," she started but Rowan cut her off.

"Tima doesn't have much time," Rowan said. "We can discuss archaeology later, once she's safe."

"I'll go now," Maliqa said.

"Thank you, Maliqa," Tima said. "May you be blessed all the days of your life and may your days be many."

Rowan had never heard Tima say anything like that, and even her student seemed to pause before she turned to make her retreat. The keys rattled in the door and there were voices outside. Soon, there was silence.

20

San Diego, California
May 19th

Lauren sat in the chair by the window. The baby was asleep in the bassinet. Five days after they'd come home from the hospital, Lauren still hadn't had a shower. She hadn't left her bedroom. She'd hardly even gotten out of bed.

She hadn't cried in the last two hours, but it seemed inevitable. She cried more than the baby. As she gazed at the little bundle, wrapped in a pink blanket, she realized the baby hadn't cried as much as she just fussed when she needed something that someone hadn't anticipated. Between everyone in the house, Sarah almost never had to wait for a diaper change, a feeding, or a burp. When she was awake, she stared at everyone and watched everything. She reminded Lauren of her Great Aunt Mary, who never said much, unless she had something important to say. Even then, she made things as simple as possible, and there was never any doubt what she meant. Sarah was very much like that.

When she wasn't tending the baby or sleeping, Lauren

spent her time doom-scrolling on her phone, looking for any mention of Rowan, Tima, or what was going on in Sudan. Andrew Miller had gone to work with Kitty to try and broker their release, and promised to let Lauren know as soon as he had word. The phone hadn't so much as beeped.

Lauren tried to reach Rowan using her own *special* means of communication, but that had only served to tire her out, and leave her in tears. She tried to blame her spiraling emotions on hormones, but she knew there was more to it. If not knowing where Rowan was wasn't bad enough, not being able to reach Henry, her mother and father, or even her brother had compounded the situation. She felt utterly alone and helpless to do anything about it. She didn't even have her cat to keep her company and soothe her frustrations.

"Mom?" Jamie knocked on the door, then peeked in. "Aunt Bahati wanted to know if you were ready for your dinner."

"Sure," Lauren said. She wasn't, but it didn't matter. She knew everyone was trying so hard to take care of her. She didn't have the heart to refuse their attention. "What's for dinner?"

"Mrs. MacIntosh made chicken enchiladas, from scratch!" Jamie called as he disappeared down the hall.

Lauren was relieved. Bahati tried, but even with Lauren's tutelage, she was not a great cook. She'd taught the kids to be kind when they were served something they didn't care for, but little Kate couldn't help herself most of the time. Kate could be brutally honest, which was rare for a little kid her age. Sam ate anything, even Bahati's cooking. He never complained and often asked for seconds. Lauren was beginning to wonder if his taste buds worked.

"Oh," Evelyn said, coming in with a tray. "Look at you, out of bed. How are you feeling?" She lowered her voice as she set the tray on the table in front of her and paused to look in on the baby.

"Like I've been hit by a Mack truck," she said.

"Maybe after dinner you'll be ready for a shower?" Evelyn sat across from her.

"Maybe." Lauren didn't know the vet's wife very well. They often stood out in the front yard comparing flower gardens or talking about kids or pets, but that was the extent of their relationship. The MacIntosh kids were much older than Lauren & Rowan's. One was about to graduate from college, the other was married and had kids of her own. Evelyn often showed her pictures of her grandkids, who lived in Omaha, on her phone. "How's my cat?"

"Improving."

"I miss her."

"Mac wanted to watch her for another day or so, just to make sure he hasn't missed anything. I'll bring her home as soon as she's able."

Lauren glanced at her phone on her lap.

"Staring at the phone isn't going to make it ring, you know?" Evelyn set the tray on the foot of the bed, then came over and sat on the tufted arm of the chair, putting a hand on Lauren's shoulder. "He's going to come home. You must believe that."

"I'm clinging to that hope," Lauren said, meaning it. "But . . . Fate is under no obligation to give us what we want."

"Do you remember what you said at Eric Sherwood's funeral?" Lauren had forgotten Evelyn and Hannah were friends from church. "You said, *it isn't our place to question the storms we must face.* You said, *storms make people stronger and they never last long.*"

"I borrowed that from another author," Lauren admitted.

"It's still sound advice." Evelyn moved to kneel beside the chair, taking Lauren's hand and holding her gaze. "You were right though. This is just a little storm. Rowan will be home before you know it. You just have to hold on to that."

Lauren swallowed back a lump that formed in her throat as tears flooded her face unbidden.

"He'd move heaven and earth to get back to you, and we both know it."

"He may have to," Lauren sniffed. "I've never been so afraid for him."

"No one's telling you it's going to be easy," Evelyn said. "But we all know Rowan is counting on us to take care of you. But do your part."

"I'm trying." Lauren took the tissue Evelyn tucked in her hand and used it to dry her eyes and nose.

"If you are truly trying, then you need to eat, take a shower and take care of yourself so that when Rowan comes home, he'll know you kept faith in him."

Lauren nodded. "But . . . maybe the shower first . . . while I still have the strength."

"I'll go put your dinner back in the oven to keep it warm until you're ready," she said. "I'll send Bahati up to help you shower."

THIRTY MINUTES LATER, Lauren was back in bed, her raven tresses bundled up in a towel on her head. Bahati sat in the chair with the baby in her arms, tickling her cheek, trying to coax a smile, with little success. "Is it normal that she doesn't cry?"

"She hasn't had to," Lauren said. She closed her eyes and laid back, warm and comfortable. She had to admit, it felt good to be clean. The warm water had done wonders. She'd used some of the soap her mother had made from the herbs in her garden. The perfume of sage, sandalwood and lavender lingered around her. "She's probably getting hungry though."

"Are you ready for her? How was your shower?" Bahati brought the baby over.

"It was amazing," Lauren said, settling in to nurse. "I've wanted one for days, but I just didn't feel like I had the strength. Surprisingly, I feel a hundred times better."

"You look like you feel better." Bahati busied herself tidying up.

"I think my cat saved my life," Lauren said unexpectedly. Her eye lifted to the foot of the bed where the Siamese typically slept. The bed felt emptier without Shadow—and Rowan—to keep her company.

"How so?" Bahati asked.

"When I was in labor, she sat in the doorway and watched, as if to say you're not alone," Lauren swallowed hard. "I'm not sure I could have made it without her."

"I've never had a cat, but she seems like a good one," Bahati said. "For a *time traveler*."

That made Lauren chuckle. She hadn't thought of Shadow as a time traveler, but the cat had come back with her from the cursed pirate ship in the Bermuda Triangle, so Bahati was right about that. "Have you talked to Rowan's parents?" The implication that she needed to convey not only the news about their newest grandchild, but the situation with Rowan was evident.

"No," Lauren swallowed hard. She didn't want to tell Martha Pierce her son had been taken hostage by a psychopathic megalomaniac. "Maybe I'll call them tomorrow. It's already late in Denver."

"It's getting late here, too," Bahati announced. "I better go see about getting the kids to bed."

"Bahati, have you talked to Jean-René?"

"We've texted," she said. "I finally got the whole story." She recounted the details from his perspective. He had a ruptured ear drum and concussion. It took several hours before they were rescued so he was dehydrated and in shock by the time they got him to the hospital.

"Is he coming home?" Evelyn asked.

"No," she said. "He refuses. He says he won't leave without Rowan."

"As soon as I'm cleared to travel, I'm taking Sarah and going to wherever Kitty is," Lauren announced out of nowhere.

Bahati gasped. "You can't."

"I know I can't go now, but if Rowan isn't home by the time I'm able to *travel*, I will, and no force on earth, or in heaven, can stop me." Lauren spoke with the conviction of a woman scorned, and no one would be able to talk her out of it.

21

Orleans Parish Prison, New Orleans
May 20th

Dauphine lay on his bunk, basking in the glory of the black magic he had woven and the results that continued to ripple on the cosmic ether over the past week. He deserved to enjoy the fruits of his efforts. Justice was delicious, yet bittersweet. He had interrupted the woman's spells and set her existence into chaos. His goal was to destroy her and her world, but his magic was not strong enough. It was enough, for now. It would have to be.

As he closed his eyes and examined the results of his spells, the perfume of brimstone came to him. "Has my effort pleased you, my Lord?" he asked, as a smile curled in the corners of his cheeks.

"Your magic is strong, my wicked and faithless servant." The deep voice resonated in his core. "Now it is time to focus your energies on those who would take arms against me and my allies. I will see you are provided with the elements and sigils needed to do my work when the moon is dark. It will not be easy."

Dauphine sat up giving his attention to the unseen demon. "You will need to see beyond the dark—to see what others cannot see—but it must be hidden from the eye of the powers of good. You must ward off the enemy and guide our allies to the weapon."

"So mote it be, my Lord. So mote it be."

"Yes, I have chosen wisely," the demon said. "See before you . . ." he started, and a flash of gold sparks erupted from the cracks in the concrete floor. They spiraled into a filagree of symbols scrolled out from the central point. "Behold the protection of Papa Legba is with you. The loa who serves as the intermediary between heaven and earth will give you strength and blesses your endeavors."

Dauphine knew this sigil well. The vèvè of Legba, also referred to as the *Devil* or the *Black Man* in Haitian Creole voodoo was the mark of the Dark Lord of all dark forces in the realm before and beyond the loa, or the gods.

"Prince of Darkness, Ash-Shaytān, Beelzebub, Ahpuch, Master of the Left-Hand Path, bless me." Dauphine fell to his knees at the edge of the vèvè, waving the smoke that rose from the sparks, using it to bathe his bare chest, and hair. "Make me the strongest bokor of your army."

"So mote it be." Enlil's wicked smile beamed in the dark corner. Then the sparks imploded. The detritus floated in the air like fiery dust motes before it twinkled into nothingness. "I summon thee, O demoness dwelling beneath the shifting sands where secrets lie. Lead those who would magnify me and bring me glory to the very gate of their destruction. Block those who would take what is mine and show them Justice, as Justice demands."

"Justice, as justice demands! O, Dark Lord, my guide," Dauphine repeated, swaying as if in a trance. "O, my Dark Lord . . . so mote it be."

"I constrain and command thee, *nolens volens*, with guile and deception . . ." the demon's chanting began to crescendo.

"I bind you my sisters and brothers who abide in this place to render aid to my evil and faithless servant, Dauphine. I command thee give him thy shape and form and the powers of thy wings and whiskers. Take him to the place where my greatest secret dwells and defend what is mine from those who would take my birthright and deny me my place at the Left Hand of the All Father."

"So mote it be. So mote it be." Dauphine swayed, sweat building over his bare chest.

"So mote it be. By my many names. So mote it be."

"Nanhi," Henry felt the energy in the universe shift. He came out of the bed and launched himself out of the house. He found his grandparents sitting by the fire with his uncle, cups of coffee shared between them. "Grandpa . . . it's time!"

John lifted a brow glancing at his wife before he looked to the boy. "It was time ten minutes ago," John rose. "It will be time ten minutes from now."

"No," Henry said. "It is time *now*. Mom is reaching out to me. I feel her. She needs me. I need your help. Nanhi, you, too."

John nodded to his wife and offered her his hand. Michael rose without effort and lifted his mother to her feet. Diana hesitated, leaning into John, standing on her tiptoes to press her forehead to his. "*Si-gwu da-na da-gwa do'hv,*" she whispered, before pressing her lips to his. *We will see one another again soon.* John nodded his acknowledgement of the vow.

She turned to Michael and reached for his cheek. He leaned into her hand and kissed it. "I'll give you a push," he said, then glanced to Henry. "Tell your mother I will cry out to the universe for answers, and I will not stop until I find the truth of it."

"Thanks, Uncle Michael," Henry said, a hesitant smile shadowed his face.

John positioned Diana in front of Henry with her back to him. Michael took a similar place behind Henry as the teenager and his grandmother clasped hands. "Picture your mother's face. Think of all the things that make you love her," John told his grandson. Then he addressed his wife. "Picture your daughter's face. See our ancestors in her eyes and take her their protection and their comfort, along with our love."

John and Michael locked their gazes on each other and allowed the strength of their magic to swirl around their loved ones, as they directed the forces to create a path to Lauren. Time and space fell away silently. It fell slowly at first, and then, all at once.

HER MOTHER often slept with the television on when her father was gone. Sarah lay in the bassinet beside the king-sized bed, watching the light of the television flickering on the ceiling above her. She had sensed the change in her mother hours before. The perfume of the cleansing herbs remained on her mother's flesh and comforted her as she nursed. Her mother seemed to relax on a level she hadn't in many months. Even in the safety of her womb, the child had fed on the magic that swirled in her mother's core. She became aware of herself and her place in the universe even as the neurons of her tiny brain knitted together.

Tonight, she felt the magic tingling in her fingers and toes, and she sensed the coming force of familiar hearts. The power of their entry into this *time-place* came with a flash of ancient *magic*, made present. The thud of two forms on the floor shook the room, and her mother sat up with a gasp, almost a shriek. "Mom!" The boy she recognized by his voice— *Henry*

—bolted to his feet. He paused to help the other woman from the floor. She knew her, too. *Nanhi.*

"Henry! Mom!" Sarah's mother cried out. There were tears and questions that were beyond her need to consider. The Universe hadn't been put to rights. Not yet. There was still much *magic* to be done, and many barriers to bringing the Creator—*The Protector*—home.

DIANA, having already examined the baby, turned her attention to Lauren. "A dark shadow cursed you," she said, surprising Lauren. "What have you done to dispel it?"

"A what?" Lauren, still stunned and emotional, couldn't seem to formulate an answer.

"That's not like her," Henry observed, holding his little sister over his shoulder.

Diana shook her head and began her inspection of her daughter, checking her eyes and laying her hand on her head. Her hair was disheveled, but it was clean. Diana leaned in and sniffed. Lavender, rosemary. *Good.* Lavender promoted a sense of calm and aided in sleep, but it also could be used to attract a partner. Considering the chaos around them, she would need something stronger. She needed amethyst.

Diana made a mental shopping list. She had such things in her room downstairs, but this was just a start. Sage, sandalwood . . . *yes, good.* Sage was for protection and purification. It removed negative energy, but there was still negative energy here. Herbs could only do so much without the proper incantations and accompaniments. Sandalwood also removed negativity, but it had to be burned.

Diana inspected the bedroom around her and then disappeared in the bathroom. In the shower she found one of the bars of soap they had made in the fall and Diana knew exactly what was in it. Lauren knew, too—had to have known about the healing properties. They often worked in the garden tending their herbs, which grew primarily in pots scattered around the courtyard surrounding the pool where the children often played on a patch of grass. Lauren was an interested pupil, but when Diana told her the purposes and uses of various medicinal plants, she got the sense that her daughter lacked a full acceptance of the true magical properties. She was happy to drink Diana's teas, but magic and medicine were often one in the same in ancient times, as they were today.

"Tell me what you know of your husband?" Diana asked. Henry had told her something had happened, but no one in John's *time-place* had a full sense of what was happening in this place in time.

Lauren swallowed hard and proceeded to convey everything she had learned from Kitty and Andrew. Diana sat on the edge of the bed to listen, nodding as the pieces began to make sense. "Kitty's trying to negotiate for his release. I'm not sure what Andrew is doing, but he said he would help any way he can."

"I do not know Agent Miller," Diana said. "But I sense he can see what others do not. That is a powerful skill. Kitty has the ability to speak peace into being, as we have seen. It will take all of us using our gifts to bring Rowan home."

"I just hope . . . I hope it's not too late." Lauren's voice cracked.

"I'm drained from our trip home, but I can sense Dad is out there, Mom. I can't tell much more, but he is alive. I promise you that." Henry had gifts his mother could not even comprehend. Diana had trouble wrapping her brain around it herself, but she'd had the same issues understanding John's powers when he was young. All she knew was they were strong, and they would progress.

"What about Dad and Michael?" Lauren looked to her mother.

"Your father is stronger where he is," she said. "And

Michael will go to the gods to intercede if he can. I must first work for you and for this little one. Then we can focus on your husband." She turned to Henry. "Have Dr. MacIntosh bring me the cat."

"The cat?" Lauren had mentioned Shadow had taken ill and was being treated by the vet a few doors over. "Shadow?"

"Just let the boy do what he's told," Diana said.

Lauren reached out and caught Henry's hand. "What about Tima?"

"They're together," Henry said. "You know Dad is doing everything to protect her."

"That's what worries me," Lauren admitted, a tear running down her cheek.

"What do you mean?" Diana asked, tucking a tissue in her daughter's hand.

"He'd do anything to protect her. Even at risk of his own life."

22

Aleppo, Syria
May 21st

Maliqa returned much later, the keys in the lock rattling just enough to alert Rowan. Even as exhausted as he was, he couldn't sleep. He lay listening to Tima moaning—delirious. He'd given her his blanket and saw that she still shivered beneath it. She slept but it was a restless, uncomfortable sleep.

She entered quietly, but when Rowan sat up, she moved to him. "I'm sorry I couldn't get back sooner. Something's going on and I couldn't get past the guards."

"What's happening?"

"I'm not sure," she said. "Trucks are lining up outside the walls of the compound. There were a lot of soldiers, but they are having a meeting. I was able to slip past the one guard who fell asleep outside the gate. I found medicine. I brought food and water, too."

She unshouldered her bag and took out bottles of water and sandwiches on flat bread that were still warm. Rowan set those aside, taking the medicine bottles she handed him. But, the labels were written in Arabic. "What are these?" He inspected the two bottles.

"This one," Maliqa said, pointing to the larger bottle. "It's an antibiotic. Doxycycline."

"How many milligrams?"

"One hundred," she said. "It is my sister's prescription. She had a skin infection. I couldn't find the ones I thought I had."

"And this one?" He held up the smaller bottle.

"Dilaudid," she said. "I took it from my father's medicine cabinet. He suffers from kidney stones. Four milligrams."

Rowan nodded, pursing his lips. "I'll need to break the pill in half," he said opening the bottle, inspecting the small round white pills he poured into his hand. It had numbers stamped on the back. The front had a groove across it, that cut across a number four. Rowan took one and put the rest in the bottle. With some effort he was able to break it in half, losing only a small portion as it crumbled at the breaking point. "Here." He handed the fragment to Maliqa, passing her the water bottle. "You'll have to give it to her. I can't reach her in these chains."

"Dr. Badr?" Maliqa tried to wake her. "Tima?"

"Tima?" Rowan raised his voice, and the woman stirred. "Maliqa has medicine for you." He handed one of the antibiotics to the girl. She helped Tima sit up enough to take the two pills with a sip of water. Tima drank greedily, but after a few swallows, pushed the bottle away and collapsed back to the ground.

"She's feverish," Maliqa said, pulling the blankets back up over her.

"You brought these just in the nick of time," he said, tucking the bottles back into her bag. "Look, all the activity you describe tells me something is about to happen. They're preparing to move us or there's going to be some type of military action. You need to go back into your home and forget we are here. You've done everything you could do to help us. Thank you. You saved her life."

"I'll help you escape," Maliqa said, excitement in her voice. Rowan could tell her pulse was racing. "I owe her that much. I will leave the door unlocked. I will create a diversion. There is a running truck just outside the gate. You go southwest towards Samandağ to the coast or northwest toward Iskenderun. There are boat captains that will take you to Cyprus or Alexandria. Once you are in international waters . . ." Rowan caught her hands and silenced her. She was frightened. He saw her desperation fueling her panic.

"Maliqa," he said. "Tima is in no condition to escape."

"Go. Get her help. I'll stay with her."

"I'm not leaving her," he said. "When she is stronger, perhaps we can escape, but it would be foolish now to try and run with her in this condition. She might not survive the effort. Look, you've given her the best possible chance at survival . . ."

"Why is this door unlocked?" A voice at the doorway caught them both off guard. The door swung open, and a dark form blocked the light. Maliqa fell back on her rump, landing with a thud. Rowan dropped the bag behind him, hoping it could remain hidden.

Scar Face cast a large shadow blocking the yellow light from the opened door. His boss pushed past him. Abdul charged forward and grabbed Maliqa's wrist, yanking her to her feet. "Who are you? What are you doing here?"

"This is my father's property." Maliqa didn't cower. "Who are you? What are *you* doing here?"

He eyed her for a long moment and didn't let go. "*You* have no business here!" He shook the girl violently.

Maliqa screamed, startled by the sudden assault. Rowan jumped to his feet. "Leave her alone! The women sent her with food."

"I did not order you to be fed!" He tossed Maliqa aside

and buried his fist in Rowan's gut. The initial blow doubled him over and knocked the wind from him audibly. Had he eaten, any food he might have had in his stomach would have been expelled. Though Rowan was at least six inches taller than the man, he was in no shape to fight. He buckled, dropping to his knees as his arms wrapped around his injured gut. A second fist caught him across the face, knocking him to the ground. "*You* have no place here!" He turned on Maliqa, raising a hand to strike her. Rowan caught him in the Achilles tendon with a blow he'd seen Lauren use when they were fighting for their lives in Mexico before Henry was born. The man's ankle collapsed, and he went down hard. It gave the girl time to roll out of the way.

"Run!" Rowan instructed.

Scar Face stepped past his boss and turned his wrath on Rowan. He kicked him repeatedly in the stomach all the while beating him over the head with a club. Rowan cowered for a moment, covering his head with his arms as he chose his moment with great care. He caught the man's boot and torqued it hard, hearing the ligaments in Scar Face's knee pop. He glanced up and found Maliqa still standing there.

"Run!" Rowan growled.

"Guards!" Abdul shouted.

"Run!" Rowan repeated, snapping the girl out of her stupor. She turned to make her escape as the door flew open. Armed guards paused, rushing in. One of them grabbed her and shoved her to the floor. Another grabbed their leader and tried to help him to his feet, but he cried out when he tried to stand, and they ended up dragging him out. Rowan was hauled to his feet only to be punched again. He collapsed but the beating continued.

"Don't kill him," he heard Abdul's command. "But teach him a lesson."

ROWAN DIDN'T REMEMBER when the throttling ended. He lay on the floor vaguely aware of his situation. Every bone in his body hurt and he suspected more than one was broken. His tailbone throbbed where a steel toed boot had struck with force. Lightning bolts raced up his spine and flashed behind his eyelids. Sparks danced in his eyes.

"Rowan . . ." Maliqa sobbed. "Rowan?"

In response, Rowan lifted his head and forced his eyes open. Maliqa sat on her knees at his elbow, leaning over him. "It's okay," he managed, his voice just above a whisper. "I've been hit harder . . . and by bigger." It was a lie.

His shoulder felt as if his arm had gotten pulled from its socket. His hand was numb. His bare ring finger lay at an awkward angle, and he forced himself to focus on it. Blood pooled on the ground beneath it. He realized the shine from the sodium lights outside was reflecting off bare bone. His rational mind began to kick in and he knew he had a compound fracture of the digit.

His training as a field medic kicked in. He could hear his instructor's voice and found himself sitting in the lecture hall along with his fellow cadets. *"Phalanx fractures are the most common injuries in the body and account for 46% of all fractures seen in a combat field hospital. Cadet Pierce. What diagnostic tools would you consider for a field assessment of a compound fracture of the phalanx?"*

Rowan didn't hesitate. "A visual assessment must identify the mechanism of injury, soft tissue injury, and determination of finger alignment."

"And what do you observe here?" The memory and reality blurred together as he gazed at the injured hand.

"Visual assessment shows there is evidence of a rotational defect," he muttered.

"What else do you need to look for?"

"Tendon, nerve and vessel damage." Rowan could hear his words slurring but he continued. "In this case there appears to be tendon rupture in the distal interphalangeal with dislocation. Nerves are harder to assess visually, but patient reports the hand is numb."

"*Pain?*"

Rowan tried to flex his hand. Pain shot up his arm and he felt light headed. "Aggh!" he growled. "Pain response . . . is 9 out of 10 . . ." he panted.

"Rowan?" Maliqa sobbed. "What can I do? How can I help?"

"*Treatment options?*"

"Non operative . . ." Rowan closed his eyes trying to steel himself. "Extraarticular fracture with less than 10 degrees angulation . . . even though there is rotational deformity."

"*That would indicate an operative open reduction,*" his instructor corrected.

"Tima? What do I do?" Maliqa cried, but no answer came from the professor. "Tima?"

"In hospital, yes, but the patient is confined in hostile territory with few resources. Field treatment indicates dorsal splinting in intrinsic plus position for three weeks or until able to reach a medical facility. Two percent of phalanx fractures will heal without surgical intervention. Further assessment will have to wait."

"*What resources are available?*"

Rowan couldn't determine. "Very . . . few." The world around him dimmed.

"*Pierce!*" The instructor's voice snapped him back to consciousness. "*Resources. Now.*"

In a moment of fading clarity, he rolled over onto his back groaning as he paused for a moment. Once he had his breath, he rolled over onto the other side, grimacing as he was able to push himself up with his uninjured hand.

Tima lay on her side, still bundled beneath her blankets. He watched her to make sure she was still breathing. When he could find the rise and fall of her body, he returned his attention to his own plight.

Maliqa leaned over him, her hand lightly on his hip. "Rowan, tell me . . . what do you need?"

"Pain meds . . ."

Maliqa saw her bag tossed in the corner and jumped up to get it. She opened the bottle and pressed one past his swollen lip. She held a bottle of water to his mouth and lifted his head so he could swallow without choking. "I have to splint this finger."

Maliqa found a fragment of splintered wood from one of the crates in the back corner. It was roughly eight inches long —several inches longer than his mangled finger. She rummaged around for anything else that might be useful but ended up ripping a strip of cloth from one of the threadbare blankets she'd brought in earlier. Rowan voiced his approval, as he clutched his hand to his chest and forced himself up against the wall so he could gain the light and see what he had to do. It wasn't going to be pleasant, and he knew it.

"*Pierce, you need to reset the bone and stitch the skin,*" the instructor's voice came as a shadow.

"No needle or thread," he panted.

"*Understood,*" he said. "*Focus on the bone. You have to remain conscious while you do it. It will be painful, but you need to set the bone, pinch the flesh and wrap it so the bindings hold the margins together, then splint it and secure that. Once you do that*—only then—*you can pass out. Are we clear?*"

"Clear, sir," Rowan muttered, still lost in the blur between reality and delusion.

He instructed Maliqa as he would a med tech. She helped him wash the blood from the finger, clearing the field so he could see what he was working with. The sharp end of the broken bone that pierced the skin was clear. She hissed and sat back on her heels when she saw the bone and jagged flesh. He gritted his teeth against the wood and pushed the bone in place, back beneath the skin. It was everything he could do not to cry out as he worked. He had the cloth strip ready.

Gingerly, he wrapped it around the finger as tightly as he could, without cutting off circulation, then added the splint. With the girl's help, he secured it with the remaining scrap of cloth, which she neatly knotted over the laceration.

"Is that too tight?"

"You'd make an excellent doctor," he said in a moment of clarity. That moment was fleeting. "Procedure . . . complete, sir," he reported back to his instructor, holding out the hand for inspection.

"Well done. Any other injuries to assess?"

"Plenty, but . . . none that appear . . . immediate," Rowan answered, weakly. He was slipping and he knew it.

"Well done. At ease, soldier."

Rowan rested his hand on his chest and nodded, then collapsed.

"Rowan?"

23

San Diego, California
May 21st

Sometime in the wee hours before dawn, Lauren put the now-sleeping infant in the bassinet. She shuffled into the bathroom. Her eyes felt sandy as she turned on the water to let it warm. When it was no longer chilly, she cupped her hands and scooped the water over her face. Her mother had rubbed her body with oils infused with herbs and the perfume of them lingered. Her muscles felt tremendously better, and she moved with an ease she'd lacked since Sarah's arrival.

After a moment's debate, Lauren decided a few more hours of rest would be beneficial. Sleep came swiftly and in her dreams she found herself in the desert, gazing up at a clear dark sky. The night air was cool, and a dry wind tossed her hair off her shoulders. Sprigs of scruffy plants grew in clumps amidst the parched earth that looked like scales on a lizard. Rocks dotted the rising plains that disappeared on the horizon. A waning gibbous moon glowed blue on distant snowcapped peaks that floated in the hot air before the dark sky took over.

She could sense Rowan was close. Her heart always knew when he was near. But the landscape and the scrubby plants weren't ones she had seen when they visited Sudan. Something wasn't right. Her impeccable bump of direction told her this was too far north to be Sudan.

Since staying home with the children, her wayfinding skills had suffered. While she knew she was somewhere in the Arabian region, her sense of place wasn't as accurate as she needed it to be. She turned at the sound of livestock interrupting the silence. A boy, not much older than Jamie, appeared behind the goats, urging them back to their home. He stopped when he saw Lauren, locking eyes with her. "Who are you?" he snapped in a language Lauren knew.

It was known as the *Language of Adam*. Aramaic was an ancient language, one of the oldest—almost three thousand years old. It was one of the first languages of Mesopotamia and remained the oldest continuously spoken language in the world. But it wasn't just one language. There were many variations and dialects. The largest concentration of Aramaic speakers was centered in Northern Iraq.

"What is the name of this place?" Lauren asked, her ability to speak the ancient All-Language extended to every dialect. *How could Rowan be in Iraq? It didn't make sense.*

"Go away! *Witch*! You do not belong here!" the boy repeated.

"Just tell me where we are and I will leave," Lauren said. The boy looked more frightened than angry. She suspected he might get in trouble if he were found talking to an unaccompanied woman in her nightgown at this hour of the night. Had she planned to *sleepwalk*, she might have put on different pajamas.

"What's the nearest city?"

He pointed northward, "Qa'im. A days walk."

Lauren's gaze followed his outstretched hand. She allowed her mind to geolocate her non-corporeal location, confirming that she was in Iraq—near the border with Syria. Bagdad was to the southeast.

Rowan had many bad memories of his time in Iraq during Desert Storm/Desert Shield. Some of the stories he still couldn't tell her, but he'd conveyed many of them. She knew he'd seen many men die, ripped apart by improvised explosives and land mines. He'd seen women and children killed by chemical warfare unleashed by their own governments.

Lauren's older brother, Kenneth, had died in Afghanistan at almost the same time Rowan was injured himself. He would never have come here voluntarily.

They rarely talked about his time in the military, but any time the Network suggested an episode in Iraq or Afghanistan, Rowan was quick to find any reason to squash the idea. Lauren found herself just as eager to avoid anything that she thought could trouble him. PTSD—along with his physical injuries—had gotten him an honorable discharge and a Purple Heart, but she'd never truly seen the effects of it for herself. He always carried himself so well it was easy to forget what he'd been through—easy for her, though maybe not for him.

Firecrackers popped in the distance. Sand erupted at her feet, and she realized it wasn't firecrackers she'd heard. It was gunfire. "Go away! "Go!" Lauren stood as the sand continued to erupt closer and closer. Men ran towards her, firing their weapons. The boy turned away and ran back into the darkness as the guns flashed and the bullets whizzed past her. Lauren stood, unfazed even as the bullets appeared to pierce her shadowy form but hit the sand behind her.

The men shouted angry words at her, and dogs ran past them, barking at her. Without thinking, she shifted into a familiar form. The spotted skin rippled around her body as she dropped to all fours and bared her fangs, hissing, whipping her long tail behind her. The Jaguar Queen would be proud of her ferocity.

"What the . . ." the men froze, lowering their weapons as she growled at them, pacing back and forth. One of the dogs made a lunge for her, and she took a swipe at it. The dog recoiled yelping, convincing Lauren she'd slashed its nose with her claw. Another started towards her, but it was a false charge and the dog stopped just out of reach. Lauren roared again, and the dogs ran back to their master with their tails between their legs.

One of the stunned men found his courage and raised his weapon to fire, but before she could leap, she found herself in her own bed, the covers disheveled.

The baby lay in her bassinet looking at her. The sun streamed through the shear drapes. That was it, Lauren decided. She couldn't stand by and let this happen without at least trying.

———

HENRY MET her at the top of the stairs with a plate of pancakes and a glass of juice. "Mom?" Lauren was dressed, had her hair braided, and the baby strapped to her body in her sling.

"Where is Andrew Miller?" she asked curtly.

"The man that came to see you in the hospital?"

"The *FBI Agent* who came to see me in the hospital," Lauren corrected.

Henry closed his eyes. "I don't know where he is at the moment, but he was with Aunt Kitty in Jerusalem."

"That's where we're going," Lauren said.

"Jerusalem?"

"If that's where your Aunt Kitty is, yes. Unless you can tell me where your father is."

Henry closed his eyes. "No," he said. "I can't find him. It's the weirdest thing, Mom. I don't think he's in a different time-place. I'm also certain he's not dead, so don't even think that. But it's like there's a wall of wind between us, like he's in a black void and there is a force keeping me from reaching him."

"I feel it, too," Lauren said. "That's why we're going to Jerusalem." Lauren took the plate from his hands and set it aside. She wrapped her arms around him, hoping the baby would be able to travel, and to shield her from any forces that might cause harm. "Now."

The world spun out from under them. Lauren felt dizzy, but Henry steadied her as the world formed before her eyes. They stood in an empty room that reminded Lauren of the interrogation room she'd been held in back in Peru before she and Rowan were married or the one in some abandoned airbase in Western Oklahoma when Kitty was accused of murdering Michael's boss. There was a single table with two chairs in the middle of the room and a two way mirror took up one of the walls. There was one door. Henry went to it and tried to open it, but it was secured from the outside. "Where's Kitty?" Lauren asked.

Henry didn't answer, but he reached through the door and unlocked it, then put his shoulder into it. It opened into a long hallway. He still held his mother's arm to steady her, and Lauren was thankful for it. She patted the baby who stirred at the sudden change but nuzzled against her chest and settled.

Down the long corridor, another door had to be opened in a similar fashion. Lauren stepped into the room and stopped. A dozen officials sat at a conference table, and all turned as they entered the room. Their jaws dropped before one of the men jumped up from the table. "Guards!" he shouted.

Lauren's eye moved to follow the woman at the end of the table as she rose. "Lauren? What are you doing here?"

"Kitty!" Lauren melted. "Oh, thank heavens."

Nothing would have kept Lauren from rushing to her

sister-in-law and embracing her, careful not to squish the baby between them. Henry was on her elbow and did the same when Kitty reached for him.

"I came to help find Rowan," Lauren said.

"Shouldn't you be home in bed?" Kitty asked, tilting her head sideway to look at the baby, only seeing the shock of black hair that stood up like a mohawk. "You look pale."

"She should be home in bed," Henry chided. "But you know my mother."

"I do," Kitty said. "But you can't be here. This meeting requires top security clearance." She started for the door, but Lauren stood fast.

"My husband and Tima aren't in Sudan," Lauren said.

A collective gasp rose from those present. "Do you know where they are?"

"Iraq," Lauren said.

"How can you be sure?" The man at the door demanded.

"Did you know he was in Iraq?" Lauren recoiled.

The man looked to Kitty, then glanced at the table behind them. He looked back to Kitty, and she nodded. "Dr. Pierce," he introduced himself as the Israeli ambassador, offering his hand. She took it. "Have a seat. What I'm about to tell you is top secret. Nothing you hear may leave this room. Is that clear?"

Lauren took the chair he pulled out for her and answered his question. "I understand." He glanced up at Henry who refused the seat next to his mother. Kitty took it, and the assembly returned to order.

"A few days ago, we were able to run a call to this so called warlord who claims to be *King of Sudan*." Lauren looked like she wanted to say something, but she caught herself and let him continue. "Our cyber intelligence team traced the call through a hundred connection points that led back to a base in Syria."

He turned to the screen behind the chair Kitty had

vacated, and he picked up the remote off the table. A picture appeared on the screen. "They're calling him the *Psychopath of Soba*."

"I heard about that," Lauren said.

"But psychopaths run in packs," the ambassador said, clicking the remote. Another man's image appeared on the screen. "Do you recognize him?"

"No," Lauren shook her head. The man looked like an Arabian dream. Not quite as villainous as Jafar from Alladin, but not quite as fake as Laurence of Arabia.

"This is Faadin al Khalid," he said. "We suspect Abdul, and al Khalid are in league with one another, but we're not really sure about that."

"What we do know," Kitty picked up the story. "Is that al Khalid has some association to Dr. Badr."

Lauren's head turned so fast her braid whipped over her shoulder. "What? How?"

"His daughter was a student at the university in Cairo, until just recently, when she dropped all her classes and returned to Aleppo. The college bursar pulled her file and there was a note from Tima that her father insisted she drop her classes and return home. Apparently he was angry she was enrolled in the archaeology program without his knowledge. We think that Dr. Badr was the intended target. Rowan was . . . collateral damage."

"That's one theory," Kitty said.

"Is there another?"

"There is," the ambassador said.

"I'd love to hear it," Lauren said keeping her tone measured.

"Intel revealed some interesting information about this *Psychopath* from Sudan. He seems to think he's some kind of reincarnation of Saddam Hussein."

"How is that possible? Hussein died in 2006?"

"Well, maybe that's the wrong way to put it. He's modeled

himself after the former Iraqi Prime Minister, who in turn modeled himself on King Nebuchadnezzar."

That made Lauren's brow lift as she glanced back at Kitty. "The son of Nebuchadnezzar, if you want to argue semantics," Lauren said.

"That's what he called himself."

"And Faadin al Kalid is of a similar mind? Is this speculation?" Lauren asked.

"That is hard to say. He's not on good terms with NATO, after the revolution he led in his own country."

"So, let's ask the question no one has answered. What are you doing to find my husband and Tima?" Lauren asked.

"Andrew went to Syria," Kitty said. "Undercover ops."

Lauren sat back in her chair, feeling deflated. "Fat lot of good that will do," she said. "Rowan's not in Syria."

"You said he was in Iraq?" the ambassador asked. "How can you know this?"

Lauren hesitated, not sure how to tell him what she knew without him thinking she was crazy. Rowan didn't have time for her modesty. "What I'm about to tell you can never leave this room. Are we clear?"

"LAUREN WHAT DO you think you're doing here," Kitty said, as they got in the car. Kitty had a suite at the King David Hotel, and there was more than enough room for all of them. One of the ambassador's assistants was picking up some things for them that they hadn't been able to *travel* with. The baby needed diapers and none of them had a change of clothes.

"I'm going to find my husband." Lauren wasn't joking either. Her mind was made—that no matter what it took—she wasn't going home without Rowan.

"Mom, you need to rest," Henry said. "The trip took a lot out of you, and you know it."

"I will," Lauren said. "But I'm going to look for your father. Tonight."

"No, you're not," Kitty said. "Maybe Henry can, but you're going to do no such thing."

"Like you can stop me," Lauren said.

"I'll . . . I'll call Michael," she threatened.

"You can try," she said.

Kitty furrowed her brow and tilted her head. "What do you mean by that?"

"Michael's stuck in another time zone with my father," she said.

Henry had to explain what had happened. "I don't understand," Kitty said. Her husband served the All-Father and Enki, his son. He had the power to master time and space. "Was it Enlil? Did he block them somehow?"

"That's one theory," Lauren said. "My mother said she thought somehow I'd been cursed."

Kitty started to repeat the word but choked on it. She tried again. "*Cursed?*"

"I don't understand it either," Lauren said. "But apparently there's a force strong enough to affect me physically. I have to think Enlil is the only one with that kind of power. It was strong enough send Henry, and Michael to my Father's *time place*, and then keep them from coming home when we needed them most."

"Mom," Henry took her hand. "You and Sarah could have died. You know that right?"

"And your father could still die," Lauren said. "I won't let that happen."

"None of us will, Lauren," Kitty said. "Look." Kitty put her arm around Lauren. "I have to believe that the gods put all of us in your path so that you don't have to walk it alone."

"That doesn't mean I don't have to walk it," she said. "I won't let anyone carry me. Rowan is . . . he's my . . . heart."

Her voice cracked. "I'll die before I let him leave this world without me."

"Nobody has to die," Henry said. "I've seen a future when you and Dad are watching the sunset over the mountains in Colorado, with all of us gathered around you. Your hair was white. Dad's hair was thin, and his beard was gray, so I know it was the future. But it's only one possible future. If we don't proceed with caution, it could be one that can be destroyed. Uncle Michael says it's my job to protect the timeline. That's what he trained me to do over these years."

Lauren turned to her son, recoiling as she did. "Excuse me?"

24

Rutba, Iraq
May 22nd

Not again, Rowan groaned as he realized he was in the back of a truck. He'd come to in a similar situation in Mexico just before Henry was born. He was drugged and bound then. This time, he'd been beaten to a bloody pulp, and he felt like it. Every jostling jolt sent lightning bolts through his pounding brain. It screamed in every muscle and bruise. He couldn't take it. He managed to get himself up onto his elbows, taking the pressure off bruised ribs and a possible broken tailbone.

He hadn't gotten into any kind of a fist fight for a long time, and it reminded him that he wasn't a young man anymore. Fifty wasn't far off and he'd gotten injured too many times in his life. His fractured finger throbbed with each beat of his heart. He felt the damp, oozing blood between his fingers.

Rowan could beat out the most daring stuntman in a battle of the scars, though there were a few fellow soldiers younger than him that could trump his history of injuries. It wasn't something he was proud of. He was the team's safety officer and medic for the first fifteen years of doing *The Veritas Codex*. He was supposed to keep others from getting hurt and treat them when they did. Somehow, he'd proven to be the one most likely to break a bone on camera.

Jean-René said the best one ever was when he shattered his ankle in Nepal. The rescue effort took over six hours, followed by a two-hour flight to a hospital in Katmandu. It took three hours in surgery, twelve weeks in a cast, and months of physical therapy before he could walk without a limp.

There were no cameras here, but it didn't make his injuries hurt any less. It was dark. He couldn't see the wounds, which was almost a blessing. He was glad Lauren wasn't here. She didn't need to see him like this. But, God, he needed to see her.

Did she know? Had she figured out what happened? Was she okay? His jaw shook with the realization that she might put herself in danger trying to find him. *She had all the help in the universe, but would her magic be strong enough to do anything to help him?* He hadn't considered that before. *Would she put herself at risk to save him?*

He hoped Lauren left it to the experts. She had children who needed her. In another month, they'd have one more who would need a mother. A father was no less important but keeping Lauren safe was his priority since the day he responded to an emergency at the Stanley Hotel and found her on the stairs, with a broken leg of her own.

As an EMT he'd kept a level head while tending the compound tib-fib facture. He'd flirted with the beautiful paranormal investigator who said someone had pushed her down the stairs. The tears in her eyes had made them sparkle. It was everything he could do not to ask her out as he was working to get her stabilized.

They'd lived a life of adventure. Adventure came at a cost. It came with scars. Jean-René had earned a few, too. His best friend had to view the world through a camera lens, which meant he didn't always see the stones in his path, or the ledges behind him. He'd backed off a ledge along the coast in Northern California and landed flat on his back in the Pacific Ocean, with a half-million dollar piece of camera equipment. The fall wasn't overly hard, but the camera smashed into his face and bloodied his nose. But that wasn't the worst of it. They were filming great white sharks below. A frantic rescue operation to get him out of shark infested waters began.

As much as he hadn't let himself think about Lauren, he'd pushed Jean-René's fate to the farthest recesses of his mind. He could only allow himself to believe he'd been rescued and was unharmed, safe on dry land.

"The first rule of survival is believing you're going to survive," he could hear his commanding officer say during the Combat Survival Training course. "Your mental fortitude will keep you alive longer than anything else." *Yes.* He held onto that. Lauren was safe at home with her children. Jean-René was safe on dry land. Kitty was working her *magic*. That's what would save him. *Why hadn't he thought of that before?*

They'd be home before the week was out. He began planning his survival and life after this horrible fiasco. He'd be more careful when he traveled. Maybe he'd cancel his summer plans and spend the rest of it with the kids. Maybe they'd pack up and go hike every trail in Colorado and spend time with his mom and dad before the kids went back to school. Henry would be off to college and John Carter would be starting his Junior year of high school. Jamie was still in elementary school, but he'd be starting junior high before they knew it. Sam and Kate were itching to get to kindergarten, and Lauren was looking into a HeadStart program for them so she could free up more of her time to commit to the show. Yes, that was an excellent plan. Now, he just had to focus on what he could do.

Rules of combat. Don't be afraid to hit first, Rowan thought, taking a deep breath and setting his jaw, willing his mind to detach from the pain in his body. *Protect your face.* Too late. His eye was swollen shut, again. He wouldn't make that mistake a third time. *Stay on your feet and keep moving.* He wasn't even sure he could get to his feet, but he made his mind up to do what he had to when the time came. *Hit hard, and haul ass.* He needed to find Tima and her student, Maliqa. They all needed to *haul ass* and get out of there.

Hours seemed to pass and nothing he did improved his situation. It was hot, and there was very little air. He continued with his mental practice. Desert survival had its challenges. Heat, direct sunlight, and the lack of shade—not to mention the lack of water—were the most obvious. There was nowhere to take cover if the enemy came in pursuit. He knew if he tried to dig into the sand he might as well dig his own grave. The sand held heat and snakes, and like his hero, Indiana Jones, he didn't particularly care for snakes. Scorpions either—much less sand fleas, mites, spiders, and centipedes.

Sandstorms were another potential hazard. He'd been caught in a sandstorm once before in Libya. No, that wasn't something he cared to relive either. The priorities would be to find shade, get something between them and the hot ground, and limit their movements. They would need to conserve sweat, and if they didn't have water, they couldn't eat. Eating required water for digestion and they couldn't spare the fluids.

"Mr. Pierce?" A very small voice came from between the cracks. "Are you awake?"

"Not by choice," he muttered. "Is Tima with you?"

"No," Maliqa said. "They put her in a separate crate. She's not answering me. I'm not sure she can even hear me."

"What are you doing here?"

"I don't know. Surely my father will be furious when he finds out how this man—a guest in our home—had treated me . . . treated us. This is not how guests are treated in Syria. Even if my father can be cruel, he is a gracious host."

"Where are they taking us?"

"Kish," she said. "He's looking for a weapon. My father told one of his generals the man is crazy. He does not trust this madman."

"Why would he say that?"

"Because the weapon is something from an ancient legend. He said something about Nebuchadnezzar and Sadam Hussein and his crazy stargate. What is he talking about?"

"More than two decades ago, America and Iraq were at war. Some say the US invaded Iraq because of 9/11 and the destruction of the World Trade Center. Others believe it was to keep Saddam Hussein from getting ancient alien technology in the form of a stargate."

"What is a *stargate*? What does this mean?" she asked.

"Mesopotamia used to be home to the Sumerians, the first civilization to exist. Archaeologists have dated it back to 3,000 BC."

"Older than Egypt." Maliqa's voice held a sense of wonder.

"Exactly," he said. "Some theories suppose that the Anunnaki—the ancient gods of the Sumerians—were actually aliens. *Stargates* were the hypothetical portals they used to travel between their worlds and ours."

"Ah! Tima had us read the Book of Enoch," she said. "I know this story . . . well part of it."

"*Enoch walked faithfully with the gods; then he was not . . .*" Rowan quoted.

"Because the gods took him away . . . using a *stargate*?" Her voice was heavy with wonder.

"So they say," Rowan said. "Tima thought she might know where the stargate was," he said, in confidence. "She thinks it might be beneath the ziggurat in Kish."

"That is where they are taking us," Maliqa said.

"Because he wants Tima and I to find the stargate, so he can use it to conquer the region and earn a place as supreme ruler of Sudan, if not all of the Middle East . . . maybe even the world. Listen," he hesitated, coming to the realization that her life was just as much in jeopardy as theirs were. "If you get a chance to escape, take it," he said. "You could be our life-line. You could get help."

"Tima needs help, '" Maliqa admitted. "But I don't know where to go. I don't know who will help us."

Rowan paused, considering a plan of action. His military training might serve her, at least in theory. "Kish is in the far southern portion of Iraq, a narrow swatch of land. "Iran is to the northeast. Kuwait is to the southwest. The Persian Gulf is south. Bagdad is way up north. There is a river that divides Iraq and Iran called *Shatt al-Arab*. If you find it, don't cross it. Just follow it to the coast. You'll have water. Boil it if you can. If not, don't drink anything that is acrid or smells bad. There's a better chance of finding help if you go that way, I think."

"How can you be sure?"

"I was deployed in Iraq when I was in the army," Rowan said. "It was a long time ago. Here's the thing, twenty-some years ago, no one mentioned a stargate. I have to believe it's nothing more than myth. But I never spent much time that far south. I spent most of my time in Al Anbar between Bagdad and Syria, at least before I got send to Afghanistan."

"How many people did you kill?"

"I was a medic," Rowan said. "I only fired my weapon to save my lives—mine or members of my unit."

"So less than 100?"

"Less than ten," Rowan said. "I saved more than 100. Lots more."

There was a long silence. "I hope you can save three more."

"I hope I don't have to," Rowan said.

ANDREW MILLER KNEW a thing or two about undercover operations. He arrived in Iraq prepared to blend in. He'd donned the personae of a Turkish business man, and presented credentials that named him as Ali Kaya, Turkish owner of a mining company looking to facilitate trade of bitumen. Iraq, particularly in the southern regions, was a major exporter of the petroleum derivative, commonly known in the United States as asphalt. Here, the naturally occurring deposits were formed from the remains of ancient, microscopic diatoms and other once-living things. *The Fertile Cresent* no longer existed as it once had, but that didn't make it any less valuable.

"Welcome to Iraq," the customs agent stamped his passport and let him past the check point.

"Well done," the voice in his earpiece said as Andrew—Ali—moved through the bustling airport. "One might think you were a native speaker."

"I'm going to need all the help I can get," Andrew said, gazing up at the messaging board, relieved that it wasn't entirely in Arabic. English was included as well. "Next challenge, renting a car."

His multi-lingual translator back in DC walked him through the process and directed him to the rental service. The agent, as it turned out, was fluent in English, but didn't speak a lick of Turkish. His coach suggested a few words to stumble over, as most native speakers did not and it made for an amusing game of cat and mouse that Andrew might have enjoyed, had the stakes not been so high. Lauren and Kitty had a wild idea that Rowan and his professor might be in Iraq. Knowing Dr. Badr and Rowan were already scheduled to go to Kish on an archaeological expedition made Andrew doubtful that they might end up in the one place they were expected to be, but knowing Lauren, he knew better than to question her theory.

When he began to suspect she was up to something—her

lies attempting to cover up her sudden arrival in Mexico—he had no idea the magnitude of the situation. It fell on him to help cover her ruse back then, but now he knew everything. Her story was more outlandish than he could have ever imagined. But he knew Lauren. He trusted her and didn't doubt she had some kind of force working in her favor. He couldn't explain it, but that didn't make it any less true.

He had done some incredible things in his life. He could make people believe he was a Turkish business man, and that was something akin to magic, too. *Wasn't it?* Andrew was relieved to find the drive to the ancient archeological site wasn't terribly far. His liaison had made arrangements for him at a guest house not far from the airport, and even arranged for his evening meal. He could get up early and make the hour and a half drive to the site where his liaison had scheduled a meeting with one of the local mining companies, as a cover. He needed to lay eyes on the site and find out what was going on, and if Rowan and Dr. Badr were seen by anyone there. He didn't know what to expect, and he didn't know what he would find.

He was glad he didn't have to make the drive tonight. His body was on the wrong side of the planet. Tonight, all he wanted was food and a bed. In the morning, he'd grab a hot shower and a coffee, then hit the road.

Everyone has a plan until they get hit in the face, he reminded himself as his host welcomed him and he realized they wouldn't be serving dinner for another hour. He was offered a coffee which he accepted with gratitude toward his host. The owner led him to a small sitting room. Pillows were scattered on the floor and a low table sat in the middle.

He'd never spent much time in Iraq, but he had studied the culture and the customs of its people. He also had an ace up his sleeve, or more properly, a guide in his ear. He knew it was considered polite to accept everything he was offered, so when one of the women in a black birkas brought in a tray of refreshments, he knew he wouldn't starve before dinner was served.

DINNER ENDED up being a long drawn out affair, with six other guests in residence that evening. It was late when he collapsed into bed, and his body completely betrayed him by allowing him to sleep through his alarm. The sun was up when he arrived at the cloverleaf where his GPS told him to exit. A convoy of military vehicles blocked the exit, and it looked like one of them had a flat tire. He sat, debating what to do, and checking the GPS for an alternate route, but found nothing. He put the car in park and got out.

"May I be of assistance?" he managed in Arabic.

"Go back to your vehicle," one of the armed guards answered. The translation came through his earpiece. Andrew was able to see that two of the soldiers were straining to get a lug nut off the truck tire, which was indeed flat. Everyone else stood around watching.

"Will this take very long? I'm late for a meeting."

The man lifted his gun but didn't direct it at him. "I said go back to your car."

Andrew lifted his hands to show he wasn't a threat. Under his breath he muttered in English, "Dang, don't blame a fella' for trying to help."

ROWAN HEARD English being spoken outside the truck where he was secured inside a wooden crate. The distinct Texas drawl had a familiar ring to it. "Hey, Cowboy," he managed, but his voice lacked the forte he would have liked to have used. He also knew there were soldiers around, so he couldn't punch it too hard either. "Hey!" he tried a little harder.

"Rowan?" His own name had never come as music to his ears. "Andrew Miller."

"Miller? What are you doing here?"

"Lauren sent me," he said, his voice coming from a lower level.

"You gotta get us out of here," Rowan said, tears flooding his face as relief washed through him.

"I'm working on it," he said.

"Hey!" Someone shouted in Arabic outside the truck. Rowan could only listen to the exchange as Miller was berated by the guards. He managed to talk his way out of it. Rowan didn't realize Andrew spoke Arabic. He'd met the FBI agent when Lauren went missing at Mount Saint Helen's and returned injured and unable to tell anyone what had happened. Miller and his partner Joshua Morrison joined them when they returned to the mountain in search of answers. Morrison died on Mount Saint Helen's at the hands of a vicious diamond thief—the same diamond thief that had kidnapped Lauren and made it look like she'd been abducted by Bigfoot. Since then, Miller had helped them catch an antiquities thief in Mexico and was present at the birth of their oldest son, Henry. Rowan hadn't seen him in almost twenty years, but he was relieved to know he wasn't alone. Lauren had sent the best FBI agent they knew to help him get home. Now, Miller knew where he was, and Andrew wouldn't leave Iraq without him, he was certain of it.

"*Eagle Base*, I need to get a message to *White Dove*," Miller said into the com when he got into the car. The liaison on the other end didn't respond. He knew the change in the formality of his request required a change of security protocols—and those listening in. He waited 'til he heard a different voice answer in his earpiece.

"This is *Big Dog*," the voice said. "Go for *White Dove*. What is the message?"

"I have eyes on *Hawkeye*. Confirm—proof of life. *Hawkeye* is alive."

There was a long pause. "Repeat message, *Eagle*."

"Repeat *Hawkeye* has been spotted."

"What is your six?"

Miller pulled up the coordinates on his GPS. "32°32'34.0"N 44°35'09.1"E," Miller said, repeating them.

"Identify support needed," Frank said.

"Hold and monitor," Miller said. "Intel is lacking."

"Do you need satellite back up?"

"Affirmative." He hadn't even considered getting a satellite on the truck. "Military convoy at this location. Third vehicle from the back. Monitor and advise."

"Any word on *Nefertiti*?"

"No," he said. "No intel on *Nefertiti*."

"Copy. Standby."

Andrew opened the car windows as the day grew sweltering hot. Unable to move until the tire was fixed, he no longer minded the delay. It gave the satellites time to convene on the location. He would have given anything for an ice cold Dr. Pepper, but he doubted anyone in Iraq even knew what Dr. Pepper was.

"Satellite will be in place by 2300," Big Dog's voice squelched in his earpiece. "Can you get a beacon on board?"

Andrew had a beacon—a low-powered carrier that could transmit telemetry data, but getting close enough to the truck to secure it might be problematic. "Negative," he said. "I have an idea where they're going, and I have eyes on them. Activating beacon *Roger-13-66-Charlie*, he said, taking the tiny device out of the pocket of his bag beside him. He hit the green button to activate it. A blue light appeared on the end and flashed, like a Bluetooth device trying to connect to another device. When it turned green, Andrew knew they had him.

"Activated," *Big Dog* said a moment later. "Advise."

Miller provided only the information he could confirm. He kept his theories to himself. Then as an afterthought, he added. "And tell *Momma Bear* I'll bring him home."

"Copy. Will continue to monitor. Advise if assistance is needed."

"Will do. Stand by."

"Standing by."

Miller took the small device and tucked it under his shirt, securing it to the back side of his shirt pocket. If his position was compromised they might find it, but this was the best he could do, for the time being.

It took over an hour for the soldiers to get the tire changed on the truck in front of the one where Rowan was being held. Miller spent that time observing and listening. His translator caught a few words here and there, but none of it seemed of any consequence to either of them.

When truck engines began to rumble to life, Miller started the rental car and rolled the windows back up, turning the AC back on. He'd run it for short periods of time, at first, to conserve fuel, but in the end it wasn't helping so he gave up. Now he turned it to max and buckled his seatbelt prepared for the journey to continue. He no longer cared about his *meeting*, but he turned the GPS back on because he knew he had to keep up appearances.

He was surprised with the first five trucks pulled out, including the truck Rowan was in, but the others didn't move. The soldier who'd chewed him out early sauntered back to his car.

"This exit is closed," he said curtly.

"For how long?" Andrew asked.

"Indefinitely," he snapped.

"But I have a meeting . . ."

"Meetings are cancelled. Go back to Baghdad. You have no business here. Not anymore."

"But?" Miller started to protest then froze when he heard multiple clicks. He looked ahead to see six soldiers with their semiautomatic weapons aimed at his car. "Why didn't you tell me an hour ago?" The man turned to his team and their weapons raised as if to fire. "I'm leaving."

Andrew put the car in reverse and backed up. The soldiers seemed satisfied as he turned and drove off. "Sounds like something changed," the translator was back in his ear.

"You could say that," Miller said, looking for a place to turn around and get off the road.

25

Jerusalem, Israel
May 22nd

Lauren put her feet up while she nursed the baby, watching the local news on the television in the ambassador's office. His staff made themselves scarce on the pretense of preparing a late dinner to be brought in. Kitty was on the phone with her boss in Washington and Henry was asleep on the sofa nearby.

Lauren had accomplished the primary purpose of her mission. Kitty had gotten word to Andrew to go to Iraq. He'd sent back a cryptic message earlier that morning that he'd gotten eyes on Rowan and could confirm he was there, and he was alive. That was enough for her—provisionally. Andrew would do anything he could to help bring Rowan home, and she knew it.

"Lauren?" She realized Kitty was standing in front of her. "Are you okay?"

"Yeah," she said, glancing at the baby. Sarah had fallen asleep. "I'm fine. What's up?"

"You were a million miles away," Kitty said, sitting beside her. "Do you want to go back to the hotel? Get some sleep?"

"No." Lauren hoisted the baby up onto her shoulder. Sarah was gaining weight, and it made Lauren's heart swell. She looked forward to handing her husband a healthy little girl when he came home. That was the image she held in her mind. It was probably the only thing that kept her functional at the moment. "I'll wait 'til we hear something from Andrew."

"Ambassador Segal is having dinner brought in for us," Kitty said. "You have hardly eaten all day. You're worrying me." She took Lauren's hand. "Are you sure you're okay?"

Lauren hesitated long enough to cast doubt. "I'll be okay when Rowan is safe," she managed to say. "Beyond that, I can't promise much."

"Your friend Agent Miller seems like a capable guy."

"He is," Lauren said. "That's the only reason I'm able to function. I trust Andrew more than almost anyone. He knows all my secrets, and he believes most of them."

Kitty angled her head with a mischievous grin. "Does anyone truly know *all* your secrets, Lauren?"

"Valid point," Lauren admitted.

"Look," Kitty squeezed the hand she still held. "Between me and Andrew, we're doing everything we can to bring Rowan home. For now, it has to be enough. Is that fair?"

"It is, but I'm not going to let you boss me around."

"I never said I would," Kitty said. "But I am going to call you out if you're not doing your part. We're going to start with dinner, and at some point, I'm taking you back to the hotel where you will take a hot bath and go to bed. I'll watch Sarah while you do it."

Lauren considered her for a moment. "When I'm ready to go to the hotel, I'll let you know."

"Have you talked to your mother since you arrived?"

"I called her after the message from Andrew came in," she

said. "I hope you told Frank how much I appreciated the message." Frank—also known as *Big Dog*—was in charge of the joint operations. It wasn't uncommon for federal agencies to work together on an important mission. Homeland Security and FBI shared similar jurisdictions in certain aspects when it came to preventing war and protecting its citizens. While Rowan Pierce might not have normally been considered a high value asset, his relationship to Lauren and his involvement in first contact with an alien species moved him up the ranks. He had information enemy forces didn't need to access. He was also a soldier, trained to endure torture and protect sensitive information.

"I did," Kitty said. "We've chatted via a secure connection. Nothing's come in since that last message this morning. We have to give him time to do his work. Undercover operations are a lesson in patience. You understand that, right?"

"I do," Lauren said.

Kitty glanced up as Ambassador Segal entered the expansive office, holding the doors for members of his team as they brought in food and set it up on the large conference table. Henry bolted up and looked at his mother blankly for a moment.

"Is it time to eat?"

"Do you have a hollow leg?" Kitty stood and put her arm around her nephew.

"Gabe doesn't eat like he's always starving?" Lauren asked.

"Only every day," Kitty smirked.

Over dinner, the ambassador updated them on other events going on. The initial purpose of Kitty's trip was overshadowed by the attack on Soba and the peace accord meetings now focused on how to manage this rogue warlord. "We all recognize that his is not a legitimate claim to leadership," Daniel said. "We're working with Sudan's existing government to identify the appropriate course of action."

"Presuming you can find him," Lauren began. "What's the recourse?"

"Sudan is not a member of NATO," Kitty said. "But if they cooperate, and we capture him, they could recognize NATO's right to try him for war crimes."

"Has that ever happened before?" Henry asked.

"It has," Daniel said. "The UN Security Council set up a commission of experts in 1992—a few years before your time, son—to gather evidence of war crimes allegedly committed by the former Yugoslavian President Slobodan Milosevic. He stood trial in The Hague."

"I learned about him in history class. He was called the *Butcher of the Balkans*," Henry said.

"A similar trial was held for the former Kosovo leader Hashim Thaçi, and three others charged with war crimes and crimes against humanity," Kitty added.

"So, his actions would be considered an act of war?" Lauren asked, thinking of the missive issued by Enki so many years ago. He told her to prepare. She'd made that her life's work for many years. She read all the ancient texts, honed her abilities, and raised five children in those years. She had been preparing as best as she could, but not knowing what to expect made it difficult. She followed the philosophy *that the best preparation for tomorrow was doing her best each and every day*. She'd kept herself in the best physical shape possible—between having babies—and she'd advanced her education. She read everything she could find about ancient Sumerian gods, legends from Mesopotamia, and other religions from around the world. She read philosophy, poetry, self-help books and even— occasionally—a modern novel.

The words of William Butler Yeats also nagged on her mind. *"Life is a long preparation for something that never happens."* Well, if this *Psychopath of Soba* had his way with it, war would come, and that could very easily unleash the powers of evil from the very gates of Hell.

Lauren knew she wasn't the same woman who'd stared down the devil, taken arms against him, and defeated him with the strongest weapon known to mankind. She wasn't as young as she was then. Her hair was graying, and she had crow's feet around her eyes—wrinkles at the corners of her mouth. *Laugh lines*, that's what Rowan called them. It was better to laugh than to cry, and they'd had plenty of years together to do both. Fortunately, their life was filled with more laughter than tears.

Lauren glanced at Sarah, who squirmed in her sling, turning her head up to gaze at her mother. She hadn't cried or fussed all day. "Want me to take her," Henry offered, holding out his hands.

"Sure," Lauren said. Henry wiped out his meal in under twenty minutes. Lauren was still picking at her food. She took Sarah from the sling and passed her off to her older brother. Henry took her and got up from the table, walking over to the window to look at the setting sun.

Returning her attention to her food, Lauren realized Kitty had a point. She needed to keep her strength up. Rowan would need her, and she had to be ready to answer the call when the time came. With that she finished her dinner while the conversation continued around her.

As she drained her glass, a woman stepped in and leaned down between Daniel and Kitty delivering a message in a tone so low she couldn't hear what was being said. Daniel and Kitty seemed taken aback and looked at one another with expressions of dread and disbelief on their faces.

"What is it?" Lauren asked when the aide left. "Did something happen?"

"The Syrian ambassador from Aleppo has asked to address the council tomorrow. He has concerns about an enemy that has attacked him in his home. His daughter is missing."

"What's that mean?" Lauren asked.

"I doubt it has anything to do with Rowan," Kitty said. "Nothing for you to worry about."

"He's petitioned to have Syria recognized by NATO— more than once. Perhaps with all the attention on Sudan he might feel like NATO could use another ally." Daniel glanced at Kitty, folding the note, and tucking it in his shirt pocket.

"Or he's afraid it's all going to blow up in his face," Henry said, turning from the window.

"Out of the mouths of babes," Daniel said, winking at Lauren.

"Daniel's right," Kitty said. "I think we've had a long day. Let's finish our dinner and go back to the hotel."

ROWAN MANAGED to hold his feet underneath him, but he couldn't stand up straight—not yet anyway. His tailbone throbbed and his head spun. "Move!" Abdul smacked him across the side of his head, making him stumble. He staggered and limped, moving away from his enemy, realizing Maliqa had found Tima. It was everything the girl could do to keep her professor on her feet and moving forward.

Rowan glanced up, as the moon appeared between the clouds, casting a blue glow on the desert landscape. The Ziggurat of Kish stood as a dark shadow in the distance. Military trucks and heavy equipment circled the site.

Shouting came from that direction, then there was gun fire. Out of instinct, Rowan dropped to the ground. Maliqa followed his example, covering Tima with her own body. The flash of the rifles illuminated the clearing as the fire-fight seemed rather one sided. The shouting seemed to subside, and as quickly as it began, the fight was over.

Abdul walked over and kicked Rowan. "On your feet!" He demanded.

Rowan moved, taking his time.

"We've secured the ziggurat," Scar Face was breathless when he approached his commander.

"Casualties?"

"None, at least not on our side," he said.

The wicked innuendo told Rowan there were casualties. Most likely innocent men and women, workers, and scientists like himself—like Lauren—like Tima.

"What of the research teams we were told to find?"

"They are here," Scar Face said.

Rowan made it up onto his hands and knees.

"Take these three." Abdul turned to Rowan, putting a finger in his face. "You will find my stargate. Find it, or I will kill every last one of you."

He shoved Rowan with a ferocity he hadn't shown initially. Rowan managed to keep his feet, but at great pains to his back. Scar Face gave him a second shove, just for good measure. He fell hard, upended, and off balance, landing with a groan. When Scar Face started towards Tima, Rowan balled up his strength and stood, blocking his path. "I'll help her."

"You can't even walk yourself." Scar Face mocked.

"No thanks to you," Rowan muttered under his breath, helping Maliqa get Tima to her feet. "We stay together," Rowan whispered between the three of them. "No matter what."

Maliqa nodded. Tima locked eyes with Rowan and did the same.

26

Ancient Site of Kish, Iraq
May 22nd

Andrew saw the flash of the weapons between the crumbling ruins, before he heard the gunfire. He recognized the sound of the artillery and knew it was from the weapons he'd seen the military brandishing that morning. It'd taken him all day to find a way to access the site. He'd abandoned his car several miles away and made it the rest of the way on foot. He took cover behind a boulder that had once formed a column that supported a massive ancient building. The building now looked like a broken LEGO building, dotted with holes where creatures had burrowed, and birds nested. A wall stood along the back perimeter of the site dotted with shadows from scrub brush that flickered on the breeze. Rocks and chat cracked beneath his boots as a figure appeared on the top of one of the crumbling structures—a sentinel with a rifle, scanning for threats. In the far distance, a cliff wall showed the dark layers of earth where ancient workers built a fortress wall to protect the temples and other structures.

The night turned cold, and daylight wouldn't warm the cooling sands for at least another eight hours. Andrew made sure he wasn't casting a shadow that might give away his position. The sentinel paused to light a cigarette as Andrew checked his own weapon. *Those things will kill you, brother. If I don't have to do it first*, he thought. More gunfire echoed across the massive site. The sentinel turned to see what was going on, but sauntered away as if it was no concern of his.

Andrew knew what the gunfire meant. If the *Psychopath of Soba* wanted something from this site, and he was willing to do anything to take over the location. It wasn't hard to figure out. Anyone who'd hidden from the initial onslaught were now being rounded up and dispatched. Resistance was futile. Lives were being lost.

Rowan wasn't at any risk of being killed so long as he served a purpose. Rowan was an archeologist, Fatima Badr was, too. The nutjob needed money. He needed someone to help him find whatever there was of value. He had reason to believe there was treasure of some kind or another. He must have intended to use Rowan and Dr. Badr to get it, by any means necessary.

"*Eagle* to *Big Dog*," he said into his com, checking his six. He waited for the change in protocol. It took a lot longer than it did the last time.

A gruff voice answered back. "Go for *Big Dog*."

"Sorry to wake you, figured it was daylight there," Andrew said, breaking protocol.

"Heroes gotta sleep sometime," Frank answered. "Figured you'd find a place to get some rack time."

"Negative," Andrew said. "I wouldn't want to miss the fireworks display."

There was a pause on the other end. "Casualties?"

"Unable to determine."

"Any sign of *Hawkeye* or *Nefertiti*?"

"Negative," he said. "I'm working on a plan. Preparing to engage."

"Negative, *Eagle*. Do not engage."

"I may not have a choice," Miller said. "Where's my eyes in the skies? Where's my bogie?"

There was a pause. "Confirmed satellite telemetry on the target identified at 0900. It's stationary, approximately 50 yards due north."

"Human count?"

"Standby," Frank said. Andrew knew this would take a minute. Getting a head count on potentially moving targets from a satellite more than 20 miles overhead. "Last orbit, visible count was twenty-six."

"I can confirm at least that," Andrew muttered to himself, freezing when he heard the crunching of footfalls running towards him. A man ran past him, a blurred shadow in the moonlight, then he heard the buzz of a bullet, and the runner collapsed less than ten feet from his position. There was shouting from the circle of trucks and more gunfire, then, it seemed to go silent. "Make that twenty-five," he muttered under his breath. "Will continue to monitor. *Eagle*, out."

He expected someone to come to retrieve the body. No one did. He waited for more than a quarter hour before he moved and peered out around the boulder. The troops were offloading cargo from the truck. No one seemed to be paying any attention to the fallen man. Andrew took a chance and moved closer, intent on checking for a pulse. However, as soon as he approached, he knew it would be unnecessary. The bullet hit him in the back of the head and the puddle of blood pooling around him told Andrew everything he needed to know.

Andrew riffled through the man's pockets, but found no identification, nothing he could use later to ensure the next of kin were identified. He also didn't have a weapon of any kind. By his attire, Andrew could guess that he was a younger man.

Most older Iraqi men went for the more traditional attire. This man wore a khaki shirt, and khaki pants. His clothes were stained with red soil, which suggested he was a worker, perhaps part of the archeology team here at the historic site. This man was slightly built, short, and dark haired. Miller remembered Pierce being tall and beefy. This man was neither. It wasn't Rowan.

ROWAN WAS FORCED along a narrow hall to an even more narrow stairway. He helped Tima as much as he could, but it was a struggle for him, too. It felt like a maze. The stairs and corridors seemed to continue forever, twisting, and winding their way into the depths beneath the ancient Ziggurat. At the bottom, he found a dimly lit room where an excavation cut another four feet into the foundation, leaving voids in the ground. He moved closer to see what they'd found, but recoiled when he realized four bodies lay face down in one of the excavations. Each had a bullet hole in the back of the head.

He turned around and put his arms around Tima and Maliqa. "Don't look."

"Is this where I will find my Stargate?" Abdul demanded, following his men and their prisoners into the room.

"Yes," Tima muttered, so softly only Rowan and Maliqa heard it.

"Maybe," Rowan said. He thought of the library they'd discovered in Alexandria while he was in college. "I'll need time to inspect the excavations."

Abdul considered him a moment. "You have twelve hours, Mr. Pierce. Maybe less. Best not to squander your time."

The soldiers left them to their work, but guards were placed at the narrow entry. "Tima," Rowan said. "You sounded so confident. How can you be sure this is the place?"

"The ancient texts I've spent my life studying . . . have lead me *here*." She spoke with an unsteady voice. Maliqa helped settle her. "*The Book of Daniel . . . The Book of Enoch . . . The Tome of Asmodeus . . . Josiah's History of the Hittites* . . . each of them tell their own version of the legend . . . of a portal where heaven and earth meet . . . where Enoch walked with god, then was no more . . . where Shadrack, Meshach and Abendigo walked through the flames but were not consumed."

"The fiery furnace," Rowan muttered. Across the room, a large fireplace was built into the stone. The hearth was every bit twenty feet wide and ten feet deep. It was taller than Rowan by almost double his height. Rowan moved passed the various excavations, finding more bodies within. Abdul's men had been busy. If there were survivors, he hadn't seen any.

"What is this?" Maliqa had never seen anything like it.

"This is a fireplace," Rowan said, running a hand up the wall. "There's soot and scorching on the stone. You can almost smell the ancient creosote."

"A city like Kish would need to feed thousands," Tima said. "A great hearth like that would be a necessity."

"But there's no wood for fires like this?"

Rowan considered that thought. "Maybe not now, but . . . this was the heart of the fertile crescent."

Rowan walked the length of it trying to work out the logistics. A cook would need access to whatever they were cooking, and the very size of this space alone would require the cook to walk through the flames to access the back of it. It would be a waste of space and fire wood to have something this large just for heating. Rowan said as much.

"It wasn't always a desert, Rowan *darling*."

"No, but still . . . the amount of fuel needed for something like this . . ." Rowan allowed his voice to trail off as he turned and paced the perimeter of the space. The scent of creosote and ancient mysteries filled the air around him. He felt dizzy and weak and for a moment he had to wonder if the air was stale. *Carbon monoxide?*

"Rowan!" Maliqa was at his elbow before he realized he was on his knees. "You should come lie down with Tima. You're too badly injured."

"I don't have time to be injured," he said, forcing himself to get up.

"But something is wrong," she insisted.

"There's something about this area," he said, moving away. "Do you smell anything?"

Maliqa took a deep breath and winced. "It reminds me of a refinery."

Rowan tried to think. "Not phosgene. Not hydrocarbon . . . hydrogen sulfide? Maybe."

"Why would an ancient temple smell like a refinery?" Tima asked, her voice echoing across the expanse.

"It could be natural gas, but . . ." Rowan's heel caught on one of the stones as he walked backward. He stumbled and fell, as the ground beneath him shuttered, and collapsed. The void was all around him and his stomach protested as he fell, tumbling ass-over-tea-kettle backwards.

27

Jerusalem
May 23rd

Kitty and Daniel were back at the embassy before dawn. The Syrian ambassador, Rafiq Zahari, arrived a few hours later, and accepted coffee and refreshments before they got down to business. "President al Khalid has authorized me to petition NATO for admission—*again*," the man said, after all the pleasantries of diplomacy were exchanged. "As a show of his good faith, I bring you a bit of intelligence you may find useful considering your current situation and the tentative nature of *The Great Accord*, after the unfortunate events in Sudan . . ." he paused. "...and *Egypt*."

Daniel furrowed his brow. "*Egypt?*" They'd done everything they could to keep news of the attack on a University of Cairo research vessel in the Red Sea under wraps. News of the tensions between Sudan and the rest of the world were too big to keep from the media, but so far, news of Rowan & Tima's plight were not being aired, so far as they knew.

"We know about your brother-in-law," he said, taking a

folder from his briefcase, pushing it toward Kitty. "And his professor."

"How could you know this?" Daniel asked as Kitty took it but didn't open it.

"Many nations come to us looking for allies," Ambassador Zahari said. "Our president is wise and listens to them all, but he is also discerning and knows when to decline aid."

"So this *Psychopath of Soba* came to your president? What did he want?"

"Money. Weapons. *Friends*."

"Don't they always," Daniel muttered to Kitty. She had the folder open and took out documents, showing surveillance photographs of Rowan and Tima, along with their captors. Rowan's face was battered, and he looked haggard and gaunt. He was unshaved, dressed in what looked like medical scrubs, but in tan. Tima wasn't in much better shape. Her hair was disheveled, and she had dark circles under her eyes. Both had bruises on their faces. "When were these taken?"

"Less than 24 hours ago," Zahari said.

"And why are you bringing them to us now?" Daniel added.

"Keep going," he pointed to the pictures as Kitty flipped through them. The last picture showed a line of prisoners being loaded into a truck. Rowan was seen looking back over his shoulder, past Tima to a young woman, also in chains.

"Three hostages? Who's the third?" Kitty asked, studying the picture closely.

"Maliqa al Kalid . . ."

"She is our president's daughter," the ambassador said. "Taken captive from her own home."

"Your president was involved in taking and hiding these hostages?"

"No," Zahari said. "Our president believes your man and his teacher were brought to our country by this rogue Sudanese Warlord as proof of his power and might. When we refused to aid his coup, he got angry and packed up his army —if you can call it that—they left without a word. It wasn't until several hours later that Maliqa was reported missing. That's when our security advisors pulled the videos and printed off these stills. Our president comes to NATO to beg for aid in returning his daughter safely. He will offer his entire army to support NATO if military action is warranted. He also has his allies in Iraq."

"Why don't you go to his ambassadors to negotiate her safe return?" Kitty asked, pushing the pictures toward Daniel for him to inspect.

"Because the *Psychopath of Soba* . . . has no ambassadors."

Daniel glanced up, then looked to Kitty. "Well, that does make it difficult, doesn't it?"

"Mom?" Henry came to Lauren just as she was nodding off. She hadn't slept well. The baby had fussed most of the night, which wasn't normal. It left her feeling restless and ill-at-ease. Long after the sun tinged her room at the King David Hotel a bright pink hue, Lauren lay wide awake.

"What is it, son?" she muttered.

"I'm going to go to the market and see what they have for breakfast. Do you want me to take Sarah so you can sleep?"

"Sure," Lauren said. "Don't be long and do be careful."

"Of course," Henry leaned over and kissed her. "If I find anything to eat, I'll bring something back."

Lauren patted his hand and finally drifted off. Somewhere in her dreams she found herself walking through a dark cavern. Her bare feet were cold against the stone floor that was damp. Water dripped like clear icy rain and collected in delicate shimmering pools. A soft glow illuminated the surface and beckoned Lauren to continue though the void. The pulse of her own heart thrummed in her ears, urging her forward. The tinkling of trickling water reminded her of their last hike in Sequoia National Park. The day began brightly, but before noon, the sun's warmth and light disappeared behind thick clouds that formed high above the trees. Rain fell in a gentle shower that continued for hours, leaving them cold and soaked. The abandoned mining village they'd come to investigate was all but consumed by the forest.

Among the sky-reaching timbers, Lauren felt the shadow of eyes on her the entire day, as something moved in the periphery of her vision. Tree limbs fell without cause behind her. There had once been a time when Lauren didn't believe in ghosts or supernatural forces. Now—after everything she'd seen—she found herself a little more open to the possibility. The scientist still felt the need for empirical proof, and data would be her path to enlightenment. She'd come home with plenty of data that day, but little proof of anything unreal.

Now, she felt eyes on her again. The shadows of missing souls seemed to follow her as she moved cautiously. "Hello?" Her voice resounded off the cavern walls coming back in a series of echoes that grew louder rather than more faint. Clamping her hands over her ears she hurried along the corridor. Rounding a turn, the source of the light became evident. A large rectangular portal filled the cavernous space.

It was a room, Lauren realized, not a cavern. The stones that constructed the wall were precise, though of varying sizes. Markings like giant sparrow's feet cut into the stones surrounding the void. The center of the rectangle reminded Lauren of the computer generated special effects in a Star Trek movie. It glowed a sickly green but was translucent with a cloudiness like smoke. It reminded her of a force field. As she moved closer, it seemed to shimmer, as if her presence affected it like drops of water rippling on a pond.

Something moved, drawing her gaze up and she realized there were vines—maybe roots—hanging down through the ceiling. They swayed in a light breeze she couldn't feel but could only sense.

As she reached the point of the cavern where a round stone indicated the center, the markings around the portal seemed illuminated. The symbols were similar to ancient cuneiform, which was used for multiple languages in ancient times, but something wasn't right. Lauren couldn't read the words.

For a woman with the gift of the All-Language, that was out of place. Over the past two decades she hadn't found a language she couldn't read—couldn't translate. This was an outlier.

She moved closer, intending to make sense of it all, but froze when a form appeared on the other side of the force-field. First it appeared as a black shadow, then as a golden-haired goddess, dressed in gossamer robes. Gold cuffs adorned her wrists and a mantle of gold and precious gems rested over her shoulders and around her thin neck.

Lauren locked eyes with her, and they held one another's gaze for a long moment. She was small, but elegantly made.

"Uh, hello?" Lauren finally spoke to break the awkward silence.

"*Aki nos dia'ü,*" she said, with a nod of her head. *Well met.*

The language wasn't one Lauren had ever heard, but she had read it in ancient texts. *Akkadian maybe?* "My name is Lauren."

"I am called *Kamadme.*" Lauren took a step back. She knew who this was. She was known by another name. *Lamashtu.*

"I see you know of me," the demoness said, smiling impishly. Despite her heart-shaped face and Cindy-Lou Who innocence, Lauren knew who she really was. The *Mother of Lies.* The *Killer of the Unborn.* The *Daughter of Anu. Sister of Enlil.* She was just as evil as her brother, if not more so.

She was so evil the legends said she bore seven names and was described as seven witches in incantations. She was the enemy of pregnant mothers and was known to steal infants from their mother's breasts, gnaw on their bones, and drain their blood. She was the Mother of Vampires, and Lauren was relieved to know that Sarah was safe with her brother, who would protect her with his very life, if necessary. She prayed it wouldn't come to that.

Great is the daughter of Heaven who tortures babies. Her hand is a net, her embrace is death. She is cruel, raging, angry, predatory. The words came to her from one of the ancient texts she'd read so many years ago. *She touches the bellies of women in labor and—with no child of her own—she takes the babies of others.* The rest of the incantation could be used to summon her brother, but Lauren refused to even think of it.

"Are you the one responsible for my recent illness?"

"The scent of your suckling is still upon you." The demon smiled but did not answer Lauren's question. "My brother bade me seek thee, and here, you come to me."

"Has your brother told you how I defeated him and his minions?"

"I don't see your sword . . . or your *Protector* now."

"That doesn't mean I can't defeat you, if you intend to challenge me," Lauren said, forcing confidence into her voice. She didn't know what her purpose was here, or why the demon came to her in her dreams, but clearly, this had something to do with what was happening to Rowan.

"Please, Mother," she said, her voice misty and saccharine sweet. "We are not enemies. Women are makers of peace, are we not?"

"Yes, but I know you for what you *really* are, and it's a whole different thing."

Lamashtu laughed. "That may be true. Perhaps that is my purpose in coming to you, to tell you of what is to be—of what is to come."

Lauren crossed her arms and widened her stance, letting one hip cock to the side. It was a pose of confidence, but also one of preparedness. If the demon attacked, Lauren would be ready to stay on her feet and lunge at the first sign of trouble.

"I come with a message . . . and a warning," Lamashtu said. "The end of days is at hand. My brother's powers grow, and his armies build. When the time comes, no force on earth can stop his onslaught, not even you."

"Is that supposed to frighten me?"

"Perhaps," she said, pacing calmly in front of the glowing force field. "But already, I have set the board to capture your King." The woman's image faded into nothing. Behind the rippling mist, Rowan appeared, standing on the other side. He gazed over Lauren's head as if studying the writing above the opposite side of the portal. Flames grew from embers in the markings around the gate. Brimstone burned in Lauren's nostrils.

Tima stood beside him, and Lauren's heart broke to see them both in such poor shape. Tima clutched an injured hand to her breast. Rowan's bandaged hand was injured, too, and Lauren feared the worst. Tima shuffled up to Rowan's side like a creature from *The Walking Dead*. A girl stood behind them, as they all gazed up at the arch of the portal.

"What does it say?" Rowan's voice came through like an echo across time and space.

"Lauren would know," Tima said, her voice gruff and faint.

"Is that Akkadian?" the girl asked. Lauren didn't know this young woman, but she seemed to be in better shape than the others. She was bright-eyed and curious.

"It's cuneiform, but hard to say what language."

"You will read it, and you will make my weapon work!" A man appeared and kicked Rowan in the back of the leg. He buckled in a pained cry that pierced Lauren's heart.

The black man with a scarred face grabbed Tima by the hair and pulled her back. He forced her to her knees then put his sword against her throat. "Read." The voice was so deep it made the ground around Lauren's feet shake. "Read!" he screamed, spittle flying on her face. Tima flinched, crying out.

"Leave her alone!" Rowan moved to charge, but his knee failed him, and he went down hard.

"Read."

The man raised the blade, threatening. Tima looked up, tears pouring over her cheeks. "I don't know this language! I swear it. I would read it if I could."

"Let her go!" Rowan struggled to get up, but men moved in and pulled him to his feet, dragging him back.

Lauren recognized *The Psychopath of Soba* as he rounded on Rowan. "Then *you* read it!"

"I don't know it either!"

"You know the words." Lamashtu slithered behind her, her lips so close to Lauren's ears she could feel her hot breath. "Tell him the words. Spare your friend's life."

"I don't know the words either," Lauren muttered, frozen, stiff with fear. Her eyes returned to the blazing symbols. None of it made any sense.

"Read the words or she dies!" The man with the sword yelled again.

"Don't do it, Rowan!" Tima said, as if he might actually be able to read them.

"Read!" The order came again as the leader leaned over Tima and screamed the words in her face.

When she said nothing, he rose and turned away, walking towards Rowan. He lifted a hand and flicked a finger. The scene began to unfold in slow motion. Rowan pitched forward, fighting to free himself as the man with the scarred face raised his sword over his head. Tima was already on her knees, sobbing, tears dampening the ground before her.

"No!!!!" Lauren cried out, unable to do anything to stop what was happening. She made a run at the portal but hit it like a window pane and fell back, landing on her rump amidst the celadon flames that grew higher. Pain echoed in her body, as her scream reverberated off the walls around her. Lamashtu began to cackle with delight.

The blade came down with a sharp twang. Lauren could hear it hit bone and slice through flesh. With a sickening thud, the professor's head hit the ground and rolled forward. Tima's eyes were turned towards Lauren. She blinked twice. And just like that, the light in her eyes was gone. It was over.

Lauren lay on the ground, stretching out a hand toward her friend and mentor, tears poured from her eyes as she cried out in agony. Her heart twisted into knots. Across the expanse of time and space, a gut-wrenching sob escaped Rowan's throat which only added to Lauren's grief. The girl rushed forward and stood over the lifeless body, horrified. "No!" she sobbed, falling to her knees, and draping herself over Tima's body. "No. No. No."

"Tomorrow, you will open my stargate, and the war will begin, or you will be next," the *Psychopath of Soba* said, and the vision faded into the flames that consumed the portal.

Lauren sat frozen, stunned and in disbelief.

The next thing she knew she was back in her bed at the King David Hotel, her pillow damp with tears, smeared with mascara. Henry came in with the baby in a sling on his chest and a mesh bag with fresh fruit, cheese, and bread.

"What's wrong?" He set the bag on the table and hurried to her mother's side.

"Aunt Tima . . . is . . . *dead* . . ." Lauren managed. "Your father is out of time."

"How? What?" Henry's knees weakened and he sat before he fell. "How did you find out?"

"I saw it happen," she said, numbly.

"What can we do?"

"I'll get dressed. We need to go to the Embassy and let Kitty know."

2 8

Kish, Iraq
May 24th

A ndrew watched the exchange from a balcony above the Great Hall where the alleged *stargate* swirled. Twenty feet below, the great device was shaped more like a wide door than the circle seen in the science fiction movie and television show that followed. Thirteen symbols, that looked like footprints made by sandpipers, glowed the same pale olivine as the surface of the portal that swirled and shimmered. He'd spent hours making his way down, level by level, through the ancient ziggurat. It took work, but he'd managed to avoid the armed guards who patrolled the passage ways. He found several bodies—left where they had fallen—in the darkest recesses of the endless maze. All but one had gunshot wounds to the head. The other had his throat slashed ear to ear. He was sure he knew now who the culprit was.

If he'd had back-up, he could to do something to save Dr. Badr, but as it was, he'd already put them all in jeopardy. Deep underground, his com no longer worked. He had no translator and no way to report back to DC. He had no way to call for help.

He knew everything rested on him now. He had to find a way to rescue Rowan and the girl. He didn't know who she was, but she was in just as much peril. After troops pushed Tima's body into one of the pits and left Rowan with a shovel and instructions to bury the dead, they left him and the girl, seemingly alone. If there was a guard in the entryway, he couldn't be sure, but he couldn't take the chance of calling out to them.

Instead, he watched, hidden in the shadows. Rowan lay curled up in a ball. The girl sat beside him with her hand on his back. She looked numb. He appeared despondent. After an hour passed, the girl rose, and took up the shovel.

"I wanted to be an archaeologist so I could find the bones of my ancestors," she said as she went to work. "Not so I could bury the dead."

Rowan sat up and wiped tears from his eyes with the heel of his hand. "Tima was more than a professor to me," he said, gruffly. "She was a mentor, a friend . . . a mother."

"She was everyone's mother," the girl said. "My mother died when I was very small." She tossed a shovel of dirt into the pit, then repeated the process a few more times. "I never knew her."

"My mother is alive and well, living in Colorado with my father. Tima didn't care. She mothered me and my wife, and cared for my sons as if we were her own."

"She told great stories," the girl said, as if this had become a memorial service.

"She was a great cook," Rowan added.

"She always smelled nice." The girl forced a laugh.

"She rattled when she moved," Rowan said.

"Haha, yes. She did love her bracelets. I never saw so many bangles in all my life."

"She was wise . . . and she was kind."

The girl stopped, leaning on the shovel as Rowan managed to get to his feet and stagger over to her. "And she didn't deserve to die."

The girl fell into his arms, and they held onto one another in their grief. Miller's heart broke. He didn't know the woman, but she was someone truly special.

"I am making you a promise right now." Rowan straightened. "I don't care what I have to do, we're getting out of here. I need you to believe that."

"I want to."

"You have to," Rowan said. "It may be the only thing that will keep us alive."

"What the . . ." Kitty sat, bowing over the pictures the Syrian ambassador left behind, flinched when Lauren and Henry appeared out of nowhere. "You could use the door," Kitty said, tucking the pictures back in the folder.

"Aunt Tima is dead," Henry said without preamble.

Kitty rose from her chair. "What? How do you know that?"

Henry pulled out the chair for his mother. Kitty realized she had the baby in the sling under her jacket. As well-behaved as her children were, Kitty couldn't understand how Lauren was able to do it all. She was always on the go, attended all her children's activities and kept a spotless home. She served as president of the PTA, more than once, and never seemed to skip a beat when someone needed something.

"Have you heard anything from Andrew?" Lauren asked.

"No," she said. "We've lost contact with him."

"Should we be worried?" Lauren asked, as Daniel entered. He had a cup of coffee in his hand.

"Ah, Dr. Pierce," he said, in greeting. "I didn't know you were here. I would have brought you coffee."

"I'm hungry," Henry said to his mother. She suspected he knew she would want to tell Kitty her news in confidence. Not everyone would understand how she'd come to learn this information.

"The cafeteria will have something to fill your belly, young man," Daniel said, lifting his arm towards the door. "Come, we'll go get you something. We can get your mother a coffee, too."

"I'll bring you back a sandwich or something," Henry said to his mother. Lauren nodded.

As soon as the door closed, Lauren leaned in. "I had a dream," she said. "Well, more than a dream . . . a vision."

"Tell me what happened?"

"I met Enlil's sister," she said. Kitty just looked at her blankly. "Lamashtu? Have you heard of her?"

"No," Kitty said. "Michael never mentioned her."

"In Mesopotamian religion, she's an even bigger baddy than Enlil."

"Wait, what?" Kitty did a double take. "I didn't think there was anybody worse than Enlil."

Lauren recapped the many names of Lamashtu, along with all her evil deeds. "I'm just glad Henry had Sarah while I was sleeping. Every mother should fear this demon." Lauren went on to relate the details of the dream and what she'd witnessed, including Tima's execution.

"Oh, dear," Kitty gasped, due concern evident in her tone. "That makes the news we've received all the more concerning."

"Tell me what you heard," Lauren said, her brow furrowed.

Kitty pushed the envelope in front of her. "The girl in the last picture, that's Maliqa al Khalid. She's the Syrian *president's* daughter."

"*President?*"

"Well, *dictator* might be a better term, but *president* is his official self-appointed title."

"How is his daughter involved in all this?" Lauren asked. "I saw her in my dream. She was with Rowan and Tima . . . when it happened."

"Maliqa al Khalid was enrolled at the University in Cairo recently. She withdrew citing a family emergency. Apparently her father wasn't a fan of her choice of majors."

"Let me guess, *archaeology?*"

"Bingo."

"Kitty, this ups the stakes, and we both know it. Rowan and Maliqa don't have much time. If he'll kill Tima, he'll kill anyone who stands in his way . . . or keeps him from achieving his goal."

"And you said he's trying to find a *stargate?*"

"I know it seems like myth, but knowing what we know, we have to take this kind of thing seriously."

"And what is this stargate supposed to do?"

"I think he expects it to be some kind of a weapon," Lauren said. "But if it involves Lamashtu, it can't be good."

"We'll try reaching him again," Kitty said. "But when there is no diplomat on the other end, the diplomatic process can be painfully slow."

"We don't have time for slow," Lauren said.

"If I could reach Michael, and my father, we could do something, but right now, no one seems to know where they are . . . or when."

Kitty considered her for a long moment. "If I remember correctly, you defeated the demon who took over Yevgeny Malakoff, a minion of the Dark One. You can defeat this Lamashtu. Right?"

"I'm not sure this is the same thing," Lauren said. "But . . . I have to do something."

The two women sat staring past each other, neither

making eye contact. Lauren's mind moved beyond the here and now, into the past when she and her brother had defeated Enlil the first time. She kept coming back to her purpose in all this. Michael had told her then that her purpose was to be a good wife and mother. She had done that and would continue to do that. He also told her to seek the truth and make wise use of it. "*When the time comes, you will know what to do, and you will have all the tools you need to accomplish your task. Allies will come to your aid, and you need not fear, for I will be with you.*" The words rolled around in her head as she tried to make sense of it all. She didn't know what to do, and she didn't feel equipped to face Lamashtu, much less Enlil, if he decided to rear his ugly head again.

"Do you think we should tell Daniel? About your . . . abilities?"

"I think it's enough that Frank knows," Lauren said. "If I have to break some diplomatic code to bring my husband home . . ."

"Deniable culpability—an ambassador's best friend," Kitty said. "In that case, we need to find a way to keep him busy. I think I can come up with something."

"I can't take Sarah to face Lamashtu," Lauren said.

"I'll keep her," Kitty said. "I protected Henry when Malakoff tried to get at him. I can do the same for her." Lauren nodded. It was the only logical thing to do. "Besides, she's such a sweet baby. I don't think I've heard her fuss more than once or twice."

"She likes being in the sling," Lauren said. "I'll feed her before Henry,and I try anything."

"Henry?"

"If I've learned anything over the years, it's that Henry is the catalyst for my abilities. I can't do much without him. He's strong and he's being trained by my brother. I need him to bring his father home."

ROWAN SAT BACK against the wall, staring at the mound of dirt covering Tima's body and the other archaeologists who were slaughtered by the *Psychopath of Soba*'s army. His anger built with every passing minute. He wanted to wrap his hands around Abdul's throat and squeeze until his eyeballs popped out of their sockets and his head came off his body. Tima's death was swift, but he would offer no such grace to the animal who had murdered her.

His anger made it difficult for him to concentrate on the problem at hand. The inscriptions on the border around the portal throbbed as if the device had a pulse of its own. A rock at Rowan's hand found its way into his fist. He stood and hurled it with all his might, startling Maliqa who'd fallen asleep nearby.

The rock hit the surface of the swirling mist with a crack and bounced off, rolling away without having left so much as a mark on the surface of the portal. He collapsed back against the wall, sliding to the floor, wincing at the pain the effort elicited. He rested his arms on his knees and hung his head, defeated.

"If we could open it, we could go through it," Maliqa said.

"We don't know where it goes," he said.

"Anyplace is better than here, isn't it?" Maliqa sat beside him. Her gaze focused on the throbbing portal. Rowan watched her out of the corner of her eye. "I do know a little Sumerian."

"You do?"

"Tima taught me," she said. "See this one." She rose and walked over and pointed at what looked like a crutch with two crutches crossing it. "That's the symbol—or the Sumerogram —for Anu. The Most High God."

"I've heard of him," Rowan said.

"But these symbols," she pointed at the next two. "This is

more of a name, so it's not just Anu. There may be some rela-tionship to Anu, but I think that's a symbol for Lord . . . and maybe that one is wind or possibly storm."

"In the movie, the Stargate created a wave of water . . . maybe this one creates a wave of wind when it's activated."

"That's possible," she said, studying the next cycle of symbols. "This one begins with the same symbol, the mark of Anu. But this is *munus*, a Sumerogram, meaning woman. This symbol kind of looks like the word Ú, or plant. I'm not sure what that fourth symbol means."

"So, that symbol means *Storm Lord* and this one is some-thing like *Plant Girl?*" Rowan asked. "Sounds like a cheap Marvel movie knock off."

"You know many of the Marvel characters are based on ancient deities."

"Thor, Loki, Sun Wukong, Uatu, Ares, Mobius," Rowan said, hearing the exhaustion in his voice.

"You know your Marvel heroes," she said, impressed.

"And anti-heroes."

"Valid point," she noted.

"Names in Sumerian are written in various ways, but most are descriptive." Maliqa turned back to study the symbols. "This could very easily mean south wind." Her voice carried a sudden realization.

"What does that mean?"

"In Hinduism, south is associated with disease and pesti-lence," she said.

"But this is Sumerian," Rowan said, not following her.

"Everything evolved from this ancient religion," she said. "Many of the more modern religions still have their founda-tions in Sumerian. God gave Moses the five books that make up the Torah in Judaism. The tablets of the Ten Commandments . . ."

"*The Tablets of Destiny*," Rowan said. Then it hit him. He

felt the blood rush from his head. The room spun and threatened to tilt. He felt heavy and very weak. "Oh, God . . ."

"What?" Maliqa turned back. "Rowan?"

"I know who *Storm Lord* is . . . and why we can't help that murderer translate these symbols."

29

Jerusalem, Israel
May 24th

Kitty found a private office on the uppermost floor of the embassy, where Lauren and Henry wouldn't be disturbed. Lauren locked the door behind them as Henry pushed the furniture out of the way, giving them space on the floor to sit while they worked.

"We have to do this quickly," Lauren said. "I don't want to leave Sarah for too long."

"We know Dad is at Kish? For sure?"

"Andrew saw him," Lauren said. "The Syrian ambassador from Aleppo had pictures. He thought that's where they might be headed."

"Okay." Henry sat down. Lauren moved to sit across from him. The two joined hands, and without discussion, closed their eyes and reached out to the universe.

Lauren could feel the darkness envelope them and she could sense Henry trying to guide her through what seemed like a maze, one without form, a void with no direction.

Rowan, I'm coming. I will find you. She didn't speak the words aloud. She didn't need to. He would know.

She felt the pressure shift and it made her body feel heavy. Opening her eyes, she found herself back in the room in the embassy, sitting across from Henry. "What? What happened?"

"I'm not sure," he said. "I was trying to take us physically, but . . . something is blocking the path. We may have to do a *mind-trip* instead."

"Did you find your father? Could you sense him?"

"No, but I thought you were close. I did get a sense for Andrew though."

"Take us to him, by whatever methods you can."

Henry nodded and they tried again.

Lauren could feel her corporeal form move through time and space. She could feel Rowan's heart and soul in the darkness and knew she was close. What she hadn't anticipated was the dark shadow that rose from the void intent on stopping her.

The laughter found its way to her ear as she dodged a blow, twisting beneath it and rounding on him with a counter attack that made contact even as her hand went numb. The laughter stopped.

"I see de powah of de Rada has found a powerful foe." Papa Dauphine's pained voice scraped like nails on a chalkboard against her already frazzled nerves. "I have done as de Dark Lord bade me. I have bidden my time . . . waiting . . . waiting for this day. I have been wronged and I demand my justice be repaid in blood."

"Was my blood not enough for you?" Lauren knew the source of her distress in labor. He had cast a spell and it had almost cost her life—and the life of her daughter. "You killed my husband once. I'm not giving you a second chance."

He came at her from behind this time, and she sensed his movement only a fraction of a second early. It allowed her not only time to avoid the second blow, but to shift into the form of a jaguar. In her feline shade she was much more lithe, but also more deadly. With the added leverage of a tail and strong back legs she pounced and laid her claws into his bare back. She buried her fangs into the flesh of his shoulder. With a bite strength of 1,500 pounds per square inch, the attack was vicious. She drew blood and tore flesh.

Dauphine let out an agonizing cry, fighting to shake her off, crying out to the dark god he served. It confirmed her worst fears. The pressure of the void around her shifted and she found herself falling *down, down, down*. Unaccustomed to the feeling she panicked until her feline instincts kicked in. She managed to flip her tail like a rudder to steer her body around and get her feet under her before landing with a thud on the hard stone floor.

She'd seen this place before. The glowing symbols around the great portal glowed chartreuse and throbbed with a pulse greater than that of a hummingbird's heart—something she hadn't noticed in her human form. The portal had more of a sheen than she'd remembered, and she moved closer, cautiously.

She could see two figures on the other side as if gazing through a mirror. The images were distorted and hard to make out. Still, she recognized one of them as Rowan. She didn't need to see him to know it was him. Her heart knew.

"Who's a bad kitty?" The female voice behind her was unmistakable, even though it had grown shriller and bird-like. Lauren felt her shoulders hunch up as she cringed, then turned to find Lamashtu, in the flesh. The woman stood on a dais of pure gold, flames dancing in braziers around her. Her skin sparkled as if it were painted in gold dust. She wore a wig that reminded Lauren of something an Egyptian Pharaoh might wear, but it too was made of braided gold threads, embellished with gold snakes, with emeralds for eyes. They swayed with her as she seemed to rock like an avatar in a video game, preparing for combat. She opened her eyes and gazed at Lauren, who stepped back. She was startled by the demon's golden eyes that seemed to be painted in the firelight. Her entire countenance did. She leaned in to inspect the new arrival, and bristled, suddenly bursting into feathers taking the form of a wicked harpy.

"Lamashtu." Lauren took a step back, stunned by the sudden metamorphosis.

"*Paw* of the Gods." The harpy laughed at her own joke. Her yellow hawkish eyes narrowed as her feathered chest swelled. She lowered her head and spread her arms—almost wings—creating a striped pattern in her feathers that reminded Lauren of a cobra's hood. She'd seen great horned owls mimic this behavior as a threat display to ward off enemies.

Lauren paced and bared her teeth, feeling the wrinkles in her lips as she could see her whiskers in her peripheral vision. A deep growl rumbled from her chest, and she flexed her claws feeling them tap against the floor.

"So, you are allied with your brother then," Lauren said, her tongue against her teeth as she hissed the words.

"Birds of a feather . . ." she screeched.

"I think of your brother as more of a serpent," Lauren said. "And he's taken Dauphine as his minion." She'd figured that out some time ago, but hadn't spoken it aloud, or even admitted it to herself. "I should have guessed as much."

"The enemy of my enemy . . . is my friend."

"What have you done to my husband?" Lauren decided to flip the switch and change the dialogue. "Where is he?"

"In the land of the living," Lamashtu said, a grumble rolled from her chest turning into a maniacal laugh.

That's when Lauren realized where *she* was, and why she couldn't read the symbols. They were backwards! This wasn't a *stargate*, it was a *portal* . . . a portal to Hell! And she was on the wrong side! *She* was in Hell! *No! No! No! This couldn't be good.* Her mind began to whir, and panic threatened to overtake her. *I have to get out of here! I can't fight her here! Not alone. It was a trap!*

The demon's laughter rose and reverberated off the stone ceiling high above. "I told my brother I could handle this. You never saw it coming, did you? Hand of the God indeed . . ."

Lauren's fear gave way to anger. *How dare she?* Lauren didn't like being mocked. She didn't like being tricked. The last demon she faced had enraged her enough to allow the energy of the gods to flow through her. She knew if she didn't do something, she'd be trapped and defenseless. She needed to escape before the demon's brother—Enlil—showed up.

Lauren knew she had a choice to make. Fight or flight? Anything but freeze. As she made her mind up, she let out a bestial roar, just as she felt the tingling of transformation as she reverted back into her human form, unexpectedly. At the same moment the pressure shifted, and a Siamese cat appeared from the shadow of a tear in the void.

Shadow? What was her cat doing here? What in Anu's name was going on?

As the Siamese cat rounded on the demoness, Lamashtu froze. She seemed to puff her chest up. This was a defense mechanism Lauren had seen all sorts of creatures enlist. *Look bigger so your enemy over-estimates your ability to defend yourself.*

"Shadow?" Lauren said as the cat ignored her and moved to sit in front of the evil deity.

"No." Lamashtu's entire attention was on the cat, as if Lauren were no longer there. Her voice quavered as if she was beset by fear. It didn't make any sense. Shadow was just a little housecat. Lauren would be twice as lethal in her jaguar form.

Shadow turned and let out a crabby mewl at her, something she'd done a thousand times since she'd come to live with them—come from a *cursed* pirate ship—in a different *time zone.*

Lauren heard a voice in her head. "Read the inscription!" The words came clearly as Shadow's instructions to her. The cat turned back to the frightened bird demon, who'd backed herself against the wall. The cat hissed and spit at the demon bird.

"Call off your minion," Lamashtu wailed. "I was just kidding. I wouldn't hurt you."

"*Mroww!*" Shadow clipped. *Now!*

Lauren turned and saw Rowan on the other side of the portal. He was on his knees while another man had a weapon pointed at his head. Panic washed over her as the monster raised the club and brought it down over Rowan's head. She looked up at the cuneiform images and tried to reverse them in her mind.

It took a moment for the image to make sense, but then she realized she needed to translate it into something more . . . ancient.

Per me si va ne la città dolente . . .

Through me is the way to the city of woe . . .

Dante had written of the *Gates of Hell* in **The Inferno**. This was the physical link between the mortal realm and the world of the dead. She knew the last line withing having to read it all. "*Lasciate ogne Speranza, vo ch'intrate* . . . Leave behind all hope, ye who enter."

"In reverse!" Shadow pounced on the demon and all hell broke loose. Feathers and fur flew in a fury as the cat took on the demon who was twice her size.

"Blessed be . . . those who . . . exit?" Lauren asked aloud. Nothing happened. She tried again. "Have hope . . . all ye who exit."

30

Kish, Iraq
May 24th

Andrew worked to find another way to the Great Hall, but every intersection was guarded by armed soldiers. He knew he risked being found and eventually returned to his hiding place. He was overdue to check in and he wasn't sure if *Big Dog* would send reinforcements or await word. He was, unfortunately, able to confirm that there were guards just inside the hall where Rowan and the girl were being held. He was trapped just as they were. He couldn't go up—he couldn't go down.

He checked his arsenal of weapons, each cleverly hidden upon his person. Beneath his local attire he'd put on a pair of tactical pants and a Henley tee-shirt with a pocket on the sleeve for a pen. Instead, he had a rambutan. He had various types of knives, razor wire garrotes, ninja stars and his handy Glock 19 semi-automatic compact pistol. It was his favorite weapon.

It was versatile and reliable, but it wasn't the only gun on him. He also carried his father's Kimber Custom, Colt M1911 single action .45 caliber pistol. It wasn't the weapon he'd pick first, but if he had to rely on last chances, his father's gun would keep him alive. He was certain of it.

He ducked behind the railing when he heard a commotion below. Angry shouts filled the void. Andrew feared their time had run out. He'd run out of options. He wasn't leaving this ancient ruin without Rowan and the girl. Still, he couldn't afford to be brash at the moment. Timing was everything.

Forcing his breath to still and his heart to settle, he moved where he could see through the cracks in the stone. The thugs were on Rowan, manhandling him and forcing him onto his knees in front of the stargate. The girl screamed and one of them grabbed her by the hair and forced her down beside him. Rowan protested and got clubbed across the side of the head for his troubles.

He landed on his face hard, with an oof that erupted from deep in his gut. The ugly one with the scarred face kicked him, then clobbered him over the head again before yanking him back up to his knees.

Andrew could see Rowan's eyes swimming behind his swollen lids. Blood trickled from his nose. Then Andrew saw something that caught him off guard. Behind the shimmering portal, Lauren stood, as if trapped inside a mirror. The wicked green flames rose around her, and a horrific demon rose behind her. Then there were two demons. One took the form of a horrible eagle, the other a vicious cat. It was a battle for dominion—with Lauren in the crossfire.

"Lauren!" He rose and launched himself over the ledge. He landed hard and rolled to his feet, startling the soldiers. He fired three shots, taking out the goons at the door before turning on the ugly one. *Scar Face* had his weapon half raised. *Pow!* Andrew got one shot in on him. The weapon fell from his hand. Rowan, though dazed, snatched up the fallen gun and lowered it at Abdul, then realizing *The Psychopath of Soba* was unarmed, turned the weapon on *Scar Face*.

"Beliel! He's the one you want!" Abdul groveled, ratting out his general. "He killed your woman. He cut off her fingers!"

Scar Face turned and snarled at his boss, then turned back, and faced down the shaking weapon. Rowan seethed angrily. It was everything he could do not to put a bullet in the man's head. "Killing you would be too easy," Rowan said with a measured tone.

A wicked smile spread across his grotesque face. "Shoot him!" Abdul shouted. "He's the one you want!" Rowan didn't hear the command. His head throbbed and blood ran into his eye. He brushed it away, then lowered the weapon. It fell from his hand as Rowan sank to his knees.

Scar Face lunged for the weapon, but before he could reach it, Andrew had one of his throwing knives buried in his skull. He pitched forward and landed in the sand of a freshly filled grave, face first.

"Andrew?" Rowan muttered, trying to force his eyes to open. "What are you doing here?"

"Lauren sent me," he said, glancing over his shoulder. Lauren stood with her hands up, opened, as if she were pushing on a pane of glass. A blaring scream filled the room and for a moment, resonated like Ella Fitzgerald hitting a high note. The portal shattered and fell away. "Lauren!"

Rowan tried to look over his shoulder, but he was too stiff and sore to accomplish the task. He folded it like a house of cards. "Rowan!" Lauren cried. She lifted her hand to shield them from the forces that moved into the room, and the Psychopath who now held a semiautomatic rifle, aimed at her husband. She could feel the fury turn to energy in her shoulder and radiate into her hand.

"Retreat!" Abdul ordered his men, already halfway to the doorway where several of his soldiers had fallen. The battle ended and the coward escaped.

Lauren let him go. Andrew rushed to Rowan, meeting

Lauren's gaze. He realized it wasn't her. It was that dang doppelgänger—like the time he'd seen her in Mexico when he'd gone looking for Rowan. "Lauren," he said, reaching for her hand, finding only mist. "I've got him. I'll get him home."

Lauren felt Henry's presence behind her. "Mom, Aunt Kitty says you need to get Dad out of there. The Syrian Army is coming for Maliqa."

"Maliqa?"

The girl stepped forward and dropped beside Andrew. Her eyes widened. "I'm Maliqa."

"The army is coming for you," Lauren managed.

"My father's army?" she asked.

"Mom," Henry insisted. "She can explain later. There's about to be a battle and Andrew has to get Dad out of there now."

"We have to get out of here," Lauren said, her voice sounding hollow even to her own ear. "Now. Hurry." She felt herself transform back into a jaguar. Andrew Miller gasped, and the girl took a step back. "Can you move him?"

"We can try," Miller said. "He's lost some weight since I saw him last."

"Follow me." She didn't know the way out, per se, but she sensed she could lead them out. She wasn't about to leave until she knew Rowan and the others were safe. Miller was able to rouse him, but Rowan wasn't in great shape. It took everything Miller and the girl had to get him on his feet, and the going was slow. He didn't even seem to notice the jaguar pacing at the doorway, ready to lead them to safety. She realized why. His face was battered, and his eyelids were swollen. His lips were chapped and split. Blood dried on the side of his head and on his filthy shirt. Lauren forced herself to focus on the escape knowing that was the best way she could help.

"*ANUBIS* TO *BIG DOG*." The radio squelch nearly startled Frank from his chair.

He reached for the toggle and pulled the mic closer to his face.

"Go for *Big Dog*," he answered. "What are you seeing up there, *Anubis*."

"Looks like freakin' OK Corral, *Big Dog*. We got armies converging on your vector from three different directions. They've got the bad guys surrounded."

"Any contact from *Eagle* or *Hawkeye*?"

"Negative," Anubis responded. There was a pause, then an excited shout. "We got gunfire! Holy Cow! *Big Dog*, this is escalating fast."

"Any ID on the opposing forces?"

"One moment," Anubis responded. "*Edwin's* checking for us."

Frank ran a hand over his weary face. He knew *Edwin* was the code name for the satellite that was monitoring the situation. *Anubis* was the operations tech monitoring the situation. It didn't matter that there were multiple satellites that would be involved in the operation, they were all *Edwin*.

"Confirmed. The bad guys flying the flag of 249." That was the telephone code for Sudan. "Forces from the north and west are flying 964." That was Iraq. It made sense it was their country. If the boys from 249 didn't have permission to be there, they had every right to defend their territories. "And #3 appears to hail from the 963." *Syria? Hm. That was a surprising turn of events.*

"Confirm 249. Confirm 964. Confirm 963?"

"Confirm on all counts," Anubis said.

"Thank you, Anubis. Let me know if you see any significant intel. Switching momentarily to White Dove."

Frank muted the call and picked up his secure cell phone. He hit her number on the speed dial. "Kitty," he said. "Your brother-in-law and his friends need you. How close are you to the ambassador of Iraq?"

"Iraq?" Kitty sounded exhausted. "I've attended a few state dinners in Baghdad."

"Make a phone call," he said. "Let him know we've got civilian hostages in the line of fire in Kish, and we need their troops to back off or provide aid."

"You found Rowan?"

"It looks like it," Frank said. The line went dead.

31

Kish, Iraq
May 24th

Andrew stopped when he heard gunfire overhead. The spotted jaguar had melted into the darkness and Lauren didn't answer when he asked her if she could tell what was going on. He knew she had an incredible sense of direction and she'd proven it by leading them out of the maze-like tunnels and hallways.

"Put me down . . ." Rowan insisted, panting. He still leaned heavily on both of them, but he seemed more cognizant than he had when they'd started up the halls and stairways of the ziggurat. "I can walk."

"You can hardly stand, Rowan," Maliqa said, grunting as Andrew let go of the injured man long enough to check his weapon. He nearly startled from his skin when Lauren's shadow appeared, again in human form.

She paused to inspect Rowan, who still didn't seem to see her. She leaned in and pressed her lips to his cheek and whispered into his ear. His head lifted, but he said nothing. With his eyes so swollen and his face so battered, she could tell he couldn't see.

Gunfire erupted outside the ziggurat. That told Lauren they were close to the exit. "Stay here," Miller ordered, drawing his weapon. "I'll try to see what we're up against."

Rowan dropped to his hands and knees, wincing, but he didn't make a sound.

"I'm coming with you," Lauren said. "Let me go first. I can see what's going on."

"Big Dog to Eagle," the voice in his ear nearly startled him. "Come in Eagle." Frank sounded weary of repeating the call. Lauren could hear the familiar voice. "Come in Eagle."

"Eagle here," he answered with a relieved smile. "I am glad to hear your voice, Chief."

"Not as glad as I am to hear yours," Frank said. "What's your status?"

"I've found *Hawkeye*," he said, "But he's badly injured. We need medevac."

"And *Nefertiti*?"

"Negative, sir. Lost in combat."

There was a silence that was as heavy for Lauren as it was for Miller. "We're under fire, but we can't see the combatants. What's the extraction plan?"

"Syrian forces have breached Iraqi territory, and they appear to be colluding to stop the Sudanese terrorists. Iraq appears to be backing them up."

"Syria?"

"My father!?" Maliqa turned. "Is it my father? Did he come to rescue me? We have to let him know you're with me, and that I'm okay. He can get us out of here." She directed the comment to Andrew.

Miller relayed the information to Frank. "I'll let *White Dove* know."

Miller stepped away from the group and turned his back, particularly to the doppelgänger as Lauren reappeared.

Miller's voice didn't escape her keen hearing. "Rowan's in bad shape, and . . . his *wife* is here . . . don't ask me . . ."

"No need to explain," Frank said. "I'm well acquainted with her abilities."

"Oh." He turned and glanced at her, then stepped back when a Siamese cat appeared at her shoulder, rubbing up against her.

"Andrew, we need to hurry," Lauren said.

"Frank's working on it," Miller said.

"Eagle, we have an exit plan . . . but . . . you're not going to like it."

Rowan managed to get to his feet, but only with Maliqa's help. Lauren had gone on ahead to make sure the way was clear. They didn't have much time. The only thing keeping him moving forward was the sense of Lauren's presence. He thought he'd heard her voice, but his vision blurred, and he couldn't tell for sure if she was actually there or if he was hallucinating.

"Okay, I've got *mediocre* news, and I have bad news," Andrew said.

"No good news?" Rowan panted.

"What's the mediocre news?" Maliqa asked.

"The Sudanese leader is pinned down at the top of the Ziggurat. Our would-be liberators have ordered an airstrike, and we've found an exit on the opposite side of the temple. It's steeper, but it's the only way out."

"Okay, so what's the bad news?" Maliqa followed up.

"If we don't get out of here in time, we'll be caught in the cross fire. We have about nine minutes before the Iraqi army unloads on this location."

"Wait," Rowan grunted, catching his arm. "They're going to bomb an ancient temple?"

"I don't call the shots," Miller said. "I'm just trying to get you home to Lauren."

———

THE SIAMESE CAT remained at Lauren's instruction. She told Andrew the cat knew the way to the second exit. To her chagrin, he didn't question her. Lauren's shadow faded upon hearing the plan. Miller assumed she might be able to do something, but he didn't have time to worry about that now. "We don't have time to argue," he started, falling in behind the cat.

Rowan let Andrew hold him up and help him through the dark hallways. When they reached the second exit, the distant sound of fighter jets could be heard on approach. The cat bolted down the stairs, turning to make sure the rest of the party followed. Her tail flicked vigorously, and she meowed as only a Siamese could—loudly.

Rowan froze, forcing his eye to focus. "Is that . . . my wife's *cat?*"

"Yeah," Miller said. "Apparently she knows the way. Come on. We have to hurry."

The stairs were steep. Andrew struggled to keep the bigger guy from stumbling as they worked their way down. The sonic boom hit a moment after the aircraft passed—just as they made it to the bottom of the temple stairs. The screaming of the incoming missiles followed and before any of them knew it, there was a massive explosion and the ground shook. Rowan pitched forward, face first in the sand, tumbling down the steep slope. Maliqa fell hard. She landed just a few inches from his foot. Andrew managed to stay upright but skidded as the sand shifted.

A moment later, everything went silent. No gunfire. No sounds of yelling or angry orders. Then, Rowan moaned.

Andrew was at his side a moment later. "Everyone okay?" he asked.

"Yeah," Maliqa said, rolling over onto her back. "I think so."

Andrew leaned over Rowan's prostrate form. "Rowan? You okay?"

There was a long pause, followed by a heavy groan. "Define . . . *okay*."

32

Bethesda, Maryland
May 26th

"May I help you, ma'am?" A woman in a pair of navy blue scrubs asked her in a deep Virginia drawl when Lauren approached the nurses' station.

"Yes," Lauren said. "I'm looking for my husband. He's supposed to have arrived this morning." Kitty had put Lauren, Henry, and Sarah on a commercial flight to DC as soon as Rowan, Maliqa and Miller were rescued by the Syrian and Iraqi armies.

Bahati and Jean-René were both expected to arrive sometime tomorrow. After receiving preliminary treatment at the best hospital in Baghdad, Rowan arrived at Walter Reed by military plane on Frank's orders. "_Diplomatic privilege for a wounded soldier_," he'd said. Henry waited in the lobby with Sarah while she napped.

"Sure." She smiled. "What's his name?"

"Rowan ..." she didn't even need to get his name out.

The woman turned and waved her back. "Sergeant Pierce

is over here in 1127," she stood. Lauren followed hesitating at the door a moment, as the nurse stepped aside to let her pass. "He's sedated," she said. "To keep him comfortable during his trip. He should wake up in a little while."

Lauren nodded and stood in the doorway as the nurse left her. It was a hot sunny day, and his room had floor-to-ceiling windows, with vertical blinds that were partially opened to let the sunlight stream in. The floors were tile, and there was a chair next to the bed where Rowan lay with his head elevated. Lauren moved gingerly, her soft-soled sandals making almost no noise as she crossed the room.

She moved to inspect him, running a hand along his bruised cheek. Stitches bisected his eyebrow, and the lid was black and blue, still swollen. Her heart broke all over again seeing him in person. It'd been bad enough visiting him as a *doppelgänger*, but to stand in the flesh beside him and to touch him, was a whole other thing.

She leaned over him and kissed his head, surprised to find he smelled like soap, maybe antiseptic. It was evident someone had gone to great effort to get him cleaned up before his wife arrived.

It took her a moment to realize his functional eye had opened to a slit, and the glint of a green iris appeared beneath his heavy lashes. "Hi," she said, having to force her voice not to crack.

"Hi," he mouthed, unable to speak.

"Welcome home." She found his hand, needing a moment before her gaze met his again. His lid closed, but his hand flexed in hers. One hand was bandaged, his ring finger splinted. Lauren was relieved to find all ten fingers still there. "I'm sorry," he squeaked, his voice breaking, a tear leaking from his eye.

"Stop that," she scolded, trying to force back her own tears. "You can't afford to expend your energy like that right now. There's nothing for you to be sorry for."

"Tima." His voice cracked.

Lauren swallowed the lump in her throat. "I know," she said. "I also know you did everything you could to help her. You couldn't help yourself. You are not responsible for any of this." She reached up and brushed his hair over, for what it was worth. It was a relief to touch him. When she ran her hand over his head and along his scruffy cheek, he seemed to melt. "Right now, you need to rest. I'm here and I'm not leaving you."

"Where ..." he started, forcing his eyes open, looking around. His vision blurred and the room spun with the effort.

"This is Walter Reed," she said. "You're back on American soil. Jean-René is on his way, too."

Rowan perked up at the mention of his friend. "He's okay?"

"He's fine," she said. "Concussion and some lacerations."

"The kids?" Rowan asked weakly, his lids dipping closed.

"They're fine." She smiled. "All of them . . . all six of them."

His eyes fluttered open enough to question her. "You have another daughter. Sarah Conner Pierce looks so much like John Carter. When you're strong enough, I'll bring her to meet you."

"I missed it?"

"Don't worry about that right now. The important thing is that Sarah's father is home safe, and she'll have her daddy to dance with at her wedding someday."

Lauren glanced up at a knock at the door. A woman in scrubs and a long white coat stood in the doorway. "I'm sorry to interrupt the homecoming, Mrs. Pierce," she said. "A moment of your time, please?"

"Rowan, I'll be outside in the hallway. Be right back." Lauren squeezed his hand, and he managed a weak nod, his eye closing again.

"I'm Captain Emrys. I'm your husband's doctor," she

introduced herself as they walked through the hallway. "Coffee?" she said, stopping at the coffee service and filling a cup for herself.

"Sure." Lauren accepted a cup and added cream and sugar to it, before falling in alongside the doctor as they walked down the hall to the doctor's lounge. It was empty and the captain closed the door behind them.

"Your husband has suffered an ordeal unlike anything he's ever experienced," she said, taking a seat across from Lauren. "How were you told?"

"I know what happened ..." she trailed off, unable to continue. It killed her to know as much as she did. "Most of it, anyway."

"We have a chart we use to evaluate the potential lasting impacts of torture. Your husband is at a very high risk for PTSD as a result," she said. "I understand he was also a combat veteran who was wounded in the line of duty over 25 years ago."

"Yes," Lauren nodded, swallowing hard. "He's had PTSD before. That's why he was discharged early."

"Has he ever had counseling?"

"Not that he ever mentioned," Lauren said. "I met him a couple years after he got out."

"The military hasn't always been the best at dealing with mental health issues after trauma such as this, but we've come a long way in the past few years, and I can promise you, your husband is going to receive the best care available—including counseling. But I want you to know, we're here to help you, too."

"Thank you," Lauren said sincerely.

"Do you and Sergeant Pierce have children?"

Lauren chuckled, lifting the corners of her cheeks. "Six."

"Oh my." The doctor smiled. "How old?"

"The oldest is 16. The youngest is just a couple weeks."

"Where are they now?"

"Henry, the oldest, and Sarah, the baby, are in the waiting room downstairs," Lauren said, staring into her coffee. "The others are home with their grandmother, in California."

"Lauren, you should know with injuries, such as Rowan's," she used his given name for the first time. "It's a marathon, not a sprint. His physical injuries will take months to heal, but his psyche could take much longer. He might seem fine, but mental wounds like his can creep up on him any time. He's going to need you more than ever, but you should know, it'll be hardest for you. He could lash out when you least expect it, and because you're closest to him, it might come directed at you. Just know, it's not him . . . it's the illness. You can call any time for help, and it won't be held against him. Protecting yourself and your children is your first priority. Let us help if Rowan is ever in crisis."

Lauren nodded, taking a moment to choose her words cautiously. "I know you deal with this kind of thing all the time, and you probably hear this too. My husband would never do anything to hurt me or his children," she said, swallowing hard. "I don't believe Rowan would ever do that, but just know, if he does, I have a very strong support system and we will get Rowan help if he needs it."

The doctor managed a smile and nodded. "We're going to give Rowan some time to rest and then begin assessing his condition. We'll develop a treatment plan that will include mental and physical therapy to help him gain his strength. He's being fed intravenously through a central line, but once he's able to begin eating, we need to get some nutrients into him. He's badly malnourished and dehydrated but it doesn't appear that his kidneys have suffered any permanent damage, though we're watching for signs of that, too. Getting him to eat is the first milestone we need him to accomplish, then we'll move on from there."

Lauren nodded, gazing into her mostly empty cup, wondering how it got that way. She only remembered taking a few sips. "Well, now," Dr. Emrys rose. "I'm keeping you from your husband," she said, standing. "I hope you're ready for a long haul."

"Whatever it takes to get my husband home."

<hr>

ABDUL BIN SALMAN entered the courtroom in handcuffs. He looked no better than his former prisoners. It was evident he'd been taken against his will by the Syrian army. The new NATO ally turned him over as a gesture of good faith. After the initial proceedings were concluded, he spoke out of turn, shouting his objections to everything.

"I consider this tribunal a false tribunal! The indictments against me are false indictments," he addressed the court at The Hague. "I have no need of council in an illegal hearing. This trial's aim is to produce false justification for crimes committed against me when my family's claim to the throne was denied in my own country. I am the rightful heir and yet this court refused to recognize my claim, my right!"

He was about to continue, when the judge reached up and hit a button. Anything he said after that was muted and went unheard by the assembly. The judge leaned forward into the microphone. "These are novel issues that have never been addressed before," he said. "Not since Slobodan Milosevic took the stand in that very seat. Hitler would have faced trial, had he not taken a coward's judgement and committed suicide."

"I am no coward!" Abdul stood and shouted, his face turning red as his hollow voice echoed over the crowd. "I am the *Hero of Soba!*"

"Sit and be silent, or I will have you gagged," the judge demanded. "Will the court administrator please read the charges?"

The court administrator stood. He opened a notebook and

took out a sheet of paper. "Abdul bin Salman, you stand before this tribunal accused of the following. On the charge of mass murder, you stand accused of committing or ordering to be committed, the massacre of two hundred of your own people—men, women, and children—during an illegal invasion on the city of Soba. On the charge of kidnapping of Maliqa al Khalid, the daughter of the Syrian interim president, you stand accused of transporting the woman across an international border with intent to torture and coerce. On the charge of kidnapping Dr. Fatima Badr, a respected professor from the University of Cairo you stand accused of transporting the woman across multiple international borders with the intent to torture and coerce. Whereas you did murder Dr. Fatima Badr in cold blood and without remorse, an added charge of murder in the first degree is included. On the charge of kidnapping Rowan Pierce . . ." the charges went on in much the same fashion and covered the injury to Jean-René, and Omar, as well as the death of Mohamed Shahara, Tima's assistant on the boat. "And for conspiracy with enemies who shall remain unnamed, you are charged."

The judge turned to the accused. "How do you plea?"

Abdul stood defiant and did not answer.

"How do you plea?"

Still he did not answer.

Then, a voice rose above the silence of the room. It was a voice Abdul had heard before. His Lord, Enlil spoke. "The accused pleads . . . guilty."

Chaos erupted in the gallery. The accused stood and shouted, "I say no such thing!"

The judge rapped his gavel on the bench. "The plea is entered, so let it be written. The accused has pled guilty. This court will reconvene on August 27th for sentencing." He rapped the gavel a final time, and the pandemonium took over as Abdul was dragged from the gallery amidst the shouting and jeering.

ROWAN GOT his first real shower three weeks after returning to American soil. He sat quietly, as Lauren gave him a haircut and trimmed his beard, which had grown so thick it was better suited to a winter in the north, than a hot summer day in Maryland, even though he had yet to go outside.

In these past few weeks, he'd remained mostly silent—speaking only when necessary—and only when direct questions were asked of him. Henry came to visit him several times, as had Bahati and Jean-René, but they all observed the same thing. He was sullen and withdrawn. He slept long through the day and was restless and troubled at night.

Jean-René took the night watch on several occasions, but most of the time, Lauren stayed up with him. Sometimes they just sat and watched television, while other times, they'd walk the halls, when Rowan's strength permitted. Lauren read to him when he couldn't endure anything more stimulating.

"How's that?" Lauren asked, stepping back to inspect her work, handing him the small hand mirror she carried in her purse.

He looked into the mirror but appeared not to recognize the hollow shell he'd become. Lauren noticed at once when his hand began to tremble and the mirror fell from his grasp, shattering on the floor. His façade broke and something in him snapped. Lauren caught him as he crumpled and began sobbing. She wrestled him up, wrapping him in her arms, holding him as he wept into her freshly cropped hair. She reciprocated and the two of them both had a long cry.

A long while later, he lay limp in her arms, too weak to hold himself up any longer. Lauren realized his uninjured hand was wrapped in what was left of her hair. She'd gone the day before to the hospital salon, as was the custom in her family, to show her respect in memory of Tima. She would sacrifice her hair to the fire at some point, but clearly, it pained Rowan more than she could have anticipated.

"A little help in here!" she called out to the nurses' station and there was a rush to get Rowan up and back into bed.

"A bit too much excitement for one day, Sergeant Pierce?" the orderly asked as he got him settled.

"A shower, clean clothes, and fresh sheets are the balm for everything. I'm sure you'll feel better after you get some sleep," the nurse added, hanging a fresh bolus of saline, slipping a little something in it to help him sleep.

THE NEXT DAY, he started group therapy. "It's worse when I'm tired," he admitted. "It hit me yesterday after I'd had a shower. My wife gave me a haircut and trimmed my beard and though it made me feel almost human, when I looked in the mirror, I didn't recognize the old man I saw there."

"It hits me when I'm driving and I look at the other cars racing by in such a hurry," one of the other patients said. "I keep wondering why they're in such a hurry. Don't they realize that they're missing out on living? It's like a rat race out there, man. When you know you're gonna die, it makes you re-evaluate your priorities."

Rowan nodded. "I'm starting to rethink my choices, too."

The counselor smiled at Rowan. "Like what choices?"

"I spend months away from home because I think," Rowan's voice broke. "I think my work is so important. Meanwhile ... my kids ... they're growing up without their father. My wife gave birth to our sixth child while I was gone, and I wasn't there to help her. And my wife ... God, my wife ... I miss her." Tears rolled from the corners of his eyes. "I just can't keep doing that. I mean, I love what I do but ... it's not worth it. Not anymore."

"So, here's the thing." The counselor nodded. "There's

not a thing in your life that you can't change if you want to. Rowan's got the right idea. Family is important. Be a good husband, wife, father, or mother. Relationships are hard, but they're necessary. One of the best things you can do is talk to those who are closest to you. Tell them how you're feeling. It doesn't just help you—it helps them, too. They're going through this along with you, so you both need it. The worst thing anyone can do is try and shoulder the burden alone."

LAUREN CAME in that afternoon with Sarah in her arms. Rowan was awake, gazing out the window. He sat up, wincing at the pain the quick movement elicited. Lauren brought his new daughter over and lay the sleeping infant in his uninjured arm. He inspected her, clearly pleased with the first impression. A tear dripped from his cheek as she kissed the top of his head. "This is Sarah," Lauren said. Rowan looked up tentatively. "Sarah Connor Pierce. Born on Friday, May 13th weighing four pounds and two ounces."

"My little *Terminator Killer*," he muttered. "*Destroyer of Skynet.*"

"She may save us all." Lauren sat on the edge of the bed.

"You know about *You Know Who*?" he asked, not looking up.

She nodded. "*The rabbit was the leader of them in all the mischief*," she muttered, repeating it in Cherokee. The baby squirmed and opened her eyes, looking up at her father, and for the first time, she smiled.

He tried to, but the expression broke into one of abject grief. He put his injured hand over his face and wept. "I can't keep going like this."

It hit her what he might mean. She looked up, concerned by this sudden change. He handed the baby back, turning away from her. His face reddened, and she could see his jaw clench. His body trembled.

"*Wh-wh-what* do you mean?" She immediately thought the worst. She had seen the counselor, too. They'd talked about the trauma he'd endured—Lauren could only imagine the details and they were haunting her dreams. They'd also talked about what the *worst case scenario* might look like. *Giving up* was one of the signs.

"The job, the travel, the months being gone from my family. I can't do it anymore."

Lauren heaved a sigh of relief. That wasn't what she expected. "Then don't do it anymore."

"Seriously?" He turned back.

"I'll take over, if you want me to." Lauren didn't know how that would work, but they could figure it out later.

"No," Rowan's brow furrowed. "No. That's not what I mean. I don't want to travel anymore. I want us to make a home and be a family ... together. If we need adventure, we can take vacations . . . *together*. All of us. No more of us being apart. I want to be with you . . . with our children. I don't want to miss another guitar lesson, Scout meeting, soccer game or dance recital. I want Sarah . . ." his voice cracked as he looked at the baby and his face twisted as tears poured down his cheeks. "I want her to know her father." He balled up his courage and fought back the tears. When he continued it was the more measured husband Lauren knew. "I want to tinker on cars with Henry, and mow my own damn grass once in a . . ." He spoke with an acerbic tone he rarely used. It caused his voice to crack yet again.

Lauren took his hand in hers and remembered his ring. She put the baby back in his arm before she reached for the clasp on the chain at the back of her neck and retrieved it. She held it up. She moved to put the chain around his neck. "Until your hand heals . . . for better or worse, for richer or poorer, in sickness and in health, forsaking all others ... until death do us part."

"As long as that's not any time soon," he muttered, as she kissed him. He kissed her back and Lauren's heart leapt in her chest. *There he was.* That was the Rowan she knew and loved. That was the moment she was certain he would be okay. *They* were going to be okay. No matter what happened from here on out, they would be fine. Rowan would be *fine.*

MICHAEL STOOD next to his father and nephew, gazing at the portal that throbbed with a pulse of its own. "So that's it? That's the stargate?" The Ziggurat of Kish had not been destroyed during the military intervention to save Rowan, but it was damaged. They had come to ensure no one would ever reach the *Gates of Hell*—that no one could summon Enlil from his prison—not through this portal.

"Dad and Aunt Tima found it," Henry explained, telling them the whole story. "You think *You Know Who* is on the other side?"

"Only one way to find out," John said, taking a step towards the event horizon.

"Grandpa, no!" Henry started after him, but Michael caught his arm.

"*Saecula saeculorum . . . sathanos . . . luciferus . . . belzebub, enlilas . . . show yourself to me!*"

The portal swirled and flames rose behind the barrier that held back the beast as it moved towards them. Even John took a step back, startled by the hideous monster as it turned towards him. Golden eyes burned like fire. "As you command, Ancient Spirit," the beast seethed, licking its fangs with a forked tongue.

"And there you will stay." Michael stepped forward. "In the Name of Anu, I bind thee! By the power of *The Three* I cast thee into the Pit of Despair where you will remain in torment for all your days, which will be many. With Anu's Power, I seal this gate that neither you, nor your minions, will cross into this world! May you rot in torment for eternity!"

The laughter of the beast reverberated, and Henry was certain that whatever his uncle was doing wasn't going to work. The beast seemed to gain power at Michael's proclamation. The flames rose into an inferno, but the beast appeared unscathed. The ground began to shake, and sand fell from overhead. Henry shouted to his uncle. "We have to go!"

Michael seemed oblivious to his cries, even as the void began to cave in around the portal, and around them. "Grandpa John! We have to go," Henry said. "There isn't . . ."

HENRY FOUND himself standing in front of the log cabin where his grandfather lived in his own time. The sun was setting and the shadows of the trees around the clearing stretched long. Michael stood beside him, and his grandfather sat in front of a fire, with his eyes closed. Henry looked at his uncle then approached and sat across from his grandfather. Michael joined them.

"Is the demon bound?" Henry asked. "For good?"

"For *now*," John said. "He has much power, but he is a coward. Cowards get others to do their bidding. There will be many who are weak enough for him to call upon. You will have much work to do."

"We will?" Henry asked.

"*You* will have much work to do."

"Me?" Henry puzzled, a sense of dread filling him.

John looked to his son. "You have been teaching him the ways of time, and place?"

"I have," Michael said. "He's a quick pupil. He is wise in his use of his powers and grows stronger with each year."

"Good, because the time has come for him to join the effort," John said. He turned to Henry. "There are demons and curses beyond the ability of our world to comprehend. It has long been my mission to seek and to destroy those who would aid the Dark Lord in his conquest—to find the weapons and charms that might aid him—and destroy them or remove them from the reach of those who would defy Anu. Now it is time. You will begin to aid us in our efforts."

"Your lessons haven't just been fun and games, Henry," Michael said. "You have been permitted to use these abilities so that you could complete your obligations in your own time-place efficiently, not so you can cheat on your exams."

"I never cheated." Henry was quick to point out. "I made the most of the time I was given. I did my homework. I never plagiarized a paper or cheated on a test. You taught me better than that."

"He is correct," John said. "And it is a good thing he has learned these lessons. You will need your education, and you must maintain your life as it exists in your time-place."

"You'll need to be careful, too." Michael put a hand on his knee. "Those who oppose us will have no mercy upon you because you're a *teenager.*"

"Will you be there to help me?"

John lifted his face to the warmth of the fading light. "My sun will set—someday—and I will help you for as long as I have the *magic* within me. I can spend little time apart from *this* world these days. It takes longer for me to regain my energy. You are young and there will come a day when you do not need my aid. Until then, stay curious, always. But be careful of those who would seek to deceive you. Remain of good heart and strong virtue."

"I will, Grandpa."

John nodded but moved to rise. Michael jumped to his feet to help the old man up. Henry realized how much older his grandfather appeared, even since they escaped the time trap they'd been stuck in. "Now, we need to get you home. Your mother and father will need your help and you will start college in just a few months."

"It's an exciting time," Michael said. "Don't spend your time going to too many keggers."

"I won't be going to any," Henry said. "I've already seen a future where I did not take those words to heart. I'm not going to repeat that mistake."

"Good man," John said, with a wink and a smile. "Now go home and help your father and mother. They're going to need you."

33

San Diego, California
Exploration Channel Corporate Offices
July 21st

"You're what?" Jacob's brow lifted as Lauren explained to him their plan.

"Quitting," Lauren said. "We're done."

"Is this because of the whole Bigfoot hunting show fiasco?" Jacob asked. Lauren had heard about what happened in Oklahoma while they were gone. A couple of drunken cowboys got wind of the production team and decided to mess with them. One of them donned a Gilly suit and tried to trick the teams into thinking he was a Bigfoot. He took a bullet in the knee and the Network decided the liability was just too much. "If I didn't say it before, I should say it now. You were right, it was a horrible idea. I've pulled the plug on the bounty hunt. It's not worth it."

"It's nice to hear you say it," Lauren said. "But no, that's not why we're quitting."

"No wait, it's Rowan's off season schedule isn't it? We can talk about that."

"Rowan needs time at home. I need time at home. You're the one who said it. What's travel without a place to call home? Well, we're going home. He's done, and it's not something that a week or two here and there can fix."

"You know if you quit, the Network can't continue paying your housing stipend." He scowled as he pushed his glasses up his nose, clearly miffed.

"We're selling the house," she said. "The realtor put it on the market the other day when we got home, and we've already had four offers on it. We're in a bidding war, and the price is already double what we paid for it."

Jacob's jaw dropped. "But ..."

"Rowan's parents were going to sell their house in Denver and go live in their RV for a while, so we're buying their house. Henry's made his decision to go to Colorado State in Fort Collins. We'll be closer to him and to the mountains. I've been offered a job with the local public television station there."

"*Public television?*" he said the words as if they were foul. His face bore the scowl of an affronted child. "Why would you ever want to work in *public television?*"

"I got my start with PBS, but this project is with the Denver affiliate, in cooperation with the Colorado Tourism Department and the Rocky Mountain Film Commission. I'm going to be doing a series of documentaries about the Rockies, and all the things to do and see. The production work is all local, and the kids can be involved, if they want to. Rowan can, too—if or when he's ready," she added. "The important thing is, we will be at home with our family, have dinner at our own supper table and sleep in our own beds ... every night."

"But ...." Jacob floundered. "What about Jean-René and Bahati? You'll be putting them out of work. You're all a team. I don't need to remind you that your contracts are tied together."

"And their contract is expired, too. Jean-René is going to

work with me and be my Director of Photography . . . *again*," she said. "Bahati is my production assistant. They're in Denver right now looking for a place to live." Jacob stood, red-faced, pacing behind his desk, having to turn away from her. "Look, I know this is unexpected and completely out of character for us, but after what Rowan's been through, you must understand."

"You're walking away from the highest-rated cable travel-adventure show in the history of the Network," he snarled. "With no notice, no negotiation, no chance of even discussing it?"

Lauren pursed her lips but held her resolve. "We've reached the end of our contract." Lauren stood. "I had our attorney review it to make sure. We're under no legal obligation to stay. I'm sorry, Jacob. It's been twenty-some years, and I'd like to say that at some point, later in our lives, we might feel differently."

"No," he snapped as he turned on her, full of fury. "You don't get to do that! You can't have it both ways. If you walk away now, you're done. Forever. No take-backs! You walk out of this office, and you will *never* work for this Network again."

Lauren shouldered her purse. "We can live with that," she said. "Thank you, Jacob. We appreciate all the opportunities you gave us." Jacob was still standing there fuming when she turned and walked out. She smiled to herself, closing the book on this chapter of their lives. There were new adventures ahead, and familiar mountains to climb.

"Just so you know, those artifacts Rowan thought were from the set of Indiana Jones? They weren't!" He scrambled to follow after her. "You know the so called Ark and all that! They're fake! They don't have the studio tags! I checked!" He spit out the words as if they were poisoned.

Lauren stopped and looked back at him shrugging. "I'm sure it was just an honest mistake, but I'll see if Rowan wants to buy them back," she shrugged. She tried to act nonchalantly but those artifacts—those sacred relics —had to go with them. She'd already instructed the team to crate them up and call the shipping company. "He has become very fond of them ... was from the moment he saw them on eBay." She'd never felt right about him putting them on his expense account in the first place. They both knew where they had come from, and the expense report was just another carefully crafted foil that could be just as easily undone. "Talk to you soon, Jacob!" She waved over her shoulder.

"I thought he said he got them on Amazon?" Jacob called after her, but Lauren never slowed.

***

"HE'S CALLED three times since you left his office," Rowan said, stretched out on the sofa with Sarah asleep on his chest. "I talked to him the first time, but when I didn't change my mind, he hung up on me. After that, I didn't answer."

"Did he leave voice mails?" Lauren smirked, kicking off her shoes, taking the recliner beside him.

"Yeah." Rowan's smile was bright today. He was having a better day, and that was encouraging.

"Maybe later, I'll make us some popcorn and we can listen to them after the kids go to bed," Lauren said with a smirk.

Rowan glanced over at her, bemused. "I'm sure I can think of something better to do with our time," he said.

"What? Like . . . pack?"

John Carter perked up from his video game. "Are we really gonna go live in Grandma and Grandpa's house in Colorado?"

"Don't you want to?" Lauren asked.

"Why wouldn't you?" Rowan added. "I loved growing up there. There's plenty of room for us, and they have the best yard in the neighborhood."

"And we can get our dog," Kate cheered. "He's waiting for us to move."

"Yes," Lauren said. "We can."

Rowan scowled. "I'll believe that when I see it," he said, glaring at the cat curled up in a sunbeam by the window. "You told me when Henry was a baby we could get a dog."

"Well, I didn't say when," Lauren said, chuckling. "But now seems like the right time. Especially if our dog is waiting for us."

Sam came over and sat on the floor by his dad. "I do have one concern," he said, sounding much older than himself.

"Oh?"

"What's that, buddy?" Rowan added.

"I've been counting, and I don't think Grandma and Grandpa's house has enough rooms for everyone to have one. Will I have to share a room with Jamie?"

Lauren furrowed her brow. "They have four rooms upstairs and two rooms downstairs."

"That's why they were going to sell the house," Rowan said. "What do two people need with all those bedrooms, when they have a house on wheels? There's enough room for everyone to have their own room, except your mother and me. We like sharing a room."

"Well . . . where's Henry gonna sleep?" Sam asked.

"Henry will have a room at the college," Lauren said. "But he has to share with a roommate."

"Three roommates," Henry said coming in from the back yard. "I'm in a quad. Oh, and if I were you, I'd put John Carter upstairs with the little kids."

Rowan arched a brow, glancing at Lauren. "Oh?"

"Yeah," he smirked, as he passed, headed to the kitchen. "It'll make it a lot harder for him to sneak out."

"Sneak out?" John Carter scowled. "I would never do that."

"Yeah, you will. Or you will try," Henry said. "You know

you're gonna do it, but I'm telling you, if you do, you're going to regret it." Henry would know.

"Dad, can I have your old room?" Sam asked.

Rowan looked to the older boys to see if there would be any protests, and only Jamie seemed to consider it for a moment. "If your brothers don't mind," Rowan said.

"I don't care." Jamie shrugged.

"Cool! It's all mine." Sam grinned.

"Well don't start counting your chickens," Rowan said. "While it is a nice house, it's going to take a lot of work for me to fix it up the way your mom likes it. I'm going up to Denver next week and get started so it'll be ready when you guys get there. You kids have to help your mom pack up here."

"Aw, man!" Kate scowled.

"The moving truck will be here soon, and your mom and I are counting on your help."

"I'll help," Jamie and Henry said in unison.

John Carter nodded. "Me, too."

One by one each of the kids sounded off, promising to help their mom with the packing.

"Well, I guess that's settled."

EPILOGUE

Englewood, Colorado
August 4th

"Rowan! That's the last of our things," Charles called up to his son. Rowan was sitting on the peak of the roof of the two-story house, hammering shingles into place. "We're going to go take everything to storage and pick up some dinner. Want us to bring you anything?"

Rowan had stopped, taking out the nails he'd been holding in his teeth. "Sure, Dad," he called back, and resumed his work, keeping the nails in his hand.

While there were still plenty of interior projects to be done, the roof was in bad shape, and it had to be replaced before the rains came. In order to do that, Rowan had installed roof brackets to attach a fall arrest system to. Once safely anchored, he set to work ripping off the shingles, replacing the decking then replacing the asphalt. "We're officially out of your hair."

Now if you'd just leave me alone and let me finish ... he muttered under his breath. "Thanks, Dad," he called down. His parents had sold most of everything they had, and what they didn't sell, or couldn't sell they were taking to storage. If they couldn't carry it in their RV, they didn't need it. The only room that remained untouched was Rowan's room, and he'd been staying there while his parents were packing up and he was working on the house. "When are you leaving for Vancouver?"

"I'm not leaving until I get to see all my grandkids. We can sleep in the RV in the driveway until then," he said.

Rowan's mother came over and stood beside her husband, holding up her hand to shield her eyes from the setting sun. "You're not getting nails in my garden, are you?"

"No, Mom," he said, shaking his head. "I wouldn't do that."

"Want me to start painting when we get back?" Charles called up.

Rowan shrugged. "If you want to," he said. "I schlepped all the paint in when I got back from the hardware store earlier."

"What room do you want me to start on?" Charles asked.

"Why don't you start in the master suite?" Rowan suggested. He planned to get their room fixed up for Lauren before she arrived. He had already ripped up the carpet and installed hardwood floors with underfloor radiant heat. He'd laid cardboard and plastic sheeting to protect it while they were painting. He'd tackled the kitchen renovation as well, and had replaced the cabinets, counter tops and had all the appliances out. What they'd removed had already been sold on *Facebook Marketplace*. New appliances were on order and would be in before the week was out. The tile, new door handles and drawer pulls were all that was left to be done, paint notwithstanding. He could work on that during the evenings. Right now, daylight was burning ... and so was his neck.

From the sale of the house in San Diego, Rowan had used

a portion of the funds to buy back his *office decor*—the sacred relics he'd sworn an oath to protect—from the Network. His parents had a finished basement, that wasn't all that finished. He planned to convert it into his office, and he had in mind a place for each piece. There was also room for Diana to have her own suite, once he had a chance to build it out. She'd announced she wanted to stay with John for a while, once she helped them get moved. The wise woman wanted to give the family time to get settled before anyone had to worry about making her comfortable. Rowan assured her she was welcome any time, and there was always a place for her in their home.

His future remained in question. While Lauren had found work, he wasn't quite ready to consider it just yet. He was already writing his memoir—at his therapist's suggestion—and thought about writing a novel. He could always do some copy writing for Lauren's television show. He'd also spent some time going through pictures he'd taken from their journeys all around the world. He had several of them printed and off to the framers, so he could hang them on the walls in their bedroom and in his office. His favorite was the one he'd taken of the family shortly before Sam and Kate's arrival while on the hunt for the skunk ape in a meadow in Oklahoma. There was also the vanity shot Jean-René had taken for their special *Family Tree* series, of Lauren—in her Native regalia with Henry in a sling on her back—and him—dressed like a Scottish mountain man. There were photos from Myanmar they'd taken the day Kate and Sam were conceived, pictures of their rental in Virginia where John Carter was born, and pictures from Mexico, Egypt, Chile, Argentina, Russia, and other points unknown. These were the memories that were most precious to him, but now, it was time to be home. *Home.*

He'd done his best all these years to put back money whenever they had it, not that they'd ever gone hungry, but with kids, money seemed to travel through his wallet like a rotating door. But with his cautious reserve, not to mention Lauren's frugal spending, they were in a position where they could afford to live without anyone having to work, at least for a while. Henry's scholarships—along with a portion of Rowan's GI Bill, if needed—would ensure he didn't have to pay a penny out-of-pocket for college, and Lauren was day-dreaming of a vegetable garden.

In his mother's ample yard, there was plenty of room to put some raised beds, and large pots for herbs, vegetables, strawberries or whatever she cared to grow. Rowan glanced down at the back yard where Francis, his mother's French bulldog, and their new rescue dog—a mix of Australian Shepard and Belgian Malinois—Indy, were laying in the shade on the cool grass, panting. They'd become fast friends and had been playing all afternoon, fighting over sticks, and chasing balls. He studied the area he had in mind for the raised gardens as he worked on the roof, glancing up at the sun, and estimating the hours of daylight the plot might receive. He wanted it to be perfect.

ROWAN HAD JUST DRIVEN the last nail into the last shingle when he heard his parents pull up in the driveway. He climbed over to the ladder and unhooked his lanyard, tying it off so it would be there when he came back up tomorrow to replace the flashing around the fireplace and inspect the bricks.

The sun was setting in the west, and Rowan was tired. He'd put in a full day's work. Before, he might have finished the roof and most of the renovations in a week, but he'd needed more time and tried to pace himself. He was getting his strength back, and the work felt good. Painting the house inside would be easy, compared to the work done, and he was looking forward to being in the air conditioning, out of the sun and the heat. He'd forgotten how hot it could get in Denver during the summer.

He met his parents at the patio door as they came out carrying brown paper bags of food.

"Guess it's a good thing you wanted to keep the patio furniture, dear," his mother said, patting his arm. "Nowhere to sit down inside. Might as well enjoy the sunset in the yard."

"Sure, Mom," Rowan said, obediently. "Let me go wash up first."

<hr>

OVER DINNER, they discussed all the things Rowan had left on his punch list. He was running out of time to get it all done before the moving van arrived. Lauren would be following with the kids. Now that Henry could help with the driving, a road-trip wasn't such a burden for her. Henry's gift of foresight had come in handy on more than one occasion, helping them avoid crashes and traffic snarls around San Diego.

Rowan hadn't been planning on his parents hanging around to help out. They'd made it sound like they were going to make a run for it as soon as they moved the last of their things out of the house. Rowan was grateful for the offer and knew his parents could manage the work. Both had the skill sets he needed—at a price he could afford. He'd pay them with ample time to spend with their grandchildren, and a promise to take care of the home they had shared for the past fifty-two years. He could only hope he and Lauren would make it that long, but they had a good start and his parents had provided him with a great example of what a happy marriage should look like.

His mom pushed a cookie over to him with a nudge to eat it. He took it and was happy to make short work of it. "Okay, so we don't have much time to wrap everything up before the moving van gets here," Rowan said, as he folded the paper napkin and lay it in the plastic container that served his food. "I think I'll get in the kitchen and finish the last of the cabinetry work tonight so I can paint in there tomorrow."

"Oh, honey," his mother gasped. "Look at you! You're all sunburned."

Rowan smirked. "This isn't news to me, Mom. I worked up on that roof for the past two days." SPF 50 was no match for the *Mile High City* sun.

"I've got some aloe vera..." she said.

"Maybe later, Mom," he said, draining the last drop of water from the bottle in front of him. "Lauren's got some stuff we got in Hawai'i," he added. "The aloe vera will hold me until she gets here."

"Well." Martha stood and collected the empty containers. "We'd better get to work. There's a lot to do before Lauren gets here with our grandkids."

THAT WAS the best time he could ever remember having with his parents. They had always gotten along great, but as he'd gotten older, he found his mother could be grating on his nerves, and his dad was still trying to tell him what to do. Now, he appreciated them a whole lot more than he ever had. He understood his parents and recognized that they only wanted the best for him and his family. The fact that they pulled their house off the market—despite having some decent offers—was proof of that.

Rowan offered them a fair price for it and would have paid double. His dad wouldn't hear about it, as long as he promised they would always be welcomed and there would always be a place to park their RV when they stopped to visit. Initially, Rowan had feared that they'd come back, park it and never leave, but he knew better. If they parked it anywhere nearby it would be in Estes Park, or over in Aspen, or Winter Park. There were plenty of prime camping spots nearby with everything a retired couple and their dog could possibly need. Rowan mused thinking about meeting them at the RV campground in Rocky Mountain National Park with all the kids in tow, putting up a tent and making s'mores around the fire. That was a pretty picture in his mind's eye.

IT WAS NEARLY two in the morning when he finally fell into bed. The kitchen wasn't finished but he'd done all the prep to paint the cabinets first thing in the morning. A rumble of thunder echoed in the distance as an afternoon storm built in the southwest and was moving in over the mountain corridor of I-70. Lightning flickered and the thunder crackled. Rowan lay listening to the storm approach, then realized he wouldn't be getting to sleep any time soon.

He reached over and flipped on the light beside the bed and picked up his glasses and his iPad.

THOMAS WOLFE SAID, you can't go back home. But Thomas Wolfe was wrong. You can. Sometimes that's the place you need to be, even when your life is pulling you in a million different directions. Maya Angelou said it best. "The ache for home lives in all of us, the safe place where we can go as we are and not be questioned." While I was chasing a dream around the world, looking for adventure and the next great story, it never occurred to me that what I was looking for was right here all along.

In just a few days, my family will join me, and the vision will be fulfilled. While I lay in my childhood room, in the house I grew up in, I can't help but think about a time when I thought this would always be my parents' home. When we finish with the renovations and all our kids are settled in their rooms, I think I shall sit on the sofa next to my beautiful wife and think, now, this is home; my home.

Rowan looked up from the screen at the bleep from his phone.

"You up?" Lauren texted.

"Yeah," he texted back. "What are you doing up?"

"Sarah's a little fussy," she said. "I think she's missing her daddy."

"Her daddy misses her, too," Rowan texted back.

"How's the house?"

"Roof's done. Kitchen's almost done. Mom and Dad are staying to help—refuse to leave until they see their grandkids."

"The movers will be here in the morning."

"Have the kids helped?"

"They've been the best," Lauren texted. "Everyone has pitched in."

"I can't wait to show you everything we've done here," Rowan yawned, taking off his glasses and rubbing his tired eyes. His sunburn felt like fire, even with the aloe his mom had provided him. His muscles ached and his stiff finger throbbed.

"Did you follow my vision board on Pinterest?" She texted back.

"To the letter," he said. "I promised I would. I got all the colors of paint you requested and the guy at the paint store wanted to know if my wife was an interior decorator."

"Maybe I could do that as a side gig, if we get tight on money. LOL."

Rowan sent back a happy face and a thumbs-up emoji.

"Better get some sleep," Lauren said. "See you soon."

"I love you."

"I know," She texted back, along with a heart emoji.

BY THE TIME the moving truck arrived in Englewood, a suburb of Denver, the painting was done, the floors were finished, and all the appliances had arrived and were installed. Rowan, the moving guys, and his dad got all the furniture put into place while his mother ran to the framing store to pick up the pictures Rowan had done. While they worked on unpacking the kids rooms downstairs, his mother went to work hanging pictures and decorating the house.

"I've watched enough *Fixer' Upper* to be dangerous," she'd assured Rowan as she headed out to the local *Home Goods* store, returning a couple hours later with a load.

"Mom?" Rowan wanted to protest, but he thought better of it. "Lauren's going to love it," he conceded and knew she would. "Thank you . . . for everything."

<hr>

LATE THE FOLLOWING AFTERNOON, Lauren's SUV pulled up in the driveway, and the kids piled out of the car, racing up to the front door, where their grandpa and grandma stood, ready to greet them.

Lauren collected Sarah from her car seat and got her diaper bag, handing it to Henry who stood by to assist. She had stopped outside Denver to change Sarah's diaper and nurse her, and she'd put her in a cute little sundress and clipped bows in her wild hair, so she'd look presentable when she saw her grandparents for the first time.

Martha inspected each of the kids and she and Charles went on and on about how big they had gotten since they'd seen them last. Charles picked up Kate and she had hugged him fiercely. "Can we go play with Francis?" she asked.

"Maybe in a bit," Charles said, as Lauren came over with Sarah.

"Oh, Lauren," Martha beamed brightly. "Oh, she is beautiful!"

Sarah blew bubbles at her Grandma, then her Grandpa. Lauren handed her over and Martha was simply beaming. "Isn't she beautiful, Charles?"

"I reckon she'll do," he said, then turned to Kate. "All right, let's go see what Francis is doing. You can meet his new friend."

"Is it Indy?" Kate beamed. "He's here, isn't he?"

"Your dad picked him up at the shelter the other day," Charles beamed.

"I told you he'd be ready to come home," Kate said to her mother.

"Let's go!" Jamie raced ahead.

The older boys followed Charles into the house, leaving Lauren and Martha to fuss over the baby.

"Where's Rowan?" Lauren asked.

"He told me to send you to your room," she said, kissing Lauren's cheek. "Come along, Sarah. How do you feel about fat little puppies?"

"I like fat puppies!" Kate and Sam chorused.

Martha left her standing at the door, bemused, and just a little perplexed. Lauren dropped her purse in the living room and made her way to the master bedroom that was once his mom and dad's room. Along the way, she stopped to inspect the kitchen, pleased at the colors she had picked out. The marble countertops were cool beneath her hand as she ran it along the white finish, tracing the marble gray flecks with her fingertips. The farm sink with the arching faucet was just what she had imagined and there was even a bowl of lemons on the countertop, just like in the picture she had pinned. A bouquet of fresh flowers sat on the dining room table, and she suspected Martha had collected them from her garden.

She found the door to the master bedroom room ajar, but it was dark. She reached for a lamp on the dresser and flicked it on. There, in the middle of the bed, lay Rowan, spread out like a starfish, snoring to beat the band. Lauren climbed up on the bed beside him. Tucking herself into the crook of his arm. She rested her head on his shoulder and her hand on his chest.

He stirred in his sleep, and sighed drowsily, pulling her into him. He kissed her forehead. She closed her eyes and mirrored his sigh. "Honey, we're home," she whispered.

"Yes, we are."

PREVIEW OF THE SULTAN'S STONE (VERITAS CODEX #8)

"I don't think you understand what's at stake," the man with the gun said, pressing the dark weapon to Rowan's temple. It was so close to his eye that he couldn't focus on it—couldn't tell what kind it was, or if the man's finger was on the trigger. The gunman's hand shook visibly.

Rowan took a deep breath and lifted his own hands, moving slowly. *Jeeze. Not him again.* His mind instantly went back to Sudan. "My wallet is in my right hip pocket. There's thirty dollars in there. Take it."

"You think this is about money?" The man pressed the barrel of the gun harder against the side of his head. His voice trembled as much as his hands.

"Let him go," the frightened clerk said, her voice trembling. "Take the money from the till. You want beer? Cigarettes? Take it! Take whatever you want! Just . . . don't hurt anyone."

Rowan swallowed hard. He couldn't help but think of his wife and children waiting at home. He closed his eyes and tried to picture Lauren's face. It came to him as clear as a full wolf moon on a cloudless night. He clung to that vision as he tried to figure a way to get back to her with all his gray matter intact.

It was just a simple trip to the hardware store—to buy a new faucet for the kitchen sink—that had taken him out on a Sunday afternoon errand. The stop at the convenience store to pick up some treats for the kids was an after-thought. He was five minutes from home—or had been —until a gun was pressed to his temple.

"I said it's not about money!" The thug screamed as Rowan came back to the present. The cashier moved as if to say something, and the man turned the gun on her. It gave Rowan his first good look at both the weapon and the assailant. Before Rowan could fully assess the situation, the weapon pressed back against his head.

Rowan could now size up his opponent and took stock of the situation. He first noticed the man when he'd walked in. He wasn't a big guy, but he was ripped. The assailant was shorter than Rowan by several inches, but the ripples of muscle beneath his olive green USMC t-shirt suggested he was strong. "You don't have to do this, Devil Dog," Rowan took a chance, assuming he was a Marine. If he were a Marine, he'd know how to use that gun and Rowan didn't want to goad him. "Just tell me what you need."

"I know who you are," he said. "You're going to help me."

"Oka-a-ay," Rowan said with some hesitation. His hands sunk down gradually. His shoulder hurt too bad to keep them up any longer than he had to. He and the boys spent the morning getting the pool closed before winter set in. His joints were starting to give out on him one by one. Years of hard travel, and one too many broken bones were catching up with him. The small $4.00 bottle of ibuprofen on the counter next to the Icees were proof of that. "Just tell me how I can help."

"I need you to make it go away," he cried. As the man's hand shook even more, the gun came off Rowan's temple. The assailant crouched down. His hands—including the one with the gun—tried to cover his ears, as he pinched his eyes shut. "It followed me home from work . . . it won't leave me alone . . . make it stop!"

Rowan turned and went to reach for him, not sure why he didn't go for the gun, but he realized a fellow military man—a Marine—in trouble. Rowan faced PTSD himself and knew the desperation that came with it. He also knew that desperation made people do desperate things. He glanced at the clerk with a look that conveyed a silent message. She nodded and moved, as Rowan turned his attention back to the Marine. Suddenly the man stood, taking a step back, leveling the gun at his face. Rowan could see now. The man's finger was on the trigger. "Stay back."

Rowan lifted his hands again. "Okay. I'll help you. Just tell me . . . what's going on?"

"I'm not crazy!" The man snapped. "Don't look at me like you think I'm crazy."

"I don't think you're crazy," Rowan said, trying to project a calm that belayed the thrumming of terror in his chest. "You said you need help. I'll help you. I just need to know what's going on."

The assailant blinked rapidly, eyeing him down the barrel of the Glock 19M. "Shut up! You can't tell me what to do." His hands went back to his ears and pain seemed to wash over him. Rowan held his gaze as he moved to take a step forward. "Stop!" The Marine snapped, pointing the gun at him again. "Both of you! Shut up!"

Rowan's eye darted to the clerk, who stood wide eyed, frozen. Her look told him what he needed to know. Now, he just had to keep the gunman talking, keep him calm. "Just tell me what's going on," he said softly. "Where do you work? What followed you home?"

The man's eyes went wide. Rowan noticed the beads of sweat gathering on his brow as he fought to control his breathing but began panting. He seemed to open his mouth to speak, but nothing came out. He swallowed hard and tried to steady the gun with both hands. "I . . ." he finally managed. "It's . . . I . . . I don't know."

"Hey," Rowan kept his tone soft. "I've been where you are. I can help you and I will. What's your name? Where'd you serve, man?"

"Lance Corporal Riggs, Benjamin F.—Marine . . . Expeditionary . . . Unit . . . Sudan." Sudan. Dammit. Rowan knew what that meant. Things had gotten a lot worse in the Middle East over the past few years. The Great Accord had all but splintered and discord was running rampant.

The region was riddled with political and religious groups fighting for control of the rich oil reserves found there, especially since the discovery of a new, untapped reserve in Sudan. U.S. foreign policy had turned heavily against the nation since Rowan's own experiences in the region, so he completely understood why this young man might be struggling. After the lengths taken to liberate the American television personality, Sudan wasn't all that happy with the United States, or her allies. They'd been taking it out on the troops there, and anyone else they could get their hands on.

Discord trembled across borders and in small cells across the globe, uprisings and civil unrest became more common. An emerging terrorist group known as Ruka D'yavola—or The Devil's Hand—led raids across Russian borders into Ukraine, Belarus, Latvia, and Estonia. A February 1st dirty bomb attack in the city of Astana, Kazakhstan—known as the coldest city in the world—killed hundreds of thousands and destroyed its beautiful landmarks. The National Concert Hall collapsed during a performance by students from the nearby Kazakh National University of the Arts. Only two victims survived to be rescued from the rubble of the concert hall.

While many died from the initial detonation, many more succumbed to the radiological contamination ejected into the stratosphere, where it was picked up by stratospheric winds and carried across borders back into Russia, and over into Mongolia. People as far away as Beijing were sickened, which enraged the Chinese government. Demanding Russia control its dissidents, they severed all diplomatic ties.

"I know what you've been through, Brother." Rowan tried to ease tensions, wishing his golden-tongued sister-in-law were here to negotiate a peace treaty one-on-one with the agitated Marine. "I've been there."

Riggs swallowed hard, blinking rapidly. His finger seemed to stroke the trigger with the lightest touch. It darted to the side of the weapon occasionally, as if the man couldn't quite figure out where to rest his finger. Conflict chased fear across the dark sweat-glazed face. The Marine's breath came in gasps. Rowan decided the young man seemed to be suffering from a physical health crisis as well as a mental one.

Rowan had been there. He recognized a man in the grips of flashbacks. He had them often enough himself. "Whose your C.O.?"

The Marine hesitated a moment, pinching his eyes shut. His hand trembled even harder. "C-c-captain L-l-lorraine Y-y-york," he said.

"Are you still active duty?"

The man seemed to blink out of the nightmare. His lips pursed angrily, and Rowan knew his answer. "D-d-discharged . . . b-b-bad papers . . ." Dishonorable discharge. Not good, Rowan thought.

"Unfairly too, I'm sure." Rowan took a step back, more so, to shift his weight and keep blood flowing to his lower extremities. His toes were tingling. Rowan felt sweat building on his own skin.

"No," Riggs swallowed hard. "I deserved it."

"You wanna talk about it?"

"Not really," the man snapped. His finger was now firmly on the trigger. "You are going to help me!"

"Yes, I am," Rowan assured him. "I just like to know who I'm working with."

"It's not who . . ." he said, swallowing hard. A bead of sweat rolled down the side of his nose and dripped off his chin onto his already-damp shirt. "I'm not the one you need to be afraid of."

"Well, you're the one with the gun to my face," Rowan said, unable to keep his naturally sarcastic nature at bay. "It's a little hard not to be afraid. Put your weapon down and we can talk. I will do whatever I can to help you."

"It followed me home from work," the man repeated, not lowering the gun. "You have to get rid of it . . . make it go away." The words were clipped, and each one individually punctuated. "I didn't do anything to it . . ." his voice rose uncomfortably. "I just want it to go away."

"What followed you home from work?" Rowan's brow narrowed.

"I don't know what it is, but it's . . . it's dark . . . it's evil . . . it w-w-won't leave me alone . . . it makes me want to do bad things . . . I don't want to do this . . . but I have to get rid of it . . . you have to help me get rid of it . . ."

"Why me?"

"It . . . knows you . . ." he said, his voice trailing off like a frightened child's.

Rowan eyed him warily, his mind running at warp speed as he analyzed the man's words and behavior, putting together his own hypothesis. Clearly this Marine was having a mental break. If he'd been discharged with bad papers, this probably wasn't the first time he'd gone off the rails. It made him dangerous. There was no way this man knew him. He might know the television personality, but he wasn't that man any more.

Still, a man needed anchors to keep him on the straight and narrow. Rowan had anchors in spades. He was a husband and a father, with a home, a dog . . . and even that darn cat. If this man had lost his career, his identity, chances were good he had lost other anchors, too. Clearly his mental health failed him. "Sure," Rowan said. "I'll help you. I just have to know what we're dealing with."

"Not what!" he shouted, pressing the gun harder to Rowan's head. Then, the man's head snapped around. A flash of red and blue lights appeared outside the windows, creating strobes of light on the dingy tile floor, sticky with spilled sodas and Icee drinks, muddy with dirt from hikers and workers boots. The sound of sirens joined the chaos, as three cruisers converged on the 7-11. The Marine whipped around, pointing the gun at the store clerk. "You called the cops?"

She screeched and flinched in terror, backing up against the counter behind her. Rowan saw his chance. He went for the gun as he shouted, "Get down!" The clerk did, and good thing too as the gun went off, right next to Rowan's ear. A screaming whine overtook the ambient sound of the room. If the clerk screamed again, Rowan hadn't heard it.

In the same move that kept the bullet from striking him, Rowan caught the weapon just over the man's trembling finger and torqued it to the side, twisting the young man's wrist enough that the nerves pinged in the hand caused his fingers to splay and open. The weapon fell into Rowan's right hand, while his left, flicked ineffectively at the man's face, unable to make contact.

The Marine turned back, and leaned into Rowan, throwing his arms around the taller man's body, taking him down. Rowan's back protested as he hit the tile floor with the man on top of him. Rowan wrestled the Marine, managing to get out from under him. Once on top, the former Army medic pinned the Marine to the floor mat as Riggs screamed in voiceless agony.

Rowan hadn't expected him to be so strong. He found himself hurled back, hitting the counter with a thud so hard it knocked his breath out. It also knocked an Icee off the counter. It landed on his shoulder as the lid split away from the cup, cracking like an egg. The cold liquid bit his skin through the fabric of his plaid shirt, but not as hard as the fist that caught him across the jaw.

Lightning crashed and the whole world seemed to go dark. Clouds blocked the sun and darkened the day. Thunder rumbled, shaking the floor. At almost the same time, another flash of lightning struck nearby and blinded everyone with its brilliance. The Marine took advantage of the moment and lunged for the gun. Rowan, deaf and blind could only sense the onslaught. He tossed the gun down the hallway, towards the emergency exit, as hard as he could. No longer armed, he fought with the only thing left to him.

Still, it was a fight for life as they grappled in a roiling ball of flailing fists and kicking feet. Rowan came out on top, wrestling the Marine face first into the floor, his knee in the middle of his back. He glanced up, looking for help. But the police officers remained outside the doors, taking a defensive position behind their cruisers where they had cover. Having just arrived, law enforcement officers had no idea who was the good guy and who was the bad guy, and Rowan knew it. His vision cleared as he held down the assailant, debating what to do next. The man bucked, startling him. He was thrown with a force so strong that he landed flat on his butt. The Marine bolted for the exit. Glass shattered when the Marine threw open the front door. He was met by the Denver Police Department.

"Freeze! Don't move! Put your hands up . . ." the words were muffled in Rowan's ringing ears. Dots danced in his eyes as he sat watching the scene unfold in slow motion. His head spun and he couldn't seem to move. Rowan could see Riggs skid to a stop, his empty hands lifting for a moment.

But instead of following orders to put his hands up, he drew a large bowie knife from a sheath at his hip—hidden beneath the t-shirt. Rowan hadn't seen that weapon and knew if the Marine had decided to use it, he'd be bleeding out now.

Riggs side-stepped out of Rowan's direct line of sight, hesitated a moment, then let out a beastly roar. Rowan struggled to move towards the door as the man charged the first police car, with the knife raised like a mad berserker. He seemed to leap into the air as gunshots rang out, windows shattered. Blood splattered the spiderwebbed glass façade of the store. Rowan could no longer see what was going on outside, but he could see the shadow of the Marine as he fell . . . and didn't get up again.

ABOUT THE AUTHOR

Betsey Kulakowski has thirty years of experience as an occupational safety professional and recently completed her degree in Emergency Management. Betsey and her husband live in Oklahoma and have two grown children. She has been writing since she could, and created her first book at the age of six cardboard cover, string binding and all.